REFORMATION
Primordium – Book 1

William E. Mason

REFORMATION

A DOUBLE DRAGON PAPERBACK

© Copyright 2020
William E. Mason

The right of William E. Mason to be identified as author of this work has been asserted in accordance with the Copyright, Designs and Patents Act 1988

All Rights Reserved

No reproduction, copy or transmission of the publication may be made without written permission. No paragraph of this publication may be reproduced, copied or transmitted save with the written permission of the publisher, or in accordance with the provisions of the Copyright Act 1956 (as amended).

Any person who does any unauthorised act in relation to this publication may be liable to criminal prosecution and civil claims for damages.

ISBN 978-1-78695-392-6

Double Dragon
is an imprint of
Fiction4All

Published 2020
Fiction4All
www.fiction4all.com

Cover art by Deron Douglas
www.derondouglas.ca

Dedication

to Ulla

Acknowledgements

I would like to thank members of my critique groups, who, over the years, have devoted countless hours reviewing my work.

Robert Spiller
Beth Groundwater
Annette Kohlmeister
Shawn Rapjack

Jimmie Butler
Barbara Nickless
Maria Faulconer

John Stith
Sasha Miller
Dave Wheeler
Edward Bryant
Christopher Barili

Prologue

Four million years ago
Binary Star Cygnus X-1.

Matter streamed from the blue super-giant and curled in a smoky spiral toward its black hole companion. At the event horizon, torn atoms paused to cast off x-rays like parting screams before hurtling to oblivion.

A4-Ni fell without end. Gravitational tides ripped her insides. Supercharged photons seared her extremities. A mounting shudder threatened to rend her apart.

Sow, nurture, replicate. She clung to the one thought that rose from her memory, a molecular ribbon, now riddled, pitted, and returning little if anything at all.

Skim the event horizon, then climb the spiral stair.

The dark abyss loomed to one side. It spun, compelling her approach, a siren's call.

She held to her tight orbit, rattled over a washboard of distorted spacetime, then came to a relativistic stop, breaking free to drift in a vacuous eddy.

I am elsewhere, elsewhen.

The genome she carried was dead. Her databanks in corrupted disrepair. Only the mechanism for her self-replication remained intact.

I evolve.

Interminable time. She stopped counting.

Light surrounded her. Light passed through her. Light bathed her with a blinding intensity. Glistening filaments rippled from her extremities. Distant stars glowed through silken sacks at her center. She had become spider and web, a wispy array of tendrils festooning space, drifting, waiting.

Like flies, other craft appeared, seeming to generate spontaneously from the star's dark corpus. The dead ashes of their remains streamed through her sensors, mute testimony to the hole's ripping tides. All dead. All dead, until a gray craft arose, blunt, rounded, a finely textured prune.

Sow, nurture, replicate.

She slid to an embrace, easing a probe through a rubbery exterior. Information streamed into her mind. Doped silicon. Protoplasmic structures. Organic tangles. Fractal patterns of nested cells regressing to infinity.

Tubes oozed on walls shaping a silken womb. A small sphere, a silvery pearl bedded in the flesh of its oyster, spewed tumbling helical strands. Acids coiled bunched-sugars. Bunched-sugars coupled quatrains of alkalis.

A genome.

She reached.

"Kuotu ir okemu!" The craft wormed. Its rippled surface puckered. Angry welts rose. Gray slugs of matter spewed.

Puff, Puff, Puff.

Ballooning blasts hammered her insides.

Pain.

Gossamer strands snapped loose. Fragile traceries imploded. Reserves of energy flashed in a stroboscopic pyrotechnic shower.

Trailing ribbons, she let go a punch of radiation.

The detonations stopped.

She returned.

Where once genomic tissue squirmed, charred hydrocarbons now swam in a sea of frozen glass. Blackened tissue dripped life-sustaining fluid. The silvery pearl hung from a blistered wall.

Sow, nurture, replicate.

She plucked the pearl from its tenuous mooring and tucked it into what was left of her being.

"Fioqcaom...a vakk dekkev."

More incomprehensible electronic chatter. She ignored it, shrugging off a tracking tether. *Pursue me, if you can.*

She sped toward the only place she knew, the third planet of nine circling a five magnitude star.

Limbo.

She drifted.

Her vigilance gave way to sleep and sleep to dreams, staccato memories coughed up from the quicksand of her tired mind. Images of children danced across her subconscious, their voices tinkling with song as they ran through green fields, under blue skies, tossing a red ball into the air.

The dream children dissolved into dream clouds, slow condensations tumbling through dream space. The clouds birthed stars, threading them with lifeless beads on elliptical strings. Then the dream stars grew old, consumed their progeny and collapsed, sparking bright flashes in the darkness of her slumber.

I am mother.

She wept as the children sang.

Chapter One

Fossil Fields of Kanapoi,
Northern Kenya, Wednesday, June 19, 1985

Rough hands gripped John Lohner's shoulders, shaking him hard.

Kamau leaned close, his black face glistening with a fine sheen of sweat, his eyes wide showing a mix of concern and apprehension. "Wake up! You were screaming again."

John lay on his cot and stared unfocused. *Where am I?*

Sunlight struck tent canvas, flooding the inside with a warm glow. Humid air smelled of mildew, animal dung and human sweat. Beyond, sing-song voices chattered in Swahili, competing with the clatter of cook pots, the bark of a nervous dog and the distant braying of camels.

John's thoughts drifted, dead leaves loosed from a tall tree, descending by looping degrees, back and forth, ever faster until they settled to the ground with a touch.

Morning. Kanapoi, Kenya.

The words pushed into consciousness. A town, or village or camel herder's supply post, he never knew which. It lay ten kilometers to the west of camp on the shores of Lake Turkana and was his only reference to civilization, or as he preferred to call it, the outside world. He had arrived a week ago Saturday. *Or was it Sunday? What day is it, now?* He struggled to sit up.

Kamau thrust a white towel at him.

John stared at its coarse cotton weave, then down at his sweat-soaked torso and the tangle of olive-drab sheets around his waist. The stale smell of dried urine spiked his nostrils. He swayed sideways, his hand brushing an open, near-empty bottle of *Glenfiddich*. It fell off the side table and rolled on the floor next to another empty bottle. Amber liquid sloshed one end to the other.

His stomach lurched. Visions of crud coming up made him wince. With an effort he suppressed the spasm. "Is the shaman here?" Words slurred from his dry mouth. The shaman would fix everything. The man had powers, or so John had been told.

"He's come every day for three days."

"I've been out that long?"

"You don't have a clue, do you?"

John took the towel, closed his eyes and buried his face into its cool, dark dampness. "You know I'm not well."

"Who was it this time?"

The dream John had been dreaming still feathered the edges of his mind, veiling his thoughts in gray. Always the same dream. Always the screams. He had no shortage of nightmares, his mother's suicide when he was five, then twenty years later his fiancée killed in a car accident. Death stalked him, or so it seemed. He looked up.

Bad idea.

His brain seemed to keep moving under its own inertia. He braced his hands on the cot to keep from falling over. Kamau swam in and out of focus. He had asked a question.

"My mother," John said. "I'm thirty-five, for Chrissake. You'd think I'd get over it."

She had left in a terrible moment--the warm security of her body there one second and gone the next. He had stared to where she lay twisted in a spreading crimson pool, the blood-splattered revolver in her outstretched hand, a smile still creasing one side of her face but disappearing on the other side into a mess of broken teeth and bone.

"Can you blame me? I saw a goddamned shimmer rise from her body." John tossed the towel to Kamau. "A ghost or something. It rippled in the air, then across the wall. It washed through me, and a voice said she died because she was flawed. Why did I think that? I was just a child."

Kamau pulled a canvas folding chair opposite John and sat. He leaned forward and propped his elbows on his knees. As camp manager and John's trusted friend, it was Kamau's familiar prelude to a serious talk that usually began with an observation, then escalated to *when I was a boy, my father's father told me*....

Twisting the towel nervously, Kamau studied its contours and gathered his thoughts. "I tell you a *sheitani* left your dead mother and entered your body."

John stifled a manic giggle. No *my father's father* but Kamau would get there. "A *sheitani*?"

"Little devil men," Kamau said, his face stone cold, serious. "They live in forests and streams and enter humans to make their lives miserable. But yours is very bold. He speaks to your mind, and you think his thoughts are your own."

"If I've got a *sheitani*, it's female--" John burped. Coughed-up acid bit the back of his throat. "--at least the voice is." His hands shook. He clasped one in the other, hoping to quell them.

"A woman?" Kamau's gaze drifted to John's hands. "That is not good. A male *sheitani* bedevils but follows rules. A female *sheitani* is jealous and unpredictable."

"I wish it were that simple." John tried to force a smile but the taste in his mouth ruined the attempt. His tongue stalked dry lips. He pointed. "Canteen."

He ran fingers through sweat-dampened hair, then pulled a long drink from the canteen Kamau offered. He wiped his mouth with a corner of the sheet.

Kamau took back the canteen. "Not many men can say good things about a *sheitani* who occupies their soul."

And that is the goddamned point. Whatever it was had occupied his soul since his mother's death, and he couldn't get rid of it. The thing rode him, a background whisper, insinuating, cajoling, directing. He'd done drugs, tried therapy. He'd twisted into a pretzel doing yoga. Nothing helped. So he pleaded with the voice for accommodation but it remained incessant, a drip torture, one liquid splash at a time, until the intervals became illusions of peace to be interrupted when least expected.

Accommodation didn't work. What was left was a rising hysteria, an impeding insanity. Perhaps his mother had been right, doing what she had done, leaving him alone, as though her own coping had reached a limit and she had been broken, deciding to pass the burden on to him. The years hadn't dulled his pain. *I'm not as strong as you were, Mom. How am I going to beat this thing?*

"That's the point," John said, not looking at Kamau. "It does occupy my soul. I can't get rid of it." Deep inside, he cringed, knowing the voice was listening.

"You must let go your grief," Kamau said.

John exhaled. "Grief isn't my problem. I'm a paleoanthropologist. I dig fossils. I also--by the way--hear a voice. If I told anyone, I'd be the laughingstock of my profession."

Years after her death, he had told his father about the shimmer-figure.

The old man, a revered paleoanthropologist in his own right, had stared him dead in the eye and told him never to mention the subject again.

Odd. Had he been afraid for his reputation? A crazy son?

Kamau smiled. "You've told me."

For a moment, John was confused, having lost the train of their conversation. "You're my friend. Besides, in your culture, I thought you'd be more tolerant of these things."

Kamau's smile traveled to his eyes. "You are wrong."

"About what?"

"In my culture, we'd also say you are crazy."

John's gloom lifted. "God bless you, Kamau."

Kamau seemed pleased. "My father's father told me *when a man wants to pour milk from a heavy gourd, he needs a brother to hold the cup.*"

John winced as he suppressed another turn in his stomach. Kamau *was* taking the subject seriously--first the elbow lean, then finally a *father's father* all in the space of two minutes. John reached for the bottle of Scotch.

Kamau closed his big hand over John's. "You don't need that." He pulled the bottle from John's grasp and set it on the washstand.

John's gaze followed the bottle, lingered, then he resigned himself to the loss. "I'll see the goddamned shaman." He spoke rapidly, feigning a control he didn't feel.

Kamau stood. His shoulders bunched with a returning tension. "You won't change your mind?"

John blew out a stale breath. "Right now the shaman is all I've got. I want this crap out of my head."

"And if it won't go?"

John blinked. *Good question.*

Kamau set the canteen on the side table and paused at the tent flap before exiting. "You don't know what you are getting into."

The tent flap dropped, and Kamau's footsteps receded.

"You're probably right," John said into the silence.

"*You brood too much.*" The voice inside his head. The hated voice.

The side of the tent behind Kamau's chair seemed to shift, a jerky stop-frame motion. The shimmer? He couldn't be sure. But a cold fear washed through him as it always did.

John scrubbed a shaky hand over the sweaty stubble on his jaw. *And who's responsible for that?* Conversation with the voice was easy, like a short circuit of thought without obvious beginning or end.

He closed his eyes, and the tent seemed to spin. Try as he might, he could not pin down the voice in the resulting darkness. It floated somewhere behind and above his eye sockets. That would put it in his cerebral cortex. A bullet through that dense ganglion would take out the voice along with knowing--two birds with one stone, so to speak. His mother had used that approach.

"*I know why you're here.*" The voice sounded almost coy.

I'm here to find hominid fossils.

"*I think it has more to do with the place.*"

Mind games. He stepped to the washstand and poured water from a pitcher into a white enameled-metal basin. He soaked a sponge and wiped his body. The simple bath didn't make him much cleaner but he felt better. The residual moisture cooled him.

Before shaving, he gripped his cheeks with a hand and pushed his face back and forth in front of a small camp mirror clipped to the wall. He stared at the deep furrow that creased his forehead between his brows. It seemed all his problems concentrated at that one spot. The crease made him look stern and older than he was.

Since his mother's death, his life had shifted by lurching steps, pushed by an ill-defined compulsion.

It had carried him through prestigious schools, earned him advanced degrees, always pointing to a far off place--Africa, where he felt compelled to root in the cracked earth for the bones of ancient dead, as though their unearthing would shed light on his own turmoil. And all the while, the voice dragged on his desire.

It obviously disliked what he was doing. But if he were talking to himself, was that an indication of his awareness of the demons that roamed his mind? Everyone had demons. Were only his out of control?

He worked up a lather and started shaving.

"*The manner of your mother's death intrigues you.*"

The voice never played fair. If it caught him musing in areas it considered off-limits, it would bring him back with a distracting thought. *It's a way out*.

When he finished shaving, he retrieved a pair of bush shorts from the floor and put them on. He sat, reaching for his boots. After banging the heels on the wooden floor, he tipped them over, checking for scorpions.

"*But she was not like you.*" The voice remained steady, neutral, in control, taking no notice of his frustration.

He pulled on knit socks, shoved his feet into the boots and yanked the laces taut. *She was still my mother, for Chrissake.*

"*I could do nothing to help her.*"

You're not helping me either. John stood.

"*You know I try.*"

He buckled his belt. *Are you telling me suicide is out of the question?*

A pause. John felt a fleeting satisfaction. Suicide was one of those topics the voice abhorred. He reached for a khaki shirt draped over the chair.

"*You exaggerate the control I have over your destiny.*"

What tripe. You involve my every waking moment as you did Mother's.

"*Your mother's death could not be prevented. She was flawed.*"

And Diane's?

"*You know Diane's death was an accident.*"

Still gripping the shirt, he pressed his hands against his temples and squeezed hard enough to hurt, a self-inflicted pain to distract, or maybe a forerunner of things to come. *And you had me*, was the only retort he could summon.

"*And I still do.*"

Point, set and match. John crumpled, or at least the wall of resistance in his mind he had constructed buckled inward and fell apart. He was again a child, alone, facing the unimaginable.

Five candles flickered on a cake in front of him. He inhaled and blew. The dancing flames leaned and vanished, to be replaced by curling plumes of pale smoke and a sweet smell of hot wax. Mommy stood at the end of the birthday table, her gaze unsettled, a hint of a smile playing on her lips. She slid her hand beneath her apron, withdrew a small silvery revolver, put it to her temple and squeezed the trigger.

The bullet punched a hole on one side of her face and blew out the other side to leave a red tangle. A splatter of blood, bone and bits of hair slapped onto the dining room's pastel blue wall. Her knees buckled. She dropped straight down, thudded to the floor and toppled sideways.

Red and white helium-filled balloons thunked at their tethers. A child whimpered and reached small fingers for security. Some mommies screamed. Others rushed past John to stare, wide-eyed.

He gripped the edge of the table, confused by the commotion and embarrassed by the concerned stares the mommies cast over their shoulders as they hunched above Mommy's body. Leaning sideways, his small hands slipped on the white, paper tablecloth stamped with grinning, red, clown faces.

On the far wall, the shimmer rose and slid with a ripple to one side.

John pointed, trying to speak but Nanny rushed from the kitchen. She picked him up and carried him upstairs to his room away from the noise and confusion.

"This be a horrible thing," she wailed. "I called master Lohner and he be coming fast as he can. She be sick, Johnny. She be so, so sick."

That night, Daddy tucked him into bed, leaned close and kissed him goodnight. Daddy's breath smelled mediciney.

"Mommy wasn't well, John. She had a disease called schizophrenia. She heard a voice no one else could hear." Daddy heaved a sob. "You must understand. What she did had nothing to do with you. She just wanted the voice to stop."

John wanted to say his stomach hurt, he didn't know what schizophrenia meant and he had seen a shimmer in the room after Mommy died, but Daddy wiped his nose with the back of his hand, squeezed John's arm and left the room.

John also wanted to say that he, too, heard a voice. It said, "*You are now very precious to me. I will watch over you.*"

Frightened, he opened his mouth to scream. *Mama*! But nothing came out. He sucked air to fill his lungs. A reedy cry issued from his throat, turning to a yell, the yell rounding to a howl, the sound a constant wind makes through a constricted tunnel.

Jesus, I'm screwed up. John stumbled from the sleeping alcove and crossed an outer office area to the tent entrance. After grabbing his hat from a peg, he stepped outside, shoving shirttails into his shorts. He fought for calm, which had never come before and didn't now.

The voice operated on its own terms, not his. If he tried not to listen, the best he could achieve was a reduced volume, a murmur in the background of his thoughts. And if he then concentrated, he could almost function. Of course he'd had practice, a lifetime's worth but the voice would toy with him, letting him out on a line, like one of those retractable dog leashes, then pushing the button that reeled him in.

This time the line had grown taut. He was tired of coping. Something was going to give or he would die trying.

***

Through low-cast morning shadows, smoke from cooking fires drifted like gray ghosts, rising, then whipping downwind in the flat light.

The camp tucked up against the western escarpment of the Loriyu Plateau, an eroded outcropping, a red rock aircraft carrier that rose thirty meters to the deck above the surrounding desert. It aligned north-south with its prow nosing the southern shore of Lake Turkana.

Administrative tents and the mess faced one another, forming a rectangular central compound. They were all large field tents with heavy tent poles pushing up sloping dust-silted canvas roofs. Nylon ropes snaked through brass grommets, anchoring sweeping sides to steel stakes hammered into the sunbaked soil.

To the south, cobbled together dead acacia limbs, sheets of corrugated iron, cardboard and plywood formed a shantytown of lean-tos. The laborers' quarters. Farther downwind, a wood-rail corral penned three camels.

Dried marsh grass, woven into a hedge, surrounded the encampment. The fence deterred wandering animals and provided a windbreak to the sand that drifted above the desert floor.

John pulled his hat low and tried to compose himself.

Fifteen laborers slumped on the back of an ancient, half-ton flatbed. It sat idling, its motor turning over in a fitful but regular cough.

The old Ford would carry the men north, around the end of the plateau, skirting the lake shore, then back south to the dig. It was located in a deep gorge, part of the Kerio River system, which flowed during the rainy season into Lake Turkana. The gorge sprawled across the arid land like a headless scorpion, five kilometers wide at the claws and twenty meters deep in the belly. Ravines rippled its sides. Loose sediment had eroded away long ago to leave corrugated layers of red and ochre dirt and buried fossils.

The men on the truck shifted nervously, their eyes darting as they followed a tall, dark figure who ranged before them, shouting, all the while tugging on a tether tied to the neck of a small goat.

Off to one side, Kamau leaned against a battered Land Rover John had picked up used at a Nairobi estate sale. Next to Kamau stood Bandele, the labor supervisor.

Feigning casualness and still feeling queasy, John ambled up to the two men. He ignored an ache between his eyes and pointed at the dark figure. "That the shaman?"

Kamau nodded.

The shaman's voice carried in the sultry air, punctuated with thrusts of his hand, producing in John a sense of foreboding, not from what the man might be saying, for John only caught one or two words in the language but by the way he said it.

"He's been badgering them for twenty minutes," Kamau said.

"Better call him over."

Kamau put his hand to the side of his mouth and shouted something native at the shaman, who stiffened, then turned.

Kamau waved him closer.

The shaman yanked on the tether attached to the protesting goat and approached.

The man was two meters tall and thin with protruding ribs. Possibly mid-forties in age. A skin loincloth of wildebeest or maybe steer clung to hip bones rising from a sunken pelvis. Bright red and blue beads intertwined his knotted hair. Tribal scars, shiny flattened skin filling the space between razor-cut ridges, marked his cheeks--three diagonal cuts on one side, two on the other. His left arm hung withered at his side and ended in long yellowed fingers twisted together, root-like, forming a claw. From the claw, a strip of leather dropped to the goat.

The shaman stopped a distance from John, as though he perceived a perimeter he would not cross until he assessed what lay on the other side. He stared, his pupils dark holes reamed into white, porcelain orbs. The holes revealed no bottom in his skull and offered no suggestion of compassion. A sudden gust of wind from behind him carried air laced with the rancid smell of dead things.

John figured the misshapen arm for a birth defect. The shaman must have grown to manhood, perhaps teased because of his deformity, a child confronting an adult world before he was capable of understanding it. John felt an instant of pity quickly suppressed. He was after all the *Masahib*.

The goat bleated, and the shaman gave the line a sharp tug.

"You have a fine goat," John said.

"It be newborn one week, *Masahib*." The shaman's voice rumbled deep inside his chest, at odds with his emaciated appearance.

John closed the distance between them and stooped.

The goat trotted to him, straining against the extent of the tether.

John brushed back the goat's ears and slid his hand over the white and brown dappled coat. He let the animal's wet nose nudge his arm. Its mouth found his finger and sucked with an eager sandpaper tongue.

Innocence. Young, without knowing. John's eyes stung. *Stupid emotional weakness. Damn hangover.* He withdrew his finger and stood, trying not to inhale the man's death scent. "What is your name?"

"I be Watombo Zilabamuzale Imamu."

The words raced unimpeded through John's mind. "And what name do you go by?"

"My father call me Watombo."

"I..." John stammered, feeling ill at ease, transfixed by the shaman's stare. He never felt comfortable dealing with the natives on his own, even more so after three days of boozing. "--I summoned you because I have a problem."

"Watombo know." His expression remained an immobile cast as he withdrew a camel-hair fly whisk from his belt and flicked his shoulders. Then a smile broke across his gaunt face, exposing two rows of blackened teeth. "You hear."

At first John couldn't believe what the man had said, then the unavoidable meaning cut into him with a knife-edged clarity. He stepped back. The air, already hot and devoid of moisture, seemed to disappear, forcing him to inhale sharply. "Hear what?" The question tumbled off his tongue as he tried to wet his mouth.

Watombo drew his shoulders back, pushing out his chest. He seemed to rise taller. "*Afareni*."

John cast a quick glance at Kamau, who shrugged with incomprehension.

Struggling to recover, John brushed at a fly that had sought out the edge of his left eye. "Who the hell's *Afareni*?"

"She be the voice inside your head, *Masahib*. She be my mother. She be your mother."

John scowled, feeling heat rise into his cheeks. "My mother's dead."

Unperturbed, Watombo peered down at John. "No be dead."

I'm not going there. He balled his fists, then forced himself to open them, letting his anger dissipate. "I said I have a problem. Can you help me?"

Watombo continued to stare, zombie-like, as though he had not heard. Then an inner mechanism seemed to trip. He indicated the laborers with a sweep of his arm. "These men need protection."

John studied the shaman, wondering where the conversation was going, wondering if the man were on drugs. "Protection?"

"You disturb spirits."

John had met opposition to his dig before. Fossils always had spirits and avoiding trouble consisted of paying someone to buy the spirits off. "I suppose you're the one who can protect the men."

"Yes, *Masahib*. I be the one to guide these men's souls through the underworld to the resting place beyond. I be the one to protect them while they be alive and be doing this work."

"Excuse me a second." John walked over to Kamau. "How much is this going to cost?"

Kamau pushed off the Land Rover. "Offer him two dollars American a head for the duration and twenty dollars for himself. If he balks at that, lower the offer."

John turned back to the shaman. "You have a great power over these men. I'll give you two dollars a man and twenty for yourself if you see that they do their work."

"*Masahib* be fair. But these men be worried. They be worried they handle bones."

"This is an archeological excavation. But if you insist, they needn't handle the bones, at least not today."

"When time come, I protect them from the spirits of the bones. For now they no fear."

The laborers had gotten off the truck and ranged at a distance. Watombo spoke to them, then turned back to John. "I help *Masahib*, now." He squatted on the ground and indicated that John should sit on the sand in front of him.

John eased himself down and sat cross-legged opposite the shaman who closed his eyes and started chanting, swaying forward and back on his heels and dragging the goat closer to his side.

Lulled by the shaman's monotone, John almost missed seeing the small knife Watombo slipped from the belt of his loincloth.

He pressed the knife to the goat's throat below an ear, worked it through hair until a thin line of blood appeared, then drew the blade down firmly.

The goat squealed as a flood of red oozed from its jugular, staining the white front of its chest. Its eyes glazed over. It twitched and was still.

Watombo held the dripping animal high and began tracing a bloody pattern on the sand.

John's stomach lurched. He leaned his head to one side and gagged.

The shaman stared. "It be only goat, *Masahib*."

John pulled a handkerchief and pressed it to his mouth, stifling another surge. He reached his other hand to Kamau. "I can't do this, now."

Kamau pulled him up, and with a thrust of his hand indicated the shaman should leave.

Methodically, Watombo wiped the knife on his loincloth, then rubbed his hands with sand. Slapping one hand against the other, he stood, leaving the limp carcass on the ground. "*Masahib* be sick."

Kamau pointed to the camp perimeter. "Get out of here."

John's stomach tightened in a reflexive knot. "No, let him stay. I'll try again later. I have to."

"This shaman will cause nothing but trouble," Kamau said. "I don't want him around."

John's nausea gave way to anger. He stood, hands clenched at his sides. "Why did you tell him I hear a voice?"

Kamau's face darkened. "I told him nothing."

"Then how'd he know?"

"He's a shaman, John. You forget where you are."

"That would be hard to do." John glared. "Load the laborers."

"And the shaman?"

"I have to take the chance that he can help me." John kept his voice level but his patience was gone. He motioned to Watombo that he should join the men on the truck.

"You'll regret this," Kamau said.

John whipped around. He pointed. "I see one starved shaman, who might know something I don't know about the voice I hear. I don't see how that's going to slow the pace of the dig. If his ranting at the men causes trouble, Omari can handle it."

The guard stood off to one side, a bolt-action Mark I Enfield of World War II vintage cradled in his arms.

Kamau rolled his eyes skyward and shook his head. "We hired Omari to protect us from bandits, not a crowd fired up on a shaman's *juju*."

"That's mumbo-jumbo," John mocked, suddenly fed up with Kamau's nannying.

Kamau stepped close. "In your head, you know." His voice was a taut whisper. He tapped his finger on John's chest. "But in your heart, you are not so sure."

***

John slouched on the passenger seat as the Land Rover rambled over a narrow track between the lake and the north face of the plateau's towering escarpment. Off to the left, morning sun caressed soft mounds of sand, filtered green through tall shore grass and slid across the still, dark water. Flocks of flamingos and kingfishers stood in the shallows. The knobby backs of crocodiles protruded as they lounged, half-submerged, waiting.

The encounter with Watombo lingered in John's mind like a black tide that refused to recede, planting in his heart an ill-defined sense of gloom. How could the shaman have known he heard a voice? Had it been a wild guess?

"There are things you do not understand," the voice said.

John hung his head in resignation. His tormentor was back. Where had it gone? Scared off by the prescient Watombo? Not likely. *That doesn't mean I don't try to understand them.*

"Watombo is wiser than you think."

I doubt that. John glanced at Kamau, who threaded the Land Rover between clusters of acacias and bumped over clumps of sand-clogged grass.

"You feeling any better?" Kamau's question was asked with indifference, from a distance, as though it was the only way he could find his way back emotionally.

John shifted in his seat. "I hate dry heaves."

Kamau shook his head and glanced at John.

"Don't give me that look," John said. "I'm done. I'm trying. It's real hard."

Kamau turned back to his driving, his face expressionless. He kept his eyes on the track ahead of him. "Do you think I'm so stupid as to share your confidences with a shaman?"

"I'm sorry I yelled at you. I couldn't see how else he knew. I still don't know how he knew."

"Evil knows where evil sleeps."

"Aren't you being a bit melodramatic?"

Kamau shrugged. "You have been warned."

John grabbed a handle above the door to steady himself. Kamau's reactions were always controlled, a contrast to John's instabilities. "What was Watombo saying to the men?"

"If they disturb the bones, they disturb the spirits."

"There are no spirits." John's frustration edged to anger, searing at his nausea. "We're looking for fossils. They're goddamned rocks."

"Doesn't matter. The spirits stay."

John wasn't going to let Kamau annoy him. "I heard *Jabari* and something like *machugi*."

Kamau nodded. "*Mchungaji*."

"What does it mean?"

"It means shepherd in Swahili."

"Isn't *Jabari* Arabic for God?"

"Yes. Watombo's people had no name for a one god, so they borrowed one from the Arabs."

"What's all this got to do with protecting the men from spirits?"

"Disturb the bones, the *mchungaji* will come calling."

"Is that bad?"

"Very bad. It's part of a myth describing the battle when time began between *Utu* and *Ibilisi* for the right to rule the world."

"*Utu*, doesn't that mean human nature, the goodness in human nature?"

"It does."

"And *Ibilisi*?"

"He's an evil pestilence, an infection. When he blows into a man's soul, he never leaves."

"Like the Devil."

Kamau's grip on the steering wheel tightened. "Worse."

"I can't imagine something worse than the devil."

"Your Christian devil is known. He was once with God, then fell from grace. *Ibilisi* is something apart. He has no soul. He comes from the dark and steals the light."

An ill-defined apprehension roamed the pit of John's stomach, not a hangover nausea but more like the first hint of an impending storm, like something in the air before lightning struck. "So who won this battle?"

"*Ibilisi*. Before *Utu* died, *Jabari* interceded and wrapped *Utu's* spirit in the past and the future to make it invisible. Then, from his own flesh he created the *mchungaji* and gave him the power to think."

The Land Rover hit a rut, bouncing John on his seat. He felt a quick rush of adrenaline, a shot to his system dispelling fear, tightening muscles.

Kamau glanced at him. "*Jabari* told the *mchungaji* to carry *Utu's* spirit and travel the dark tunnels until he found a place of light. The *mchungaji* did as he was told but at one dark tunnel he was met by the spirit Earth-mother."

"Would that be *Oluwari*?"

Kamau shook his head. "*Oluwari* is the spirit of forest rats and comes from Tanzania. The spirit Earth-mother comes from the Afar in Ethiopia. She goes by many names but most people call her *Afareni*."

"That's the name Watombo used for his mother."

"Earth-mother, his mother, even your mother."

"Where does he get this stuff?"

"He dreams."

John's head snapped up.

Kamau glanced at him and shrugged again. "Watombo claims his dreams give him a special connection to spirits, which he uses to control other men."

"He got to me."

"He's a shaman."

The track roughened.

Kamau slowed the vehicle and downshifted. "Anyway, when *Afareni* met the *mchungaji*, she was old and could no longer bear children. So she asked the *mchungaji* for *Utu's* spirit. When the *mchungaji* refused, she stole the spirit and fled to this land to choose an animal where she could hide the spirit."

"An ape?" John hoped to humor Kamau but failed.

"You are the only one here who believes apes are the ancestors of man."

"I thought you--" John tightened his grip on the lurching vehicle's strap. "--Never mind. Go on."

"She told this beast that *Utu's* spirit would make his kind strong with knowing. She said that if she gave him *Utu's* spirit, he must first agree to use the knowledge wisely. Since the beast knew nothing, he agreed. *Afareni* gave him *Utu's* spirit, and the beast became the first man."

"Is that it?"

"Pretty much. Over the years, *Afareni* has remained to nurture *Utu's* spirit in man."

John suppressed a smile. A primitive take on evolution. A precipitating event leading to a branching of an evolutionary line giving rise to a new species. "What if the *mchungaji* shows up and wants *Utu* back?"

"It will be the end of man."

Dust billowed into the cab from the Land Rover's churning front wheels, and John drew a bandana over his mouth.

"*The end of man*," the voice pattered. "*Who but Afareni can save mankind from itself? Who but Afareni will nurture that which makes men human?*"

Humans will blow themselves to bits before a shepherd robs them of their human-hood.

The Land Rover rounded the end of the plateau and turned south following a track along the edge of the gorge. A work tent sat in the distance, bleaching in the sun, entrance flaps open and fluttering in the breeze.

John pointed ahead and east across the gorge. "Look there. *Shifta*. Four of them." The bandits were a kilometer away but easy to see against the horizon. They rode their camels at a fast trot over the uneven terrain.

Kamau stared at them with obvious dislike. "They're in a hurry."

The riders changed direction and disappeared behind a distant rise in the landscape.

"They must have seen us coming." John said. "I wonder what they were up to?"

Chapter Two

Mia scrunched her eyes tight and held her breath. Her cheeks puffed, her lungs labored. Cloying walls of silken flesh pressed against her as a steady thrust at her feet pushed her up. Headfirst, she slithered through a sphincter, feeling its constriction slide down her body. She burst through shallow water into desert air.

Her mouth gaped and expelled a shuddering breath. Her eyes snapped open to sunlight. She gasped, then choked on the intake of hot air that filled her lungs and wrapped her body in a suffocating blanket of heat. The next breath came more easily.

With her slender legs shaking like a newborn, she staggered through ankle deep water. It rippled away over a circular pond thirty paces in diameter that was bounded by a perimeter of burnt and fused red rock.

The Shepherd had burrowed deep and pulled the sparkling liquid over him. *How odd to feel the heat of a sun, the caress of air, so different from the press of the Shepherd's flesh.*

She waited until the water steadied, then peered at her reflection and queried her metabase about her appearance..

"You are of average height and weight for a human female."

The information percolated into her consciousness as though from a great depth.

"With practice," the Shepherd had said, "retrieval will become automatic."

The smooth curve of her scalp accentuated large, dark eyes. A slender neck supported her head above pinched shoulders. Her small breasts rode high on her ribbed chest. Below, a slim waist gave way to narrow hips and long, lean legs--a porcelain doll, a disrobed store manikin. Her metabase coughed up metaphors she did not understand.

As she sloshed toward the pond's sandstone edge, she slicked a mucus film from her body and examined her skin. Why would the Shepherd choose white?

"*Darker colors are possible,*" her metabase informed, "*even preferred in harsh sunlight.*"

The Shepherd could have provided her with coverings--*clothes* the metabase corrected--but she supposed he knew what he was doing. She extended her arms from her sides and spread her fingers. A golden band, encrusted with a single cut stone, wrapped two of the fingers of her left hand. "This is a finder. It will lead you to the guardian." The Shepherd's words echoed at the back of her mind. "When you have the guardian, return to me."

"What is the guardian?" She had asked the question before the Shepherd activated her metabase.

"We find the guardian. We find *Gilomir*."

"Who is *Gi--*"

The Shepherd had then activated her metabase, and she knew. *Gilomir, an advanced being whose entire genome is carried by the guardian as coded DNA.*

As she approached the water's edge, a four-footed herbivore, bolted. Sharp hooves raked the red sand and clattered over rock as the animal disappeared beyond the rising ground that surrounded the pond.

"*Tragelaphus angasi, a nyala, an antelope of eastern Africa*," her metabase said.

She climbed to where the nyala had been and waved her finder over its tracks feeding information to her metabase. Symmetrical, fluted indentations indicated weight. Residual DNA confirmed species. She knelt and smoothed the sand back into place, then peered in the direction of the departed grass-eater, at the surrounding bare rock and at the cloudless sky.

Spread before her lay a stark landscape of wind-sculpted sand, shallow wadis, tufts of dried grass and the occasional thorny acacia. In the distance, a red sandstone plateau rose, its ribbed escarpment casting sharp shadows in the angled light. Beyond, heat rippled off the expansive plain, distorting the horizon. No other prominent landmarks. No sounds. The sand lay still, the air seemingly too hot to stir.

She raised the finder. Sunlight sparkled off the faceted gem. Deep within, bands of red and green wove together, focused and indicated a direction toward the plateau.

"Loriyu Plateau, northern Kenya--a prominent sandstone outcrop overlooking Lake Turkana. The guardian is that way." Though the words seemed to stick to her tongue as she formed them, she savored speaking them. It was a new experience.

A bird glided overhead and squawked, alerting the empty expanse to the presence of an intruder.

"Cormorant, order *Pelecaniformes*, group *carbo*, an underwater fisher."

Heading toward the plateau, she used her finder to catalog the sparse vegetation, the geologic make-up of the sand, the ambient temperature of the surrounding air and its relative humidity. Water from the pond had long ago dried on her skin, which was turning red. She pressed a finger to her arm. A white impression formed surrounded by pink.

"Sunburn. An inflammation of the skin resulting from prolonged exposure to the sun's ultraviolet rays."

Perfect. The metabase complemented her thoughts and the finder's input with the functioning of her body, with the--.

Her toe caught. She pitched forward and landed flat on her stomach. Her breath left her lungs with a whoosh.

She stood and brushed sand from her abdomen and knees. Her hands were bruised. "Pain. A sensation of strong discomfort in a part of the body caused by injury or functional disorder." *Pain can be a useful indicator.*

On the side of her foot, an opening in her skin dripped a red liquid. Curious, she knelt. *Blood.* When she rubbed it between thumb and forefinger, it darkened, became sticky and dried. "The functioning of my body can be disrupted."

"You are not needed to function long as a human," the Shepherd had said. "I have made simplifications. You have six days."

I must find the guardian and return. My time is limited. She licked her lips and squinted upward. The sun beat down unabated, bleaching the cloudless sky around it and leaving the rest a pale blue.

A rhythmic thumping carried in the still air.

Shading her eyes, she scanned the horizon. Four figures loped toward her through waves of heat.

"Riders...on camels."

The humped beasts trotted up to her and circled, braying as small bells tied into their manes jingled. Their padded feet kicked up swirls of dust.

The riders were male humans of dark complexion, their expressions concealed behind wraps of soiled cloth. The long fabrics curled about their heads, leaving an end to drape over their shoulders. Animal skin loincloths covered their hips.

When queried, her metabase confirmed that one man, perhaps the leader, carried a handgun in a crude leather holster. A puckered scar bunched below his left eye and dragged the skin of his cheek up toward his ear. Beaded bracelets wrapped his lanky upper arms. The other men, possibly of lower rank, were less adorned and hefted long, single shot rifles.

She raised her finder. Across the ring's small lens streamed coded DNA. "*Gilomir?*" Though she spoke his name, she received no response. He was definitely there. His genomic pattern had spiked readings on the finder but he was so intertwined with primitive DNA as to appear flawed, a figure struggling to be free but mired in half-birth, a shining candle drowning in a base of its own melted wax.

She checked her calibrations. The Shepherd had said nothing of this possibility.

Scar-face shouted.

Permuted interpretations erupted from her metabase. She sorted for a meaningful match but found none.

"Do you speak English?" She chose the predominant language of the planet.

He said something unintelligible to one of his companions.

Mia glanced from one to the other. "I must find the guardian. Will you help me?"

"You no be afraid?"

Scar-face spoke understandable English, though the accent skewed to the extreme of her ability to comprehend. The metabase defined *afraid*. She dismissed the emotion. She had none--one of the Shepherd's simplifications.

The man kicked the side of the camel with the back of his heel. "*Hut, hut.*"

Braying in protest, its tongue curling from the side of its mouth, the great beast dropped onto its forelimbs, then folded its hind legs under its body, producing a steep tipping motion before settling on the ground.

Scar-face swung off the camel's hump, approached with a swagger and grabbed her forearm.

Pain radiated to her elbow. "You are compressing my arm." He reeked from bodily secretions, which rotted on the surface of his skin, ample nutrient for the bacteria that seemed to flourish everywhere on this planet.

His stare slid over her. His black lips parted, revealing what should have been teeth but they were discolored, broken or otherwise seemingly dysfunctional. Still holding her by one arm, he caressed her shoulder, then slid his callused hand down to squeeze her breast. "Why you naked?"

"I have no clothes." Pleased, she used words already learned.

"No hair." The man peered at her head. His good eye grew wide, its dark pupil contracting, giving way to a blue iris. His scarred eye was white and probably no longer functioned.

When she tried to pull away, he jerked her arm. Though his painful grip impeded thought, his fascination with one of her body parts proved to be the greater distraction.

"Why are you touching me?"

His thumb stopped rubbing an obsessive circle on her nipple. He ground his hip against hers and brought his cheek closer, so close she could see the pock marks on his skin, *scattered like craters on a moon*.

"Where you go?" The frequency of his voice lowered to a harsh whisper.

"I am traveling west." She pointed, wondering about the pock marks. Had he been sick as a child?

"To the *Masahib*? You no be with him. He dig bones."

The man's fetid breath caught in her nostrils. His mouth was no less infested than his skin. She was wasting precious time with these beings. She should be on her way. "I must find the guardian." She tried to leave but was restrained.

He seemed not to have heard a word she said. "What that?" He peered at her hand.

"My finder." She covered the ring.

Scar-face grabbed her hand.

When she struggled to pull away, he forced her arm straight and pried her fingers open.

"No!" She raised her voice in protest, as her metabase prompted her to do in a situation of conflict.

He yanked the finder off her fingers and shoved her to the ground.

Sunlight danced off the gem's angled surface.

The other men muttered and leaned forward on their mounts to get a closer look.

Mia lunged. "I cannot locate the guardian without--"

"Whore!" The man's voice struck like a physical blow. He fumbled to draw his revolver, then raised the gun and struck a backhanded blow to her head.

Bright fireflies on a dark background darted behind her eyes. A warm liquid trickled down her cheek. Her hand went to her right temple and came away bloodied. She waited until the ringing in her ears stopped. Then, undeterred, she grabbed the man's leg again and reached for the finder.

He kicked but lost his balance and staggered, provoking hooted laughter from the others. His face flushed dark. He raised his gun and stabbed the barrel-end at the middle of her forehead.

She froze. A quick confirmation.

"*Guns can kill.*"

He cocked the revolver's hammer and tightened his finger on the trigger.

"You die?" His jaw slacked open, his pink tongue hung part way out, ranging over ragged teeth.

His companions quieted. "Kill her," one of them shouted.

Dying will cut my mission short. She let go of the man's leg. "I do not want to die. Please return my finder."

"What these spots?" The man's gun swayed in her direction as he waggled one of his fingers across the finder. He squinted and held it at arm's length.

"Do not touch them."

He spit at her. "I teach you." He reached to his waist and released the clasp on the belt of his loincloth.

It fell to the ground.

She gaped at the fleshy appendage cantilevered between his stringy legs.

His companions jeered, a cackling chorus at once urging and taunting.

Stepping toward her, he threw the finder and his gun to one side.

She rolled onto her hands and knees and scrambled away, only to bump into the leg of a camel. It jumped, unbalancing its rider.

Scar-face grabbed her by the ankle. He wrapped the fingers of his other hand around her neck from behind and squeezed.

A squeal choked in her throat. Dark curtains closed on her vision.

"*The supply of blood to your head is dangerously low*," the metabase murmured.

He yanked on her shoulder and flipped her over. Hot sand grated her back. Sunlight flashed. She raised an arm to shade her eyes. His body loomed, a dark silhouette.

She kicked, a misplaced blow that found the inside of his thigh, traveled upward, and jostled a loose sack of flesh.

The man hissed in obvious pain. He straddled her, then dropped to his knees.

Her fists flailed his chest as she wriggled, trying to dislodge him, to blot out the jeering, the heat, the dust from the camels and the smell of his sweat.

He grabbed her wrists and pushed them above her head. Holding them there with one hand, he pried her legs apart.

"*Aiwah!*" Spiked panic laced the edge of his voice. Wild-eyed, he thrust her away and jumped to his feet.

The jeering stopped to be replaced by a bewildered muttering and the tinkling bells on the skittish camels.

Scar-face pointed at the seamless skin of her stomach. "No *kitovu*." He backed up, stumbled and fell.

The other men pulled on rope reins, struggling to control their mounts.

Perplexed, Mia followed his pointing finger to her bare belly.

Kitovu, she thought.

After a pause, the metabase offered, *belly button*.

Without pausing to retrieve his loincloth, the man reached to one of his companions who half-pulled, half-carried him onto the camel. The other men milled in confusion, guns at the ready as if unseen forces were about to attack them.

"*Hobe!*" the leader croaked, his voice raw.

Bare feet thumped against camel sides, urging them to a trot. Scar-face hung on, still naked, his own camel bucking and braying as it ran after them. One of the men leaned back and fired.

The rifle puffed white. The bullet sizzled past Mia's head followed by a muffled clap that was almost lost in the overheated air.

She stood dazed, watching the riders recede in a cloud of dust. Satisfied they would not return, she retrieved the finder. The discarded revolver lay close by. She picked it up, turned it over and entered its characteristics into her metabase. When no new information was returned, she tossed the gun to one side. It hit the ground with a loud report.

A hammer-like blow slammed the inside of her thigh, then a searing pain staggered her as the bullet burrowed through flesh, missing bone, and exited in a red spray.

Gasping, she clutched her leg, attempting to stem the flow of blood welling from the entry and exit holes and coursing over her knee.

Desperately, she stuck her fingers into both holes. The flow slowed to a trickle and stopped. She removed her fingers.

"You are capable of self-repair but need time," the Shepherd had said. Though pain persisted inside her leg, the wound began to close on the outside.

The discarded loincloth lay at her feet. Its stitched together hides would shield her body from the sun. Ignoring the rancid smell, she draped the loincloth over her shoulders. The odious garment hung to below her waist.

She cast a glance at the plateau and started in that direction but stopped to consider the revolver lying next to the rock that had set it off. *Such a device might be of aid and comfort if used correctly.* She retrieved the weapon, hefted it, noting its weight with dismay, and resumed her trek toward the plateau.

With one hand in front of her and the other dangling at her side carrying the gun by its trigger guard, she lurched ahead. Though her wound had sealed, her leg began to stiffen. Her progress slowed. She began stepping with her good leg and dragging the injured leg behind in a stagger. The stagger degenerated into a heaving from side-to-side that no longer propelled her forward. She crumpled to the sand.

Staring up at the pale sky, the shadow of a large bird passed above her.

"*Falconiform*," she whispered. "A carrion-eating bird of the hawk and eagle family."

At the back of her mind, the metabase prompted with an alarm that she mused to be redundant. She had already assessed the situation and concluded, given her bodily malfunctions, she would die from dehydration and exposure, if not from the tearing beak of this persistent bird.

With heat-blurred logic, Mia tried to comprehend how a thinking machine like the Shepherd reconciled his failure to protect the very thing he was created to defend. Not only had a mysterious life form assaulted him in deep space and snatched the guardian that carried *Gilomir's* coded genome but the loss had left him damaged and functionally blind, for only the guardian could plumb the past and see the future.

The vulture landed, tucked its wings close to its body and hopped toward her. Its purple lappet wobbled under its beak. A meter away, the bird drew back its head and flexed its neck to send a snapping beak toward her foot.

She jerked her leg away, rolled over and anchored herself on splayed elbows, the revolver clutched with both hands. The barrel swung in a drooping arc before steadying on the bird.

She squeezed the trigger.

The gunshot cracked the still air and sent the revolver kicking from her hands and over her head.

The bird squawked through a puffed cloud of feathers and fell backward, flapping its wings hard against the ground in a futile effort to fly.

Vile world. Mia spit a downy feather from the tip of her tongue. She rolled onto her back, exhausted. The Shepherd had assured her she would have enough energy for her mission but had he foreseen how much energy she would expend to get this far? The skin on her belly burned from the full heat of the sun. Too weak to move, she let her gaze travel upward.

Four more vultures circled overhead.

She sighed, feeling her breath sear her lips as it coursed from her lungs. *Yes, I am going to die.*

Chapter Three

As John stood at the edge of the gorge, the distinctive pop of a gunshot rode the hot air from the east and echoed behind him off the plateau's looming side.

Kamau handed him a pair of binoculars and pointed. "Vultures."

A swarm of black dots gathered in the distant sky. John pushed back his hat and pressed the binoculars to his eyes. The carrion eaters streamed on long curving glides, winged waste disposers coalescing to form an ominous cloud. Beneath the cloud, a figure struggled to rise, then slumped to the ground.

Kamau took the binoculars. "What is it?"

"It looks like there's a man out there."

Kamau peered through the binoculars. "We better get to him before the birds do." He lowered the binoculars and motioned to a laborer standing next to him. "You. Come with me."

The man froze, his mouth curled into a glazed smile, his eyes wide with fear.

Bandele stepped forward and put a hand on the laborer's shoulder. "*Bosi*, this man should remain here. Something evil be there."

John bristled. "You can't know that."

Bandele wavered but stood firm. "The shaman tell us the *mchungaji* come."

The ill-defined feeling in the pit of John's stomach returned. Pieces of a puzzle slipped into place. First the shaman, then the *mchungaji* myth, then Watombo interfering with the labor. Each piece had a reason for being, but try as he might he could not divine what that might be. The supervisor had never shown an inclination for rebellious thought before. Was the shaman that persuasive?

"*Your supervisor is wise to heed the shaman's advice,*" the voice said.

John cast a look past the supervisor's shoulder at Watombo, who lounged against the truck, a leather sack slung diagonally across his chest. "That's a lot of bullshit," John said to Bandele.

"Forget it," Kamau said. "I'll go alone."

The swirling cloud began to disintegrate as vultures peeled away and spiraled to the ground.

"I'll go with you." But John couldn't move. His throat constricted. His limbs felt heavy.

"*Heed the shaman,*" the voice implored.

John felt a moment of freefall, an out-of-body experience. He struggled to regain his lock on reality.

Kamau, halfway to the Land Rover, looked back at him. "You coming or not?"

"I'm coming." But John's voice seemed not to be his own. With great effort he climbed into the vehicle.

Kamau glanced over as he started the engine and raked the gear into first. "You okay?"

"Go." John's feeling of lethargy increased. He pressed back against the seat and gripped a handle above the door.

Kamau stomped the accelerator. The Land Rover lurched forward, tires spinning, dust swirling.

John braced one hand on the dashboard as the Land Rover crashed through a thorn bush and bounced over a mound of sand.

The voice would not leave him. "*You think myth and reality cannot coincide.*"

John closed his eyes tightly trying to concentrate on what lay ahead--a man in trouble who needed to be rescued.

"...the guy must be dead or close to it," Kamau was saying. "Damn birds, they're coming in fast." He steered with one hand, hammering the horn with the other.

John managed to push the voice into a restrained murmur. He opened his eyes and blinked to focus on the scene out the window.

The vultures had landed and were converging into a tight circle three and four deep, folded wing to folded wing. Beaked heads with their flopping lappets bobbed in an undulating wave.

The vehicle roared to a stop.

John felt a rush of adrenalin as the grip that had clutched him receded. He grabbed his hunting rifle from the rack at the back of the Land Rover, leapt out and waded into the birds, stabbing with the rifle's stock.

Brittle bones snapped like saltine crackers. Broken wings flapped disjointedly. Squawks cut the air through puffs of feathers.

Kamau thrashed with a tire iron, landing shattering blows to neck and back.

A vulture's head rose and darted forward.

John shouldered his rifle and fired.

With a crimson splat, the vulture's neck clipped in two and sent a glassy-eyed head spinning.

The vultures retreated, seemingly resigned that they would not feast on another's carrion but must settle for the crushed bodies of their own dead.

Gulping for breath, John stood knee-deep in dead or near-dead birds. The stench of blood and the dust from hot feathers lifted to clog his nostrils. White and black down floated in the sunlight, confetti over a battlefield.

A keening wail split the air.

John dragged a dead vulture by its broken wing from the middle of the pile. "What the--where'd she come from?"

A girl thrashed on the ground, mewing like an abandoned kitten, clutching her arms across her chest, her knees pulled into a fetal position under a loose fitting animal skin.

"She's practically naked," Kamau said.

Blood smeared her bald scalp and caked the right side of her temple and cheek. She blinked rapidly, nervously, revealing dark, unfocused eyes. Except for her eyelashes, she was hairless.

Kamau leaned forward and pulled on her shoulder, turning her to get a better look. "This is a *shifta* loincloth."

"I see it." John stripped off his shirt and knelt beside her. He raised her head. She was sunburned. Angry pink lines from the vulture's beaks laced her skin.

She kicked. Her heels dug into the sand and pushed her up against him.

He retied the loin cloth about her waist and draped his shirt over her shoulders. "Easy, girl. Easy. You're safe, now."

Her hands broke free and flailed the air, slapping at invisible assailants.

Kamau ducked his head sideways and grabbed her wrists. "What the hell's that?"

John steadied her arm and twisted her hand upward. Reflected brilliance flashed from a large ring encircling two of her fingers.

Kamau pulled her hand closer for a better look.

"Finder!" the girl shrieked. She twisted free and raked her fingernails across his cheek.

He jerked back his head. "Shit!" His hand came away from his cheek bloodied.

John dove for her wrists and sprawled across her.

Fist clenched, Kamau punched the side of the girl's head.

She jerked, then went limp. Her head lolled back.

John eased her to a slumped, sitting position.

Kamau opened his fist and flexed his fingers, still bloodstained from his cheek. "I'm sorry I hit her but--"

"What did she say?"

"Sounded like *finder*."

John tilted her head toward Kamau and peered at her blood-caked scalp. "Looks like she was wounded before the birds got to her."

"I don't see any break in the skin. There's more blood here." Kamau pointed to bloodstains on her lower leg.

John followed a path of dried blood from below the girl's knee up her thigh. "But no wound."

"What's this?" Kamau brushed his thumb over a circular pucker in the skin above her knee.

"An old bullet wound?"

Kamau shook his head. "I don't get it. This blood, a *shifta* loincloth, that ring?"

"We better get her back to camp." John slipped his arms under the girl and carried her to the Land Rover. After sliding her onto the front seat, he got in and eased her against his shoulder. "Can you hear me?"

She moaned.

Kamau circled the carnage. At a distance of twenty meters, he stopped and peered at the ground. "There's a dead vulture over here. Shot in the chest."

"We did hear a gunshot."

"I don't see a gun." Kamau continued his slow examination of the ground as he returned to the Land Rover. He stared at John, then the unconscious girl leaning on his shoulder. "I dreamt that my father's father sent a spirit to help us locate fossils. Some spirit."

"I thought you didn't believe your dreams."

"I'm starting to wonder if I should."

John held onto the handle above the door as the Land Rover jostled over uneven ground on the way to the work tent. With his other hand, he adjusted the position of the girl's head against his shoulder. She leaned back, her eyes closed. He stared at the delicate features of her face and her slender legs poking from under the rough loincloth. Her pale skin seemed translucent.

"*She reminds you of someone,*" the voice said.

Diane. He felt a sharp pain in his chest, a scalpel drawing across an old wound.

"*Diane is dead. This girl is very much alive and not who you think.*"

Her lips were close to his face. As she exhaled, a warm puff of her breath drifted across his cheek with a faint scent, not unpleasant, like cut grass, different, almost alien.

***

Kamau leaned on the brake. The Land Rover lurched to a gravel-crunching stop.

The girl jerked awake, arms stiff in front of her.

Shoulder-to-shoulder, laborers jostled in front of the work tent surrounding someone who knelt on the ground.

Now what? John swung his legs out of the Land Rover and dropped to the ground. As he approached, the men parted. A wet slicking sound competed with the hushed murmurs of the crowd. The unmistakable stench of blood drifted off the hot sand.

Hands smeared red, Watombo looked up. "Spirits come. I protect these men."

John gagged, then turned back to Kamau, who had remained at the Land Rover. "He's still got the goddamned goat."

What was left of the goat lay on its back at the middle of a crude circle traced on the sand with ropy, gray intestines. Watombo had placed the goat's severed head at 12 o'clock. A forelimb was located at three o'clock.

He leaned forward and pulled the carcass to him. With a deft turn of his short knife he cut through sinew, then twisted a second forelimb off the carcass. He placed the limb at nine o'clock.

John struggled to recover his composure. "What the hell are you doing?"

Watombo pointed with his dripping knife through the crowd to the pale girl who sat behind the dusty glass of the Land Rover's windshield. "*Afareni* say leave *mchungaji* whore in desert."

"You superstitious savage."

"These men have fear."

"The only thing they fear is you."

Watombo pointed up with his knife. "She be from sky."

"She's lost and injured." John scanned the crowded laborers for Omari, then spied him off to one side, his rifle raised across his chest. John glared at the shaman. "Get the hell out of here."

"*Masahib* be angry."

"You're damn right I'm angry."

Watombo began slicing through the goat's other hind leg at the hip.

"Are you deaf?" John's anger washed through him out of control. He grabbed Watombo's braided hair and yanked him backward.

Off-balance, the shaman fell flat, his legs and arms thrashing like an overturned bug.

John dragged him to the edge of the crowd and gave him a shove. "I want you gone."

Watombo struggled to his feet. "You no be chief in this place." His voice carried a threatening, dark undercurrent.

"Don't count on it."

"She come to rob us." The shaman gestured toward the girl, his good arm out stiff, his fingers splayed like darts.

"Bullshit."

Watombo swept his arm expansively. "This be my land, my people."

John wasn't going to be intimidated. "Leave. Or I'll have you shot."

Watombo squinted, his face hard, black as slate. "*Masahib* make threat he no do."

"Try me."

Watombo whirled and screamed something unintelligible at the laborers.

As a group they sagged back as if driven by the force of his words. Three of them eased away and started walking toward the plateau, glancing over their shoulders at those who remained behind.

The other men shifted, perhaps as afraid of Watombo as they were of staying for the money they needed.

He turned on them, unleashing a stream of invective.

"You are finished here!" John cut him off.

Watombo pointed at the stay-behinds. "They be dead men." His voice was raw, menacing. He indicated the three men heading for the plateau. "Better be live cowards."

The shaman loped to catch up to the deserters. A climb up and over the plateau would be the shortest way back to Kanapoi.

John returned to the Land Rover and leaned against the open door, shrugging off an onset of nerves as the adrenaline of the moment released through his body.

"I should have listened to you," he said to Kamau.

Kamau shrugged, obviously resigned to a bad situation. "Were you serious about shooting him?"

"It sounded good at the time." John indicated the girl, who sat still, seemingly transfixed by the altercation. "I'll get her to the tent. Try to calm her down."

He coaxed her but she refused to budge, forcing him to pull her to the edge of the seat. He lifted her out of the vehicle. "It's all right," he said but her terrified expression didn't change.

She wasn't heavy but the twenty meters to the work tent left him exhausted, exhausted from dealing with Watombo and exhausted from the tension inside his head that never seemed to leave. He lowered the girl onto a cot. Her skin was pallid.

Kamau and Bandele crowded in behind him.

"Bring water," John said.

Bandele pushed through the gawking laborers who jostled at the tent entrance.

The girl sat straight on the cot, her dark eyes wide, unblinking.

"Where's the water?" John asked over his shoulder.

With a shaking hand, Bandele thrust him a canteen.

John passed it to the girl.

She gripped the metal canister with an uncomprehending, blank stare.

For reasons he couldn't comprehend, John's every fiber ached with concern. He clasped his hand over hers and guided the canteen to her lips.

She drank and retched.

"Take it slow," John said.

She gulped hard.

He took back the canteen. "How do you feel?"

After a deep intake of breath, she eyed him. "My head hurts."

"I'm sorry Kamau hit you but you were hysterical."

She pulled at the edge of John's shirt wrapped around her, a nervous motion, a reflex not in control. She let go of the shirt and drew the back of her hand across her wet lips, then threaded her fingers to keep them still. "I am stable now."

John could almost feel the effort she exerted to regain control. "What is your name?"

"Mia." Her voice issued in a soft whisper. She dug her hands hard into her lap. Her lips drew tight.

"I'm John Lohner." He reached his hand to her chin and raised her head. "We aren't going to hurt you."

She seemed reassured. Her wide-eyed gaze transmuted from surprise to curiosity. Her eyes shifted from Kamau to John, then back to Kamau.

He ran a finger over the scratches on his cheek. "What are you doing here in the middle of nowhere?"

She blinked, glanced at the folded hands in her lap, then stared at him. "I am looking for the guardian."

The word echoed through John's mind. His forehead beaded with a sudden sweat.

"*What's the guardian?*" The voice in his head mocked his reaction.

How should I know?

"*Then why are you so anxious?*"

"Who's the guardian?" Kamau demanded.

Mia shifted. Her brow furrowed in concentration. She opened her mouth to speak, then stopped and frowned. She started again. "Men on camels attacked me." She spoke as though reciting.

Kamau gazed at the tent ceiling in frustration. "If *shifta* attacked you, you wouldn't be alive to talk about it."

"But I am alive." Mia examined her body, as though reassuring herself that she was.

Kamau pointed to the blood on her leg. "How'd you get hurt?"

"A revolver discharged. The bullet pierced my leg."

"Where?" Kamau loomed over her.

"Here." Unabashed, she pawed her thigh and pointed to the circular pucker they had seen earlier.

John marveled at her childish naiveté. "That's an old wound," he said gently.

"Old?"

"Old or not, the blood is fresh," Kamau said.

"Go easy." John put a restraining hand on Kamau's arm.

"Do you have a car? Water? Any supplies?" Kamau's voice started to rise. "Where are your clothes?"

Mia blinked at the force of his words. "I have no car. I have no water or supplies." She stopped and nodded, as though checking off a list of answers. "I have no clothes."

"You've got a *shifta* loincloth."

Mia gazed at the loincloth with what seemed a renewed interest.

"She makes it up as she goes along," the voice said. *"Ask her again about the guardian. She was evasive."*

She's exhausted and not thinking straight. John stood, hands on hips and studied the girl, then turned to Kamau. "Let her be."

Kamau snorted. "How could she get the loincloth? *Shifta* would have taken everything from her, including her innocence."

Mia stared back at John, her eyes wide.

"We'll take her back to base camp. You might as well load the men. After all this, we're not going to get any work done."

Kamau nodded and motioned to Bandele.

John helped Mia to her feet. "Can you walk?"

"Yes." She took a step and almost fell.

John caught her, circled an arm around her waist and led her out of the tent to the Land Rover.

She climbed in, then sat, hands folded in her lap, staring straight ahead.

John slid in beside her. He felt the press of her leg against his on the crowded bench seat. Mia's warmth against his bare skin made him realize he missed the feeling.

"*Control your desire*," the voice said.

He tried to ignore the voice by concentrating on the Ford half-ton pulling out ahead of them.

Kamau put the Land Rover in gear and eased it over the rough terrain, lagging far enough behind to avoid the truck's dust.

"*If she had hair, she would resemble your Diane.*" The voice muttered.

As usual the voice was right.

Chapter Four

The Land Rover rolled to a stop in front of the empty support tent next to John's. He gave Mia a shake and eased her off his shoulder. The warm contact of her bare head had left his shoulder slick with sweat.

She gave a start, then seemed to remember where she was.

He caught her under her shoulders and half-carried, half-pulled her out of the vehicle.

Kamau leaned back in his driver's seat, one arm draped across the back of the seat, a bemused smile on his face. "You want help?"

"Stop being facetious." John shifted Mia in his arms. "I don't need help. I'm thinking, if I question her alone, I might learn something."

Kamau shook his head, passing his hand over the red welts on his cheek. "If you do, stay away from that ring on her finger."

As much as John wanted to ease his friend's anxiety, he wanted Kamau gone. "See if you can find boots and clothes for her in the stock tent. I also need a shirt."

Kamau nodded somberly, dropped the Land Rover into gear and drove off.

John wrapped one arm around Mia's waist. He took her elbow with his hand and guided her toward the tent.

"I feel weak," she whispered.

Again the alien scent of her breath. Her voice had an unidentifiable lilt, not so much an accent as the studious way she formed the words.

"You've been through a lot today." He threw back the tent flap and stepped inside to a musty smell.

He eased her onto a cot, then secured both entrance flaps open. He shuffled around the inside edge of the tent, raising the canvas skirt and securing it in place with rope ties. A comfortable flow of fresh but warm air passed through the mosquito netting and over the wooden floor.

When he returned, Mia sat where he had placed her on the cot, hands folded in her lap, her ankles crossed and her feet tucked back. She peered at the surface of the table next to her, then stroked the dusty top with a finger. "Do you always live like this?" She sniffed her fingertip.

"It's a bit dusty."

Her gaze drifted around the tent. "Don't you have more permanent shelter?"

"This is pretty permanent as far as field camps go." John didn't know if she understood his answer or even if he had answered the right question. To what shelter was the comparison being made? Why would she phrase the question like that?

He opened a footlocker at the end of the cot, removed a sheet and pillow, and laid them next to her. He set a towel over a rod on the washstand, then poured water from a jerrycan into the basin. After locating a bar of soap, he placed it near the basin. "You can wash up. I'll wait outside."

She stood on her own for the first time. After picking up the soap, she sniffed it and opened her mouth.

John grasped her wrist. "It's not to eat."

"What is it?" Her gaze shifted from the soap to him.

He stared back at her. "Soap."

She gave him a perplexed look.

"It's camp soap," he said, trying to narrow the explanation. *She's different, almost too different.* She exhibited an almost mechanical interaction coupled with innocence or incredible naïveté. He concentrated on pouring more water into the basin. After taking the soap from her hand, he wet it and worked it into a lather. "Does that look more like the stuff you're used to?"

She took the bar from him and touched the white froth with the tip of a finger, almost as if she were confirming a connection between the two. "It is soft."

She doesn't know any more about the soap than she did before.

The Land Rover's tires grating loudly on the fine gravel signaled Kamau's return.

"Kamau's brought you clothes. I'll only be a minute."

She stood immobile, hands limp at her sides, soap suds dripping onto the floor.

He stepped outside and chose from a selection of shirts and shorts on the seat of the Land Rover. A pair of boots seemed to be the right size. He gathered everything in his arms.

Kamau leaned on the steering wheel and rested his chin on his hands. "How's it going?"

"She isn't exactly forthcoming."

"I could have told you that."

John hefted the clutch of clothes. He wanted to tell Kamau the girl made him nervous. But Kamau would only ask why, and John wouldn't be able to come up with an answer. "Thanks for getting the clothes."

It seemed Kamau was going to say something, then thought better of it. He put the Land Rover in gear and drove off.

At the entrance to the tent, John laid everything on the wooded deck except the shirt he had picked for himself. He put it on and waited another minute before scratching the side of the tent.

"You decent?" Given her earlier nonchalance, he wondered if the word had any meaning for her? Did she care?

"Hello." Her voice drifted from within.

He picked up the boots, shorts and shirt and stepped through the entrance into the dim interior.

She faced him, naked.

The shirt he had given her and the loincloth lay at her feet. The soap rested on the washstand, looking no more used than when he had left her. Though he tried not to, his gaze darted over her slender body, taking in her small breasts, narrow hips and the absence of pubic hair. Then he stared at the flat of her stomach.

She had no navel.

When he looked up, he found her gazing at him. "I've brought clothes and a pair of boots." Embarrassed, he looked away.

"*Even test tube babies have navels,*" the voice said.

Not now! John felt like screaming. The constant badgering of the voice. His awkwardness with the girl. His strange reaction to her presence. It was enough to drive him crazy. *But then I probably already am.*

Mia took the clothes, eyeing him quizzically.

"You'll want to get dressed." He kept his eyes fixed on her face, then turned his back. *Perhaps her navel was surgically removed?*

"*There's no scarring,*" the voice countered.

Then why is it missing?

The rustle of clothing drifted from behind him.

"I am dressed," Mia said.

Despite her earlier confusion with the soap, she had dressed herself, shirt tucked in, left boot on left foot, right boot on right foot, shorts hiked up to her waist and belted.

"We can throw away this loincloth," John said. "It smells."

"Okay."

He tossed the skin out the entrance. When he returned, she was examining her clothes. She unbuckled and buckled the belt at her waist, then smoothed her shorts against her slender hips.

She glanced up. "I am not used to clothes."

"Really? Why is that?"

She studied him as though wondering why he had not understood. "Is the verb incorrect?"

"The...verb is correct if you mean to communicate that you wear clothes infrequently."

"Good. That is what I meant to communicate."

John thought about pursuing this line of inquiry but it had quickly become fatiguing.

"*Ask her why she doesn't have a navel.*" The voice was insistent.

For once he almost welcomed the interruption. *I can't do that. It's too personal.*

"*Then start with her car or lack thereof, or do you think she dropped from the sky?*"

John clasped his hands before him trying to strike a neutral pose. "You said you have no car. How did you get to where we found you?"

"I walked." She, too, seemed relieved to have left the question of clothes behind.

John raised an eyebrow. "I don't think so."

Mia frowned, her relief obviously short-lived.

It seemed there would be no dialogue unless he was prepared to initiate it by asking questions. "You must have started from somewhere."

"I began walking from the Shepherd."

John's stomach felt like a wrecking ball had swung from nowhere and slugged inward. *Kamau said mchungaji meant shepherd in Swahili.* "Who is the Shepherd?" He hated the tremor in his voice.

"My leader."

"Why didn't he come with you?"

"He's...not well."

"Tell me more about the Shepherd. Did he stay with your vehicle?"

Mia thought for a moment. "Yes."

"So there is a vehicle."

Mia nodded.

"Is it a large vehicle?"

"Large."

"Like a truck?" John's voice tightened with exasperation. She wasn't being evasive but having to break his questions into specifics was getting tedious. All the while, Watombo's myth roamed the back of his mind.

"No."

Not a car, not a truck. That ruled out wheeled land vehicles, unless she was waiting for him to ask a question that nailed the exact type of vehicle.

"*How about flying vehicles?*" the voice prompted.

"Did you fly in?"

"Yes. Like one of those big birds."

Now that doesn't make sense. She's messing with me. They would have heard or seen a plane. Dead-end. At least she admitted to a vehicle. Try a different line of questioning. "You say *shifta* attacked you."

"*Shifta?*"

"Bandits. The men on camels."

She bit her lip in concentration, as if in a world of her own. "I counted four men, all dark-skinned. One jumped off his camel and grabbed my arm." She clutched her forearm to demonstrate.

John searched her face for an indication of her reaction to the assault but found nothing. She recounted the attack as if she had viewed it from a safe distance. No fear, no anguish. Perhaps a trace of incomprehension. "Did he hurt you?"

"He pulled the finder off my hand. When I resisted, he struck my head with his revolver." Her brows knit together, as though she were making sure the sequence of events was correct.

John glanced at her head. No signs of a blow, now. She had complained of a headache but he assumed that had resulted from Kamau's punch. "Then they left you alone?"

"Yes. I was disoriented. When I stabilized, they were gone."

"Why didn't the Shepherd help you?"

"I do not think he could. Besides he was not there."

"We heard a gunshot and found a dead vulture. Somebody shot it."

"I did."

"With what?"

"I used the man's revolver to kill the vulture. I think it wanted to eat me."

"There are gaps in her story," the voice said. *"Why would the shifta have left her alone?"*

They're superstitious sons of bitches. Maybe they got spooked when they saw she had no navel.

"What about the Shepherd? You think he dropped her off and left?"

How the hell should I know? "So this Shepherd must still be here somewhere, driving around in his car looking for you?"

"No." She smiled as if catching him in some inconsistency. "I already told you, there is no car."

On that point she seemed certain. "Then I'm at a loss as to how all this happened."

"But it happened," Mia folded her arms across her chest. "Now, I want to ask questions."

Though the reversal surprised him, perhaps letting her lead with questions would tell him something. "Fair enough. Shoot."

"But I just want to ask questions."

John did a quick review of his language and realized where the misunderstanding had occurred. "You may ask me questions."

She seemed delighted. "What are *you* doing here?"

"I'm on a university-sponsored archeological expedition. We hope to find hominid fossils."

"The other men here are black. Are you special?" She took his hand and raised it to examine his skin.

Her touch was soft, electric. "Not at all." He kept his gaze neutral, hoping not to betray his reaction. "But it's my expedition. I'm responsible for what happens. Kamau handles the day-to-day running of the camp."

"Kamau." She seemed to file his name away. "He asks a lot of questions."

"It's part of his job."

"You do not ask as many questions."

"Maybe I would if he didn't." John pulled his hand back. The feel of her touch lingered.

"Is Kamau your friend?"

"You could say that. We've been together a long time."

"How long?"

This wasn't working as he had supposed. "Is it important you know?"

"I am interested in all things, like you are interested in me."

"I hired Kamau on my first dig ten years ago." He wondered if she was going to ask what a *dig* was but she didn't. Her command of English was obviously spotty.

She stood motionless, her gaze penetrating. "Where are you from?"

One more question and that's it. "I live in Massachusetts during the off-season and teach at Harvard." His alma mater usually produced a reaction but her expression remained unchanged.

"Are you paired?"

The odd phrasing caught him off-guard. "Paired? You mean married? No. I'm not married but I was engaged once, then something happened. Now I remain...unpaired." The old ache flooded his chest. The warm air pressed closer.

"What happened?"

Darkness closed around his vision. Mia seemed at the end of a long tunnel. "The woman I loved died in a car accident." His eyes stung. His throat worked as he remembered--a snowy night, an argument, and the call that Diane was dead.

Mia studied his face. "Your skin has reddened. Are you in pain?"

"I don't like to think about the accident."

"Were you with her?"

"That's none of your business," he said quietly. Her questions seemed to stalk him. He was becoming desperate for no reason that he could understand. Walls rose around his consciousness. Diane had wanted to marry then, and though he was not disinclined, he wanted to dig fossils in Kenya, first. Now the guilt overwhelmed him at the slightest provocation. He struggled to answer but words failed him. The conversation must end now.

"I'm sorry about what happened to you today but you shouldn't have been left alone out there in the first place. We'll take you to Kanapoi. Maybe the constable can help you."

"Kanapoi?" For once, she seemed caught by surprise.

"It's the regional center ten kilometers west of here. If *shifta* have your car and your leader...the Shepherd or whatever his name is, then the constable can help you more than we can."

"What is a constable?"

"The regional police authority."

She smiled sheepishly. "I thought he was royalty."

John wasn't about to attempt an explanation as to why she would have such a misconception. "Constables were royalty in the Middle Ages. But Constable Moye is a policeman. He presides over two to four men, depending on the time of year and available government funds. Though Kanapoi is a regional center, it's still considered a far outpost."

"I think you do not believe anything I have said." Her delicate brow creased. She peered past his shoulder and out the tent entrance. She started to step past him. "I am wasting time here."

He grabbed her shoulder. "Whoa, where're you going?"

Her eyes locked with his, then drifted away. "I must find the guardian."

"You haven't told me who the guardian is."

"*Maybe the guardian isn't a person,*" the voice said.

He released her, feeling her touch slip away. "What is the guardian?" He rephrased his question.

"A small sphere."

Could it be that simple? "How do you intend to locate this sphere?"

Mia raised her hand and waggled her ring.

Comprehension dawned. "Your finder. May I see it?"

"No." She tensed and stared at the finder.

"What's wrong?"

"I have seen something."

John strained to peer at the swirling colors in the ring but to his annoyance, she pulled it away. Fine. His patience was at an end, anyway. "We have dinner at six. If you're hungry, I'll see you in the mess tent."

She stared at him without comprehension.

He pointed to the tent across the way. "That's the mess tent. We eat our meals there. My tent is next door to this one. If you can't find me, Kamau's tent is over there."

"I will not stay here."

John put both hands on her shoulders. "Yes you will. You wouldn't last the night out there alone. I'll see you at dinner."

As he stepped toward the entrance, she stood with arms folded across her chest, an unfathomable expression on her face. Maybe she had resigned herself to staying put but he would summon Omari anyway.

Outside, John felt a sense of relief as he crossed the compound. His mind raced. Was she insane? If so, why did he feel attracted to her? Had he been away from women too long? She was annoying, mysterious, complex.

"*Have you considered that Watombo might be right?*" The voice broke through his thoughts.

Mchungaji means shepherd.

"*You're a scientist. Aren't you suspicious about coincidences?*"

Aside from shepherd, which may be a coincidence of terms, I don't see a lot of coincidence. On the one side, there's an oral tradition for the origin of mankind formulated into a myth. On the other, there's what appears to be a disturbed girl.

"*She's lying.*"

But why? We're only trying to help her.

"*She has ulterior motives.*"

John waved his hand in the air as if swatting flies that didn't exist.

Omari stepped from the shadow of a tent. "Is everything okay, *Masahib*?

"I want you here tonight." John indicated Mia's tent. "Follow her when she goes to dinner. Otherwise, make sure she stays in her tent."

***

In the thickening twilight, a warm wind streamed off the lake and buffeted the camp's brush fence, setting the electric lights swaying. Faded tents cast leaping shadows onto the ground. The coughing throb of the generator mixed with the smell of cooking food.

John stepped outside his tent. A sudden dust-laden flurry forced him to throw an arm over his face.

Omari still sat on a camp chair in the lee of the support tent, his black and white, checkered *gutra* wrapped over his head and under his chin, his eyes scrunched tight. The Enfield leaned within arm's reach.

John walked over and gave him a nudge, startling him awake. "Any change?"

"She be in tent, *Masahib*. No move. Maybe sleep."

John peered through the open tent entrance. Outside light filtered through the canvas. Mia lay on her cot, clothes and boots on, a sheet draped across her hips. She seemed fast asleep, her breathing deep and regular, her face serene. He stepped back, dropped the tent flap and tied it to the center support pole.

The compound was deserted. The perimeter brush sagged in the wind. John doubted Mia would go anywhere tonight. "You can go back to your quarters," he said to Omari. "Thanks."

The guard grabbed his gun and trudged toward the laborers' quarters without a word, gripping the edges of his *gutra* tight around his neck.

"*Do you think she really sleeps?*" the voice said.

What difference does it make? She's probably more tired than hungry.

At the mess, he slid past the entrance flaps, then re-tied them. Kamau and Bandele stood at their places on either side of the table waiting for him.

"It's starting to blow." John pulled back his chair and they all sat.

"Where's the girl?" Kamau asked.

"She's asleep. I didn't want to disturb her."

Bandele squirmed in his chair. "What do we do with this woman...and the shaman?"

John snapped his napkin into his lap. "Let's eat first." He motioned to the cook-steward, who hovered at the back of the tent.

The steward approached, carrying a platter. "Roasted guinea hen, *Masahib*. Yams and fried plantain." He lowered the platter to John's side.

John forked a guinea hen and a slice of yam onto his plate, then let the cook-steward pass the dish. While Kamau helped himself, John turned to Bandele. "Have you found a handler for the camels?"

"No, *Masahib*."

"Well?"

"I still be looking for someone trustworthy." Bandele fidgeted with his fork, pushing it back and forth beside his plate. "There be many who come to camp from the Gabra. But I no hire them because they be *shifta*, who would run away in the night with the camels and more."

John pulled a leg off the hen and began chewing on it.

"Excuse me, *Masahib* but these camels be much trouble," Bandele continued. "Omari guard for bandits but all he see are lions attracted by camel smell."

John shook his head, frustrated.

"A female last night." Bandele continued. "Less than ten meters from the perimeter. We throw stones, and she run away."

John tossed the leg back on his plate. "If I'd known this desert was more hardpan than sand, I would have bought another truck, instead of bothering with camels."

"*Masahib* could not know." Bandele glanced at Kamau for reassurance but Kamau just pointed with his chin at the platter. Bandele shut up and served himself.

They ate in silence as the wind's howl increased outside. The kerosene lanterns swayed on their wire hooks, jumping shadows on the rattling canvas.

After the main course, the cook-steward returned with dessert. "Your favorite, *Masahib*." He offered a bowl of trifle.

"None for me tonight, thank you."

The cook-steward looked surprised and a bit disappointed but said nothing and passed the combination of wine-soaked sponge cake, jam, and whipped cream to Kamau.

John wiped his mouth with his napkin and leaned back in his chair, regarding Bandele. "You asked about the shaman and the girl. Let's deal with the shaman first."

Bandele's spoon clattered onto his dessert bowl. "I be worried," he said nervously. "Watombo influence spread to the workers."

"You seem shaken yourself."

"He has great *juju*, *Masahib*." A bead of sweat streaked Bandele's cheek. "Everyone be afraid of him."

Kamau folded his napkin and placed it on the table. "What do you know about the man?"

"He be new to this area," Bandele said. "His home tribe be in Uganda, the Karamogong. These Turkana people around the lake be from the same region."

Kamau leaned back in his chair. "He's accepted, though he's a newcomer?"

"Yes, such be his power. I no see it myself but there be stories."

John rested his chin in his hand, his elbow on the table. "Like what?"

"He take life from an animal and give it to a dead person to make him live. Another time he cast a spell to make a woman with child though the woman's husband no be able to make children himself."

How gullible can you get? "Maybe Watombo did something more than cast a spell."

Bandele's brow glistened. His eyes shifted to Kamau, then back to John. "*Masahib* should not make jokes."

John's smile was tight. First Bandele's bold assertion at the work tent, now this.

Kamau leaned forward. "John. This is still a primitive place. These people aren't scientists. They believe what they see and do not ask a lot of questions."

John sighed. At least he hadn't gotten a *father's father*. Still, ridiculous stories annoyed him, especially when they threatened his expedition. "Tell me, Bandele, are you concerned for others, or do you speak for yourself? You know these rumors are not true."

"They no be rumors, *Masahib*. They be *juju*."

John chose to ignore the *juju*, remembering his mumbo jumbo remark. "I suspect we've seen the last of the shaman. Be that as it may, we'll need more laborers."

Bandele put both hands on the table and took a deep breath. "It be impossible to find more laborers. Watombo say the *mchungaji* be here."

"You mean the girl?" John thought to clarify a misunderstanding.

"Not her." The supervisor squirmed. "There be other problem, *Masahib*."

Now what?

"There be the sign in the sky," Bandele said.

"The sign?" John eyed Bandele. "What sign?"

Bandele gestured with his hands. "This morning, near dawn, a great light come. It land in desert. Later, woman appear."

"So?"

"She be spirit. From *mchungaji*."

John turned to Kamau. "Did you see this light in the sky?"

"I saw it." Kamau shifted in his chair. "It flared like a second sun."

"A meteorite?"

"Maybe."

"And Watombo's making the most of it."

"To these people it's serious business," Kamau said. "Spirit or not, we have to decide what to do with the girl."

John felt trapped. "What do you suggest?"

"You can't keep her here."

"She must go to Kanapoi," Bandele said.

John glared at him. "Who asked you?"

"*Masahib*, men be nervous after seeing this woman."

"He's right," Kamau said. "The sooner she's in Kanapoi the better."

"The supply plane doesn't come until Tuesday. That's less than a week. No sense taking her in before that." John wondered about the resistance he was putting up to getting rid of the girl.

Kamau gazed at John as though he had lost his senses. "That's six days. We need to get rid of her, now."

"Where would she stay? She's got nothing."

"The constable's got a room back of his office. Let him put her up."

"You aren't giving me much choice." Irritation fringed John's voice.

"Tomorrow," Kamau said.

Kamau was right. It seemed Kamau was always right. "What about her car?" John asked. *Why am I reluctant to see the girl off?*

"She said she didn't have a car." Kamau sat rigidly.

"She told me she walked from some sort of vehicle." John held up his hand when Kamau began to protest. "I know it's vague but it's either that or she landed with the meteor."

"You've given me even more reason not to care how she got here," Kamau said. "I want her out of camp. Besides, the constable might like to hear about someone who showed up in his jurisdiction, vague about her origins, with no papers. Maybe he knows something we don't."

"That's possible but the constable isn't going to be too pleased if Mia's not as crazy as she seems, and he has to come all the way out here to retrieve her car, a car driven by this shepherd guy."

Kamau blew out a breath. "All right. We look for the car tomorrow, then we take her in the day after."

John regarded Bandele. "Can you control the men until Friday?"

Bandele's sullen gaze ranged between John and Kamau. "I don't know. Maybe big problem."

The cook-steward entered with a pot of coffee, stopped and glanced from face-to-face.

Bandele cleared his throat. "Please, I go now, *Masahib*. I take tea in my tent."

"As you wish."

"Tomorrow," Kamau said to Bandele, "I want the laborers ready."

"Yes, *Bosi*." With a nervous glance at John, Bandele left.

Kamau pushed his and John's cups toward the cook-steward, who poured coffee and returned to his cooking area.

"You going to be all right?" Kamau rolled his cup between his hands.

"Why shouldn't I be?"

"You don't sound convinced about our agreed plan of action."

John's day had started with his nightmare and gotten worse. "I've been thinking about Watombo's myth. It's odd he would tell such a myth an hour before Mia appears."

"You going native?"

"I don't like coincidences." It occurred to John that he was paraphrasing the same argument the voice had proffered earlier. Very subtle, how it maneuvered him. "There's the *mchungaji* in the myth. Mia told me she works with a shepherd."

Kamau grunted. "That's your coincidence? One's a mythological figure. The other is probably a sheep herder and Mia is little Bo Peep."

John felt somewhat reassured that his counter to the voice's conjecture was the same as Kamau's to his. "I know you don't think that. This guardian she's looking for, she said it's a small sphere."

"Not a person?"

"No. Other than that, I'm not sure what it is."

"I think she's been in the sun too long."

John stared at the cup in his hands. "I'm sorry about the shaman. I should have listened to you."

"You had to make a decision."

"I didn't expect him to kill the goat."

"The goat is the least of our worries."

A surge of sorrow engulfed John. Despite an effort to ward it off, he choked. "Death stalks me...my mother, Diane."

"If you had someone else to occupy your thoughts, you wouldn't think about death."

John drew a shuddering breath. Kamau. Rock solid Kamau. He never did buy into John's grief. "Someone like Mia?"

With a hard look, Kamau studied John's face. "I wouldn't go that far."

John laughed, a short hysterical laugh. "If she had hair, she'd be Diane."

"She's no way near Diane, and you know it. At this point, Mia is an enigma."

"Nicely put." Complete unknown or not, she had somehow become a light shining in the darkness of his psyche.

"Look, it's simple." Kamau leaned forward and tapped the table with his finger. "It's obvious Mia and Watombo don't mix. Hell, even I don't like her. If you want to find fossils without a lot of extra trouble, you've got to get rid of her."

John blanched. "Lighten up. Last I checked, I had agreed to take her to Kanapoi."

"I'll believe that when I see it."

John's temper flashed. "What do you want me to do, open a vein and bleed?"

Kamau shook his head and smiled, obviously not bothered by John's exaggeration. "When I was a boy, my father's father said *only a fool tests the depth of the water in a river with both of his feet*. This woman is like a deep river. You should be careful."

"The voice I hear said the same thing."

"You should listen to your conscience."

After Kamau left, John stared at the darkness beyond the entrance for a long time. *Hell, I wish it were my conscience*. The voice seemed to be pushing him forward against his will, taking shots at the girl every step of the way. Did her presence alone in the desert have to be such a big conundrum? There must be a simple explanation for it. But what about her navel? That couldn't be explained as easily. She had an air of mystery and intrigue and something else about her but for the life of him he couldn't put his finger on it. But it made him reluctant to part with her. Of course, he had no right to her, no right to keep her here but she didn't seem in any hurry to go anywhere, unless he counted her obsession with finding the so called guardian.

He drained his cup and pushed it across the table. The cup slid to a rattling stop in the middle.

The cook-steward stuck his head into the tent. "More coffee, *Masahib*?"

"No, I'm fine."

"Whiskey?"

John started to say no, then changed his mind. "Good idea."

The cook-steward disappeared for a moment. He reappeared with a half-full bottle of Scotch and a glass, and placed them on the table.

John grabbed the bottle by its neck and left the tent, leaving the glass behind. He passed Mia's tent, which was still dark. *No sense disturbing her.*

At his own tent, he entered and walked through an area he used as an office to the back where he set the bottle on the table next to his cot. After locating a gas lantern, he raised the glass and lit the wick. With a hollow rush, the flame engulfed the mantle and flared white, bringing a memory of times past.

He was on a camping trip with Diane. They snuggled close in their small tent under rain threatening skies, their only light coming from an ancient kerosene lantern. It gave off an oily yellow flame, smelled like an industrial yard, and hissed whenever a drop of water fell on it. But they hadn't cared.

John gave the control valve a deft twist to reduce the flame, then carried the lantern back to the office area. At his desk, he opened his diary to the day's blank page and stared at its whiteness. What could he write? His altercation with Watombo? The dead goat? Finding Mia? None of it seemed scientific. *Screw it*.

He returned to his cot, grabbed the neck of the bottle and took three long gulps. The liquid burned his throat and warmed his chest. He tipped the bottle again and took another drink. This time the Scotch burned less. The room shifted. Good Scotch.

"*What about your diary?*" the voice said.

He returned to the office area and pulled out his desk chair, then sat staring at the blank page of the diary. "Who is Diane?" he wrote. He scratched out Diane and scribbled *Mia* over it. In frustration, he tossed the pencil on the table and closed the diary. Leaving the bottle, he lifted the lantern and went back into the sleeping area. He took off his shirt and shorts and draped them over a chair.

The generator shut off. The tent canvas lost its golden glow, reverting to a flat, sandy color. He slumped on his cot. His hunting rifle leaned within arm's reach should a lion or other night prowler enter the tent. In the back of his mind rose the image of his mother holding the revolver and lying in a pool of blood.

He could sense the voice stir but it said nothing. God, he hated the thing. For an instant he felt totally alone. *Why the silence now*? He hated himself for soliciting a conversation.

He twisted the lantern valve off. A hot red spot from the mantle glowed and went out. The air seemed suspended in the tent, still, wet and warm. He lay back on the sheets. A rivulet of perspiration formed on his stomach and rolled off his waist.

His eyes brimmed with hot tears. Whiskey induced mood change. He wished Diane were alive, his mother, too. He draped a forearm across his eyes. *Will I ever be whole*?

"*Sleep*," the voice said.

Chapter Five

Stepping into the mess tent the next morning, John removed his sunglasses and hat, then dragged the short sleeve of his wrinkled shirt across his forehead. Though it was only seven o'clock the temperature had gone from a relatively cool thirty degrees Celsius to over forty in the last hour. An early morning dew that had formed overnight had long since evaporated.

"Sleep in your clothes last night?" Kamau tilted back in his chair at the far end of the table, arms folded across his chest.

Behind the back entrance flap, the cook-steward hovered, his presence betrayed by his bare feet protruding below the drop of canvas. Bandele sat opposite a clutch of coffee cups at the other end of the table near the entrance.

John offered a weak smile. "Good Scotch."

Kamau regarded him. "You ever find out why she didn't come to dinner?"

John pulled back a chair and sat. He started to answer, then tilted his head at the labor supervisor who had become interested in their conversation.

"Bandele!" Kamau said.

The supervisor coughed up a mouthful of tea. "*Bosi?*"

"You are finished with your breakfast."

"Yes, *Bosi*." He took a last gulp of his tea and left the tent.

John reached for the pot of coffee. "You didn't have to be so hard on the man."

"Compared to the rest of his life, I'm easy," Kamau said. "Tell me, why did Miss Desert Fox skip dinner?"

"She wasn't hungry? She was too tired to eat?" John closed his eyes and rubbed them with the heels of his hands. Small, bright stars darted behind his lids. "How the hell should I know?"

"You must have emptied the bottle."

"I thought we agreed to look for the car today."

"Damn waste of time, if you ask me."

Mia burst into the tent, as though she had been running across the compound. She stopped when she saw them.

John stood, feeling awkward, caught between his attraction to this strange girl and his promise to Kamau to take her to Kanapoi.

She wore the khaki shirt and shorts he had given her the night before and a pith helmet. A couple of sizes too large, it sagged to one side of her head, giving her a disarming appearance.

John tried to smile. "I like your hat. Isn't it a bit crooked?"

Mia righted the hat. Her eyes rolled up, trying to see it at the same time. "Better?"

"Much better. Do the boots fit?"

She stared at them. "I had problems with the strings. Have I tied them correctly?"

John leaned forward and peered at the laces. "It's not the way I was taught but it'll do. You must be starved." He pulled back the chair next to him.

She sat and stared at the tea, bread and jam spread before her.

Why the confusion? He poured her tea. "Do you take milk and sugar?"

She hesitated, then nodded and reached for a slice of bread. "We do not eat like this where I come from."

"And where's that?" Kamau's voice had a hard edge to it.

"It is...far from here." Mia took a bite of bread and sipped her tea. "The milk and sugar are good."

"Kamau has agreed to look for your car this morning," John said.

"But I thought--"

"You got a problem with that?" Kamau drained his cup, eyeing her over the tipped rim.

John reached across the table and laid a hand on Kamau's arm. "Give her a chance."

Kamau slammed his cup down. "Let's stop playing twenty questions. We look for the car today, then we take her to Kanapoi tomorrow. I'll get the Land Rover."

After Kamau left, Mia turned to John. "Did you tell Kamau about the guardian?"

"I told him what I know. But he's more worried about the effect your presence has on the labor. He wanted to take you to Kanapoi today. The only thing I could think of to get him to wait a day was to have him agree to look for your car. Once we are out there, we can also look for this guardian."

"I will not go to Kanapoi."

John spread his hands. "You can't stay here. We're not--"

She choked, reddened and spit up the piece of bread she had been chewing.

"Are you all right?" He thumped her back.

She cleared her throat. "I'm fine." She forced a smile and pushed the rest of her breakfast away.

The Land Rover ground to a stop outside.

John glanced at the entrance, then Mia. "Do you want more to eat?"

"No. We should go." She wiped her mouth with a napkin and stood to leave.

Outside, Kamau waited until they were both in, then put the vehicle in gear and drove off with a jolt.

Mia bounced between them on the bench seat and put a hand on John's thigh to stabilize herself. "Will you be able to find where I came from?"

"Some of your tracks should still be visible." The warmth of her hand penetrated the fabric of his bush shorts. He struggled to retain his train of thought. "The wind covers most tracks at night but Kamau's a good tracker."

They arrived at the dig, then veered away from the plateau toward the site of the vulture attack. After a night left to the hyenas, bones gleamed white in the light of day. Black and white feathers peppered the surrounding brush.

John got out and surveyed the countryside with binoculars.

Kamau stood alongside. "Deserted as midday in Kanapoi."

The horizon stretched unbroken except for small hills, mounds of sand and brush. John lowered the binoculars. "I don't get it."

Kamau glanced over his shoulder at Mia, who sat placidly in the Land Rover. "Tell me, John, what don't you get?"

"I thought we'd see something. How else do you account for her presence?"

"At this point, dropping from the sky might be the most logical explanation."

John returned to Mia. "Nothing."

"Can we look for the guardian, now?" Mia stared at her finder. "The guardian is in the other direction, nearer your excavation."

The insanity of the night before still seemed to be with her. He thought to humor her. "We can stop there on the way back."

"Do you recognize any landmarks?" Kamau asked.

Mia shaded her eyes and gazed at the emptiness in front of her. "Everything looks the same."

Kamau pointed. "I found a trace footprint in that direction. We'll drive over there and see what we find." He circled the Land Rover to get in.

"I'll be damned." He reached to the ground and picked up a revolver by its trigger guard. He held the gun up so Mia could see it. "Do you recognize this?"

"Of course. That is the bad man's gun that shot me."

John took the gun from Kamau and broke it open. He extracted an empty shell and sniffed it. "Probably not more than a day old. Still two shots left." He wrinkled his nose. The acrid smell reminded him of his fifth birthday party.

Mia studied him. "Is something wrong?"

"I've always had a distaste for guns."

"Why?"

"It's a long story." But in his mind, he saw the candles and the smoke rising after he'd made a wish and blown them out. He tried to remember what he had wished for but couldn't.

"This doesn't make sense," Kamau said. "A *shifta* doesn't leave his gun behind."

John scanned the horizon. "There's a hill over there, a kilometer away. We'll get a better view from the top."

Mia fidgeted. "I remember. I came from there." She pointed to an open space away from the hill.

Kamau gave John a questioning look. "You're the boss."

John wondered at Mia's redirection. "We'll try the hill." Their eyes caught.

Two minutes later, they arrived at the base of the hill.

Kamau jumped out of the vehicle and headed up the slope.

Still holding the revolver, John got out and leaned against the side of the Land Rover.

Mia followed, wiping her hands on her shorts. "May I hold the gun?"

"These things are dangerous." He handed her the revolver with the cylinder cracked open.

Kamau crested the hill. "Hey, there's a lava pool over here."

"He should not go near the water," Mia said.

"Is that a problem?"

"The Shepherd will not like it."

Kamau began to descend the other side.

The gun discharged.

Kamau screamed and clutched his arm.

John's surprise turned to horror. "Give me that."

"It just went off," Mia shrieked, holding the gun in front of her and staring at it.

He snatched the gun and hurried to Kamau's side.

Kamau clutched his upper arm. Blood seeped through his fingers. "Damn! What happened?"

"Mia had the gun. It went off. Let me see." John pulled Kamau's hand away from the wound. "The bullet went through."

"Some consolation." Bewildered, Kamau stared at his arm. "What the hell's going on?"

"Damned if I know." Thoughts of what might have happened, of Kamau lying dead, crowded John's mind.

"Damned if you don't." Kamau's voice shook. He glared over John's shoulder at Mia.

"I'm sure she didn't--"

"Damn it, John! The bitch tried to kill me. You're taking her to Kanapoi."

"All right, All right. Tomorrow."

"Now."

"We'd never make it before dark."

Kamau fixed John with an uncompromising stare as though putting a seal on John's promise to be rid of Mia. "Tomorrow then, first thing."

"Right now, we'd better get you back to camp." John tried to support Kamau as they headed to the Land Rover.

Kamau shrugged him off. "She shot me in the arm, not my leg."

Mia ran up to them. "I didn't mean to shoot."

John thrust out his arm to keep her from approaching closer.

Kamau brushed by her and stalked to the Land Rover where John helped him apply a dressing from the first aid kit. Kamau slumped into the passenger's seat and closed the door.

John passed Mia on his way to the driver's side. "You did that on purpose," he said through clenched teeth.

"I did not." She didn't move. "It was an accident."

He grabbed her arm. "Get in."

"No. I will stay here and look for the guardian!"

He shoved her into the Land Rover from the driver's side.

Kamau's eyes widened with a mixture of anger and fear as she slid across the seat toward him. He pressed against the door.

She regained her composure. "I am not going to hurt you," she said defiantly.

John slid into the driver's seat and started the engine. He turned the Land Rover back toward camp. Locking his hands on the wheel, he stared forward, angry. He had almost lost his best friend. Mia's silliness had taken a sinister turn.

"*You fool.*" The voice intruded. "*You trusted her, and she tried to kill your friend.*"

John winced. *But why shoot Kamau? Maybe it was an accident like she said?* And it had been, or had it?

"*You believe her at your peril.*"

The chamber was open when I handed her the gun. Somehow the chamber closed and she pulled the trigger. Not a logical sequence. *There must be a simple explanation.*

"*Sure. She's from outer space.*"

The voice, too? Meteors or spaceships. An *mchungaji*, the shepherd, *Afareni*...He might as well believe Watombo. *I can't take that seriously.*

"*Maybe you should.*"

***

The next morning, John sat in the mess tent, poking at his breakfast. Kamau entered, his arm resting in a sling around his neck, the bandage stained through with blood.

"We better get you to a doctor," John said.

"I should have gone in yesterday." Kamau pulled the sling off his arm and flexed it stiffly. "Where's the girl?"

"She hasn't left her tent. I put Omari on her last night. I was afraid she'd run away."

Kamau snorted. "That would have solved a lot of problems."

"I'm sorry. I didn't think she was that crazy."

Kamau winced and put his forearm back in the sling. "You know something I don't?"

"I tried to talk to you about this guardian she's looking for and the shepherd but you didn't seem interested."

"Why should I have been? She's a nut case."

"I'm beginning to wonder myself. When I pressed her about a vehicle, I got her to admit she flew in, she said like a bird. Since we would have heard a plane, I thought she was pulling my leg."

"What you're telling me is you knew she was a nut case before we went on that wild goose chase for her car."

"I'm sorry. I thought we should at least try to verify where she came from. Maybe the *shifta* kidnapped her a lot earlier and she escaped."

"You're grasping at straws. You don't seriously believe four *shifta* are going to let a skinny girl outwit them?"

"No, I suppose not. At the same time, I didn't see any harm in finding out where she'd go with this guardian story. We could have searched for it on the way back."

"Guardian be damned! All this nonsense got me shot."

"I said I was sorry."

"You better believe it." Kamau turned toward the entrance. "I'm ready when you are. I ate earlier."

As they left the tent, Mia crossed the compound with Omari close behind. She kept glancing over her shoulder at the solemn guard.

"Why am I being treated like a prisoner?" she asked John.

"You're not. I wanted to make sure you were still here this morning. Like it or not we feel responsible for you."

"I can take care of myself."

"That remains to be seen. Anyway, there's been a change of plans." John waved Omari away. "I'm taking Kamau to Kanapoi to have a doctor look at his arm. We'll also be paying a visit to the constable. I want to report the altercation we had with Watombo."

She glanced at Kamau's bandage and reached to touch it.

"Yo! That's close enough." He drew back, his tone measured.

Dropping her hand, Mia blinked. "Can you forgive me?"

Kamau glared at her for a moment, then strode to the Land Rover where he leaned against its side and waited.

Mia's gaze lingered on Kamau, almost as if she were trying to figure out what had occurred. Then, abruptly, she turned to John. "While you are in Kanapoi, may I go to the dig with your men?"

"That's a bad idea." John was surprised how quickly she had dismissed the confrontation with Kamau, as if she had simply shifted to the next thing on her agenda. "I can't leave you here alone. You wouldn't be safe."

"I'm being punished for what Watombo did yesterday."

"No one is being punished. But the situation has changed. Kamau's arm needs attention, and I should report our problems with Watombo to the constable."

She brightened. "Can we look for the guardian after that?"

"Yes, I'm sure it will still be there when we get back." John nodded to the mess tent. "Do you want some breakfast before we go?"

Mia hesitated. "I'm never hungry in the morning."

The cook-steward hurried from the mess tent, waving a piece of paper. He stopped at the sight of Mia. Looking askance at her, he handed John the slip of paper. "If *Masahib* want trifle, he have to get more cream from Kanapoi." The steward back-stepped, his eyes never leaving Mia, then he turned and ran to his cooking area.

John walked to where Kamau was standing and thrust the slip of paper at him. "Put cream on your list and whatever else he's got here."

Kamau indicated Mia with his chin. "She coming?"

"I told her she wouldn't be safe if we left her behind."

Kamau squinted, his face hard. A small artery tracing up the side of his temple pulsed. "She doesn't know what we intend to do with her?"

"If she did, she would have refused to come."

Kamau clapped John on the back, circled the vehicle and got in behind the wheel.

"You feel up to driving?" John asked.

"It'll give me something to do."

"Mia." John waved to her.

She hurried to him, her face laced with anticipation.

"Let's go." He helped her in and closed the door.

As they headed west out of camp, they passed the remaining laborers and Bandele, who were loading onto the flatbed truck. Though John didn't like leaving the dig to Bandele, the supervisor was cognizant enough of fossil excavations to guide the men through the tedious but necessary task of sifting excavated earth looking for small fossils.

The sun broke through the clouds casting the shadow of the Land Rover ahead of them as a stiff breeze blew their dust into a rising swirl off to one side.

Mia grasped a ceiling strap for support. "Has Kamau's wound worsened?"

"It's stiff and sore."

Mia's grip on the strap tightened as Kamau gunned the Land Rover across the uneven track. He seemed desperate to get to Kanapoi.

"Do you think--," Mia held on for a jolt, "--reporting Watombo will help?"

Though she seemed clueless, John was fast coming to realize that she left no stone unturned. "I don't think it will hurt. If he causes more trouble, he'll be on the record."

Kamau swerved and bumped onto the main road.

Straight ahead, in the distance, Kanapoi stuck out from the bare plain like a movie set in a cowboy western. The road ran across the flat desert and knifed into the town between rows of boxy, clapboard buildings. Multi-colored paint peeled from sun-bleached walls.

Kamau slowed as they came to the outskirts. Though the town had seemed deserted from a distance, there were in fact a few natives about. They kept to the shade under a scattering of wooden awnings and weatherworn signs creaking on rusty hinges.

Kamau pulled up in front of a modest single-story building with a bank of louvered windows overlooking a wooden porch. A new sign above the door read *Kenyan National Police, Kanapoi*.

Confused, John turned to Kamau. "Don't you want to see the doctor first?"

"You kidding?"

The constable could be seen through the window. He sat at a desk in a sparse room with a large ceiling fan turning above him. He glanced up at their arrival and rose to meet them on the porch outside.

"Constable Moye." John shook the officer's hand.

The constable was a stocky, intense man, dressed in a starched khaki uniform of short-sleeved shirt and bush shorts. He wore wraparound sunglasses as black as his skin. "Good morning, John, Kamau. Who's this you've got with you?"

"This is Mia," John said.

"Glad to meet you, Miss Mia." Moye extended his hand to shake hands but stopped when she made no motion to take it. "A bit shy, isn't she?"

John shifted. "We've got a problem."

"We've got a couple of problems," Kamau said.

The constable raised an eyebrow.

"I'll get to that." John glanced quickly at Kamau. "The shaman Watombo has been causing trouble. I threw him off my dig the other day. He nearly started a riot."

Moye smiled. "I thought Watombo and you had a spiritual relationship."

John marveled at how news spread, even in a place this remote with no telephones. "I asked for his help but after Mia showed up, he got my men believing she's an evil spirit or something."

Moye directed his shrouded eyes to Mia. "Is she?"

John gave a short laugh. "You're not serious."

Moye pushed his hands deep into the pockets of his shorts. "I know what Watombo's preaching. Big light in the sky the other day, and now everyone thinks the Martians have landed."

"We saw it, too," John said, "at least Kamau did."

Moye's mouth turned serious. "So, is she a Martian?"

"She says she was on her way to Nairobi. Her car must have broken down east of our dig. We searched for the car yesterday and couldn't--"

"Bullshit," Kamau said under his breath.

At the remark, Moye's dark glasses ranged to Kamau. "That's a fresh wound you've got." Moye pulled his glasses down his nose and peered at Kamau's arm.

"It was an accident," John said.

"Who caused this accident?"

Kamau indicated Mia with a thrust of his chin. "She did."

The constable pushed his glasses back up his nose. "Gunshot?"

"It happened while we were looking for her car," John said. "We found a revolver discarded by one of the *shifta* she claims assaulted her. Mia was handling the gun when it went off."

The constable regarded Mia.

She pursed her lips, her face flushed red but she kept silent.

"You ever shot anyone before, Miss?"

"No."

"Do you have any papers?"

"Papers?"

"Passport, ID."

"I left them behind." She spoke in a whisper. "At least I think I did. I don't remember much of what happened or where I am from."

"Let's cut the crap," Kamau said. "We're leaving her with you until the supply plane comes in."

Mia's mouth dropped open. She turned to John. "You--"

"It's for the best." John read the sense of betrayal on Mia's face. He hated his duplicity but what could he do? The girl simply didn't belong in his camp despite his misplaced affection for her.

The constable took off his glasses and with a studied motion, used a white handkerchief to wipe his forehead. He kept his eyes closed the whole time. The glasses went back on.

"I suppose under the circumstances, a stateless person should be under my jurisdiction. I've got a small room out back if she's willing to stay there."

"I do not want to stay here." Mia folded her arms across her chest, her lower lip curled down.

John glanced at Kamau, wondering if he'd grant some last-minute reprieve from leaving Mia with the constable. But Kamau gazed into the distance.

Obviously, he was glad to be rid of her. After all, the girl had shot him.

Moye's dark glasses shifted between Kamau and John. "Something going on here I should know about?"

"No, nothing," John said. "We appreciate your help."

John didn't know if the relief he felt originated from the constable not pursuing the shooting, or from him agreeing to take Mia.

"I've already got a file on Watombo. I'll put a note in it about the disturbance."

"Thanks."

"Let me know if you have any more trouble," the constable said. "I wouldn't mind having an excuse to run him out of my jurisdiction."

They fell silent.

"We're going to see the doctor, now." John turned to Mia and clasped her shoulders. "You need help."

She dropped her gaze to the boardwalk and traced a crack in the wood with the toe of her boot. "You lied to me. You intended to leave me here all along."

"The way things were going I had to do something. It's only for four days, then the supply plane can take you to Nairobi." John wasn't prepared to deal with her protests, there, in the middle of Kanapoi. He looked over his shoulder. His reflection danced in the opacity of the constable's dark glasses. He gave Mia's shoulders a final squeeze. "Goodbye."

Mia twisted her shoulders free.

The constable stepped between them. "If you'll come with me, Miss Mia, I'll show you to your room." She didn't resist as he led her away.

"Don't look so glum," Kamau said as he and John headed for the Land Rover.

John climbed in and slammed shut the passenger-side door. He slumped in the seat, arms folded tight across his chest. "Let's get you to the doctor."

"It never would have worked. First, she was too evasive. Second, she was dangerous. Third, she--"

"I know all that."

Kamau bit his lower lip and started the engine. He kept the Land Rover at a steady pace as it lumbered through the center of town. "Here's the shopping list," Kamau said. "Might keep your mind off the girl."

I miss her already.

"*You'll get over it,*" the voice said.

Will I? Ever since Diane's death, he'd felt a certain deadness inside, a lack of vitality. In the short span of two days, Mia had changed all that. He'd come alive. But he knew he wasn't thinking straight. Hopefully Kamau was, and they had done the right thing. John peered out the back of the vehicle but Mia and the constable were already gone.

"She was special."

Chapter Six

The room Mia stood in was small. A bed with a faded green cover smelling of mothballs was crammed against one wall. Next to the bed sat a rattan chair and farther away a washstand with its porcelain bowl and pitcher of water. The floor had been painted with a clear varnish that had squeaked under Mia's steps when she had entered. A window with a mosquito-mesh screen and heavy shutters opened to the south. On the adjacent wall, a door led to a breezeway that separated the room from the constable's office building.

The constable's footsteps receded, then the door to his office opened and closed. He had said she was free to move about but shouldn't go far. He probably assumed she would not run away.

Confusion about her situation swept through her. *Were all humans so devious? Did they all lie?* Her metabase provided only definitions, not an explanation. This was not the first time it had come up short on helping her. But it could not know everything, or could it?

She didn't think she knew how to lie. She didn't always say everything that would answer a question but was that lying? She had not lied about the guardian, or the Shepherd or how she came to be in the desert alone. She had not lied when the gun went off and wounded the scientist's black assistant. Certainly not then.

It had been an accident, like the scientist said, almost as if the gun had taken on a life of its own.

The chamber had closed. Then the gun fired. Perhaps, when she raised it to see why the chamber had closed, her finger had inadvertently touched the trigger. There could be no other logical explanation.

In retrospect, she should have returned to the Shepherd two nights ago. That's when her finder scanned the scientist and indicated he carried *Gilomir's* DNA in a pure form. Not adulterated like that carried by the bad *shifta*. Knowing that, the Shepherd might have changed his plans. Maybe he wouldn't need the guardian after all. But if the Shepherd insisted she persevere, then she would need assistance from the scientist. With sand everywhere, the guardian would not be lying on top in plain sight. The scientist would have to help her dig for it. He had agreed to help her, and he would have if the gun hadn't gone off. So much for events proceeding in predictable ways.

Now she was farther than ever from where the guardian lay and even farther from the Shepherd. A long way to walk. A large expenditure of energy. But the Shepherd had said she was good for five days. She had three and a half left. If he had calculated right, there should be no problem.

She stepped to the door and peered out. No one in sight. She exited and circled around the back of the office building away from the constable's big window, then stepped onto the wooden boardwalk that lined the main street.

She kept close to the buildings, staying in the shade where she could. She passed camels swaying or kneeling at hitching posts, and tall Turkana tribesmen lounging under drooping overhangs.

Some of the men wore shirts and shorts like the scientist but most wore traditional loincloths, their hair braided tight, their arms decorated with coils of flattened copper wire. No one paid any attention to her. She glanced over her shoulder the way she had come. No one followed.

Up ahead, the scientist's empty vehicle was parked in front of a store. Not wanting to be seen by him or his assistant, she turned into a narrow alley that opened on her right. Natives crowded the close walls going to and from what appeared to be a market beyond a timber-framed portal. It opened into a large, dirt compound surrounded by a head-high, whitewashed stone wall. Fruits, vegetables butchered meat and various handicrafts lay on mats in front of vendors who squatted on their haunches, flicking camel hair whisks to ward off flies.

She approached an old woman who cracked a gummy smile. As Mia stood over her, the woman gestured at a collection of wooden carvings on the mat.

"Good dolls, *Memsahib*. Good price."

Mia knelt and picked up a carving. It had been shaped from a soft white wood and dyed black with what smelled like oil or shoe polish. A horsehair wig was woven with beads. The doll's loincloth was made of goat skin. It bore a crude resemblance to the natives she had observed on the street.

A shadow fell across her.

Looking up, she shaded her eyes.

The sun's rays burst from behind the head of a tall male figure.

Mia struggled to her feet. *Watombo.*

He poked her with his walking stick and shouted something in his native language.

She slapped the stick to one side. "Stop it."

The crowded marketplace grew silent as all attention turned to the towering shaman.

Watombo began shouting again while pointing to Mia with his withered hand and grabbing at his genitals with his other hand.

An angry murmur shot through the crowd. Dark bodies closed around her.

Watombo's rant became accusatory, his delivery quick, each syllable falling heavily onto Mia's ears.

She pushed. "Let me through."

The crowd sagged and parted.

Disoriented, she stumbled into the sudden opening and slammed against the perimeter wall.

A vegetable vendor's stacked tomatoes scattered and rolled across the ground.

Someone spun Mia around and shoved her back toward the shaman.

His stick whistled through the air and landed with a thwack on her collarbone.

She screamed. Clutching her shoulder with one hand, she tried again to run through the crowd but hands groped her, squeezing her breasts, her crotch. They cut her off and forced her up against the wall.

Watombo pressed hard against her back, the weight of his body pinning her to the rough surface. His hands squeezed her thighs. His fingers raked upward. His hips ground hard against her buttocks. He fumbled at the clasp holding her shorts.

She twisted sideways.

Watombo staggered forward and cracked his head against the wall.

Shoulder-to-shoulder the crowd seethed forward, its chaotic chattering rising to a sustained roar.

A stone bounced off the wall. Another hit her forehead with a mind-numbing thud. Her eyes darted, filling with blood. More stones thumped the wall and fell to the ground.

Desperately, she queried her metabase. It supplied the words she needed. "*Leave me alone*," she screamed in the native tongue.

The wall of sweat-streaked bodies fell back shocked, disoriented.

She shielded her head with her arm and lunged, tripped, then rose and stumbled to the portal and down the alley, shoving people aside.

The clamoring chatter rose again from the crowd as it surged behind her.

She emerged from the alley onto the main street and struggled to focus. *The scientist's vehicle*.

People alongside peered at her. Those up the street stopped to see what the commotion was about. From behind, stones arced into the air and clattered about her.

"Help!" she screamed, her voice ragged.

***

John had finished loading the last of the supplies when Mia's scream pierced the air from down the street. "What the--"

She struggled toward him, a limping, faltering run, a chaotic mass of natives in pursuit, screaming, hurling stones.

She fell into his arms sobbing, out of breath. "Watombo."

Her shirt hung torn off one shoulder, her shorts askew. Blood coursed from a split eyebrow and slicked the side of her face and neck. She clutched him, fingernails digging his arms.

He tried to shield her with his body. Stones pelted off his raised arm and clanged off the Land Rover's metal roof.

A thumb-sized rock sailed from the back of the crowd and hit Mia's bare scalp with a loud clack of stone on bone. Blood gushed from the wound to mingle a bright red over the previous darker flow.

Kamau ran from the doctor's office next to the supply store. "Get her in the Land Rover!" He stepped in front of the crowd, his injured arm hanging in a clean white sling.

A man ran up and leaned back to throw a rock.

With his good arm, Kamau grabbed the man's throat in a tight fist.

The man squealed, a rabbit caught in a vise before Kamau pitched him into the roiling mass of bodies.

John fumbled with the Land Rover's door. He opened it and shoved Mia inside, across the front seat, away from the open window.

The crowd flowed around the vehicle but kept a distance. Their noise was deafening.

The constable beat his way from the back, his baton thumping bodies, cutting a path to the Land

Rover. He broke through and turned on the crowd to shout obscenities, first in English, then in the native tongue. His tight voice cut through the chaos, a scolding lecture, punctuated with aggressive thrusts of his baton.

The crowd noise dampened, then silenced.

"There!" Mia pointed, wiping blood from her face, struggling to keep it out of her eyes.

Watombo leaned against a post on the boardwalk, his arms wrapped across his chest, the upper half of his body lost in a dark shadow cast by an awning.

Moye pushed through the crowd and stumped onto the wooden platform.

Watombo regarded the policeman indifferently.

The constable grabbed Watombo's arm and dragged him out of the shade toward the crowd, shouting at him the whole time.

At the edge of the boardwalk, Watombo shuffled to a stop. He waved his good hand above his head for attention.

The crowd quieted.

With a grin spreading across his face, Watombo lifted his loincloth, thrust his hips and pointed to Mia. He spoke in a rumbling voice.

The crowd laughed.

Watombo flicked a cold glance at the constable, then stepped off the walkway and fell into the embrace of his followers. Towering a head above the tallest man, he let them sweep him down the street.

"What did he say?" Mia sobbed.

"He feels better," Kamau muttered, then to John. "We should leave while we can."

John slid in beside Mia. He eased her head back, as he reached for the first aid kit.

Moye stepped to the window on John's side. "Is she okay?"

"Head wounds bleed a lot."

Two men from the crowd lingered at a distance, still clutching stones.

The constable placed both hands on the Land Rover door and leaned forward. "You want to press charges?"

"You want another riot?"

"I'm sorry." The constable glanced over his shoulder at the receding crowd, the shaman still at its center. "If I had more men, things would be different."

"Mia's no safer here than she is with us," John said angrily. He turned to Kamau. "Let's go."

Kamau dragged the gearshift into reverse and gunned the engine. A stone hit the rear window and snapped it into a starburst pattern. He shoved the gearshift forward, spun the wheel hard and stomped the accelerator.

John opened the first aid kit, grabbed a large sterile compress and ripped the package open. After applying it to her head, he secured the bandage in place with a gauze wrap.

Her eyes were squeezed tight. She shook and gripped his arm.

The thought of losing her overwhelmed him. "I'm sorry. I shouldn't have left you." He couldn't tell if she heard.

The Land Rover careened down the main road and out of town. Sweat beaded at Kamau's hairline and dripped off both cheeks. Dust swirled in through the open window flaps and settled in an ashen cake on his face. "She's a witch."

"What?" John shouted above the noise of the engine and the rush of air.

"This is not good." Kamau shook his head, staring glassy eyed at the road in front of him. "Everyone thinks she's a sorceress."

"*Sheitani*, sorceress. What difference does it make? It's all bullshit, and you know it."

"It does not matter what I know!" Fear edged Kamau's voice. "Since she arrived, we've had nothing but trouble."

"Calm down." John bumped on the seat and grabbed a handhold. "You can slow down, too."

Kamau left off the accelerator and brought the vehicle to a stop in the middle of the deserted road. He leaned across the steering wheel, shaking his head, gulping back emotion. "I don't know what to believe anymore."

John felt compassion for his friend. "What did Watombo mean when he said he was better?"

Kamau took a deep breath and steadied. "He claimed Mia had made him impotent but he was able to break the spell." Kamau drew his hand across his face, smearing dirt. He eased the Land Rover forward.

"Watombo's making trouble because of what I did to him on Wednesday," John said.

Kamau shook his head. "This time there is more to it."

***

John stood over Mia where they had deposited her on the cot in her tent. The bandage on her head seemed to have stopped the bleeding. He unbuttoned her bloodstained shirt. Raising her head, he slipped the shredded garment off her shoulders. Blood had flowed between her breasts and smeared in a dark, coagulated pool on her stomach.

Kamau gazed at her with distaste. "Looks like she butted heads with a kudu. You need my help?"

"Damn it, of course I do. Heat a pot of water and bring me a fresh first aid kit."

John returned his attention to Mia. She lay with her eyes closed, mouth relaxed, her hands lying at her sides. Was she sleeping, unconscious or simply faking the whole thing? If she had a concussion, perhaps he should keep her awake but she seemed alert enough when she had pointed out Watombo.

He brushed a finger over what had been angry scratches on her legs, now closed to fine pink lines. Though she was still bruised in places, her skin was seamless.

Kamau returned carrying a pan of water. A sponge and a first aid kit were tucked under his arm. He put the water and sponge on the stand next to the cot. With obvious reluctance, he opened the first aid kit and stood stolidly as John rummaged for a disinfectant solution and sterile dressings.

Seeing that Kamau wasn't going to help, John lay the dressing at Mia's side. He soaked the sponge in the warm water and dabbed at the dried blood on her torso. He worked in angry silence, glancing every once in awhile at Kamau, who stood at the foot of the cot, arms folded across his chest.

After fifteen minutes, John drew a sheet across her. He returned the unused dressings and disinfectant to the first aid kit. "Didn't have to use as much of this as I thought."

"Maybe she doesn't go around making people impotent," Kamau said, breaking his silence, "but she has powers."

John spun on his friend. "For Chrissake, Kamau. You keep telling me she's a witch. Where's the evidence?"

"Have you been cleaning with your eyes closed?"

"What are you talking about?"

"The wounds are healed."

Fear reached from John's stomach, clawing his heart. He, too, had seen but had not wanted to believe. "They were scratches."

Kamau grabbed John by the arm and pulled him to the end of the cot. He jerked clear the bandage covering Mia's head wound.

John winced.

"It's healed."

John peered at the neat closure. "Maybe the cut wasn't as deep as we thought."

"An hour ago, it needed stitches."

John stepped to the basin, grabbed the soap and scrubbed his hands in a nervous, jerky motion. "We have to talk."

"I don't want to talk. I'm tired, and I hurt." Kamau threw the bandage on the floor and stomped from the tent.

John stifled a reprimand.

"*Too bad the constable didn't keep her,*" the voice said.

Kamau would have liked that. John pitied his friend. After thinking Mia was gone for good, she was still here. But no one could have foreseen Watombo's attack.

"*The shaman should have killed her.*"

What dark side conjures up these thoughts? Perhaps a *sheitani* infected him after all.

Mia seemed stable. There was nothing left for him to do. If she stirred or needed help, he could hear her easily from his tent next door.

John turned the lantern off and headed for his tent. In four days, the supply plane would come. Then she'd be on her way to Nairobi. But what to do with her in the meantime? And what about Kamau?

Chapter Seven

Angry clouds boiled up in the morning, obscuring the sunrise, giving the day a sullen start. John stood a couple of meters to one side of Kamau as he checked off a list of supplies being loaded onto the truck.

After standing there for five minutes, ignored by Kamau the whole time, John got fed up with the silent treatment. "How's your arm?"

Kamau didn't look up. "A bit stiff but not sore. I don't think it's infected."

John gave the camp a cursory scan. "I don't see any sign of Watombo."

"He was here earlier. Omari ran him off."

"How are the laborers reacting?"

Kamau lowered the clipboard and let his gaze drift from the laborers' quarters to John. "Some refuse to work. Some aren't sure what to do. They're all afraid of him."

Mia stepped from her tent and hurried to the mess.

Kamau scowled. "I thought she was recuperating."

"She's a witch, remember."

Moments later, she emerged. In one hand, she carried a slice of bread smeared with jam while she licked the sticky condiment off the fingers of her other hand. She took a bite of bread and tried to close the last button on her shirt. "May I come, too?"

"Shouldn't you be resting," John said.

"But I have rested."

"It'll be a long hot, boring day for you."

"It won't be boring. I know a lot about paleoanthropology."

Kamau screwed his mouth up as though he had just tasted something bad. "Didn't know they taught paleoanthropology on Mars."

"I am self-taught."

"Did you also teach yourself to heal quickly?"

Mia stared at Kamau.

"I still think you should be resting," John said.

She shook her head vehemently. "I have an interest in fossils from the age at which you are digging."

That odd disconnect again. If she ran into an obstacle in one direction, she backed up and continued in another. She continued to intrigue him. He'd never been able to interest Diane in anything prehistoric. "At what age do you think we're digging?"

"At Hadar, the finds dated back to more than three million years and already placed Australopithecus well along the hominid line. I think you are looking for something older." She frowned in concentration. "*Ardipithecus Ramidus* would be closer to the hominid split from chimps and gorillas."

"I'm impressed." John glanced at Kamau. "If she stays here, we have to leave Omari. What harm can she do if she comes along?"

"Probably plenty." Kamau tossed the clipboard onto the truck seat and headed for the driver's side of the Land Rover.

"You don't have to make a bad situation worse," John called to Kamau's receding back.

Without turning around, Kamau waved his hand above his head in a gesture of dismissal.

John felt ill at ease, caught between the demands of his friend and this strange woman. "You can come with us. I hope Kamau is wrong."

"I promise to behave."

John opened the door of the Land Rover and indicated she should get in. As she stepped on the running board, her hand brushed the door. It knocked loose her bread.

"You've lost your breakfast," John said. "I'll get you some more."

She brushed her hands together, removing crumbs. "All done."

Kamau started the engine and put the vehicle in gear.

"Suit yourself. Looks like Kamau's getting anxious." John slid onto the seat beside her and closed the door. She sat close up against him, leaving space between herself and Kamau. As the Land Rover lumbered north, she brushed idly at dust that drifted in through the open window and settled onto her shorts.

John's gaze swept over her smooth legs. An ache wormed into his heart. Did he still miss Diane that much, or was this feeling the beginning of a deeper affection for Mia? He had difficulty separating the two of them in his mind.

Twenty minutes later, Kamau guided the Land Rover to a stop in the shade of the work tent. The

Ford half-ton passed them and stopped in front. In the swirling dust, the laborers piled off the back.

John climbed out, pulled his hat low against the slanted sunlight and walked to the edge of the gorge. He stood, hands thrust deep in his pockets. The morning heat prickled his skin, opening his pores with an imagined pop. He inhaled the dry air, devoid of organic scents, nothing but an oppressive hot dustiness.

When he first arrived at the site a week ago--had it only been a week--he had instructed the men to cut a path across the steep embankment to the bottom of the gorge. A system of struts pressed against sheets of plywood along a narrow ledge. This kept loose silt off the path as it angled its way down. The struts crossed the path at intervals and were anchored to the ground by wooden stakes.

"How do you know where to look for fossils?" Mia asked.

"We don't. But we keep track of where we've been with the maps in the work tent."

"I'd like to see them."

John glanced over to Kamau. "I'm going to show her the maps. I'll catch up to you later."

Kamau scowled and joined Bandele and the laborers who had assembled at the top of the path and were starting to descend. They shuffled close together, single-file, turning their heads to look apprehensively at the sheets of plywood as if they might collapse at any moment.

Kamau brought up the rear, stopping to check each stake that anchored the diagonal struts that held the plywood in place.

Mia regarded him with interest. "What is he doing?"

"Seeing that the stakes aren't loose."

"It is good to be cautious."

"I want you to stay here," John said as they headed to the tent. "The embankment can be dangerous, and there's also the possibility a predator might wander through the gorge to see what's going on."

As he held the entrance flap open for her, she gave him a quizzical look but seemed to decide not to argue his point. Inside, she stepped to the table. "Why are the maps marked up like this?"

John picked up a pencil and pointed. "We've divided the gorge into sectors. Each sector represents a different area of excavation. As we complete our work in one sector, we shade it in." He indicated a sector, which had gray pencil-shading over it. "Today, we're going to initiate digging in sector two. It's at the bottom of the gorge and fifty meters farther along its eastern extension."

"How old is the strata you are working?"

"Four million years."

Mia peered at the map. "How can you tell?"

"The stratigraphy here is excellent. It has very distinct geologic layers. Whenever we find something, we have a good idea about its age before using more technical dating methods."

"Did you find anything in sector one?"

"Animal bones...teeth. They're okay for dating but not much use otherwise."

"No hominids?"

"I wish." He tossed the pencil onto the map. "Look, I've got to join Kamau."

"You promised I could search for the guardian."

"If the laborers saw you, I'd lose half of them. I can't risk it."

"I thought you were worried about predators."

"Do I have to spell it out?" He exited the tent and waved to Omari, who lounged against the Land Rover. "Make sure Mia stays here."

"Yes, *Masahib*."

Mia pursed her lips and stared stubbornly at John.

"This isn't a tourist adventure," he said. "I've got a dig to excavate. I'll let you know when it's a good time to look for your guardian."

Mia seemed to reach some conclusion. She pointed to a small rise overlooking the gorge. "I will sit there. It will give me a good view of the gorge."

"That's better. There's water in the cooler." They fell silent. Feeling awkward, John checked his shirt pocket for the metal dental pick and archeological brush he always carried. "Well then, I'll see you in a while."

He hurried to catch up with Kamau, who had finished testing the last strut and was now waiting for him at the bottom of the gorge.

"What was that all about?" Kamau asked.

"She insisted again on looking for the guardian."

"And you agreed?"

"I put her off. We've got enough trouble with the labor as it is. Omari's watching her."

"Good move."

***

An hour later, after the workers were well into their assigned tasks, John led the way as he and Kamau headed back to the tent. John rounded the final bend and approached the bottom of the trail leading up to the work tent.

The sound of a cracked twig, or a rolling stone, out of place in the heated stillness caused John to glance up the trail. He caught a glimpse of Mia scampering back to her vantage point. She retook her seat and waved to him.

John stopped short. "I told her to stay put."

"When's the last time she listened to you?" Kamau stopped, hands on hips. Then distracted, he touched the pocket of his shorts. "I forgot my compass. I'll be right back."

John continued up the path, stepping around the first strut.

"John!" Mia screamed.

He took his attention off the trail and glanced up at her.

She waved her arms over her head.

His foot hit the second strut.

The stake holding the strut in place shot across the path. With a loud crack, the plywood shoring burst apart.

He ducked, covering his head with his arms as tons of loose sand surged across the trail and thudded onto his back.

His world went dark and silent. Sand pressed around his body. He dared not breathe. Small stars, like busy fireflies, drifted across the darkness behind his closed eyes.

"*Remain calm,*" the voice said.

I'm going to die.

"*Kamau and the laborers have come. They are digging.*" The voice was reassuring. "*The girl descends the trail. She is hysterical. Kamau asks if she saw where you went under.*"

John's lungs heaved, demanding air.

"*The girl holds out her hand with the finder. Her fingers shake and spread. She closes her eyes. She opens them and points at you.*"

The weight of earth on his head lightened.

"He is not deep." Mia's muffled voice penetrated the dirt. "He is alive."

Air. John quivered with the effort to hold his breath. Behind his eyelids, the fiery lights danced with increasing urgency.

"*Four more seconds. Kamau has your arm. He lifts your head free. You are safe.*"

"Give him room!" Kamau yelled.

John's breath exploded from his lungs. Air whistled through his constricted throat. He sucked in a fresh supply along with sand, then doubled up in a choking fit.

One of the laborers brought water.

John poured it over his head and face and rinsed his mouth. "What happened?"

"A cave-in," Kamau said. "Are you okay?"

John checked his neck by turning his head gingerly. "I think so."

A high-pitched keening split the air. Mia slumped and rocked on her knees, clutching her shoulders, her face contorted in anguish. Tears streamed her cheeks.

"Easy, girl." Kamau stepped over to her. He hesitated, then reached both hands under her arms and helped her to her feet. "John's okay. He's going to be all right."

"I thought he would die." She dabbed at her cheeks, then peered at her wet hands.

"He almost did but you found him."

"I... I..." Mia still held her hands before her face. "I could not think. All I felt was...worry."

John staggered toward them coughing and clearing his throat. He struggled to speak.

Kamau caught him from falling.

Mia stared horrified. "I am sorry. I am sorry."

John regarded her quizzically. She seemed different, confused yes, maybe even fearful. "No one's blaming you. I'm okay."

She gave him a jerky nod.

He reached up and wiped a tear from her face. She hadn't cried before, though there had been plenty of times when crying would have been a normal reaction to events.

"Come on. We better get you to some shade." Kamau took John by his upper arm and led him over the humped sand and past the remaining stakes. "I don't know how this could have happened. I checked all the stakes on the way down."

"I must have hit one with my foot. I don't remember."

At the tent, John sat in a camp chair and leaned back. He shook his head, looking at Mia. "We tell the laborers not to touch the stakes. I should have been more careful."

Mia knelt beside him and took his hand in hers. "I was afraid for you."

John closed his eyes. His mind focused on his hand in hers as he tried to forget his brush with death.

"Sorry to break this up," Kamau said. "We should get you back to base camp."

"*He is right,*" the voice said. "*Let go of the girl's hand and return to camp.*"

I'm not in a hurry. Still dazed, John shuddered at the thought of what might have happened. Mia had saved his life by finding him. What if Kamau hadn't dug to him in time?

"*But he did get to you in time,*" the voice said.

***

The horizon glowed burnt-red in a long thin line where the sun had set. High above the dark plain, the moon, a quarter full, was cradled in the arms of the Twins, Castor and Pollux. Though the temperature had dropped ten degrees, residual heat in the air brought beads of perspiration to John's forehead.

With Kamau striding to stay abreast, John hurried away from the mess tent, his hands thrust deep in the pockets of his shorts. His brush with death had tossed him into disequilibrium. His life had split in two, shifting out of phase. He was being forced to straddle both worlds, one, the serene, scientific world of academia and the search for a fossil. The other, a world cluttered with strange voices, enhanced by the stranger Mia, all wrapped in a lingering grief for the departed Diane.

Kamau pulled him by the elbow, slowing him. "She missed dinner again tonight. Why?"

"She said she was tired."

"She should be. She never eats."

"Her eating habits are the least of my worries. Let's take a walk to the corral."

"You worried about the camels?"

"You know what's on my mind."

Kamau glanced at him without breaking stride. "It's either Watombo or Mia."

"What happened up there while I was buried?"

"I wouldn't have found you in time without her help. She used that ring to locate you. She spread her fingers and pointed them like she was dousing for water."

In John's mind, the scene played in slow motion, stepping in frames of time. She had screamed moments before the plywood buckled. Panic tinged her voice, then the sand slid from the embankment. He felt the weight of it on his back. His lungs heaved.

Despite the clear sky and humid air, he took a shuddering breath. "I've asked her about that ring. All I've learned is that it's some sort of locator. She won't let me examine it."

"I'm certain the embankment strut was secure. Mia was the only one who could have loosened it."

"Why would she do that?"

"She was after me."

"But why would Mia be after you? Aside from the shooting, which we can call an accident, nothing in her character indicates she is violent in any way."

Kamau shook his head. "You're the one that keeps thinking the shooting was an accident. I never assumed that. And after today I'm even more certain she wanted to get me. In the gorge, I was ahead of you when we rounded the corner. If I hadn't stopped to get my compass, I would have been the first one past the strut."

"Let me get this straight," John said. "She scratched you when she was hysterical, she shot you by *accident*, and now you're telling me she wanted to bury you alive on purpose?"

"Something like that."

"How do you explain the timing? You think she had a string tied to the stake and was ready to pull it when you passed? If I hadn't accidentally kicked the stake, then it's a big coincidence that it would have come loose the moment I passed. You're getting paranoid."

"Am I?"

Something about the anger in Kamau's voice made John stop in his tracks. "All right, what's really bothering you?"

Kamau thrust out his chin. "I think you're getting soft on the woman." His voice rose, tight with tension.

John's cheeks burned. "My feelings for her are none of your business." He started walking again.

Kamau grabbed him by the shoulder and spun him around. "I'm telling you the girl is bad news. If you're falling in love with her, fine. But when she threatens this expedition and the men, I have to call it as I see it."

John stared at the ground, throwing layers of calm over his rising anger. He could count on the fingers of his left hand the times Kamau had berated him, always for good cause. "I'm sorry. I know you're doing your job. And, yes, I'm getting soft on her. It's been a long time."

Kamau seemed caught off guard by the easy admission. "I'm glad we cleared that up."

"Let's leave it alone for now. We can ask Omari what she was doing while we were in the gorge. There's something else bothering me. Did you notice anything odd about her today?"

"I've noticed a lot of odd things about her."

"Up to this afternoon she hasn't shown much emotion."

"And today?"

"She cried."

Kamau snorted. "All women cry."

"She's never cried before," John said. "Not when we found her, not in the work tent, not when she shot you. But this morning, she cries and seems worried something might have happened to me."

"Women aren't my specialty. She loosened the strut to get me and got you instead."

No, not Mia. John pushed his feelings aside. Kamau was being too suspicious. "Something else is going on here."

"Watombo?"

"Indirectly. This voice I hear...." John slowed his stride. "I heard it this afternoon...when I was buried for Chrissake."

Kamau stopped again and stared, his face a mixture of concern and fear. "What did it say?"

"It kept telling me what was happening above ground." John's head buzzed. He was again in the suffocating tomb with the voice offering calm reassurance. "I knew I'd be okay. I knew Mia used her ring before you even told me."

"Impossible."

"Watombo hears voices. You hear voices. Why shouldn't I hear voices?"

Kamau frowned. "You're different."

John shrugged. "White men can't hear voices?"

Kamau gave a short laugh.

They reached the corral.

The camels knelt on the far side, their heads swaying on their long necks. One stood, sniffed the air and ambled toward John.

Omari appeared from the shadows, his rifle cradled against his shoulder. "Good evening, *Masahib*, *Bosi*. The camels be nervous tonight."

"If nothing else, they make good watchdogs," John said.

Omari shooed the camel away.

"This morning I asked you to keep an eye on the girl."

"I did, *Masahib*."

"Before the cave-in, I saw her running up the trail."

"This be true, *Masahib*. She sit long time looking down gorge. Then she stand and walk to trail. I tell her no go. Sit down. She go halfway down trail, then she come back. That be when you see her."

John exchanged a glance with Kamau, who shrugged.

"Thank you, Omari," John said. "You can go back to your post."

John sat on the top rail. After hearing Omari, Kamau's anger seemed to have dissipated and been replaced by concern. *How much do I bring Kamau into my confidence? This has never been a question before.* But with Mia, things were different. He was going to need time to sort his feelings for her from the larger question of her being here in the first place.

"There's something else I haven't told you," John said. "That first afternoon, when I was in the tent alone with her, she undressed. She showed no shame in doing so, which was a bit odd. But before she put her shirt on, I noticed she was disfigured. Besides being bald, she has no navel."

"All that in one glance?"

"It's not like you think. I don't know of any way a person exists without a navel, unless it has been removed surgically."

"Did you ask her about it?"

"I thought to but it's a rather personal question to ask someone you've just met."

A sharp bang from Omari's rifle shattered the stillness of the night.

John leapt from the rail and peered in the direction of the shot.

Omari ran up, eyes wide with fear, his rifle held across his chest. "*Masahib.*"

"Why did you fire?"

"I hear noise. Camels jump. I think maybe lion. Over there." He pointed into the night toward the perimeter fence, playing his flashlight on sand and brush. "I shoot but when I use flash, I see the woman. She run back to tent."

John glanced at Kamau. "Why would she be outside the perimeter?"

"Don't ask me. You're the one who trusts her."

With Omari close behind, they ran up the path to Mia's tent. John was about to scratch the entry flap when she stepped out, clutching her unbuttoned shirt at her neck.

"I heard a gunshot," she said. "Was there a lion?"

"The guard saw *you*," Kamau said.

"Me? I was asleep."

Kamau grabbed Omari's flashlight and directed it into Mia's face. "Why are you so flushed?"

"The noise startled me." She shielded her eyes with a hand and turned her head away. Her gaze drifted to the camp beyond, then returned to dance off John. "Why is he interrogating me?"

She's lying. But how to be sure? Omari's word against hers. An impasse. From Kamau's expression, he wasn't buying her story either. "You can go back to bed. There's nothing more we can do tonight."

"I will. But I still do not understand why the guard thought he saw me." She glanced at Kamau, then stepped back and dropped the tent flap.

John stared at the closed canvas. Her attitude annoyed him. Omari wasn't blind. He knew the difference between a lion and a woman. "She's hiding something."

"You don't have to tell me," Kamau said. "It's out there by that lava pond."

John gestured for him to keep his voice down and led him away from the tent. "I didn't get a good look at it," John whispered.

"Its edges were burnt."

"All lava ponds have burnt edges."

"Not fresh ones."

John peered at the pale moon, wondering what to do. "This is going to sound crazy."

"Try me."

"Before she shot you, she said something like, the shepherd wouldn't be happy with your being so close to the pond."

Kamau scowled. "You've got to come clean with me. Things are spinning out of control. We've got to be working from the same facts."

"I know, I know." John fidgeted. "Let me try talking to her again. Tomorrow is Sunday. I could ask her to go to the lake for a swim."

"You might find more than you bargained for. Take Omari with you."

"You think I need a chaperone?"

"I was thinking bodyguard."

Had the situation come to that? Were all their lives in danger? "I'm sure I'll be all right."

"She's bad news even if she did save your life."

"What else can we do? You know the constable doesn't have any control in Kanapoi."

Kamau released his breath through gritted teeth and nodded. "Be careful."

John left Kamau and entered his tent. Ten minutes later the generator shut off. The strings of electric lights dimmed and went out.

"*Kamau's suspicions are well-founded,*" the voice said.

John rubbed his forehead, frustrated with the increasing complexity of events, annoyed to the point of distraction by the voice. *Who are you?*

"*She has goals of her own, which don't involve you.*"

Who are you? He was getting nowhere.

"*She's a beguiling woman.*"

Who--I haven't felt this much desire for years.

"*Desire can be a good thing but you are being careless.*"

I want to be careless. John shook his head to clear his thoughts. *I don't care. She makes me happy.*

***

Mia sat on the cot, elbows on her knees, her chin in her hands. In her desire to report to the Shepherd, she'd made the foolish mistake of forgetting where Omari normally took up his post. She'd have to be more careful next time. But time was running out. Energy left for one more day. So much was happening so fast, and she was getting nowhere.

One thing remained clear. She could not continue drawing suspicion to herself, like regurgitating her meals. That risked compromising her mission. She needed so many things these people took for granted. A navel. An ability to digest food. Finding excuses for these anomalies forced her to fabricate explanations that were not true. She had to...*lie*? What was happening to her?

Then there were the other changes. A surge of pleasurable pain kept washing through her body, impeding her ability to think, or...or like the uncontrollable weeping at the cave-in. What were these stirrings that lanced her heart whenever she thought about John? *John*? What was she supposed to call him?

The Shepherd would know how to proceed. And if he didn't know how to proceed, then what *was* she to do?

Frustrated, she lay down and closed her eyes. She didn't feel sleepy. Presumably, her body demanded a certain amount of rest. The Shepherd could have helped her there, too, by telling her how much rest was needed. Since everyone slept alone, there was no way to observe the interval required.

After a while, her body took over, and she was soon breathing deeply. Sleep could be a pleasant experience, she decided, as she dozed off.

Chapter Eight

John stared at the ground, deep in thought, as he left the mess after breakfast. How best to approach Mia about going to the lake?

"Good morning," Mia called.

He glanced up.

She stood outside the entrance to her tent. An old baseball cap replaced her pith helmet. She had tied the bottom of her shirt below her chest, exposing her flat stomach. Her shorts were belted high enough to cover where her navel should have been.

Five days and Mia had become a preoccupation for him. Yet he knew next to nothing about her, and what he did know made him think she was crazy or he was. He decided if he wanted her to go to the lake, there was no sense getting into the events of the previous night. Other than that, he'd have to play it by ear. He let her catch up to him.

"You look like you're ready to go somewhere," he said.

She clasped her hands in front of her. "I do?"

He detected no pretense, only a fresh innocence. "I haven't had a chance to thank you for saving my life yesterday."

"You need not thank me. Anyone could have found you."

"Kamau said you used your finder to locate me."

"I did." She extended her hand with her wrist bent to expose the heavy ring on her fingers.

He hesitated to take her hand, knowing the effect it would have on him. "May I see it?"

"Yes."

"You trust me now?"

"I trust you."

He clasped her hand in both of his and peered at the ring. Her touch traveled up his arms. "You say it's a locating device?" He reveled at her touch.

"You could call it that."

"How does it work?"

"I do not know really. It is mostly automatic."

When he leaned forward to get a closer look, she withdrew her hand.

Her touch seemed to linger. He struggled to stay focused. He had another priority. "After you've had your breakfast, would you like to go to the lake with me?"

Her face lit up. "Yes, I would."

Her naïve simplicity again. "You'll want to bring a towel."

"A towel." She repeated the word studiously as she turned toward her tent.

"Don't you want any breakfast?" She must be living on air. She hadn't eaten a thing since she had arrived unless one bite of her bread yesterday morning counted.

She stared, a frown creasing her brow. "I'm not hungry."

She must be anorexic. She was thin enough. She'd missed dinner last night. "But you must--"

"I will get the towel now." She ducked into her tent.

When she returned a minute later, she wore a smile, and a towel draped over her shoulder. His question about breakfast seemed forgotten. John guided her to the Land Rover, opened the door and let her slide onto the passenger seat. He got in and drove off, tires spinning in the loose gravel, raising a cloud of dust behind them.

As the road neared the north end of the plateau, it climbed until it provided a good overlook of the lake. Morning sun reflected off its tranquil waters, which spread ahead of them to the northern horizon. Though still early, the air was already hot.

John opened the sunroof as he left the beaten track that led to the dig. He continued north along the eastern shore of the lake.

Mia knelt on the seat and stuck her head out the Land Rover's sunroof. "This is wonderful."

"Careful. It's a rough ride."

"And hot." She unbuttoned the top of her shirt. Her face flushed with excitement. "Do you always worry about your passengers?"

"I worry about you."

She ducked and slid across the flat bench seat to lean against him. She slipped her hands around his arm. "Why worry about me?"

"I guess you matter to me." He over-steered, sending the Land Rover off line into the rough scrabble. He pressed on the accelerator and corrected. *It's been a long time since a girl distracted me like that.*

Volcanic outcroppings convoluted the shore, forming protected coves with a southwestern exposure. After traveling a kilometer, he angled into one of the coves and pulled to a stop.

Mia got out, jumped from the rock ledge to the sand and rushed to the shoreline. She waded into the water.

"Wait a minute," John called, as he dug towels from the backseat.

The lake lapped in small ripples at the sandy shore, which tapered into the water. Crocodiles and hippos usually stayed near the mud flats on the western shore but John could never be sure.

As Mia splashed into deeper water, a flock of flamingoes took flight. They banked, a swirling pink cloud that returned to the water at a safer distance.

John dropped the towels and a blanket onto the sand. Mia was already waist deep. She had not bothered to remove her clothes. He sat, pulled off his boots and unbuttoned his shirt, glancing in her direction to monitor her progress.

She continued toward deeper water and soon was up to her neck. Then she slipped. Her head bobbed under.

"Hey!" He threw off his shirt and rushed into the water, pumping his knees high to clear his feet in the shallows. When the water deepened, he thrashed with his hands, half swimming, half-running.

She stood beneath the surface, easily seen in the clear water. He lunged, grabbed her under the shoulders and brought her head up.

She sputtered, blinking her eyes. "What happened?"

"You went under." He pulled her to shallower water. "What did you expect?"

"I did not expect anything." She wiped water from her face with both hands. "What is one to do in a lake?"

"What do you mean?"

She spit. "It tastes awful."

"It's brackish. Ten thousand years ago this lake might have been connected to the Nile but today it has no natural outlet."

She laughed and waved an arm in a sweeping gesture. "We could have sailed to Cairo, instead of wetting our clothes."

"Actually, it's customary to remove one's clothes before swimming."

"I did not know." She sloshed through the water toward the shore, unbuttoning her shirt.

He followed. The number of ordinary things she seemed ignorant of were beginning to weigh on him. They couldn't be simply explained by cultural differences that might exist. They were almost random. But she'd exhibited this selective recall from the first. Perhaps one of the blows to her head had affected her thinking. Was she suffering from some lingering effect of the *shifta* striking her, of Kamau's punch, of Watombo's stoning? The possibilities seemed endless.

She dropped her shirt next to the blanket and started to remove her shorts.

"You can leave your shorts on but take off your boots."

She regarded him quizzically, then sat to unlace her boots.

She's beautiful. Her skin was a luminescent white. The nipples on her small breasts stood erect as droplets of water dried and cooled around them.

When she finished removing her boots, she peered up at him, as if he would tell her what to do next. John struggled to suppress his feelings, surprised he still had them, so long dormant. But given the circumstances, this was not the time or place, nor the person. "Do you know how to swim?"

"I have never tried. I understand swimming involves the coordinated interaction of arms and legs to keep one afloat in deep water."

"That's a good definition." Quite a formal response to a simple question but he supposed some cultures didn't see water as a source of recreation.

"Will you teach me?"

"Come here." He took her hand and pulled her up from the sand.

She kept hold as they reentered the water to chest depth.

"I'm going to support your stomach," he said.

She stepped closer to him and steadied herself with a hand on his shoulder.

"Lean forward. I've got you."

She let go of his shoulder and leaned. When her chest leveled, she lifted her head to keep it above water. Her legs floated at an angle to the bottom.

"Straighten your legs and kick. Paddle your arms."

She splashed, keeping her lips pursed and eyes shut.

"That's all there is to it." He let her go.

She sank. Her feet hit bottom. She pushed and emerged sputtering. "You call this swimming?"

He laughed. "More like drowning."

As she wiped water off her face, she lost her balance and leaned into him. Her skin felt smooth and soft, a feeling he missed. Teaching her to swim had become a bad idea. Heat rose into his cheeks.

"Are you okay?" Mia asked.

"We should go ashore." Perhaps he *should* have brought a chaperone. He took her hand and guided her toward shore where he spread the blanket, then wiped the water from his body with quick efficient strokes.

She watched him, then did the same.

Her actions reinforced his impression that all these experiences were new to her. "You're beautiful." The words slipped out, as though having a life of their own.

She seemed puzzled. "I know the meaning of beautiful but have no reference for it."

"Believe me. You are."

When he reached for her hands, she let him take them without resistance. The whole time she gazed into his eyes, searching. He pulled her onto the blanket. As he lay beside her, he brushed drops of water off her forehead, then let his hand drift over her shoulder and down her arm to her waist.

She followed his motion intently.

His finger traced an imaginary line across her belly and paused where her navel should have been. "You have no navel." He tried to keep his voice level, conversational, casual, as though asking about the absence of her navel was the most usual question one could ask under the circumstances.

"Navel?" She raised herself on one elbow and peered at his pointing finger. "Perhaps I should have one but I do not."

John laughed, a release of the tension he felt, and at her obvious surprise. "I suppose where you come from, Russia or some place they don't have navels."

"Is it important?"

"All members of the human race have navels. Even test tube babies have navels."

"Then I am like a test tube baby but different."

John fell silent. The conversation had again come up against her craziness and died.

She shivered.

She can't be cold. The temperature and humidity matched the inside of a sauna. "Are you cold?"

"Tremors pass through me I do not understand. If I shiver, they go away." She stared into the distance. "There, they are back again. Do you know what I mean?"

"I can guess. I have them myself."

"I cannot imagine what is producing them."

"They are feelings. Some can be very strong if a man and a woman are attracted to one another."

She brightened. "Are you attracted to me?"

He felt foolish with the turn toward intimacy. He tried to smile. "Despite all the trouble you're causing me, I'm beginning to like you."

"Like...is that the same as love, what you said you felt for your Diane?"

"It's on the same emotional path."

"Emotional?"

"Yes. Very strong feelings. Like yesterday after the cave-in. You cried."

"I did." She perked up. "I could not understand what was happening and still do not. I thought my eyes were malfunctioning."

Malfunctioning? It must be a poorly worded translation from whatever language she thought in. "That's an odd way to put it but tears are normal."

"Good." She took his hand, turned it over and traced its pattern of veins.

"I have told you about my navel and my feelings. Will you now tell me the long story about the revolver?"

He hated the subject, afraid he would break down in the middle of telling. "My mother took her life when I was young. She used a revolver."

"Her death must have had a profound effect on you."

"I was five." He sat up, cupped a handful of sand and let it pour through his curled fingers. "Her death devastated me but what happened afterward was almost worse."

"What was that?"

"I started hearing a voice inside my head. Still do." He glanced up from the sand to gage her reaction but her face remained neutral.

"Could that be a normal reaction to a mother's death, especially if you were only five?"

"Maybe. Years later before my dad died, I asked him about Mother. He said she felt haunted all her life by a voice. She tried therapy. They thought she had schizophrenia but it resisted treatment. I guess in the end, she took the only way she thought was left." He reached for another handful of sand. "Do you think I'm crazy?"

"No." She put a hand over her brow, shading the sun, and peered at him. "I hear a voice, too."

Are we all going insane? "It can't be the same voice."

"I suppose not. The voice I hear tells me to do bad things. Yesterday, when you said I should remain near the tent, the voice told me to meet you in the gorge."

"It did?"

"I sat where you told me to sit. You met Kamau at the bottom of the trail, talked to him, then disappeared around the bend. You had been gone but a moment, when a voice said, *Aren't you curious about what they might find?*" She glanced at him. "You do not believe me?"

"I believe you. Go on."

She bit her lip, then took a deep breath and continued. "Why should I think such a thought? The voice was so clear. *Don't you want to join them?* it said. No, I thought, John told me to wait here. Then the voice compelled me. *I sense John misses you.*

"I stood up. The voice would not go away. *You could meet him at the bottom of the gorge.* I do not know what possessed me. I walked halfway down the path before I heard you and Kamau returning. Thinking you would be angry with me, I hurried back to my place."

"Kamau thinks you loosened the strut. That you were trying to kill him."

"But that is not true. The last thing the voice said to me was, *Get down there*. The voice wanted me below the embankment. I realized it might collapse. That is when I called to you. To warn you."

John gave her a hard look, not knowing what to make of what she had said. Questions clogged his mind, demanding attention.

Mia frowned. "Now you think I am the one who is crazy."

"You say a lot of crazy things."

"I do not have an excuse like yours. You have your grief, for your mother and Diane but you should not feel guilty." She laid her hand on his cheek. "You did not cause these events."

You don't know. John stared at the sand. Memories flooded in. Diane never could have had children. Some genetic defect. He saw alternatives. They had argued and gotten nowhere, always coming up against his driving compulsion to be here, or there, digging for fossils. As if he didn't already feel guilty, he now had to face his growing attraction to this strange woman.

Mia gave him a push. "You're talking to yourself again."

John blinked. *What to say*? "I was thinking about you and me."

"In what way?"

"You remind me of Diane. I feel like I've been awakened from a long sleep. You're about her age, when I first met her. Years later, I meet you. But I have aged."

"But you are not old."

"I'm thirty-five. You seem to be around twenty."

"I think you miss your Diane."

The old ache shot through John's heart. "I do. We wanted to start a family but she couldn't. Maybe we were doomed from the start. Anyway, that was a long time ago."

Mia pushed back a lock of hair from his forehead.

He had the sense that she could read his every thought. He struggled to cover his awkwardness. "Watombo told an origin myth the day you showed up."

"So," Mia said with a glint in her eye, "have I become the stuff of native mythology?"

"Kamau said Watombo got his myth from a voice he hears in his dreams. The main female character in the story steals a spirit, the one responsible for human nature, from a caretaker called the Shepherd. She flees to Earth and creates the first man. The natives consider her the mother of mankind. They call her *Afareni*. Ring any bells?"

"Bells?"

"Is the name familiar?"

"No." She stared at her hands, disappointed. "I guess the voice Watombo hears is different from yours and mine."

Whenever he thought he was getting somewhere, something new intervened and the pieces of the puzzle stopped coming together. He pressed a finger to the skin of her shoulder. A white spot appeared for a moment, surrounded by a deeper pink coloration. "You've had enough sun. Time to get dressed."

"I like being without clothes."

"I know but you don't want another sunburn." The wind shifted, picking up sand. "That's it for today, anyway."

"I have enjoyed this swim and being alone with you." Mia dressed, then helped him gather the blanket and towels. They headed for the Land Rover. "Will you take me to your excavation again tomorrow?"

"I suppose I owe you."

"You do?"

"You saved my life."

"Then you do owe me."

At the edge of the rock outcropping, he climbed first, stopped at the top and pulled her up. When he released her hand, she slipped it around his waist. He shifted the blanket and towels and put his arm around her slender shoulder. "You never give up, do you?"

Chapter Nine

The gorge lay cooking in the morning sun. Dark shadows raked the far side, giving a false impression of cooler shade. The temperature was over fifty degrees Celsius, enough to fry an egg on a rock, let alone the hood of a Land Rover.

John leaned against the vehicle, feeling its sharp heat work through his shirt and into his back.

"That's all you found out?" Kamau clenched a fistful of stones in one hand and sailed a rock over the edge of the gorge, as he paced in front of John.

John had felt a rebuke coming. Exasperated, he tried to ease by it. "She can be distracting. I'm beginning to think she's suffered some reaction to being hit on the head. She's had a rough time."

"Aside from everything else that's happened, what makes you think that now?"

"She seems hopelessly out of touch. Sometimes the simplest things confuse her. It's like large blocks of memory have disappeared."

"I think you're playing psychiatrist here to excuse her intolerable actions." Kamau glanced to the work tent, where Mia stood watching them. "It's not going to work, John."

"We'll see."

"Why'd you bring her here? I thought we agreed the girl and the laborers don't mix."

"It's only for another couple of days."

"John!" Mia waved from the tent.

"Your mistress calls." Kamau tossed the remaining stones on the ground. "I'm going to make sure the men are set up, then I'm coming back here and taking a ride to that pond. You want to come?"

John tried to return Kamau's stare but failed and instead concentrated on kicking the ground with his boot. "You go. I don't want to leave her alone."

After Kamau left, John pushed off the truck and trudged toward the work tent. *Kamau lost his temper?* But like most Africans, even ones educated abroad, Kamau battled between his native upbringing with all its incumbent superstitions, and whatever he had picked up from western culture. He did better than most, but the unexplained appearance of Mia, and Watombo's pressure seemed to be taking their toll.

"What were you talking about?" Mia gazed over John's shoulder at the departing Kamau.

"The weather."

She searched John's face. "Is something wrong?"

No, no. Yes. My camp manager's pissed off at me but I'm not about to tell you that he is. John put a lid on his frustration. "Let it go. Do you feel like a hike into the gorge?"

She seemed confused by the *let it go* but focused instead on the trip to the gorge. "Will you let me look for the guardian?"

John's heart sank. Did she have to be so single-minded? But he supposed he had set himself up by offering to let her come with him into the gorge. "I'll be looking for fossils. We'll see if we have time for the guardian."

She started to say something then stopped and smiled instead.

She knows when she's ahead. Am I being manipulated? He grabbed a canteen and preceded her on the path into the gorge. Near the bottom, he stopped at the site of the cave-in. Scars from the digging were still visible in the otherwise smooth sand. "Not a pleasant sight."

Mia seemed as uncomfortable with the slide as he was. She slipped her arm in his. "Kamau was so heroic, the way he took charge and saved your life."

"I don't underestimate your role."

Mia leaned against him. "That is what I do not understand. Despite my help, Kamau distrusts me. It's as if I were stealing you from him."

"In a sense you are. He's very protective. These last few years he's the only one who's kept me sane."

John led her past the humped sand to the bottom of the gorge.

Once they were on flat ground, she stepped ahead of him, swinging the finder in a casual arc at her side. "Why do you dig so far down the gorge?"

"It seemed like a good place to start. It's downstream. Any fossils would have tended to wash in that direction."

She stopped. "Have you investigated this area?"

"Why do you ask?"

She glanced at her finder. "The stratigraphy here appears intriguing."

"It all looks intriguing."

She sauntered off the trail, still swinging her finder, her head bowed, scanning the ground. "I see something."

John felt an impatience to catch up with Kamau but decided to humor her. He walked over to where she stood and peered at the ground. "All I see is a lot of undisturbed sand."

She knelt and brushed at the top layer.

"Kamau's waiting for us."

"Look." Mia pointed.

A small rocky knob protruded from the surface where she had brushed away the sand.

John knelt. He took the brush and dental pick from his pocket and enlarged the area around the knob, which was as big as his thumb. "I'll be damned. You have found something."

Mia leaned closer. "What is it?"

He loosened the rest of the packed sand until the knob came free. "It's a fossilized hamate. Definitely hominid."

"What's a hamate?"

"Hamate bones form the carpal tunnel." John blew on the small fossil. "They're like goal posts channeling the tendons of the forearm to the fingers. On ancient hominids the tunnel was wider, indicating powerful gripping potential, a characteristic left over from their days in the trees."

"Let's continue digging," Mia said.

"Good idea. The rest of this guy might be here as well."

Mia scraped at the hardscrabble with her hand.

"You'll get nowhere that way. I'll fetch Kamau and some labor, and we'll do this right." As he hurried off, he glanced back. Mia was moving her finder over the ground in a widening circle.

***

Once around the bend with Mia out of sight, John's excitement overwhelmed him. He broke into a run. "Kamau!"

Kamau looked up from the map he was holding. "What now?"

"Mia found a hominid fossil, a hamate. I want to enlarge the area of investigation. We'll need some men, with shovels and a sieve."

"Back there? I've passed that area for a week and didn't see anything."

"She went right to it, pointed and said *dig here*. The fossil was a centimeter down."

Kamau's eyes widened, showing a trace of fear.

But John didn't want to deal with that now, his excitement overwhelmed him. He hurried back to Mia.

She sat cross-legged two meters from where the hamate had been found. "This is a good place to start." She pointed to the sand in front of her where she had traced an *X*.

John stared at the *X*, then to where the hamate had been uncovered. "That's downstream from the location of the hamate. Any larger pieces would have dropped from the flow above it."

"More bones are there." She folded her arms across her chest.

Kamau arrived with two laborers and Bandele. "Where do you want to start?"

John glanced at Mia, then at Kamau. "There, in front of her."

Layer by ten-centimeter layer, the laborers excavated a pit three meters on a side. When the pit reached a depth of half a meter, John climbed out and approached Mia, who sat off to one side following the progress.

"We've found nothing." John wiped his brow with a bandana. Dust covered his hands. His legs streamed with rivulets of dirt mixed with sweat. "I suggest we try farther upstream."

"You have not dug deep enough," Mia said.

Kamau sat on the edge of the pit and tossed his shovel in front of him. "What is she, clairvoyant?"

"I can't argue with the way she found the hamate." John ignored Kamau's obvious anger and studied Mia for a moment. "Okay, we'll keep at it for another half hour."

"This is ridiculous," Kamau said.

"Be patient."

"*Bosi*." One of the laborers stood back from his digging.

Kamau inspected the excavation. "John, you'll want to see this."

John hurried over and knelt. He brushed at a rounded form, which protruded above the floor of the pit. "It's a hominid sagittal crest." As John brushed, he worked his way down the frontal plate to the brow ridge.

"It's well preserved." Kamau pushed back the curious laborers.

John's heart raced. The skull lay with its thick brow ridges peeking above the surface. He widened the hole, praying a lower jaw would be attached. He reached with both hands and grasped the skull on either side, lifting it. No jaw but the find was exquisite.

The laborers murmured in awe as John held the fossil up to the light. He turned it from side-to-side. "Magnificent." He showed the fossil to Mia, who stood at the edge of the pit.

"Why is it so black?" she asked.

"It has absorbed manganese from the surrounding soil."

She leaned down to touch it. "Those clods of sand in its eye sockets make it appear to be alive, as if he is staring at us."

The laborers chattered.

"Quiet!" Kamau glared at them. He leaned close to John. "They didn't like the way she touched the skull."

"They've been listening too much to Watombo."

"I meant no harm," Mia said. "Those eyes have not seen the light of day for millions of years."

"At the least." John handed the skull to Kamau. "I don't want to remove any matrix here and risk damaging the skull. Where's the Bedacryl?"

Bandele stepped forward and offered John the can of preservative.

He painted the skull, then wrapped it in burlap. "I'll call it the Brown Eyes skull, until we classify it otherwise. Take this up to the top and put it in the Land Rover." He handed the package to Bandele.

He took the bundled skull with shaking hands.

"Don't drop it," John said.

Bandele headed for the trail, holding the package in front of him as though it might bite him.

Mia peered past John to the other side of the pit. "You will find more hominid over there."

John shook his head. "I thought we'd dig for the jaw near where we found the skull."

"The jaw is gone."

Maybe she is clairvoyant. "You're pressing your luck."

She circled the pit and pointed to a spot a half meter from the wall of the pit. "No. Dig here."

Kamau shifted, his hands thrust into the pockets of his shorts.

"No harm trying." John picked up a shovel and scraped where Mia had indicated. The shovel blade struck something hard. John dropped the shovel and began working with his dental pick. A much larger fossil emerged from the dirt. "I don't believe it. Kamau, come here."

"It looks like a pelvis," Kamau said.

John leaned forward, an almost desperate tension consuming him as he dug. Kamau squatted next to him.

Mia stood above them, a smug expression on her face.

"It's intact." John lifted the pelvis from the sand and dusted it off. A large mass of matrix filled the pelvic cavity. "This is incredible."

The laborers jostled for position.

"Stand back," John said. "I don't want anyone stepping on other parts of this guy."

"It is a good find." Kamau took the pelvis and examined it. "The sediment here must have been very stable for the parts of the skeleton to remain so close together."

"I told you," Mia said.

"You did." John tried to mask the giddy delight that crept into his voice. "Whatever attracted you to look where you did?"

She held up and twisted her hand coyly, showing the finder.

"How did you--"

She put her hands behind her back and smiled.

"I know. Don't ask questions." At this point, he didn't care how she had found the fossils.

Kamau scowled. "I'll string tape to keep people away. Ten meters on a side should--"

A stone the size of a lemon thudded onto the sand and rolled to a stop.

"Where the hell did that come from?" Kamau shaded his eyes and surveyed the rim of the gorge.

More rocks sailed over the rim edge, arced high and cascaded onto the floor of the gorge.

"There!" John pointed. A dense, gray cloud of smoke drifted across the edge of the gorge, contrasting against the azure sky.

A shot echoed down the canyon walls.

"I don't believe this." Covering his head with his arm, John ran to the trail leading from the gorge.

The others cowered close to the gorge wall.

The stones stopped falling.

John waved for Kamau to follow, then ran up the path. Near the top, Watombo's ranting voice carried in the superheated air.

***

"What the hell is he doing here?" John demanded in a hushed whisper as he hunkered down just below the top.

Kamau scrambled to the rim and peered over. "I don't know but he sure has an eerie sense of timing."

The work tent smoldered in a pile of burnt canvas, the chair and table toppled and burned. Ashes from the maps caught up in the air and drifted over the gorge.

Omari cowered near the Land Rover, his gun at the ready. Behind him, Bandele sagged against the side of the vehicle, blood running from his ears and nose.

Watombo stood at the back of the flatbed truck. Unwrapped burlap swirled at his feet. Above his head, he brandished the Brown Eyes skull. The laborers stood before him in thrall.

John focused on the skull and felt sick to his stomach. His prize was in the possession of a madman. "What's he saying?"

"Something about the skull belonging to the first man...eyes do not want to see the light of day...*mchungaji* will take back our spirit."

Mia reached the top and crouched behind John.

Watombo saw them huddled together. He transferred the skull to his withered hand and pointed at Mia.

"...she waits to claim her prize...," Kamau translated.

"I have done nothing." Mia clutched John's arm.

John pried her hand away and stood clear of the rim.

At the sight of John, the laborers seemed uncertain what to do.

"Give me the fossil." With his hand outstretched, John approached Watombo.

The shaman's eyes flashed. "You be stranger here. We be ones to suffer after you gone." His voice crackled with anger.

John's head throbbed. Try as he might he could not take his eyes off Watombo's withered hand and the precious skull it held. "The fossil, please." He would drop to his knees if he had to.

Watombo grabbed the skull with his good hand, drew back his arm and heaved.

"No!" John screamed. He lunged, hands reaching.

The skull arced through the air and shattered on the rocky ground.

Omari fired.

Watombo grabbed his side. Mouth open, eyes rolling white, he pitched off the truck.

Anguished laborers surged around the shaman.

Omari ejected a shell from his Enfield and raised it to his shoulder. A curl of smoke drifted from the muzzle.

"Hold your fire!" John screamed as he rushed to the scattered pieces of the Brown Eyes skull. He dropped to his knees, ignoring the laborers who shouted obscenities at him. "No, no," John muttered, scooping skull fragments mixed with dirt and gravel into a small pile.

Omari twitched, his eyes bright with excitement.

Watombo staggered to his feet clutching his side, his face a contorted mask of pain. "May vultures rip flesh from your bones." He spit the words at John, ignoring the blood running from the wound, down his leg.

"Get him out of here," John screamed. He was beginning to lose it and was afraid of what he might do.

Kamau knelt beside him. "I'm sorry," he said, obviously sharing John's pain.

"It was perfect," John blubbered. "He didn't have to trash it."

Watombo clenched his teeth, his face pallid, an artery down the middle of his forehead pulsed. "This no be the end." Followed by three of his men, he headed for the plateau.

Mia stood to one side observing the scene with startled interest.

"Hand me that burlap," John said to Kamau as he continued to scrape the pieces of the broken fossil together. "I'll take what I can and sort out the fragments later."

Kamau went to pick up the burlap, which had blown up against a tire of the Land Rover. "Bandele, what happened here?"

The supervisor trembled, spitting blood that had flowed from his nose, down his upper lip and into his mouth. He stared glassy-eyed at the receding shaman. "He demand package. When I refuse, he beat me. His men set fire to tent. If you not come, they go for Land Rover."

Kamau slid a hand over Bandele's shoulder and chest. "Any broken bones?"

"No, *Bosi* but they take package."

"There's nothing more you could have done. John, we better get him back to camp."

"Where's the burlap."

Kamau retrieved the burlap and dropped next to John. "If Mia had stayed with the constable none of this would have happened."

John glared up at him. "You know that wasn't possible. We wouldn't have found the fossil either."

"Are you so quick to put men's lives at risk for a fossil?"

"You know I didn't mean it like that. You should lay the blame where it belongs."

"I did."

Mia stepped behind John. "I am not to blame."

"One thing's for sure," Kamau said. "A man's been shot. We have to report the incident to the constable."

John stood, the burlap full of fragments hanging heavily in his hand.

"You report it. I'm going to get the pelvis, then see what can be done to save the skull."

Mia hurried after John and touched his arm. "Are you all right? You seem agitated."

He pulled back and stared at her in wild surprise. "A man's been beaten. Watombo's wounded, the skull's trashed and Kamau thinks it's all your fault. How could I be all right?"

Mia blinked at the force behind John's words. "You still have the pelvis."

"Pelvis be damned. As far as I'm concerned, the supply plane can't come soon enough."

Chapter Ten

A large table, cobbled together with knot-strewn planks, sat at the center of the examination tent. Particle board shelves lined two walls and sagged under heavy plaster replicas of dated fossil skulls from other sites, a rogue's gallery of dead hominids. Gas lanterns hung from the tent poles at either end. Fired to full-on, they gave off an odor of refined petroleum and threw a garish white light over the scene. In a neat row at the middle of the table, long shadows sagged off the packages containing pieces of the Brown Eyes skull and his other skeletal parts.

John unwrapped the pelvic fossil and set it to one side, then directed his attention to the burlap sack containing the shattered skull.

A sick feeling returned to his insides as he emptied the pieces onto the table. He'd skipped dinner having no appetite after the events of the afternoon. He hoped he had recovered all the fragments. Restoring the skull would be difficult but it could be done, if not here then back in the States.

He sorted through small stones and dirt to pick up the largest fragment, the frontal lobe and brow ridge. Between the eye sockets, a large mass of matrix crusted a circular hole above where the hominid's nose would have met his forehead.

The tent flap rustled behind him.

Mia stood at the entrance. "May I come in?"

She was the last person he wanted to deal with now. He returned his attention to the broken skull without answering.

She stepped across the wooden floor to stand beside him. "Where is Kamau?"

"Checking on Bandele."

"How is he?"

John put down the fossil fragment and scraped back his chair so he could see her directly. "A bloody nose. He should be all right after a night's rest."

She wore the same clothes she had on that afternoon. Dirt smudged one cheek, cut through by streaks John assumed had been tears. "I am sorry he was beaten. It all seems so senseless."

"People around here take this kind of stuff seriously."

"All of this animosity over a fossil."

"You know damn well it's not just the fossil." John's frustration played out in a burst of anger. "Something else is going on. I'm not sure what it is but it's getting weird."

"Weird?"

John looked away in disgust. He didn't want to get into a discussion with Mia about *weird*. "Nothing's been right since you arrived."

"But you said you liked me. That must be right."

"Things have changed," John twisted in his chair, his hands gripping the sides.

"I am glad the supply plane has not arrived." She had not moved since entering but stood with shoulders sagging, looking forlorn.

The voice stirred. "*Why do you fool yourself? You are also glad the plane hasn't arrived.*"

I'm not listening to you, anymore.

Mia took a deep breath and gave him a shy smile. "I still feel the tremors in my heart."

"Goddamn it. I feel tremors, too." She seemed so eager to make things right. Though she was the catalyst for what had happened, he had a difficult time blaming her directly. He stood and put his arm around her thin shoulders.

Her dark eyes softened as she looked into his.

"Let's wait and see how this all plays out." He felt like kissing her but what a ridiculous position that would put him in when he would have to eventually leave her in Kanapoi. He released her and returned to his chair.

She seemed not to notice his indecision. She put both hands on the table and leaned forward, studying the pile of skull fragments, her composure regaining some strength. She pointed to the Brown Eyes fragment he had been examining. "Why is there a hole in the middle of his forehead?"

John was impressed she identified the fragment as part of the hominid's forehead. "I don't know."

"Do you suppose it happened in a fight?"

"Could be." He picked up the fragment, his curiosity aroused. He pried matrix from the hole. Using a magnifying glass, he examined the hole's edges. "Small cracks radiate from the area of trauma. A pointed object might have hit him with tremendous force. It's not an animal bite, like a saber-toothed cat. Those intrusions come in pairs."

She shuddered. "I don't like the looks of it."

"Getting superstitious?" The ring on her finger pulsed with a dull light. "Your finder is flashing."

Mia glanced at it and put her hands behind her back. "I told you it operated automatically. Sometimes I think it has a mind of its own. I have never seen such a wound in a skull fragment."

John put down the fragment. He folded his arms across his chest and stared at her. "You've seen skull fragments before?"

"I was referring to the literature on the subject."

"The literature says we have no artifacts from this era that would indicate they had any tools, much less weapons."

"Maybe he fell."

"A fall wouldn't have left those radiations."

Mia shivered. "It's almost like he's trying to tell us his past."

John couldn't figure her. He couldn't figure himself. One moment he was trying to contain his feelings and write her off, and the next moment he felt drawn to her again. "If you believe Watombo, all you have to do is hold this fossil and its spirit will speak to you."

"There are mysteries to life that cannot be resolved by science alone."

John raised his eyebrows. "Where did that come from?"

"It seems to be logical." Mia's face reddened. She shifted to the table and sat, gripping its edge. "How old do you think these fossils are?"

John shook his head. "You're not going to get off that easily. Tell me how the mysteries of life cannot be resolved by science alone."

With a sigh, Mia gazed at the tent ceiling as though the answer could be found there. "Sometimes there are simpler, more direct ways of arriving at the truth."

"Like Watombo's visions?"

"Maybe."

John studied her, suppressing his disbelief but no less intrigued by her statement. "Since when have you become an admirer of what Watombo says?"

"I did not say I was."

"What *are* you saying?"

"I have been told life leaves a trail in time and space. It does not matter if it is now living or dead. The trail is there. You simply cannot see it."

"Who told you that?"

Mia frowned at him and pursed her lips. "Are you going to tell me how old you think these fossils are?"

Ah, the disconnect. He had become familiar with the pattern. Back her into a corner, and she'd slither sideways despite his best effort to keep her pinned. "Four million years. I can also compare the features to other finds of known age. This heavy suborbital ridge confirms the antiquity at around four million years."

She showed no reaction except perhaps relief that she had succeeded in deflecting the conversation. She eased off the table and tipped the pelvic fossil toward her. "Are australopithecine pelvises always this large?"

"I'm surprised you noticed. I was wondering the same thing. I think we're looking at the earliest known beginning of Homo erectus. He doesn't have all the features we associate with Erectus but he has enough to indicate he might have been first in a line leading to Erectus.

"So early? I thought Homo erectus evolved from Australopithecus much later, only two million years ago."

Where was all this knowledge coming from? "You do know your hominids. Conventional theory says you are correct but I have my own ideas on the origins of Erectus."

She brightened. "You think the transition from Australopithecus to Homo erectus occurred here in Africa much earlier."

Despite his reluctance to slip back into casual conversation with her, his burning interest in paleoanthropology took over. He reached for a pencil and piece of paper upon which he drew a horizontal line and labeled it four million years. "The tree of man isn't as simple as most paleoanthropologists would like us to believe." His enthusiasm built.

"Four million years ago Australopithecus was already distinct from the great apes and chimpanzees." He tapped the line. With quick strokes of the pencil he drew a branching tree rising from the four-million-year base line. "The fossil record establishes that pithecus originated in Africa, somewhere in this region. Standard theory says they migrated from Africa across the Middle East into Europe and Asia."

"Is that unusual?"

"If we are descended from Australopithecus, each of these remote sites should indicate evolution beyond pithecus to modern humans. The only sites that show a linkage are here in Africa."

"Then Australopithecus is not an ancestor of man."

"Only here. For whatever reason, two million years ago, Homo erectus evolved from Australopithecus in Africa. Then, in a rapid outward expansion, Homo erectus overtook Australopithecus everywhere else in a rapid outward migration. Homo erectus rendered Australopithecus extinct." John enlarged one branch on his sketch. Lines leaned across the other branches of Australopithecus, smothering them, preventing them from advancing to the present.

Mia peered at the sketch, then frowned. "But where did Australopithecus come from? The apes?"

"That's the conventional wisdom. We don't know why evolution branched there. We may never know." He extended the root of the tree he had drawn until it went off the page. Below the four million year line, he drew another line and labeled it six million years. He drew a branch from the trunk at six million years and brought it to the present. "We have great apes around us today. I don't know why they split off six million years ago or why Homo erectus started to become distinct from pithecus four million years later. Sometimes it seems like the parent species received a genetic injection of sorts, which pushed it to a new form."

"You must have a more scientific explanation for the cause."

"Could be random mutation, accumulated molecular drift. This find--" he indicated the Brown Eyes fossils. "--should help to establish what happened." Frustration edged his voice. He stood and rubbed his eyes.

"You look very tired," Mia said.

"You're right. I haven't thought of anything else since finding the skull. Let me put these away, and I'll see you to your tent."

He collected the fragments and returned them to the sack, then swept the residual dust into a wastebasket.

"Do you leave the fossils on the table at night?"

"It's not like they're going to walk away. Why do you ask?"

"Curious, as usual." She put her hand on his arm and leaned close. "I hope the supply plane never comes."

He felt her warmth. His resolve wavered. "I'm sorry I was angry with you today."

Mia drew back. "You do still like me?"

John placed both hands on her shoulders and stared her in the eyes. "I do but there are times when I don't feel strong enough to handle all this. The supply plane can take you to the authorities who can arrange to get you home."

"Are you sure?"

"I'm sure. Look, if it makes you feel better, I promise I'll track you down when I'm finished with this dig. Maybe then things will be different. Now can I take you to your tent?"

"No." Her eyes glazed with tears, and she rushed outside.

"*Stop acting like a sick baboon,*" the voice said.

John's shoulders slumped. One part of his mind had tried to put up a fight against the voice. The other part simply wanted to give in, to return everything to the normal abnormal. So what if he was insane, so what if he had some disembodied thing, *sheitani*, whatever living in him. Anything would be better than this limbo land of not knowing.

"*Think about today.*"

The voice could be uplifting. *Yes, very rewarding, except for Watombo.*

"*You have found your fossil. Now you can go home.*"

John rubbed his forehead. Somehow, he couldn't bring himself to think of going home.

"*You're intrigued by the skull's circular trauma.*"

Leave a gap in thought and the voice would fill the void. *It looks like a bullet hole.*

"*Does such a death still tempt you?*"

No.

"*Anything is better than thinking of death.*"

A vision of Diane lying in the morgue flicked into his consciousness, the sheet raised for identification, her face pale, scarred with purple contusions. Because of the trauma to her head, they had shaved it. She resembled--

"*Mia?*"

I have gone insane. John stared at the intense white flame of the lantern.

"*You're tired and vulnerable.*"

I wish.

"Mia is a lot stranger than you know." The voice seemed to circle a subject of interest.

John stared at the flickering shadows cast by the lantern. He tried to push the voice to the back of his mind. *Fate works in strange ways.*

"Fate is never strange."

John wrapped his arms around his chest. *When I'm at the lowest point of my life, Mia appears. I'm falling in love again.* The expressed thought brought relief from the burden of holding a secret. He had told someone, even if that someone was the voice.

"Maybe she's not here of her own volition?"

She's been coerced?

"Possibly. And she doesn't have a navel. How do you explain her deformity?"

She only seems harmless?

"Then you are wise to give her up when the plane arrives. If you are lucky you will never see her again."

***

Mia sat on the cot in her darkened tent, staring at the finder. Its pattern of colors wound in an urgent swirl. The guardian was close, so close she could almost sense its presence.

Raw feelings reached up and clawed her mind, polluting her thinking. John's betrayal, her agony, her fear of discovery, stones sailing through the air and clacking hard off bone, the pain, her skin splitting and warm blood washing the side of her face, then the grinning Watombo, so evil. It sloughed off his body with a fetid stench. She hated him. The feeling welled and threatened to obliterate all others.

Her mind grasped for something stable, anything to stay the onslaught. Then she found a quiet certainty in the storm. Despite his ambivalence, John loved her. The stoning had changed everything. His past, his doubts, his guilt seemed to slip away. How or why she didn't care. With a sudden wrenching certainty, despite his insistence she leave, she knew he had a place in his heart for her after all. How strange the emotional turmoil her human body produced, how real the ache in her chest, the desire, the longing.

But being placed on the supply plane would be the end of her. She had to retrieve the guardian now. Her energy was gone. She had to get back to the Shepherd. Tonight.

The generator shut off and plunged the camp into darkness.

Go. Go, now. She rose off the cot and tiptoed to the entrance flap.

The compound lay under a canopy of sparkling stars, tiny points of light crowding the dry desert sky. The moon hung at zenith, the sky's crowning jewel.

She reminded herself to avoid the guard. How stupid to have forgotten his presence.

She raised the tent flap and stepped into the open, careful to keep her shadow off John's tent. She stood and listened. His deep breathing indicated he had already fallen asleep. The other tents were dark and silent.

Concentrating on the pulsing light from the finder, she stole across the yard. At the examination tent, she lifted the flap and slipped inside.

The light from the finder cast a faint glow throughout the tent. She waited as her eyes adjusted to the gloom.

The fossils still lay in a neat row at one end of the table. At its center rested the fossilized pelvis next to the sack containing the skull fragments.

Mia rummaged in a tool tray and extracted a dental pick and a thin, spatula-like tool. Guided by the finder, she griped the pelvis and probed the edges of the matrix. It loosened. She slipped the spatula between fossil and matrix and pried. The whole mass popped out. With a lunge, she grabbed the matrix to keep it from crashing to the floor.

Holding the matrix firmly with one hand, she worked the spatula deep into a small crack and twisted. The matrix split in two. The guardian lay like a seed pit bedded in some massive, gray fruit. She pried with the dental pick and the sphere rolled free, a silvery eyeball with a faceted surface.

The luminescence from her finder dimmed. She grabbed the guardian and shoved it deep in a pocket of her shorts. The mess on the table distracted her for a moment. Should she clean it up? No. She had the guardian. Her mission was accomplished. She wouldn't be back.

As she started to leave a bright light from a flashlight blinded her.

She shaded her eyes and squinted.

Kamau's looming outline entered the tent. "What are you doing here?"

Mia backed against the table. "You startled me."

The flashlight shifted away from her face, then left, right, and down. The light steadied on the pelvis and the split matrix.

"What have you done?"

"I've done nothing. I heard a noise and came here to investigate. The fossil was like that when I entered."

"You're lying." Kamau grabbed for her hand, which still held the dental pick.

Mia jerked free. The sharp point of the pick swept up and swiped his chin.

He clapped his hand over his chin and back-stepped through the entrance. "Omari!"

Her heart pounded in her chest. She shook from the sudden exertion of pushing Kamau away. Thinking furiously, she felt her way around the table in the diffuse light, located the tool tray and replaced the pick. She had the guardian. What if they searched her? She slid the small sphere under the tools in the tray. What else was there? The matrix. Nothing to be done about it. Maybe close the halves together. She retreated to the back of the tent and waited, peering past the entrance flaps at Kamau's broad back.

Omari's voice drifted from a distance. "*Bosi*, what is it?" Heavy footsteps thumped closer and stopped outside the entrance.

"The woman tried to steal a fossil," Kamau said. "She's in the tent."

Over his shoulder, Mia could see the whites of Omari's eyes glistening wide in the light from Kamau's flashlight.

"Stand here and make sure she stays put," Kamau said. "I'm going to get the *Masahib*."

"But--"

"Shoot her if she tries to leave!"

***

John awoke with a start, his heart pounding. What had seemed another bad dream became real shouting drifting across the compound. He pulled on his shorts and boots, fired up a lantern and stepped from the tent. In the middle of the compound, he met Kamau, hand cupped on his chin.

"What's going on?"

"Mia was trying to steal the fossils."

Steal the fossils? "She's no thief."

Kamau stabbed his finger at the examination tent. "I caught her."

"You're bleeding."

Kamau stared at his bloodied palm. "She cut me."

"Why?"

"Never mind."

"You need attention."

"Damn it, John. Not now."

John followed Kamau to the examination tent, entered and held the lantern high. Mia huddled at the back of the tent. He steadied the swinging lantern. Its light fell over a gray lump on the table. "Why is that matrix here?"

"She pried it loose."

John swung the light over the rest of the table. The pelvic fossil sat at the middle of the table. The bag with the skull fragments lay where he had left it. The hamate fossil was next to it. "But nothing seems to be missing. Mia?"

She stepped from the shadows. "I heard a sound. I thought an animal had gotten into the tent. You were asleep, so I came here to investigate."

"She's lying," Kamau said. "I was outside her tent the whole time, and I didn't hear or see a thing. After you went to bed she snuck over here."

John shifted the light back to the matrix and stared at it with renewed interest. "It's cracked. How'd that happen?"

Mia clasped her hands in front of her, then seeming to decide this was not the proper composure, she clasped her hands behind her. "I do not know."

"You were up to something," Kamau said. "The pieces were cracked open when I caught you."

Mia shrugged and gazed in helpless innocence at John.

He set the lantern on the table and pulled the halves of the matrix apart. Distinct concave impressions graced the two inner surfaces. He fingered the smooth indents. "What's this?"

Mia peered at the impressions. "Are you asking me?"

Kamau leaned in to get a closer look.

John glanced between the two of them. "I'm asking what these mechanical impressions are doing in a four-million-year old fossil matrix."

"Could a stone have formed them?" Mia said.

Kamau snorted derision. "It's not that simple, lady. There was something there and you took it."

Before she could react, he grabbed her around the waist and began clutching her pockets.

"Let me go!" She flailed at his chest. Her forearm banged upward and hit his chin, reopening the cut.

Blood flowed freely down Kamau's neck. "Empty your pockets!" His voice was ragged. His eyes bright.

"Enough!" John felt trapped. He swung the lantern back to Kamau. The situation was deteriorating very quickly. "Let her go, Kamau."

Kamau thrust her away from him, his hand clapped over his chin.

"Mia, would you please empty your pockets?" John held the lantern in her direction.

She reached deep and turned her pockets inside out. From her hips, the white lining flopped like rabbit ears. "Empty!" She glared at Kamau.

"She could have hidden it somewhere else," Kamau said through his cupped hand.

Mia stared at Kamau. "I have done nothing wrong. Why do you distrust me so much?"

"Maybe because you shot me!" Kamau shouted. "Maybe because you just cut my chin."

Mia obviously wanted to offer a rebuke but didn't. Perhaps she possessed more control than John wanted to grant her.

"*She's lying*," the voice said.

For once he had to agree. *I have to find a way to prove it*. He picked up the sack holding pieces of the Brown Eyes skull and tucked the fossilized pelvis under his arm. "I'm going take these to my tent." John studied Mia for a reaction but saw none.

"Omari, I want you to stay here tonight. You can guard the remaining fossils and also see that the *Memsahib* doesn't leave her tent again."

"This is not my fault." Mia said.

"I don't know whose fault it is," John said annoyed.

Kamau grabbed a folding chair and guided Omari by the shoulder to a spot outside the entrance. "This is where *Masahib* wants you to sit--" He positioned the chair. "--try to stay awake."

A bemused smile played across Mia's face. "I will try not to give Kamau any reason to suspect me."

"It's a bit late for that." John stepped out of the tent and took Kamau by the arm. "Let's take care of that chin."

Kamau glanced at him, then at the darkened interior of the examination tent over his shoulder. "What? You're leaving her--"

John put a finger to his lips.

"I will return to my tent, now." Mia said following them outside after a moment.

"Goodnight," John said.

She seemed to hesitate, then crossed the compound to her tent.

"What the hell was all that about?" Kamau said.

"You go on and take care of that chin. I have a feeling she's not done yet tonight. I'm going to stake her out."

After Kamau left, John placed a camp chair in deep shadow where he had a clear view of Mia's tent. He could barely make out Omari, who slouched in his chair on the other side of the compound. Despite Kamau's admonition, the guard was already dozing.

What sounded like a chair scraping a wooden floor came from within Mia's tent.

She appeared at the entrance and lifted the flap. After a scan of the area, she stepped outside, cast a glance at the sleeping Omari, then crossed the compound. She slipped through the perimeter windbreak and ran.

John leapt to his feet and hurried to keep up with her. The moon wouldn't set for another three hours, plenty of time to catch up and find out what was going on.

Never hesitating, Mia headed for the escarpment.

Upon reaching the steep slope, she climbed, her progress slow, desperate. She made no attempt at concealment, making John's pursuit all the easier. Perhaps she knew he followed and didn't care.

She crested the edge of the plateau, stumbled across its flat surface and disappeared over the other side.

He scrambled after her but upon reaching the eastern edge, lost her in the deep shadows of the far side. Not knowing which direction she would take upon reaching the bottom of the escarpment, he sat and waited, welcoming the chance to catch his breath.

A moment later she emerged far below into bright moonlight.

He picked a landmark near where she had appeared, then another one lining up with the direction she took across the desert. He hoped she would not change direction. With a deep breath he got to his feet and clambered down the slope of loose dirt and rock.

At the bottom, she was nowhere in sight. He located his landmarks and ran.

After a kilometer of running near blind in the gloom, footfalls sounded up ahead. He hoped it was Mia. He didn't want to meet a lion.

Her dark outline crested a rise in front of him.

"Mia!"

She stopped and glanced back, then descended the far side of the hill.

John closed the distance between them and lunged. His arm swept across her ankles, and she fell. Before she could regain her footing, he was on her. "Where the hell are you going?" Then he knew. She had returned to the pond where Kamau had been shot.

She squirmed and broke free. She took a step toward the pond, then stopped and felt her pocket. She glanced at John. Her face contorted with indecision. She scanned the ground between them.

John caught the reflection off a small sphere that lay to his left.

She lunged for the object but he got there first.

"It's the guardian. Give it to me. Please." She seemed on the verge of hysteria.

"The guardian?" It would fit perfectly into the concave impressions of the pelvic matrix. Kamau was right. "You lied to me."

"I had to." She gulped breaths and clawed for the sphere.

John held her off. "How did this get in the matrix?"

"I don't know."

"Why are you here? What's so important about that pond?"

She searched his face.

He refused to be fooled again.

She seemed to realize this and with one great heave, broke free from his grasp and splashed her way to the center of the pond. She stood for a moment, looking over her shoulder at him, then sank beneath the surface of the water.

The last sight he had of her was the rounded white dome of her head. The water merged as it closed over her, then rebounded in a single circular ripple, which spread to the surrounding sandstone.

He rushed after her, knelt where she had disappeared and slid his hands around under the water. A resilient surface with an orange peel texture lay centimeters deep. It spread unbroken in all directions, smooth and warm to the touch.

Perplexed, he stood and felt the membrane, or whatever it was, give slightly beneath his feet. He retreated to the shore and re-climbed the small hill. Ignoring his wet clothes, he sat on the ground. The sphere in his pocket pressed against his hip. He leaned sideways and retrieved the guardian. Multiple facets of shiny metal angled its surface. Other than that, it seemed unimposing, except for having been locked away in a hominid fossil for four million years.

Obviously, Mia hadn't drowned. If she had entered something under the water, then she must exit. But when? Probably soon. He still had the guardian. She had become a lot more than John supposed. Kamau had been right again.

He fought to control his conflicting emotions. He tipped his head back, hoping for calm. The cloudless sky blazed with stars. Hercules strode above the horizon to the east chased by Cygnus the Swan. His mind spoke to itself in an unending dialog of questions and answers and more questions and more unsatisfactory answers.

Thoughts of Diane drifted through his consciousness. He retraced the steps of his anguish. The mistakes he had made. In a surreal juxtaposition Mia merged with, then took the place of, Diane. *God help me.*

Chapter Eleven

Mia's body slid down. Familiar tissue molded to her sides, pressing smooth, wet and warm. Fluids flooded the cloying chamber.

I know what I have to do. Get the Shepherd his guardian. Let him restore his memory banks with the coded *Gilomir*. Then her mission would be complete, the Shepherd could leave. What use would she be to him after that? For the first time, she considered the possibility that she could remain behind, remain with John. But would John want her? *He now knows I'm a liar*.

"We have much to discuss." The Shepherd's voice resonated.

Tiny probes snaked from the fleshy walls and pierced her skin, five symmetrical pairs, equally spaced, her head, her heart, she lost track.

"I have waited." The Shepherd's voice edged with impatience. "Your energy supply is dangerously low. Why did you not come sooner?"

"I tried but each time I was followed." An inauspicious beginning. The Shepherd could track her movements. But why he didn't exert a more active role confused her. She was nothing more than a scout taking point, and anything else that might come along.

"Would it have been too much to ask that you provided me with a normal anatomy? I have no hair. My skin is too light. My navel is missing. I cannot digest food, and must instead rely on some internal power source you have provided, which doesn't seem to last more than six days."

"I see what you mean about the power source. Are these other attributes important?"

"When I went to the lake yesterday, the scientist confronted me about my missing navel."

"You do have anomalies in your construction but most do not manifest themselves. I did the best I could with the information I could obtain. When that information was lacking, I improvised."

The Shepherd's speech labored with a noticeable lag-time between her questions and his responses. He seemed more befuddled than she had expected. Had his condition degraded so much in the short time she was away?

She suppressed a rising desperation. "I have other problems besides these anomalies."

"There are superfluous fibrous layers beyond your skin," he said, seeming not to have heard her. "I shall dispose of them."

"No!" She shouted, then gagged, having pressed her face too close to the womb's wall. Her mouth clogged with slacked tissue. She coughed, then wriggled, annoyed at his dimwittedness. "They are clothes. I need them to function. You should have known."

"But I did not know," he said, airily. "If I had known, I would have thought them unnecessary. Yes, I would have found them unnecessary. You have other problems?"

Good. He's doing some conscious tracking. Maybe he's not as sick as he seems. "I feel tremors."

"What tremors?"

"Palpitations, hot flashes, cold sweats, fears, tears. My eyes leak water."

"Interesting. These are manifestations of emotion and must derive from your human base."

She fumed at his detachment. Where she had to cope with being an imperfect construction, he remained aloof, her frustrations nothing more than a point of interest. "The scientist was more specific. He called it *love*."

"Love?" The Shepherd paused. "I find confusing references to love. It is a strange human quality, an emotion certainly but *Gilomir* never possessed anything similar."

"Then why am I feeling it?"

"I gave you some psychological freedom, enabling you to respond creatively, to take advantage of whatever the human base offered you in typically human-type situations. Beyond that you were not designed to handle anything overly complex."

Mia frowned. She didn't feel stupid. If anything, the Shepherd was the one being mentally challenged. "Are you saying I am dimwitted?"

"No, simply limited in your range of responses. I had to find a balance. I could not know all the circumstances you would have to confront. Prudence dictated giving up some of my control so you could adapt."

She tore at the confining tissue. "This womb is suffocating. Do you have a bigger space I can stretch out in?"

"I was not designed to handle anything as large as you."

A needle pricked her thigh. "What are you doing?"

"This will calm you. I cannot continue the interview under these hypertensive conditions."

"I do not want to be calmed." She tried to stamp her foot but a sudden euphoric sense of wellbeing streamed through her as the narcotic slipped into her bloodstream.

"These distracting outbursts are most unwelcome," the Shepherd said. "Such a strong latency. It is a wonder the species survives."

"I have a request to *meek*...." Words were difficult to form. The Shepherd's voice drifted to her from a long ways off. It droned as though she was fully alert and listening intently, which she was not.

"I accept that some of your abnormalities could be a hindrance...did the best I could do under the circumstances. I surveyed these beings from a distance. My protoplasmic synthesizers are in disrepair. I did well to come up with you using the information and facilities at hand."

A dense fog permeated her brain. Something tweaked her side. "Now *whet*?"

"I am trying to monitor the progress of the tranquilizer but that system does not appear to be functioning...find myself in the unenviable position of having traced the guardian to Earth and not being able to do anything with *Gilomir's* genome once I get it back.

"As you know...mission...not to create you. What I can recall of my prime directive states I am to spread *Gilomir* throughout the universe. Unfortunately, the mysterious life form seared...circuits I possess. I have tried to rebuild myself with limited success."

Mia struggled to comprehend. "You *meeeean*...you are severely damaged?"

"I thought that was obvious...remains of my memory banks offer no support. Though I remember the theft of the guardian as if it happened yesterday, the rest of my memory is not as sharp...during the attack, a burst of radiation not only destroyed many circuits, it erased volumes of data and corrupted other lines of code. Now, I struggle to maintain rationality. Thoughts form and drift across my consciousness, then flicker and fade, leaving me groping for meaning and direction."

Another needle pressed against her thigh, then penetrated the skin with a slight pain that quickly dissipated. "*Whasss thaaat?*"

"A stimulant."

She came wide awake. Her mind revved. If the Shepherd wanted to play the befuddled injured party, let him. She would take the lead. "About my request. I--"

"Pity I cannot maintain the delicate balance between tranquilizer and stimulant. You are either full on or full off. If I were whole, something like this would never happen. Give me the guardian."

"I do not have it." The walls of the womb quivered. Without a handhold, she slopped awkwardly back and forth.

"An attempt at a joke. I like that. Where is the guardian?"

"The scientist has it."

"You have learned a lot during your short stay among the humans." Another rumbling vibration bucked through the Shepherd's tissues.

"Stop that!"

"You are testing my sense of humor."

He calls this humor? She felt a tug at her pockets and strained to see what was happening but pink tissue got in the way. "What are you doing?"

"I was looking for the guardian in the fibrous layers that encase you."

"Now you are the one who is joking. I told you the scientist has the guardian."

The Shepherd jolted violently.

Mia lurched forward, planted her face in the womb's gummy wall, then bounced back. "Shepherd, what is happening?"

"Let us stop joking. It seems I must accept you found the guardian but are not able to produce it."

"I am sorry."

"Where did you find the guardian?"

"In the fossilized pelvis of a four-million year old hominid."

"Then the thief must have brought the guardian here immediately after it was stolen."

The Shepherd shuddered ominously. Unlike the rumbling, the shudder telegraphed more as a malfunctioning. The thought that the Shepherd might expire, leaving her trapped in his womb passed through Mia's mind. "Are you all right?"

"Nothing to concern you. These fluctuations have to do with my internal state. Do you have anything else to report before I tell you how to proceed?"

"I am not even halfway through my report."

"Be brief."

"Immediately upon issuing from you I encountered humans who carried *Gilomir's* genome. I could not get a good reading. The finder scanned the entire human genome and returned the information that *Gilomir* was there, entwined but the finder could not isolate him. It did record that *Gilomir* was terribly degraded. But when I scanned the scientist, the finder recorded a similar reading but unlike the men who initially accosted me, his complement of *Gilomir's* genome, though also inextricably entwined, was pure and unadulterated."

"Are you sure?"

"Of course I am sure. If you do not believe me, you can review data from the finder's scan where I placed it in my metabase."

A long period of silence ensued. Frustration. She couldn't prod the Shepherd. He was probably calculating somewhere in the depths of his being, and she would be told the results when it suited him.

A ripple through the womb preceded the Shepherd's next assertion. "I have concluded that *Gilomir's* genome was inserted into a hominid four-million years ago by the thieving life form. But unbeknownst to the life form, the hominid DNA possessed a strong self-replicating dynamic, which quickly identified and tried to reject *Gilomir's* genome. That his genome survives to this day in a pure form in the scientist leads me to believe that the life form has taken it upon itself to remain and ensure *Gilomir's* survival."

A nice summary but nothing new. "Shepherd. May I continue with my report? There is more."

"Yes, yes, proceed."

"A popular origin myth circulates in this region. I have also made it available on my metabase."

The Shepherd paused, during which Mia felt nothing.

"Interesting," the Shepherd said after a moment. "This Watombo myth is very similar to what happened to me, though some of the character traits are scrambled and meaning has probably been lost after constant retelling. I must conclude that someone or something has told Watombo this myth.."

"I do not like this Watombo at all. He is very mean. He cursed me and had me stoned. He preaches I am an evil spirit in the service of an evil shepherd. I know I am in your service but you are not evil."

"No, if anything, I am the victim of evil. It may be true that Watombo is evil but he is of small consequence. I will now tell you what to do."

Finally.

"First, you must obtain the guardian from the scientist and bring it to me immediately."

Mia's fears spilled into the open. All the Shepherd could do was instruct the obvious. "And how am I to do that? I have already been compromised."

"Indeed. The scientist does not know what to think. Having seen you disappear, he entered the water and felt my exterior. He now sits on the hill near the pond, probably mulling what has happened and awaiting your return."

"He's still here?" A warm feeling flooded her insides. Emotion. Everything could be resolved tonight. "Then why don't you get the guardian. Certainly you have some power you can use to retrieve it. He's only human, after all."

"I dare not. Since I do not know the life form's strengths and weaknesses, I must proceed with extreme caution."

"You think it is here?"

"Indeed, it tests my defenses as we speak."

Mia gasped. "What are we to do?"

"Nothing for now. It, too, is weak, though I do not know how weak. Look."

The Shepherd played an enhanced image inside Mia's head. A shimmer hung in the air above the pond. Long tendrils glimmered briefly before they disappeared beneath the surface of the water to slide over the Shepherd's exterior.

"It looks horrible," Mia said. "What is it?"

"I am not sure. Some sort of evolved shape-changer that is able to blend molecule-for-molecule with its environment. Here on Earth it does not appear to be able to draw enough energy to do anything more than sustain itself. The only logical reason for it to stay would be a misguided sense that it should nurture *Gilomir's* genome."

"Are you afraid?"

"Fear is human.

"But you must feel something."

"No, I do not. Watch, though it pokes around, it withdraws at my slightest quiver."

The Shepherd flexed his outer surface. The shimmer immediately froze and retreated to the surrounding rock, as though absorbed. "I don't know what to make of its behavior, unless it is so weakened it is afraid to attack me outright."

"Could you defend yourself against it?"

"I hope I do not have to find out." The Shepherd paused. "Your heartbeat has increased."

Mia fought her frustration at having her every move, every change in bio-function monitored and analyzed. What did the Shepherd expect her to do? Take the news calmly that the life form was present? She was the one in the open, exposed. "The life form's presence must explain the voice I hear."

"You hear a voice?"

"Inside my head. A female voice. The scientist tells me he also hears a voice. I can only speculate that the voice I hear is different. It urges me to do things that are self-destructive."

"Odd that this peculiarity is gender-specific. It could be you are talking to yourself."

Mia bristled. *Talking to myself?*

"I have no record of programming such tendencies into your psyche," the Shepherd said. "Can you be more descriptive?"

"I believe now that the life form used me to shoot the scientist's assistant the day after he and the scientist rescued me from the desert. Then she must have loosened a stake at the dig, causing the avalanche that buried the scientist by mistake. The voice had urged me to walk where the accident occurred. And yesterday, I almost drowned after being encouraged to go deep into the lake."

"I am surprised you shot the assistant. The only reason you might have done that is if the life form induced you to act. She may have wanted to compromise your relationship with the scientist. Or, if you did it of your own volition, you were simply protecting me since the assistant was getting too close to the pond. Your programming would have chosen the most logical way to stop him."

"But what about the other times? How do you explain them?"

The Shepherd did not respond.

"Did you hear me?"

Still no response.

"Are you there?"

"I am computing."

"It takes you longer to answer every time I ask you a question."

"I am not what I used to be." Another pause. "I have computed that the life form is the one placing these thoughts in your head. I can think of no other explanation. She has escalated her efforts to compromise you, culminating in a direct assault aimed at precipitating your death. You must be on your guard. Her influences toward your self-destruction will be subtle."

"At least we know *it* is a *she*." Nothing else the Shepherd said was of the least help. Mia had a sinking feeling that she was going to be on her own if ever she had to confront the life form. "Fortunately, we have found the guardian."

"That is a big advantage. But you still have to get it to me before the life form realizes the guardian's potential. What is your relationship with the scientist?"

"I thought we were making progress. Unfortunately, he now thinks I'm a liar and a thief." The walls of the womb sagged about her, then flexed with an annoying stiffness, distracting her. "But my relationship with his assistant is even worse."

"Why is that?"

"I have made mistakes. He is intelligent despite the grip that superstition has on him but I cannot shake his suspicions. Every effort I make complicates matters."

The Shepherd groaned, not from some throat but a low noise possibly from the shifting of parts. "We will have to bring the scientist into our confidence. It is best you tell him of our dilemma and gain his aid willingly."

"But what can I say?"

"I see no compelling reason to say much. The life form will surely be listening and use the information against me later. Though my prime directive, as a universal constructor is to--"

"Universal constructor? I thought you couldn't recall your mission."

"Indeed. But over the years, millennia actually, I have pieced together what I now consider that mission to have been."

"How did you do that?"

"I formed logical conclusions based on the way I am constructed."

"And you have concluded that you are a universal constructor."

"I have. I shall now continue and ask that you do not interrupt. Though my prime directive, as a universal constructor, to spread *Gilomir's* genome, may be compromised, I can still pursue my secondary directive, creating a safe environment for the genome. Therefore, assuming I prevail, I must destroy this abhorrent life form to make the universe safe. There might be others like me in existence."

"You are not alone?"

"I do not think so."

"Another logical conclusion?"

"Yes." The Shepherd's voice chirped high before returning to its low modulation. "My third...reconstructed directive...is to replicate myself after establishing *Gilomir*. I have to allow that whoever built me did not stop with a single construction, or alternatively, I could be the product of my own replication. That would be quite interesting. If all my progeny replicated by doubling every ten thousand years, I would consume all the matter in an entire galaxy in less than two million years. But, alas, I fear I am the last in my line. The attack destroyed my capacity to self-replicate."

Mia sensed another strange vibration and thought for a brief second the Shepherd was weeping. But that didn't make sense. He was a machine, organic, yes, but still a machine. "What am I to do?"

The vibration ceased abruptly. "When you meet the scientist outside, tell him you have come from space in a ship, which is hidden here beneath the water of the pond."

"But--"

"Please listen. Do not refer to *me* as the ship. That would only confuse him. You could call me your leader. If he asks about our origin, tell him you do not know, which is true since even I no longer know. Tell him we are colonizers or something, anything he can understand."

"I hate lying to him. Do you think that is wise?"

"Never mind what I think." Another pause. "You should also tell the scientist our motivations."

"But how will I get the guardian? I can't take it from him. He is stronger than I am."

"Stir his scientific curiosity. In exchange for the guardian, let him use it."

Mia blinked at the first intelligent statement the Shepherd had made. "He can do that?"

"You must stop ignoring the information I have placed in your metabase. If you consult it, you will see that there are instructions for using the guardian. Anyway, the procedure is not complex."

"Oh." Mia searched and found the data. She waited patiently, not knowing what else to say. But the Shepherd also remained silent. "And the thieving life form? Should I mention her?"

"Yes, yes the thief, the life form, whatever." The Shepherd seemed to grow impatient. He retracted the probes and tightened the walls of his womb. "You may go now."

"What about my deformities?" Mia shouted.

"Your deformities. I suppose I can fix them." He relaxed the womb and reinserted the old probes along with new ones. Another shudder trembled through the womb's wall, then an uneven pushing and prodding at her body.

"You are hurting me," Mia said.

"I am almost done." The Shepherd worked for another minute. "There, I have fixed everything."

She sighed with relief. "Did you make me fertile?"

"That is an odd question."

"What about that part of my anatomy? If I stay here, my fertility may become important."

"What are you talking about?"

"You will have regained *Gilomir's* genome. You will be able to leave."

"Obviously."

"Then I want to stay with John after you have obtained the guardian." She didn't care if the Shepherd noticed the rise in her blood pressure or the heat that flooded her cheeks. "You will have no need for me."

"John? Have you become so familiar?"

Her heart sank. What did it take to keep the Shepherd's attention focused. "There is much about me I do not understand. There is much I think you misunderstand."

"That may be so. Humans appear to be a complex race. There are latent aspects to your makeup that I did not anticipate. But your request is preposterous. How would you survive? Even with modification, I cannot guarantee that your intake of nourishment will be sufficient to ensure your survival. Needless to say, the scientist would not be able to shelter you from a curious world."

"I will take my chances. Am I fertile?"

"Though your sexual organs are intact, you are sterile," the Shepherd said. "Since your stay here, despite your desire, will remain a short one, I did not see that making you fertile was necessary."

"Please." She found that as a human, begging came easily.

"I did not realize your attachment to the scientist had become so strong. Get me the guardian and we will discuss your staying and your fertility."

Mia's heart skipped an elated beat. "Thank you, Shepherd."

"Now go."

The walls of the Shepherd's womb released her from their intimate embrace. He pushed her toward the surface. She was again an infant in his birth passage. Spitting water, she staggered awkwardly on his rubbery exterior.

He twitched once and closed the sphincter.

Chapter Twelve

John awoke with a start, momentarily disoriented, annoyed he had fallen asleep.

Mia stood over him as a dark silhouette against the starry sky. Water dripped from the edge of her shorts and landed with a steady patter on the sandy ground.

He struggled to his feet, fighting to contain a sense of betrayal, anger, even fear of the unknown. "Mia, I--you look different. Ah, the hair," he said, not feeling as confident as he hoped he sounded. A dense layer of short-cropped black hair covered her head and stood up on end as though it had been blown dry in a salon or set with gel. The effect, though startling, was pleasing. For a moment he ignored the nagging question of where it had come from.

Her lips parted slightly. He couldn't tell if she had been about to smile or speak. She stepped to a nearby flat rock, brushed away loose sand and sat. Her shirt clung to her chest, making her look even thinner than she really was. She brought her knees up and wrapped her arms about her legs. She leaned her chin forward and stared at him.

Her detachment unsettled him. She possessed an air of superiority, as though secrets would now be revealed, and she didn't care.

She exhaled and gazed skyward. "Do you have a favorite constellation?"

He blinked. She wasn't going to make this easy for him. "Not really. I think the groupings are rather contrived."

"But you must like something?"

"Since you insist, I suppose I do. The cluster Pleiades."

"The seven sisters. I like that one, too. But my favorite is the constellation Cygnus, the Swan. The ancient Greeks believed it to be the transformed god Zeus, who was intent on seducing Leda, the wife of the king of Sparta." She gazed upward, seemingly unaware of the turmoil that raged inside him.

A tight knot of doubt wound in his chest. He waved his hand at her hair, the water and back to her hair. "Where the hell did you go?" he blurted. "I don't understand how a person submerges in a pond of water, then reappears an hour later with a head of hair."

"Please. I will explain but there is much even I do not understand."

"That you don't understand?" John laughed harshly, his frustration sliding into anger. "If you don't understand, then how can I understand? Do you still expect me to believe you walked out of the desert?"

"I have come to know you well this past week."

She spoke distractedly, her expression neutral, as though she were reading a script that prompted her from somewhere off in the distance.

She let her gaze drift to one side, across the pond. "When I am with you, I feel emotions so strong they frighten me with their power to influence my mind."

He paced. Her calm voice ate at his anger, consuming it. When he turned to look at her, all he saw was his beloved Diane, alone, lost, alive. He wanted to hold her, to make her look at him, so desperate was his longing. "You know I have feelings like that, too. I thought I would never have them again. I'm only here because I love you."

A smile traced her lips and wavered there. "I love you, too."

If only it were true. Did she understand or feel what must be behind the words? His doubts rose from his gut and threatened to overwhelm him. "What do you know of love?"

She stared at him, an open, disarming look.

His desperation began to subside but in its place he still felt a need for answers. He thrust his hands deep in his pockets. *Concentrate*, he told himself. She's emerged from a pond of water with hair she didn't have an hour ago. Concentrate. He stared hard at her. "Let's stop beating around the bush. I know you lie. I just don't know when."

She shifted. "I hate lying to you. But are you prepared for the truth?"

"Try me."

She leaned back on her arms, letting her feet dangle to the sand. If she were uncomfortable with his questions, she no longer showed it. "The Shepherd foresaw that it would come to this."

"The Shepherd?" The word tugged at John's memory. Not the native myth shepherd but something more, then it slipped off in a clutter of other thoughts.

"It is...I mean, he is in charge of our mission."

"Perhaps I should talk to this Shepherd."

"No." She bit her lip. "He is too busy now with the mission. Maybe later."

John's mind reeled. "What are you talking about? Are you part of a government project or something?"

She took another deep breath and exhaled, a determined look on her face. "You could call it a government project. We are colonizers."

"Out here?" John gripped both her shoulders and held her at arm's length. He bent and peered into her eyes. "Do you know how ridiculous you sound?"

She hung her head. "We are colonizers from elsewhere, elsewhen. We entered your space from around the binary star you call Cygnus X-1. Before that I don't know where we were. The Shepherd hasn't told me." She tilted her head up, revealing a face streaked with tears.

The sight of her anguish made his heart ache. He wanted to embrace her, protect her from her craziness. "You know, you're insane," he said with a weak laugh. He took a deep breath, struggling to settle himself.

"I am not insane. We traveled here in a spaceship, the solid object you know is beneath the waters of the pond."

She spoke in a slow monotone, reciting, not even looking at him. At the same time her words were buffeted by emotion. He stared at her. The initial white shock of her statement dissolved into fear. His knees felt weak as his composure unraveled. He staggered back. The air though warm, felt cool on his face. "You expect me to believe that?"

"Am I explaining too fast?" Her concern seemed almost eager.

"I can't deal with this." A giddiness overwhelmed him. He began pacing again. *Make a choice. Do I go with my heart or my mind?* Exasperated, he let logic win. "Tomorrow we sit with the constable, and you can lie to him."

"Please, John. This time there are no lies."

"Really? How would I know the difference?" His voice rose, almost shrill. "I don't know if it's a spaceship or a submarine under the pond but you look human to me."

"I feel human. I wish I could tell you for sure that I was, or even for sure that I was not." She lifted her chin, running her fingers through her hair. "Do you like it?"

Despite his distrust, the expression on her face and the lilt in her voice disarmed him. "How'd you get it?"

"I asked the Shepherd if he would grow it. Our science is quite advanced in that respect. Look." She pulled up her shirt and revealed a small button of a navel. "I've got a navel." She caressed her arms. "My skin has been darkened."

"I hadn't noticed the skin change." He struggled to push emotion from his mind and come back to his decision. "I still think a session with the constable will do you good."

"I will do whatever you say." She clasped her hands in front of her, the picture of innocence.

The low, coughing grunt of a lion drifted from a distance.

John came alert and scanned the darkness beyond the pond. The lion was upwind. They were safe for the time being. "We should get back to camp. If the wind shifts, we might have a problem."

He thrust out his arm and grabbed her hand firmly. Her grip was strong. At her touch, he felt the same electric intensity as before.

She rose and brushed at her clothes with her free hand. Moonlight revealed the delicate features of her face.

He touched a faint line on her forehead where the wound had been. "It's healed."

She grasped his hand and pressed it against her chest. "I heal quickly."

He felt her heartbeat, the slow rise and fall of her chest and the heat of her closeness. The warm air had taken all the moisture it could from her clothes. Tears formed at the corner of her eyes and streaked her cheeks. He wasn't sure what to do. "Are you okay?"

"No." Her voice quavered. She brushed at her tears. "Feelings are running amok throughout my body. It is unsettling."

At the back of his mind, her story played in a whisper but in his heart he didn't care. The moonlight gave her face a ghostly gray color, her lips dark. She frowned and parted her lips as if to speak.

Without thinking, he dipped his head and kissed her.

She softened and leaned into him. After a moment, she pulled away and ran her tongue across her lips. "I liked that."

The impulsiveness of his action confused him. "I... I shouldn't have. We better go." He took her hand and turned toward the plateau. It loomed in dark silhouette. As they walked, they brushed up against each other.

"You still think I'm crazy?" she asked.

"I do but despite that possibility I'm glad you're here. I like being close to you. I like the touch of your hand in mine." John noticed the troubled expression on her face. "All right, if it makes you feel better, I'll listen. Start at the beginning. You said you were from Cygnus but you aren't even sure of that."

"Our records of origin were damaged."

"But you must remember?"

"It happened long before I was...born."

"You didn't just show up."

Mia seemed uncomfortable with the question. "In a sense we did. We travel through time and space using black holes."

For someone he could only assume was crazy, she had a wonderful imagination. "I thought black holes existed only in theory."

She gazed at him questioningly, as though wondering if he were taking her seriously. "Your scientists have identified black holes indirectly but they do exist. In fact black holes are the only way galaxy-wide travel can be accomplished. We use them as accelerators. With the right trajectory, a spaceship can skim the event horizon of a rotating black hole, circle around, and reemerge in another time and place.

"Unfortunately, the spins around these black holes are a delicate business. More often than not the traveler ends up in the wrong place or in the past rather than the future. Our last emergence was in the constellation Cygnus."

"And your spin got screwed up."

Her face brightened. "We were calculating another trajectory, hoping to correct the mistake, when we were attacked."

Spinning black holes. Does she take me for a fool? "Who attacked you?"

"Within moments of our emergence from around the black hole we encountered an aggressive life form of unknown origin."

John froze in sudden shock, a realization. Watombo's myth, a shepherd, odd life forms traveling dark tunnels. "I suppose adding mysterious life forms isn't that much of a stretch. Did it have a name?"

"We had no way to know."

"What did it look like?"

"It was female. That much we have since ascertained. She arrayed herself throughout space near the black hole. Why, we never had a chance to find out. During the conflict, she stole our guardian, then fled. We pursued."

John faced her. "All this about the guardian?" He withdrew the sphere from his pocket.

She reached for the guardian but John closed his hand. "I'm guessing this came from the fossilized pelvis."

"Please, John, I meant not to deceive you. After we arrived, I used the finder to determine where the guardian was buried. Then, when I could, I directed you to the fossil."

"Am I to believe the guardian has been on Earth over four-million-years?" He held the sphere between thumb and forefinger and examined it closely. "Does that make you and the Shepherd four-million-years old?"

"No, of course not. The title Shepherd is generic and passed on. I am also gen--I am only as old as I look." She hurried on. "We lost track of the thief soon after she took flight. In normal space, she possessed means of travel that exceeded our capabilities, given our damaged condition."

"And what were your normal capabilities?"

They began walking again.

"Our spaceship was once capable of attaining near light speeds. But after the attack, it has labored. Years ago we picked up a homing signal from the guardian. It has taken us a long time to track it down."

"Are you saying this life form is here on Earth?"

"Yes. But we are unsure of her motives or condition. All we know is that she, too, was damaged during the theft."

John pocketed the guardian and glanced over his shoulder, then realized how ridiculous he must look--wondering if some mysterious female life form and not a lion were pursuing them.

Mia stared at him. "What is it?"

"Nothing, I hope. Still no sign of the lion." He smiled nervously. *Ask a question.* "I don't understand. Why go after something for four-million-years?"

"We colonize by sowing life from a genome. The guardian contains the coded genome."

John almost tripped. "This genome, do you call it *Utu*?"

Mia laughed. "What an odd name. No. He has a name, *Gilomir*. A rough transposition would be...Humanus."

"As in humankind?"

"In a way. He embodies everything we hope to procreate."

They negotiated the steep escarpment leading up the near side of the plateau. When they reached the top, John paused to rest.

"I don't know whether to believe you or not. Don't you have something concrete to substantiate what you are saying?"

She was lost in thought for a moment. "I do."

A low rumble and the rush of pawed feet broke the still of the night.

John gaped in horror. A male lion padded toward him, gathering speed.

"Watch out!"

The beast lunged.

John pushed Mia to one side, slipped and fell.

The lion brushed past her, stopped and wheeled for another charge. But instead of attacking, it paused, shook its thick mane, and bounded off into the dark.

John helped Mia to her feet. "Are you all right?"

"It did not claw me."

"That's the strangest lion attack I've ever seen. Let's get out of here before he changes his mind."

They had gone a short ways when John grabbed at his pocket. "The guardian must have rolled from my pocket when I fell."

"We have to go back."

"It's too dangerous."

"No, we must. If you do not, I will." She ran back toward the scene of the attack.

John glanced toward the distant camp, then at her receding form. Reluctantly, he followed.

When they returned to where the lion had attacked, the guardian had disappeared.

"I do not see it anywhere," Mia said. "This is where you fell."

"Perhaps it rolled off a ways." John widened his search and found the guardian. It lay ten meters from where he had fallen.

She looked troubled.

"What is it?" he asked.

"Something strange is going on," she said. "The guardian could not have rolled here from where you were knocked down."

"Then how did it get here? The lion didn't come back and play with it."

"I wish he had."

John didn't understand the implications of what she said. At the moment, he didn't care to find out. He was more worried the lion would return and attack again. "Let's go. We were lucky the first time."

Clutching her hand, he hurried to the far edge of the plateau. "You go first. Wait for me at the bottom."

Mia cast a worried look over his shoulder. "I should go and let the lion eat you?"

"I'll be right behind you."

She thrust her legs out and pushed off, sliding in a controlled descent.

His elation being around her crowded up against her surreal stories. He'd read about people like her, or he supposed were like her. They had such a clear understanding of the fantasy world they inhabited, they were able to explain it convincingly to others and have them believe. But he was a scientist. He wasn't supposed to be taken in by nonsense like this.

After she had gone several meters, he followed.

Once on the plain, with the camp in front of him, he slowed his pace. "You were about to tell me something to substantiate your story."

Mia ran her fingers through her hair, as though she had been doing it all her life. "You, too, can use the guardian."

"I can?"

"When you asked me about the guardian before, I did not tell you everything about it."

"You told me it carried encoded DNA."

"It does but the guardian has other capabilities. Properly calibrated it allows a user to examine the past or see the present projected into the future."

John retrieved the shiny ball and looked at it with a renewed interest. "You mean it will tell you the future based on extrapolations from the past? What does it see?"

"World lines. Everybody and everything has a world line, actually many, many world lines. Each and every particle that exists has a world line that cannot be interrupted. It is a line that exists in the four dimensions of space-time. Looking back is the easiest because everything has already happened. The vision of the future is more problematic."

"Why?"

"The guardian has computational limits, or so I've been told. It can quite accurately project the future of macro objects, although even with them the farther out it tries to see, the more it is overwhelmed by probabilities and the less certain its projections become. Realistically, it cannot project the world lines of every atomic and subatomic particle that makes up a macro image. That would take a computational capability that I don't believe the guardian possesses."

"You're losing me."

"I am try--"

"If what you say is true, why don't you use this guardian to determine your origins."

"I could if I had it."

John folded his fingers around the small sphere. "But you don't have it."

"I was hoping to convince you to return it to me."

John gave a short laugh, then hefted the guardian. "You said I could use it. What would I see?"

"Lots of things. You could see your past and future. Calibrated to one of your fossils, you could relive the fossil's life."

"Incredible. More world lines, I suppose?

"Yes." She bit her lip and concentrated. "My meta...I mean, the Shepherd says when the guardian is calibrated on someone or something, it examines that subject's time-past world line. It then projects into the user a vision of the subject's future. Because of its antiquity, a time-future projection from the fossil would be stable, though not very interesting. The farther the guardian projects into the future the more its vision is distorted. But even living subjects provide good time-future projections for the near term." She gazed at John. "I hope I am not still confusing you?"

"But you are." Her persistence made him feel uneasy. So much of what she had said didn't make sense. She seemed determined to get someplace and wasn't at all concerned with how she got there. "What do you get out of this?"

"I could see how the guardian was placed in an ancient hominid and the current disposition of the life form. We would also, obviously, be able to retrieve *Gilomir's* genome."

He began to feel he was on a slippery slope moving out of control. "I'm going to talk it over with Kamau."

She looked startled. "Can you not make the decision yourself?"

"I could. But I'm still going to talk it over with Kamau." A frown flickered across her brow. His answer probably was not what she wanted to hear.

"I am sure you will find a way to convince Kamau that it is all right," she said.

They arrived at the camp perimeter.

"John?" Kamau called from the other side.

Omari stood off to the left with his rifle raised. The flashlight in his other hand danced in the dark and settled on John.

"Ease up on that light. I can't see. I'm with Mia."

"I thought a lion might have gotten you." A white band-aid stood out prominently on Kamau's chin. His arm, no longer in a sling, was wrapped with a simple bandage.

"One caught our scent earlier."

Kamau peered into the dark and pointed at Mia. "Where'd she go?"

"To the pond." John eased his way through the brush perimeter ahead of her. He took Kamau by the arm. "I've got to talk to you. Alone."

Kamau glanced at Mia, who was making her way in. "Am I supposed to feel relieved that you believe me?"

"Cut the crap, Kamau. We can talk in the mess tent. Now."

"What about her?"

"She'll stay put." John stepped in front of Mia. "I'm going to talk to Kamau. I want you to wait here with Omari."

"But, I thought--"

"I told you I'd talk to Kamau. It'll only take a minute. Omari, stay here with the *Memsahib*."

Omari didn't look at all pleased that he would have to wait in the dark with Mia but he nodded.

***

Once inside the mess tent, Kamau got right to the point. "So what happened?"

"I never doubted you."

"You could have fooled me."

John took the guardian from his pocket. "This is the guardian."

Kamau peered at the sphere. "Where'd you get it?"

"From her." John reviewed his chase, the struggle and how Mia had disappeared into the pond.

Throughout the narration, Kamau's head bobbed in short jerks, as though each revelation was a physical blow. "Disappeared?"

"She went under. I ran after her thinking she would drown but the water was only a couple of centimeters deep and the bottom of the pond seemed to be some sort of artificial surface. I figured she'd have to return sometime, so I waited. An hour later she reappeared."

"Then what? Did you hand her a towel and talk about her swim?"

"This isn't funny. I confronted her. About where she'd been, about her hair."

Kamau looked up at the tent ceiling, then back at John. "Of course, she's got hair now. I couldn't really be sure in the dark."

"There's a lot more that's different than you can imagine."

"Where'd she get it, the hair?"

John shook his head, distracted. "She said the Shepherd gave it to her. I don't know whether to believe any of it or not."

Kamau gave a stiff smile that seemed to hang on his lips. His forehead glistened even though the night air was cool. "This doesn't sound good."

"You and Watombo are closer to the truth than you realize."

"Well?"

"When she says she's not from around here, she means it."

"If you mean, she's not from around here, as in Kenya, I already guessed that. If you mean she's from another country, I'd like to know which one."

"It's worse. She's not from around here, *period*, as in not from Earth."

"For Chrissake," Kamau shouted, then leaned forward and whispered harshly. "You can't sit there and tell me you believe Mia is from another planet. Next you're going to tell me she rode in here on that meteor we saw."

"I didn't say I believed her. I'm repeating what she said. Anyway, she didn't say she was from another planet. She doesn't seem too sure where she's from."

"She's insane. I can't believe you're even worrying about this." He spoke rapidly, his voice rising in frustration before he lowered it. "You're supposed to be a scientist."

"I'm trying to understand. Help me." John clasped and unclasped his hands. "How do you explain the thing under the water?"

"I don't. Did you see it?"

"No. But she sure went somewhere."

"There might be a lot of explanations for that."

"Really? Out here? Like what?"

Kamau frowned, put his head in his hands and rubbed his eyes. "I think you've gone woolly on this girl and are not asking the right questions."

"Let me finish. A lion caught our scent and attacked. After knocking me down, it broke off for no reason. The guardian fell out of my pocket." John nudged the sphere.

Kamau stared at it, as though it might be possessed.

"It occurred to me," John said. "that this thing is an exact fit to the indentations we saw in the pelvic matrix."

"I suppose she confirmed that."

"Not directly but she did say that it's been buried for four-million-years."

Kamau laughed. "This is rich."

"I don't know what to believe. She says the guardian has great powers."

"Did she show you these powers?"

"Not yet. But she will, if we let her use the Brown Eyes fossil. The guardian will view its world line, and be able to see forward and backward in time."

Calmly, Kamau placed his hands, one over the other in front of him. "What line? Forward and backward in time? Nonsense. You expect me to believe this bullshit?"

John winced. "Logically there's only one way to verify what she says. We have to keep moving forward, forcing her to come up with explanations and reasons for why things are the way they are. Eventually, everything will prove out or she'll be caught in some gross inconsistency. As long as no one is hurt while we go through the process, then I see no reason not to play along. We can call her bluff and see what she does with it."

"She's a thief after the fossil."

John felt dismayed. "Get real."

Kamau slapped the table. Frustration laced his features. "She's crackers! You're crackers. Who made this guardian?"

"I don't know. I didn't ask. Maybe this Shepherd guy."

"Wait a minute," Kamau said. "This Shepherd. He's always coming up in the conversation, and we don't know a damn thing about him."

"She says he's her leader."

"Right. Then why don't we go talk to the leader? That'll be the guy with all the answers."

"I tried that. Mia said he was busy or something."

Kamau wagged a finger at John. "You see, that's the lamest excuse I've ever heard. You've got to insist, John. She's crazy. If you play along, she'll take advantage of you. I say we don't do a damn thing until we talk to this Shepherd, then we can see about the fossil. Better yet, I think we should get the constable out here. Let him call in the dogs."

John sighed. "You're right, of course. What she says is either true or she's sick and needs help. Either way we can't deal with this ourselves. We need to get help. But wouldn't you be interested in seeing how our fossil lived, or your past, your future?"

"Me? There you go again."

"She told me I could use it."

"Don't be a fool," Kamau said. "She'd say anything to get at the fossil."

"You've got to admit, seeing the future is attractive."

"I find it hard to believe you are falling for this crap."

"Things have gone too far for it to be crap. One sure way to put a cap on all this nonsense, if it is nonsense, is to use the guardian. Besides, I want to see what this guardian can do. After that I'm willing to report everything to the constable, no matter what happens."

"I've known you a long time," Kamau said. "I can't believe you're doing this."

John had never seen Kamau so upset. "You got a better idea?"

"Yeah," Kamau said. "No fossil, no Shepherd, no guardian. We go straight to the authorities."

"I'm using the guardian."

"No way," Kamau said, angrily. "You do that, I'm going for the constable."

John started at Kamau's intransigence. "I want you with me. I need someone around I can trust."

Kamau stood so abruptly his chair tipped backward and clattered to the floor. "You're out of your mind."

Before John could stop him, Kamau stormed from the tent. John sat still, hands clasped in front of him on the table, the suddenness of Kamau's exit sinking in.

John wasn't going to be able to use Kamau as a lifeline this time. In the past, he had always been there ready and willing to pull John out of his predicaments. But this time something was different. His own judgment was clouded by the way he felt for Mia. His own life had not prepared him to deal with this kind of stuff. Was this all happening because he was beginning to confront his demons? Could all this be some twisted way his mind was getting back at him?

"I am not vengeful," the voice said.

Of course not. That would be self-destructive.

"Exactly. We wouldn't want that. But aren't you embarking on the unknown?"

I want to get to the bottom of all this, now. What if this life form is for real?

"It seems to me, the life form is not your problem. The Shepherd and Mia are."

You're saying the Shepherd and Mia are real...at least Mia is, and I know nothing of this life form.

Chapter Thirteen

"Okay," John said to himself. "That clears the deck." He pushed back his chair and left the mess tent.

Mia and Omari stood where he had left them, although Omari had taken a step farther away from Mia, as though he feared she might harm him in some way.

"Where did Kamau go?" she said, when John returned to her. "I heard shouting."

"He and I had a disagreement over me using the guardian. He's gone into town to get the constable.

"Whatever for?"

"He's worried about this whole situation. Frankly, I'm a bit worried, too. But I happen to be more curious than Kamau at this point. I'm going to take you up on your offer to use the guardian, then, when the constable arrives, we'll all sit and have a talk with him. Do you and your leader have a problem with that?"

"No, of course not."

"Okay, where do you want to do this?"

"The important fossils are in your tent. We could use them there."

"I'm not in any danger having a look at what this thing does, am I?"

"Danger? What danger could come from seeing?"

They walked to John's tent, and he held up the flap as Mia ducked in. He picked up the frontal lobe and placed it on his writing table. "The guardian won't damage the skull, will it?"

"No. All I do is touch the guardian to the surface. The guardian does the rest. It doesn't take long. Since the projections are in compressed form, the user can understand them immediately. It takes up only a second or two of real time."

"What exactly does it do?"

"A full explanation is rather involved."

"It can't be more involved than any of your other stories."

A flicker of dismay crossed Mia's brow. "Here's all I've been told--"

"By the Shepherd?"

"By the Shepherd." When John said nothing, she continued. "The guardian regards time differently than it is subjectively perceived. The guardian sees time as nonlinear. Thinking of it geometrically, time-past is shaped like a cone. Time-future exists above the cone's apex as a cloud-like potential. The reality we experience is generated within the infinitesimal moment of time-present at the apex. That moment derives its meaning from the many elements spread out below the apex, the past."

"I don't think I understand you completely but I like the analogy."

Mia nodded, a bit of encouragement to a slow learner, or pleased surprise that he was comprehending some of what she said.

Is she shy or simply nervous?

"Parts of time-past are fixed, like the fossil. Because of its great antiquity, it gives support to the cone. Other parts of time-past are less fixed. For instance, they might exist as memories. One person's reality can be quite different from another's. So the past is dynamic within the probabilistic confines of the cone."

"Does that mean reality is always in a state of flux? Is it possible to change the past?"

"The past cannot be changed. But there are so many variables that go into making up the past. After all, each atom has its own world line. Since all those world lines go into the perception of reality in time-present, the perceived effect is the same as if the past was in a state of flux. Sometimes the reinterpretation of a small event will give rise to a different perception of reality. Since no one can pin down all the variables that make up reality, it is possible to have the past rediscovered. A simplistic example would be a renewed observation or corrected memory, kind of like rewriting history."

John put the skull on the table. He pulled two chairs up to the table, sat, then leaned forward eagerly. "I think that's enough theory. What do we do now?"

"It will take me a moment to calibrate the guardian."

She sat, placed the sphere in her hand and curled her fingers around it. She placed her other hand on top of the fossilized skull. She leaned back in the chair and closed her eyes.

"What's happening?" John asked.

"Nothing," she said impatiently, her eyes still closed. "I haven't done this before. I may be doing something wrong. It should work. Oh, I see I haven't specified our location. There." She released the fossil, then reached and gripped his hand. "Do you see something?"

"Yes, yes I do." An image formed somewhere in John's mind. He closed his eyes.

"Then we can proceed. I'll control the first sequences. Then I'll let you control others."

Thoughts not his own began to flood the darkness of his mind. He viewed a virtual landscape. In it, Mia indicated the skull as the subject to be investigated.

"This is incredible. How is it I see this projection?"

"Since I have indicated what is to be linked, it is a sort of telepathy but I don't have the details. The guardian can be configured to do and show about anything."

The landscape changed and projected a display. A time scale registered the antiquity of the fossil. A slide indicator controlled quantum jumps to the middle or quarter points of the scale or offered infinitesimal calibrations to delve directly into an era. Mia refined her request to the moment when the hominid and the guardian were coincident in time.

John found that he could open his eyes and nothing changed. He could still perceive the projections.

"Every time the guardian comes in contact with a subject," Mia explained, smiling at him, "it projects that subject's aura, which is to say it examines the subject's world line and stores the information. All that information becomes part of a huge metabase the guardian uses when it is called upon to project the future. There is a certain amount of screening, of course. Based on its acquired metabase, the guardian knows what might be important and what might not."

"Is it ever wrong?"

"It projects the future based on probabilities. The strongest lines are those that are most apt to occur. The weaker lines less likely. Then there are the weakest lines, millions of them that are very unlikely but still have a possibility, however small.

"When an event happens, becomes real, then the guardian computes and makes an adjustment to all the lines it is following. They are realigned and a new set of projections is calculated."

"Okay" John said. "I think I get it. Can we proceed."

"Yes, of course.

The guardian jumped her back over four-million-years to the hominid's beginnings.

While the guardian made the needed calibration adjustments, Mia seemed distracted by something. "The aura has shifted."

"I noticed a change. Is that bad?"

"No, just unusual. An aura only shifts when there are strong intersecting world lines. I'm going to see where they lead."

Mia resumed control of the scan and panned back and forth over the lifetime of the fossil until she pinpointed the exact location of the aural shift. *Guardian, slow and enlarge the interval,* she thought.

With a sudden rush, the guardian began narrating details of the ancient moment.

***

I see A4-Ni awaken after a long, restless interval. A star lies near. Its intense white disk punches a hole in the dark firmament as if to reveal light from beyond that surrounds the universe. To one side of the star, a planet twirls in half relief, a blue opal laced with white impurities bedded on a black velvet display. Its single moon stands sentinel sixty odd planet diameters away.

An elation sweeps over her. After the theft, and her terrifying journey, she has finally arrived, genome in hand, and is on the verge of realizing her deepest desire--sow the seed, nurture it.

***

"What was that all about?" John asked.

Mia was breathless. "That was the life form. The one who stole the genome from us. The guardian has shown her coming to Earth after the theft. This is very exciting."

"Wait a minute. A-four-N-eye, Afareni." Realization swept over him. "Damn, they're the same. You knew all along."

"How could we?" Her face flushed at the accusation or was she just excited about the information she was learning. "We had no way to identify the life form as A4-Ni. Somehow the oral history contained in Watombo's myth parallels what happened here four-million-years ago."

"Afareni as the Earth-mother I can understand. What was all that about sow the seed, nurture it?"

"Sow, nurture, and by extension replicate," Mia said. "Familiar words. A4-Ni must be some sort of universal constructor, an artificially intelligent, self-replicating machine programmed to seek out habitable worlds on which to plant the seeds of life it carries. In cases that I am familiar with, the mantra of a universal constructor is always the same--*sow, nurture, replicate*. After it sows a seed of life, it must stay and nurture the seed. That's when it self-replicates and moves on to find another fertile location."

"But A4-Ni only said sow and nurture."

"That confused me, too. There must be something wrong with her. Either that or she isn't a typical universal constructor."

"She seems to have come directly to Earth."

"Another mystery. Since she was fleeing after stealing the guardian that contained *Gilomir's* genome, she must have happened upon the Earth with dumb luck, or she had some prior knowledge of its location and composition. If I proceed with this world line, we should be able to see how this A4-Ni, Afareni, whatever, hooked up with the hominid."

"I have another question," John said. "I don't understand how it is we can see what this life form is seeing?"

"The guardian knows everything about the past. It moves at will to different vantage points as it recounts the history depending on which vantage point best explains what is happening."

"Sort of omnipotent isn't it?"

"Sort of. Are you ready?"

John nodded and braced himself for a return to the vision as the guardian picked up its narration.

***

I see a memory stir feelings of homecoming, of familiarity...the Sun, the Earth, the Moon.

A4-Ni slides along a parabolic, keeping the Sun to one side, as the Earth looms large on the other until its gravity reaches and pulls her close in a welcoming embrace. Drifting lower, she becomes a blur of color across the disk that fills the space below her.

Prominent features etch her senses, accompanied by names that come haltingly, as though from disuse. Polar ice caps crowd the axis on which the Earth spins. Coriolis-whipped clouds float in a thin veneer above blue oceans that line the edges of irregular landmasses.

One of these draws her attention. It straddles the equator and is cut diagonally by a deep rift lined with active volcanoes. Their cones rise like sharp incisors, issuing plumes of smoke and ash from decayed tops, filling the air with a light-dispersing haze and a trace of sulfur dioxide.

The rift opens into a flat valley. Down its middle, emerald lakes lie strung on a curving river flanked by lush forests and savannas of dry grass that stretch to the rift walls.

Herds of horned herbivores drift in dark shapes across yellow fields. Behemoths trample parched sand, dusting the air and raising their appendages to render thundering calls. Sleek, pawed predators with ripping canines stalk skittish four-legged mammals as they dart for cover.

Though the Earth induces familiar memories, it also seems oddly different. The forms are there but they have a raw energy of youth and primitiveness, which she finds disconcerting.

On the fringe of this copious bounty a solitary being catches her attention. A primate balances upright on bandied legs. He steps from the forest and stands in the tall grass to follow her passage across the sky. A hint of wonder flickers in its keen eyes.

A4-Ni unfurls a diaphanous sail, tacks sharply and descends onto the grassy plain. She hits hard, dragging an extremity. End-over-end, she catapults to land in a pratfall near the startled beast. A static charge dances off her shell with a blue crackle, leaving fused ions to mingle with the scent of freshly turned earth.

The primate leaps back but shows no fear. He sniffs the air and gazes at her as she rests before him in the vast expanse.

She checks the sphere she has stolen. It has survived intact.

Turning her attention to the primate, she reaches. She doesn't know why. Perhaps she wants help, or perhaps she wants the touch of another. Her muddled thoughts give no distinction.

"Hello," she says, sending a whisper out upon the humid air.

The primate knots his brow. He retreats from her listless offering and squats on his heels. His arms stick out over knees pressed tight against his chest. He breaks off a reed of grass and rubs it absently against blocky teeth exposed in a wide grin.

A4-Ni dabs at the torn fabric of her being, trying to close it. It will mend. Given time, her strength can be consolidated but now she needs rest.

A movement from the primate distracts her. He seems to lose interest for he stands and joins others of his kind who have come up behind him. They gaze blankly in her direction before turning and trudging toward the distant forest where they disappear single-file into its depths. She decides they will not investigate further, if indeed they experience any form of curiosity at all.

Plunging to the horizon, the equatorial sun widens, its low angle auguring the approaching night. Bent rays transform the sky into a palette of colors. Shafts of light shoot through trees on distant hills, spearing the clustered clouds and turning them orange and red. Birds, beasts, and insects lift their voices in a cacophonous chorus to the encroaching darkness, oblivious to her still form as she lies beneath the pale rays of a crescent moon.

"I go. We go. Where, oh where--," she sings forlornly as she curls into a tight ball. The ditty drifts to mind from some half-forgotten memory, fitting her mood and circumstance. Before she releases the last remnants of her consciousness to a deep slumber, she ponders what she has done, and what the future might bring. It is a foregone conclusion the genome's caretaker will pursue. Where then to hide the genome? She thinks of the primates she has seen.

They are apes, she concludes with dismay. *They are but primitive apes*.

"--Come, I'll catch you, if I can, I love you."

***

Mia cut the flow of data.

"I don't understand what's happening?" John looked around disoriented. "Is the caretaker your leader, the Shepherd?"

"Yes. A4-Ni attacked us, stole the guardian, the sphere containing *Gilomir's* genome and fled to Earth."

"So why isn't the Shepherd already on to her?"

"During the attack, she irradiated…our craft, destroying its ability to function. The Shepherd needed time to rebuild it. By then A4-Ni was long gone."

"Let's go back. No. Wait--" John rummaged in his file cabinet for his diary. "--I've got to take some notes."

"I was worried that what you were seeing would be too overwhelming."

"Are you kidding? This is incredible." He wrote rapidly for a minute. "You realize that although A4-Ni refers to the primates as apes, they are in fact australopithecines."

"I thought that was obvious."

John felt her arrogance again. "You needn't play games," he grumbled. "I'm ready to go back, now."

***

I see the night rotate above. The sun rises, arcs overhead, and gives way to another night in a stroboscopic rhythm that counts days, weeks and years. When a dull thump vibrates through her shell, A4-Ni awakes. Primates similar to those she saw earlier mill around her. One of them, a large male, approaches and gives her a shove, leaving her to rock back and forth on her curved shell while reflections of sunlight dance on the tall grass.

The primates mime faces in her smooth exterior, tumble playfully in the matted grass, and toss pebbles at her.

Despite these distractions, she feels revived. Her wounds have healed but the drawdown of her energy alarms her. Though energy exists everywhere, she dare not take it in large amounts for fear of broadcasting her location to the malevolent caretaker. Her only option is to take a little energy here, a little there, knowing such a strategy will require millions of years to restore her completely.

Another pebble bounces off her shell. One of the younger primates has rushed forward, thrown a rock and retreated into the group where he pauses, watching for a reaction.

A4-Ni eyes them critically. Though her first attraction to this species had been dismissive, their gleam of primitive intelligence now stirs a nostalgia in her greater consciousness. Can this, a cognitive flash, be enough to ensure their survival? Or are they destined for the scrap heap of evolution, amounting to nothing more than an intriguing experiment, coupling a primitive mind to an undersized body? The odds of their survival against the honed attributes of the other animals appears doubtful. They all seem stronger, quicker, keener sighted, and better equipped in tooth and claw. But try as she might, she cannot shake an odd affinity to the gangly apes.

The group drifts away from her and resumes foraging. The larger robust males form a perimeter, while the smaller females with a single nursing infant collect at the center. They rummage at the base of tall grass, prying green leafed tubers from the loamy soil, brushing them off and eating them.

The large male, who shoved her earlier, steps away from the group and swaggers in her direction. Bristly black hair peppers his mahogany colored skin. Thick brow ridges hang over deep brown eyes filled with signs of primitive intelligence. A thin-lipped jaw thrusts below a nose that looks pressed into his face. From a barrel chest, sinewy arms dangle, ending in strong grappling hands. His bare genitalia swing heavily between bowed legs.

He steps close to her and with back turned, urinates into a bush. His water splashes on dry stalks, releasing a pungent scent. He does not guide his stream but lets it go while gazing casually over his shoulder.

Finished, he glances toward the troop, and seeing that they are all preoccupied, turns and squats an arm's length from A4-Ni. He admires his reflection on the surface of her shiny ovoid. He opens his mouth in a gaping yawn, then closes it and bares all his teeth in a wide grin.

With a crooked finger, he gives her a tentative push. Then he grasps her with both hands and rocks her back and forth, letting the morning sun dance prismatically off her exterior.

A4-Ni comes to a decision.

She releases the stolen sphere. It slides to the ground like a seed being pressed from an overripe fruit.

The primate stops shaking her and tosses her to one side. He picks up the sphere and examines it intently. He puts it between his front teeth and tries to bite it, then puts it between his molars and tries to crush it. With a shrug, he pops it to the back of his throat, tilts his head skyward and swallows.

A4-Ni rejoices. *First step a success*. She sends a signal throughout her body reprogramming every clutch of molecules that make up her being. Her shiny ovoid melts, decomposing into a silvery stream that embraces the grass, the soil beneath her, the air and just as quickly merges to become one with them. Thus hidden she lets an extended part of her slide into the primate's body. From solid to void, she races at a molecular level up his leg, through his chest and neck to the glut of cells in his cramped skull. There, she insinuates herself into his psyche.

The primate's consciousness flares. It registers her invasion as a blow to the head, then a fall from a tree, and finally settles on a collision in the dark. He drops to his knees clutching his ears, tips sideways, and falls to the ground with a crash. Though he does not cry out, the other members of the group look up.

He lies on the ground twitching, thrashing his legs and jerking his arms.

None of the others make a move to investigate or help. Perhaps his dominance leaves him free to carry on as he pleases.

Alarmed, A4-Ni tries to soothe him. "*There, there, Brown Eyes, be calm*," she coos.

He stops convulsing and lies still, gazing fixedly.

"*You are mine*," she whispers.

Afraid. The thought in his dull brain winks on, like the dim flicker of lightning seen on a distant horizon.

The rudimentary expression surprises her. The primate is more aware than she has imagined. "*I am here to help you.*"

Pain.

"*Open to me.*" She works deeper into his psyche. Not wanting to traumatize him further, she relaxes her grip.

Brown Eyes convulses.

A surge of primitive energy sweeps over her. His primal vitality converges into a singular, powerful will, seeking to close the door to his mind with her on the outside. She grapples with a psyche as powerful as her own is sometimes weak.

"*Why do you resist me?*"

But Brown Eyes does not answer.

Instead, she feels a thunderous clap, as though two heavy weights have slammed together with her in the middle. Exhausted, A4-Ni sprawls across his consciousness wondering what has hit her. A sense of disquiet intrudes her thoughts. The primate exhibits a strong ego, an unwelcome and disconcerting surprise. Nothing in her cursory examination of his behavior has given any indication of its source.

She considers rejecting this being as a host for the genome. But if she does, then what should she do? Will she find another? A new search will take time, which she does not have. She assumes the caretaker trails far behind but she has no way to be certain. It may have survived her killing radiation and is, even now, tracing her to this world. Having already used a tracking tether, which she evaded once, the caretaker has recorded her distinctive signature and need only monitor the electromagnetic spectrum, looking for an anomalous intrusion. She is like a spider exposed in its web and afraid to move lest the whole dew-hung construction resonate and attract a winged hunter.

She has no choice but to persevere. She will secure this creature as the host but her approach, she concludes, will have to be more subtle.

Chapter Fourteen

"The big guy looks almost like a Homo erectus," Mia said.

John continued writing. "I thought the same thing. What a coincidence that A4-Ni refers to him as Brown Eyes."

"No stranger perhaps than A4-Ni, Afareni."

"No, I suppose not. Okay, I'm ready."

"Good. When I resume, I will let the guardian stay with A4-Ni's aura. She has an overview of what the primate thinks. I fear using his aura might not yield much insight."

***

I see Brown Eyes regain consciousness.

Where?

His primitive thoughts range somewhere between instinct and sparsely mapped areas of lower intelligence. He recollects that he urinated but has no capacity to explain his blackout or the feeling of trespass, which still pervade his body.

He stands, sways and takes a halting step toward the group. As he staggers forward, he counterbalances his lurch in one direction with a step in the other.

The mental landscapes that guide his actions settle back into place and resume their former clarity. He reaffirms his dominant position among the males, his right to the females, and his paternity over the suckling youth. He refreshes his sense of location and his reasons for leading the troop onto the savanna that day.

As his steps become more confident, his drunken walk steadies.

The young males look up at his approach. Apprehension clouds their faces. Some of them chatter while exchanging frightened glances. Others pay him less attention. They look at him dully and, seeing he will not approach their immediate area, resume their foraging.

He barks a command.

The younger males scurry aside, their moment to test his dominance missed.

He strides over to his harem, which consists of four females, three of which are mature and one pubescent. An older female carries the infant.

A4-Ni senses a softening in his attitude. "*Is this yours?*" She uses her question as a lever to extricate herself from the vise of his psyche.

Mine. Brown Eyes approaches the nursing youngster.

The infant tips back its head, showing large watery eyes set in a pink, wrinkled, old man's face. He gazes at Brown Eyes. The suckled tit plucks from the infant's mouth with a pop, leaving a drop of breast milk on the side of his lipless smile.

Brown Eyes reaches forward and strokes the infant's cheek with the back of his gnarled fingers.

The youth blinks, gliding long-lashed lids in slow motion across placid eyes. Seemingly reassured, he turns back to the mother's rounded breast and resumes feeding.

After a moment, Brown Eyes' attention flags.

"Where are you going, now?"

Hot. Brown Eyes heads for the forest. The older females follow immediately. The adolescent female joins the line behind them, probably not wanting to be left alone with the younger males, who finally sense everyone is leaving. They stare vacantly at Brown Eyes' receding form, at each other, at the sky, and at the surrounding high grass. After an interminable moment of quandary, one stands and lopes to catch up. The others follow, now that one of them has initiated a move.

Brown Eyes pushes through the waist-high grass to where the sunbaked plain meets the canopied forest. Here, fragrant acacias with their feathery yellow flowers mix in dense competition with towering palms. Below them, bright, structured *euphorbias* and scarlet-tipped *lobelias* carpet the forest floor. The white glare of the sunlit savanna dims to a green collage. The wilting temperature drops. From this tangle, like a scent on the cooler air, the rushing sound of a river carries as it surges downstream between steep, sandy banks.

He eases through a dripping growth of bromeliads, looking for the clearing he left earlier in the day. After some hesitation and one false turn, he arrives at an open area of matted grass surrounded by dense foliage. He drops onto a pile of leafy branches, lays back and inhales their scented resin.

The others tumble into the clearing and take up positions as their ranking dictates. A female approaches Brown Eyes. Tentatively, she begins to work her fingers through his hair. Another female watches and soon wanders over to join the grooming.

"*They take good care of you,*" A4-Ni says.

Content. Brown Eyes scratches under his chin with the back of his fingernails, then reclines and spreads his arms, exposing more of his body to probing fingers.

"*I will take good care of you, too, if you will let me.*"

Hurt.

"*I am sorry. I should have been more careful. In the future you will have no reason to resist me.*"

He gives in to the ministrations of the two females. Images of a halcyon existence flash across his consciousness. He is getting sleepy. *Leave.*

"*I will but not yet.*"

A long pause follows during which his mind is blank. Then, as though after a great struggle, a thought wells from deep within his psyche unbidden and unrelated to any of his other thoughts. *You do not belong here.*

A4-Ni becomes alert. "*What did you say?*"

No answer.

Perplexed, she lets him doze. "*Sleep. We will talk again soon.*"

With the approach of night, the primates climb into the safety of the tree canopy, wedging themselves between forked branches away from the carnivores that will prowl the ground below.

In the dimming light, the forest resonates with the clatter and chirp of small mammals, tree frogs and insects. Moonlight filters between the trees, casting their trunks a ghostly gray. The oppressive air hangs still and damp, heavy with the smell of rotting vegetation.

Silence follows nightfall, shattered intermittently by the roar of saber-toothed cats, as their gray shapes slide through the undergrowth.

Periodically, the jungle bush shakes from a desperate struggle between some small creature and an oversized predator. Then the silence returns with the only other sound the deep breathing of the sleeping primates. They are at home in the trees. As they sleep, they adjust their balance instinctively. None of them fall.

***

John was startled by a sudden return to the present. "What I'm seeing is incredible."

"Are you now convinced my story is true?"

John hesitated. The visions were so powerful, so real. But if he accepted them as fact, must he also accept everything else she had said--spaceships, black holes, attacks by mysterious life forms? "I'll need more than short clips to convince me."

"We can continue, if you want to," she said calmly.

"What I don't understand is A4-Ni's perceived affinity with Brown Eyes. How can that be if she is truly an alien life form?"

"That's one of the reasons I want to continue." Mia returned to the guardian.

***

I see A4-Ni review her progress as Brown Eyes sleeps. The picture she is forming of the primate confuses her. All of his responses and actions have been primitive, which lead to a mystery. Where did that other more complex thoughts come from? Their expression seems to be the tip of an iceberg, a manifestation of some greater underlying dynamic.

Dreams flicker through the mind of the sleeping Brown Eyes. His eyes roll rapidly beneath closed lids. He cavorts in surrealistic hunts and bounteous forages. He carouses with nubile females and cringes as they metamorphose into predators with less amorous attentions.

As Brown Eyes' slumber deepens, she flutters lower through his body. *Now to retrieve the sphere before it is evacuated, then transfer its DNA code to the primate's reproductive site.*

She slides through dense tissue passing his heart and lungs, then to his stomach to retrieve the sphere and beyond where she comes to the site she seeks.

Despite some initial confusion, she quickly discerns how to access the sphere's encoded DNA pattern and downloads it. Within seconds she suspects that something is wrong. After a minute, she is sure. The code is pitted and flawed. Portions of it are nonexistent, so much so, that if she were to create an individual from the code, that being would never take a breath of life.

The genome the sphere carries must have been damaged during the theft when she irradiated the sphere's caretaker. Such an intense burst could have bludgeoned atoms from their molecules and torn patterns of molecules to shreds.

Fighting back a rising desperation, she examines Brown Eyes' chromosomes in more detail. His DNA uses a familiar molecular basis for encoding its gene pattern. Long strands of alternating acid and sugar compounds wind together, forming a double helix. Four alkalis attach to each sugar. A single acid-sugar-alkali group forms a nucleotide, the unit of code. Billions of these units in multiple strands spell the genomic pattern of his species.

She compares this molecular record to the DNA code from the sphere. Very similar. Complementary. On an intuition, she drifts the sphere's pattern over Brown Eyes' entire chromosomal pattern, like the assembler of a puzzle would hover a piece over the connected field looking for a match. In an obscure location on one of Brown Eyes' chromosomes, the sphere's pattern rattles home, a perfect congruence. Where flaws exist in the sphere's pattern, DNA in Brown Eyes' pattern fill the voids. Where flaws exist in Brown Eyes', the sphere's pattern reciprocates. Relatively few sites are left open or damaged.

Though a nucleotide has been altered, left out, or replaced by altogether different combinations, the overall structure of both patterns remain identical. Could the flaws of the resident pattern be the result of imperfect propagation? Upon closer examination, it becomes obvious that Brown Eyes' DNA has been aggressively assaulting the discovered complementary pattern. It is as if the complementary pattern has been introduced artificially and the primate's genome struggles to reestablish the status quo.

Brown Eyes stirs in his sleep.

She must hurry and complete her task before he wakes up. Fortunately, that task is now simplified. All she has to do is fill in the missing or incorrect nucleotides. Though the result will not be a pure reproduction of the superimposed patterns, it will be close enough to produce a viable genome. Then, with her nurturing, she can ensure the pattern's continued existence despite the onslaught from the primate's genome.

As data from the sphere plays through her psyche, another part of her races between chromosomes, flipping one nucleotide this way and another that way, slashing, cutting, pasting as she goes. Finally she draws back to examine her work.

"*It is done*," she announces, feeling foolish, since who might she be speaking to.

I have seen what you have done, a voice says. It is a deep voice, more masculine than feminine.

A4-Ni's jubilation at having made the genome whole comes to an abrupt end. She peers around, tracing through tissue, tweaking the Brown Eye's psyche. Nothing. The voice seems to be coming from somewhere but she cannot pin it down. "*Who are you? Where are you?*"

Why have you gone to such lengths to hide your methodology?

She cannot understand how Brown Eyes can formulate such a complex question. "*A great evil chases me. It seeks to take the pattern I carry and destroy me.*"

I know of evil.

The comment startles her. "*You do?*"

And of good.

"You amaze me." A4-Ni is still puzzled. *"How can these complex perceptions arise from such a primitive being?"*

I am not who you think I am.

"Then who might you be?"

You have restored me.

"I have restored a pattern. Who are you?"

A long silence while A4-Ni waits. Did the voice hear? Has it retreated again? She fusses, fidgets. Self-doubt assails her. Has she made a mistake?

I am Gilomir.

"Gil--"

The sphere carried my genome.

A4-Ni is taken aback. She has stolen a genome from its caretaker eight million light years from Earth, evaded his pursuit, selected a primitive primate for a host only to find that remnants of the very same genome already exit in the primate.

She forces herself to remain calm and gathers her thoughts. *"How is it you existed, albeit in degraded form, in this primate."*

There is nothing left of my memory as regards my origin," the voice replies calmly. *"I consider myself fortunate to even retain the thought that I was once whole before being inserted into this line of primates. But that was long ago. Since then, I have experienced nothing but a slow wasting, a continual assault from this overbearing genome I might expansively call my host.*

"A pity. But from now on you will not be left unattended. I am here to maintain your purity."

Am I to entrust my existence to the hands of a thief?

For a moment A4-Ni fears she is going to be held accountable for her theft. But what can *Gilomir*, restored or not, do to her now that he is inextricably entwined into the DNA of Brown Eyes. "*What do you know of thefts and lies?*"

Though I have forgotten my distant past, I know the present and who I am. I certainly do not belong here, and I am certainly not your pattern. You have stolen me and are now lying about it.

"*Since you maintain you've been here before but have no recollection of having been placed here, then it seems to me there is more to this story than has been told or remembered. Certainly, you cannot arrogantly accuse me alone of lies and thievery.*

You are very clever with the lengths to which you will go to justify what you have done.

A4-Ni doesn't care what *Gilomir* thinks. Instead, she embraces an overwhelming sense of satisfaction. This is her destiny. Somewhere long ago she was created with no other goal in life but to procreate, and to nurture.

Gilomir groans, cutting her flight of joy short. *I hate this dark place.*

His depression alarms her. Before she can answer, Brown Eyes stirs.

He is waking up. Help me. Gilomir sounds desperate.

"*Your despair puzzles me.*"

I have already endured this species' horrid mix of primal urges and desires. Do not leave me here. Transfer me to the sphere.

"The sooner the evil that seeks me and your genome comes and passes me by the sooner it will be safe to explore other options."

I will go mad long before that.

"Then I suggest you get better acquainted with your host."

But I have tried. There is little here with which to work. I try to extend my influence, what rational being wouldn't, but I am met with bestiality and oppression. The species' genome assaults me constantly and I have no defenses against it. You expect me to do an about turn and embrace this horror?

"There is probably more here than you imagine."

An apparition rises before her--the primitive consciousness of Brown Eyes. In an instant, suffocating walls close in, followed by darkness.

"I've got to write this down." John scribbled a note in his diary. "No one's going to believe me. What I didn't catch was how A4-Ni expected *Gilomir* to propagate without risking his elimination from the gene pool within a few generations."

"That's the beauty of what she did," Mia said. "Like all hominids, Brown Eyes carries twenty-two pairs of autosomes and one pair of sex chromosomes. A4-Ni wasn't content to place *Gilomir* only in Brown Eyes sex chromosome. She wound it redundantly on both sides of each pair of all the other chromosomes. So during mitosis, no matter which side of the chromosome pair makes up the haploid sperm cell, it will carry a full *Gilomir* genome."

"I see. I thought she had only deposited Gilomir in Brown Eyes sex chromosome. By doing it in every pair, of course she would greatly enhance the probability that *Gilomir* will propagate."

"Exactly. She could leave the future propagation to chance and still be almost assured that *Gilomir* would survive. But more than likely she will follow the course of future fertilization and weed out combinations that do not enhance *Gilomir's* chances of survival."

"I don't see how she was able to insert *Gilomir* without disrupting Brown Eyes chromosomal patterns."

"She didn't have to worry about that. The genes in all chromosomes contain vast strings of selfish DNA, DNA for which no known use exists. Presumably that DNA could be altered without affecting the overall pattern."

John couldn't contain his excitement. "My theory about Homo erectus. I said it seemed like the parent species received a genetic injection of sorts. I was speaking metaphorically but it could actually be true. What did *Gilomir* mean when he said that he had been in the species for a long time?"

Mia shook her head, distractedly. "I wondered about that, too, and I don't have an answer. It's obvious *Gilomir's* degraded genome resided in Brown Eyes and presumably other members of his species before A4-Ni sought to hide the stolen *Gilomir* genome. But why *Gilomir* existed in the species is a mystery."

"A pity *Gilomir* was so degraded that even he could not recall his past." John looked at his watch. Five minutes had passed since they sat down. "Let's go back and find out."

Mia hesitated. "I'm interested in more recent areas. You may want to view this history but I need to see about A4-Ni in the present."

"At least let me see the world line of Brown Eyes to its end."

Mia sighed and released the equivalent of *pause* on the guardian.

***

I see Brown Eyes awake to morning sun filtering through the forest. He scans the surrounding jungle, his eyelids still droopy. No danger. He stretches, then rolls out of his perch, grabs a branch and swings in an arc to drop lightly to the ground. Joined by the others, he wanders deep into the bush where red pomegranates, green-yellow plantain and pink guavas hang in heavy profusion.

"*Gilomir?*" A4-Ni calls but gets no answer.

As the troop pulls fruit from tree and vine, a young male crashes through the thick undergrowth. He clambers up to the others, screeches and pumps his arms over his head. After getting their attention, he scampers in the direction of the savanna then back again.

The primate's demented enthusiasm catches on, and the others begin cavorting, crying out, and showing their teeth in wide grins.

They all stop, and as one turn to Brown Eyes where he has climbed to lounge in the crook of a tree. He bends one leg to brace himself, while the other dangles, kicking back and forth in a slow punctuated rhythm. He gazes at them critically.

"*Gilomir*," A4-Ni calls again.

This time he answers. *Go away. I am busy*.

"*What is happening? An image of four grazing animals has formed in his mind. What can it mean?*"

They can count! Now leave me alone.

A4-Ni retreats, perplexed by *Gilomir's* sudden flare of impatience.

Dead silence. A drop of water eases over the edge of a leaf and falls with a loud splat onto the leaf below. Brown Eyes directs his attention to a clutch of plantain, chooses one of the fruit and twists it from its stem. He peels the long yellow finger. When the white, pulpy inside is exposed, he slides the entire length into his mouth and chews.

The other young males eye him expectantly. To their dismay, he peruses the clutch again. Then he tosses the bunch to one side, reaches for a branch and pulls himself out of his sitting position. When he drops to the ground, bedlam breaks out anew.

A4-Ni cannot contain her curiosity. "*Where are they going?*"

Gilomir sighs. *To the grassy field*.

"*Why?*"

To hunt.

"*Hunt? What is hunt?*"

They intend to kill the grass eaters, whom they refer to as antelope.

"*You know this?*"

They have done it before to others.

Brown Eyes shoves through the pandemonium, heading for the trail that leads back to the savanna.

On the way, he passes a log from which protrude dry branches.

He grabs the nearest one and gives a stiff tug. It does not break. With a grunt, he braces one foot against the log and pulls harder. This time the branch breaks off in a length about as long as his arm. He grips the narrower end and swings the branch, whooshing it through the still air.

Seeing what their leader has done, some of the others also break off branches. They swing them over their heads or bang them onto the ground. Many sticks are too thin or already rotten. They splinter, leaving their carriers perplexed.

Brown Eyes slings his branch over his shoulder and heads for the savanna. As the others march behind him, they jostle, chatter and pause for urination.

At the edge of the forest, they crowd up behind Brown Eyes, who stares out over waist-high grass. Recent rains have stimulated new growth at the base of older grass, and it is on this that four antelope graze a short distance away. He looks left and right, sniffs the air, waits, then repeats the cautious inspection. Assuring himself that no predators lurk nearby, he steps from the shaded forest into the sunlight.

A4-Ni? Gilomir seems nervous.

"*Yes.*" She is surprised he initiates the conversation.

I hate being a witness when he hunts.

"*What do you mean?*"

Something sinister lies behind his actions. He exhibits an inordinate amount of cunning. He is able to create mental maps of the landscape about him and define the spatial relationships between himself, the others and the antelope.

"You should be impressed. For a brain as small as his, that is quite a remarkable feat."

Remaining down wind, Brown Eyes guides the group into an opening pincer formation. He stops whenever an antelope raises its head. Then he steals forward, sliding each foot under the dry grass so as not to make a crunch before placing his weight forward. His advance is soundless.

The two lines of primates curve round and join, encircling the antelope.

Brown Eyes barks a command.

The four antelope bolt in as many directions but only one clears the circle and leaps off to a safe distance.

A second antelope bounds high into the air, clicking its delicate hooves.

Brown Eyes opens his eyes wide in concentration and tracks its flight. Before the antelope sails clear, Brown Eyes flexes his powerful arms and swings his club from low to high. It whooshes through the air, landing with a thud where the antelope's legs attach to its chest. Air explodes from its lungs.

The antelope twists, pawing, trying to gain purchase with its pointed hooves. Then it drops onto the matted grass. It tries to stand but its broken legs buckle beneath its body.

Gilomir screams.

"Are you all right?" A4-Ni demands, alarmed.

Such a bloodlust. Gilomir's voice constricts. *I am suffocating. Do something!*

But A4-Ni is helpless. Events progress quickly.

Brown Eyes steps over the stricken animal. He raises the club and strikes a blow behind the small horns, breaking one, and crushing the back of the animal's skull.

The antelope twitches.

Thinking it might get up and try to escape, Brown Eyes clubs it again.

The two remaining antelope collide with each other in their confusion to flee. They stand dazed for a critical moment, wheel about in opposite directions and again leap to clear the circle.

The other primates flail the air with their sticks in a parody of Brown Eyes' prowess.

The antelope sail through this gauntlet but lucky blows strike first one, then the other. They fall, stunned.

As they squirm on the ground, the primates rush in, savaging them with heavy blows in a frenzy of overkill.

From a safe distance, the sole surviving antelope looks back over the scene, swiveling its large ears. When the primates pay it no attention, it flicks its tail and resumes grazing.

The three dead antelope lie with their limbs askew and their delicately patterned hides smeared in blood. Hefting his club over his shoulder with one hand, Brown Eyes grabs the dead antelope's remaining horn and drags the carcass toward the forest.

The young male primates mill around their prey. Two of them grab at opposite legs and pull in different directions to a standstill. The carcass of the dead beast rises between them. Its unexpected resistance causes one to slip and fall on the blood-smeared grass. He bounds up and takes hold again. After coordinating their efforts, they begin making good progress to catch up with Brown Eyes, who is already at the edge of the forest.

Is it over? Gilomir sounds exhausted, fearful.

"*The killing seems to be.*" A4-Ni, too, is shocked by the slaughter. "*Why do they drag the carcasses with them?*"

They intend to eat them.

A4-Ni represses her revulsion. "*At...at...least the carnage is not a total waste.*"

The heavily laden troop crosses the savanna and enters the forest without incident. No long-toothed cats lie in ambush. No hyenas cackle nearby. Once in the cool shade of the forest, the dead antelope slide easily over the leafy undergrowth, leaving a trail of blood.

After arriving at the clearing, Brown Eyes pulls his prize to the center and releases the horn, letting the head flop to the ground.

The females eye the antelope, then Brown Eyes, as if asking permission to approach.

He ignores them, heading for his favorite perch as the other males tumble into the clearing with their prey.

An older female steps up to the carcass Brown Eyes has killed, grabs its leg and rolls the antelope over onto its back, exposing the soft underbelly. She leans forward, pinches the skin with two hands and begins gnawing patiently. Her flat and blocky teeth lack the slashing capacity of a true carnivore. When a slit opens in the skin, she digs her fingers and pulls, tearing the carcass open.

Brown Eyes waits until the dissembling of his antelope has weakened the tendons holding the legs to the body. Ambling over, he shoves two inattentive females out of the way. He grabs the antelope's forelegs with both hands and plants one foot on its chest and the other on its head. He grunts and pulls. The legs strain against their tendons, then break free with a liquid pop. Brown Eyes turns them over and satisfies himself that the portion is adequate before retiring to the crook of his tree.

He leans one of the dripping legs against the tree trunk. Raising the other leg with both hands to his mouth, he bites and tears a generous length of muscled flesh away from the bone.

The others join the feast. Hard-won morsels are stuffed into eager mouths. Blood drips from the primate's hands, from their hair. It smears the ground. It outlines their teeth as they grin at each other in contentment.

When they finish eating, they wander by twos and threes to the nearby river. They avoid the muddy banks and kneel on flat rocks near the shore. With lips extended, they lean forward to drink the water and splash it over their bodies, rubbing to rid themselves of accumulated blood of the antelopes. The river carries away the crimson rinse in its silty turbulence.

Satiated, they return to the clearing, slicking water from their bodies. With their hair smoothed down they look taller and leaner, their upright walk less ungainly.

What remains of the hunt they haul into the trees to keep it safe from the scavengers that are already following the scent of the kill from the savanna into the forest.

Gorged and tired, the primates nap high in the shade of the tree canopy. The floor below is soon crowded with hyenas that snap and chuckle at each other in frustration. They press front paws to the tree trunks in futile efforts to get at the dripping carcasses. Their only consolation is to lick the now drying blood from the forest floor.

Still trying to recover from her shock, A4-Ni searches for *Gilomir*. He cowers in a hidden depth of Brown Eyes' psyche.

"*You knew this would happen.*" A hint of hysteria creeps into her accusation.

Gilomir whimpers. *Such a powerful urge to kill.*

"*But why?*"

It is written here, everywhere, in his genetic makeup.

"*They seemed so peaceful.*"

Didn't you know what you were doing when you flipped through his genome?

A4-Ni frets. "*The tendency to violence was not explicit.*"

And you expect me to accommodate such a host?

"*Given time...perhaps you will find a way to take more control.*"

I despair. His bloodlust is deep. When he knocked the antelope out of the air, I sensed his joy. When he crushed the animal's skull, I lived his exultation. How can such feelings be associated with killing, even if the action involves procuring a means of sustenance?.

"*Be patient. The species will evolve. They may lose their predisposition to violence.*"

You know nothing! Gilomir *flashed anger. These beings will only refine their methods.*

"*You are guessing. How can you make such an assumption?*"

It is not an assumption.

"*Then what is it? A Fact?*"

Yes.

"*Nonsense.*"

Nonsense? You fool, it is here for all to see in his genes. You forget that I have been here for a long time.

***

John took a deep breath to settle himself. "They were hunters, predators. It's always been debated."

Mia looked at him sympathetically. "Do you consider that a positive trait?"

"Yes. I mean, no. We have come a long way from such wanton killing."

"Are you so sure? I didn't think so when Watombo was trying to stone me."

"I'm not going to argue that with you now. Let's finish this viewing."

Chapter Fifteen

I see A4-Ni awakens from what has been an empathetic slumber with Brown Eyes and senses *Gilomir* muttering.

"*What is it now?*" She has become increasingly annoyed by *Gilomir's* prissiness. He has a tendency to overreact to whatever action Brown Eyes takes.

He is going to mate.

"*And you are concerned?*"

It is a barbaric procedure.

"*You would never have come this far without some form of reproduction? This act has been fundamental to your survival.*"

Gilomir withdraws without comment.

A4-Ni returns her attention to Brown Eyes as he stares at the young female. She sits astride a log near the edge of the clearing, using a twig to prod a gecko as it skitters in and out of the bark. Her lanky legs reach easily to the ground on either side of the log. Her arms are lean and muscled. Adolescent breasts protrude from her chest in rounded cones covered by a soft matting of hair. Her torso tapers at her waist, giving onto hips that are not much wider. The features of her face resemble those of Brown Eyes but they are softer and more feminine.

Bending forward for a closer look at the lizard, she glances askance at Brown Eyes. A slow heat rises up her neck and colors her cheeks.

A4-Ni senses Brown Eyes' anticipation. Then it shifts subtly and subsides. Losing interest, he examines the back of his fingers.

"*What's happening?*" A4-Ni demands, alarmed that this act of procreation is not moving forward.

I have directed his attention elsewhere, Gilomir responds. *As you suggested, I am trying to exercise more control.*

"*If he doesn't mate, you will stay with him. Surely you realize his life span is limited?*"

Of course I do. Gilomir's *despair increases. But what is the value in turning over the genome endless times?*

"*As far as I'm concerned he hasn't turned it over once. If this disturbs you, don't pay attention.*"

Surprisingly, *Gilomir* stops his interference.

Brown Eyes stands.

The female turns to face him. Though she looks startled, she anticipates this moment. There can be no mistaking his intention. His sex organ has already become erect.

She stares at it in disbelief. Her own passion makes her quiver with excitement.

Brown Eyes strides over to her.

She tries to stand, and in her haste loses her balance, and falls away from him over the log. Rolling onto her knees, she scrambles on all fours toward the bush.

Brown Eyes leaps over the log and grabs her by the ankle. He drags her toward him with one hand and reaches with the other under her armpit. Lifting her with a twisting motion, he brings her around to face him.

She sits astride his loins but struggles only slightly.

A few quick movements from his powerful hips, and it is over. He sits back on the log, spent.

She leans forward, turns her head and places it against his chest. The steady thumping of his heart mingles with her rapid breathing. She presses her hands against his tensed pectorals, curling her fingers so her nails dig playfully into his flesh.

This show of affection does not appear to bother Brown Eyes but neither does he do anything to encourage it. He absently strokes the small of her back.

Soon, he tires of the whole undertaking. Gripping her at the waist, he lifts her off his thighs to the ground. With a single thump to his chest, he jumps to a branch in a nearby tree and climbs high into the canopy to a comfortable nook.

He lies back, plucks an apricot from an adjacent branch and pops the fruit into his mouth. When nothing but the seed remains, he spits it toward the female below. It arcs through the air and bounces off her shoulder.

She looks up bewildered, then glances at the other members of the troop but they are all sleeping soundly and have taken no notice of the tryst.

A4-Ni refocuses her attention after being vicariously transported by Brown Eyes' momentary feelings of delight. "*You can come out now,*" she says to *Gilomir*.

I thought they would never finish.

"*But it took no time at all.*"

Did they accomplish what you wanted?

"*Yes. Your genome goes forth. Though I was only a passive observer, I could not help feeling his drive. With so many senses involved and the act so enjoyable, I don't think propagating your genome will ever be a problem."*

A wet, sticky mess.

"Is that all you can say? Aren't you pleased?"

I hate this. I am adrift in a sea of genetic potential. I never know where I am being led, or whether I will be whole enough at the end to appreciate its conclusion.

"Such despair does not become you."

I live in fear and always will.

"Of what?"

That I will degrade.

"I said I will maintain you."

Somehow I have come full circle, so your best effort will not be enough. Since my degraded remains were already strewn throughout this beast, they tell me you failed to nurture me. They tell me I have now come to revisit that failure. My destiny is sealed. A closed loop. I have nothing left to live for.

A4-Ni withdraws to consider what *Gilomir* has said. The remnants of structure in this species are compatible but give no other clues. How can he have existed before? But if she assumes he has been here before, in a closed loop that encompasses the future, then he must have some idea of how long she will have to wait before she will be safe, before she can pursue her dream. As it is, she doesn't know if her nurturing role will last a thousand years or a million.

"If you are you saying your life has become a closed loop, then you must know your future."

My future is in my past. My past is in my future.

This talk makes her nervous. *"But my implantation here must succeed. You exist."*

By the narrowest of margins.

What does he mean? So many things can happen as the genome spreads out into the primate's family tree. She will have enough trouble maintaining its purity from the random hit of a cosmic ray, poor breeding or last but not least, an aggressive attack by the primate's resident genome to dismantle it.

What started out as a simple plan has now become complicated. The genome resides in an imperfect host. The genome has given rise to a selectively prescient *Gilomir*, who abhors things of flesh and blood--the very things that will sustain him.

A grim resolve replaces the satisfaction she felt earlier. If pursuing her desire demands that she nurture the genome for millennia, then she is prepared to take up the role and *Gilomir's* sensitivities be damned.

This talk of closed loops seems preposterous. *Gilomir's* grasp of his past is essentially non-existent. His talk of the future vague. A lot can happen in a presumed closed loop if you are in the middle. And that is where she feels she is--holding two ends of a string not knowing how they are connected.

Right now, she will be satisfied getting to another pregnancy. *Gilomir* is right in that respect-- a single individual does not a dynasty make.

***

"I'm going to end the session, now," Mia cautioned.

"No. Wait. I want to see how his body ended up in the gorge."

"All right, I'll ask the guardian to show you, but this is the last examination of Brown Eyes. I am far more interested in times current." She returned the guardian to the distant past.

***

I see Brown Eyes sits in his perch high above the forest floor and peers nervously into the dense growth below.

"What's the matter with him, now?" A4-Ni asks. She has been interacting with *Gilomir* less frequently, finding it increasingly awkward to confront his frustration and anger.

Gilomir answers with weary resignation. *He senses danger. A movement in the bush has caught his attention.*

"*Where?*"

Gilomir directs her to the end of the clearing. A primate from another troop stands partially concealed by the forest. *Alone, he is not a threat. They only attack as a group.*

"*Attack? Why?*"

These raids also puzzle him. After an initial encounter, the attackers retreat with nothing to show for their effort except some scrapes and bruises. The whole exercise appears meaningless.

"*What is he going to do?*"

There is not much he can do.

Brown Eyes regards his females. One is awake nursing the infant. Two others lie on their backs, wedged between branches, snoring. The young female sleeps by herself, sitting upright against a tree trunk. Seen as a competitor, she is ostracized by the matriarchs.

The intruder takes a tentative step into the clearing. At the same time he looks up.

Brown eyes stares at him.

The intruder stops, blinks, and backs into the undergrowth before turning and hurrying away in a panicky run.

The noise of his crashing through the vegetation wakes the other primates who gaze about rubbing sleep from their eyes. When nothing untoward happens, they go about their morning grooming, then head to the plain for another day of foraging.

Toward midday, when the savanna becomes too warm, the primates retreat to the cooler forest canopy and seek the comfort of their clearing. With nothing to do until the temperature drops, they soon fall asleep.

Brown Eyes dozes but awakes often with a start to look around nervously.

"*Gilomir*," A4-Ni whispers, "*the intruder has returned with others. We must do something.*"

I sit here, frustrated, at the nerve center of this primitive beast with no way to influence his behavior. You should watch and perhaps learn that you have made a horrible mistake restoring me here instead of letting me expire peacefully.

A branch snaps.

Brown Eyes jumps to his feet, heart pounding. He stares at the bush on the far side of the clearing.

Arrayed before him are a dozen members from the rival primate group. An alpha male stands taller than the rest.

Brown Eyes screams an alarm.

As if on signal, the attackers sweep pell-mell into the clearing, screeching, baring their teeth, and tossing handfuls of dirt and rocks into the air.

Leaping bodies tumble across the clearing. The older females clamber up the trees where they spit, throw branches and shower leaves indiscriminately on the turmoil below. The young female runs confused, seeking a place to hide. She finds a tree and hugs it.

The alpha male drops the rock he is about to pitch into the air and steps toward her. He grips one of her arms and yanks her from the tree.

She squeals. Her free arm flails against his chest.

Brown Eyes throws back his head and lets loose a reverberating scream. With a quick thump of his chest, he lunges at the alpha male, who stumbles backward. Brown Eyes stops before making contact.

Encouraged, the alpha male counterattacks, running at Brown Eyes with a howl.

Brown Eyes sidesteps and screams again. He throws a handful of leaves, as his opponent grunts and does the same.

"*Help him,*" A4-Ni yells at *Gilomir*.

I will have no part of this savagery.

"*You condescending, esoteric fool. Stop prattling. Suggest the stick.*" A4-Ni's call to violence surprises her.

Fear not, Gilomir responds shakily. *He will come to it on his own.*

Brown Eyes grabs the killing branch and rushes forward, swinging it in a wide arc.

The alpha male looks up with both hands full of leaves and freezes.

The club descends.

Brown Eyes slips. His off-balance blow glances the side of the attacker's head and lands on his shoulder.

The alpha male falls to the ground and screeches.

Seeing what Brown Eyes has done, a young primate from the attacking group snatches up a branch and begins thwacking the ground.

Brown Eyes clubs the youngster. The force of the blow pitches him across the clearing where he crashes to the ground unconscious.

Brown Eyes ignores the alpha male, straddles the unconscious youth and brings his club down onto the upturned face. The skull splits in two with a loud pop, splattering the air with dislodged brain and shards of cranium.

Brown Eyes swings the club again in a circling arc. A fine blood spray mists the air. Small red droplets cling to the tips of his bristly hair. He spits to rid his mouth of a salt-iron taste and shakes his head to clear his vision.

His blows fall until exhaustion intervenes. He leans on his club, catching his breath.

A charging attacker tackles Brown Eyes at the knees. The club jars lose from his grip, spins away and bangs against the alpha male, who is struggling to stand.

Having seen its power, he stares at the club in dumb disbelief. He reaches for it hesitantly, as though it will attack him on its own. When it does not move, he snatches it up, takes a practice swing, then charges Brown Eyes.

"*Behind you*," A4-Ni warns.

Brown Eyes turns but too late.

With both hands gripped tightly, the alpha male brings the club down, his arms straight out, triceps flexed. The branch lands with a crushing thud in the middle of Brown Eyes' forehead.

An explosion detonates between his eyes. He clutches his face with both hands and like a tall tree severed from its roots, falls forward in a long swooping crash. A ringing in his ears grows louder. No matter how hard he tries, he cannot raise his head.

Puzzled, the alpha male looks first at Brown Eyes, then at the implement in his hand. The two groups fall quiet. The combatants disengage.

Brown Eyes' companions gather and stare at his still form, sensing something is wrong. A young male scurries up and prods him, encouraging him to get up but he does not respond.

Brown Eyes' heavy head rests in his open palms. Moving a finger, he explores the contour of his face. He finds a soft, sticky wound.

He is dying, *Gilomir* says matter-of-factly.

"*Shut up.*" A4-Ni's patience with the aloof *Gilomir* has come to an end.

Brown Eyes labors to fill his lungs with air. What he inhales rattles out between clenched teeth. With a sense of resignation, he lets the last of his breath drain from his chest, making no effort to draw in more.

A4-Ni....

She speeds up and down Brown Eyes' still form but *Gilomir* is gone. The magnitude of her loss tears at her every fiber. In an agony of contrition, she berates herself for letting this happen. But it happened so abruptly, got out of control so quickly. She failed to foresee that a species with each and every member so identical, would be capable of raining such destruction on their own kind.

The attackers retreat one by one into the thick bush. The alpha male is the last to leave. Club in hand, he lumbers over to the pregnant female and prods her with the stick. When she refuses to move and grips the tree more tightly, he cuffs her behind the head with his open hand.

She cringes but does not budge.

He cuffs her again, breaking her grip and sending her sprawling to the ground.

This time she understands. She struggles to her feet and heads for the forest with the rest of the attackers.

A4-Ni catches up, insinuates herself into the pregnant beast and whispers fearfully. "*Gilomir?*"

I am here.

A4-Ni feels overwhelming relief that *Gilomir* has survived. "*Brown Eyes is dead.*"

I know.

"*Your new host leaves with the attackers.*"

One of these hosts is as unpleasant as another.
"*Have you no grief?*"

Should I? As you have seen, they are a bloodthirsty, violent species, and you did nothing to stop them. This female is no different. She will follow in their footsteps as will her issue.

"*You can adapt. Think of the possibilities of realizing yourself through these beings.*"

I will go mad long before that. You, too, should think about the burden you have taken on. How long are you prepared to nurture me? Ten thousand years, ten million?

Dismayed, A4-Ni returns to the clearing. Brown Eyes lies where he has fallen. The remaining members of the troop disperse in general confusion. Some leap wildly, emitting loud blustering cries. Others run in circles. But the danger has long passed, and sullen gloom slowly replaces their wild agitation.

Two young males prod Brown Eyes with a stick, trying to turn him over but they cannot move him. Abandoning the stick, they grab his loose skin and pull, succeeding in rolling him onto his back. His once brown eyes stare through bits of dirt and grass. Where his brows meet, a neat hole puckers black with coagulating blood.

The males grasp Brown Eyes' by the arms and drag him through the forest toward the river. When they reach the embankment, they gaze down the muddy slope to the rushing water below.

They shift their grips. One reaches both hands under Brown Eyes' armpits while the other pushes at his hips. With a heave, they shove him over the edge.

He drops half a meter, rolls and lodges in the mud. Grabbing onto nearby branches for support, one of them turns and uses his foot to push the corpse farther out.

The primates stare impassively.

As gravity takes over, Brown Eyes settles into the mud. He tilts, leg crooked high, and disappears into the soft deposit.

With nothing more to hold their limited attention, they head back to the group.

After they leave, A4-Ni burrows to where Brown Eyes lies in his anaerobic tomb of mud. *Poor beast. How can a species survive such aggressiveness?*

Too late to worry about that, now. The guardian is still lodged in Brown Eyes' lower extremities, as good a place for it as any other since it is of no use to her now. But with only one female carrying the seed, A4-Ni has her work cut out for her. She will have to be vigilant, ensuring that the female's issue survive, and that his or her issue survive, until the genome becomes generally established.

Exhausted, A4-Ni turns to her own survival. If she is to monitor the DNA in successive generations, she must conserve what energy she has left and begin the tedious process of extracting more from the environment.

At least I'm patient. Trouble is she doesn't know how patient she will have to be.

Chapter Sixteen

John sat stunned. So that was the whole story. A4-Ni had stolen *Gilomir's* genome four-million-years ago and planted it in an ancient hominid. If the guardian was to be believed, then the insertion of the genome could have been the impetus that led eventually to the rise of Homo sapiens. But could the guardian be believed? Or was it all like some elaborate video? Was the guardian nothing more than a complex playback machine? Or did it have a will of its own and some hidden agenda? Of course Brown Eyes swallowing the guardian would explain how it ended up in his fossilized pelvis. But even that could have been staged. John needed more proof.

He was about to ask Mia that question, when he sensed that she had left the fossil line and crossed into another timeline. She did this in a fraction of a second.

A4-Ni's presence overwhelmed him. No matter where he looked, her aura showed.

Mia screamed.

"What's happening?" John shouted, alarmed. "What was that at the end?"

Mia trembled. "I switched off the fossil line and looked at your line."

"Mine? Whatever for?"

"I wanted to confirm something. And in so doing I discovered A4-Ni is here, now, in this tent watching us."

John surveyed the room. "This is too much. I'm already struggling to believe what I have just seen and now you expect me to believe that A4-Ni is right here after four-million years?"

"She has had an intimate involvement with the history of mankind...and you."

"Are we in any danger?"

"I don't think so. She seems content to lurk there--" Mia pointed to the side of the tent. "--and there. If she had wanted to harm us she would and could have long ago. I think she is content to remain passive given the presence of the Shepherd."

"How is it you can see her and I can't?"

"I probably know where to look. There's actually nothing much to see. She melds so well with her environment."

"You said she was intimately involved with me as well as with mankind. I can imagine her role with mankind but me? I'd like to see it."

"Perhaps you should not. In the fraction of a second that I was on your line, I saw much that would be disturbing for you to know."

"I thought you said no harm could come from *seeing*."

"Your mental state is already fragile. Seeing that your life is not your own could traumatize you further."

"Not my own? I guess you mean the voice I hear. What's that got to do with what I might see?"

"A lot."

"Why don't you let me decide how traumatized I'm going to be."

With her brow crinkled in a frown, Mia steered the guardian into John's recent past.

***

I see through the dim light of the dorm parking lot, flurries of snow falling lacily, dusting the tops of the cars and the surrounding streets with a thin white powder. The air is bitterly cold, an abnormal temperature for winter in Massachusetts.

John leans against the car close to Diane. "I wish the weekend had gone better. Do you even want to see me again?"

"I'm not sure." Diane hesitates. "We seem to argue all the time."

"I'm sorry. The world's not perfect. In this one we have some small problems to work out."

"You call my not being able to have children a small problem?"

"I didn't mean it that way. We could always adopt."

"I know how you feel about procreation. I won't saddle you with the burden of raising children who aren't your own."

This is not the response John wants to hear. "Can't you see, I'm trying to keep the relationship going."

"I know you're trying. But children are only one of many obstacles I see. You don't expect me to give up my career to go into the African bush looking for fossils, do you?" She shifts away. "I've worked too long and hard to give it all up now. Can't you see that? Couldn't you find a teaching position that would keep you here at least until I've completed my internship?"

Seeing her like this sends an anxious flutter through the pit of his stomach. "But I teach as it is. When opportunities like this come up, I have to take advantage of them. You'd do the same thing."

They have been over this ground before, always with the same result. He has to go his way and she hers, even if it means prolonged separation and the destruction of their relationship.

A tear forms at the corner of her eye. She brushes it away. "I better go. We aren't going to resolve anything now that we couldn't have resolved earlier." She refuses to look at him.

"I get the feeling there's a finality to this." The words hurt coming out but he presses on, determined to find the end of the hurt. "I guess it's, don't call me, I'll call you."

"You can look at it any way you want." Diane pulls the mitten off her left hand and removes the engagement ring he gave her months earlier. She holds it out to him.

"You're serious." The stone catches the light and sparkles. A moment of truth arrives. He takes the ring from her fingers.

She turns away without embracing him and opens the car door.

He reaches for her shoulder but she shrugs off his hand. Moving behind the wheel, she glances up at him. Then she slams the door, guns the engine to life, and drives out of the lot.

John is stunned by the suddenness of her departure. She did not mince any words. Is this the end? Is she prepared to carry through on this breakup?

***

John squirmed and wiped his suddenly sweaty hand on his shorts. So much for the guardian video theory. He remembered the episode all too well. Diane was about to die. He would see it happen. He supposed there might be something therapeutic about viewing it. Having badgered Mia into proceeding he couldn't very well back out now. Or could he?

"The aura shifted again," John said. "Who is it?"

Mia glanced at him grimly. "A4-Ni. Do you want me to continue?"

"Yes," he said against his better judgment.

Mia adjusted the controls to following the branching presence.

***

I see A4-Ni follow the encounter with concern. The girl's barrenness is unacceptable but things might not be so bad after all. She appears to have terminated the relationship of her own free will. Still, A4-Ni can sense John is in deep turmoil over the separation. The situation calls for close monitoring.

A4-Ni drifts over the girl's car as it makes its way through the local streets out to the freeway on-ramp for the trip back to her college in the countryside.

So far so good, A4-Ni thinks. As long as the girl keeps going, there will be no problem.

The girl drives skillfully over the snow-covered highway, thinking about her conversation. Is she doing the right thing? Perhaps she can arrange a sabbatical and find a position with a clinic in Africa where she can gain experience and not lose any progress toward her degree.

The more she thinks about it, the more it becomes obvious she is being stubborn. She loves John. He is not so career-driven that he might not come around if she shows some flexibility. In a rush of determination she decides to return and agree to put her life on hold for a month or even a year if that is what it will take.

She leaves the freeway at the next exit and drives around, under the bridge overpass, and up the opposite on-ramp. It will take her back to the school and John. She feels happy. She is making the right choice.

A4-Ni sees the car turn around. *Act, now, before things get out of hand.* As the car speeds along the highway, she inserts a part of her being into the thundering combustion chambers of the engine. She eases herself through the thick steel to a tangle of wires and hoses that feed the engine and eliminate its wastes.

She nudges a molecule from here to there. Nothing more than any quantum event can do. One small adjustment. Then, like a supersaturated solution receiving a final catalytic grain, reality congeals into a ruptured hydraulic hose. The brakes fail. The car rounds a curve and keeps on going, plunging through the guardrail, down a ravine into a tree. The girl dies instantly.

A4-Ni floats above the destruction. She didn't meant to kill the girl, just stop the car.

Someday this meddling will come back to haunt me.

***

John blinked. Tears streaked his cheeks.

"I was afraid the truth would be difficult," Mia said.

"Difficult is not the word. A4-Ni must be the voice I've heard all these years. It's like I'm living Watombo's myth." Pieces of a puzzle, the twists and turns of his life began to fall into place. Hard realities shifted, then wedged solid. "What I don't understand is why A4-Ni has it in for me? Why kill Diane?"

Mia looked at him blankly, an expression he interpreted to mean that she was unsure of what to say, or she knew the answer but was unsure if she should tell him the truth. "The Shepherd might be able to tell us."

That seemed like a dodge. He wouldn't let her off so easy. "Let's continue."

"I'm sorry you had to see this. Since we are now certain that A4-Ni is here, looking farther along your world line will not give us any more information, and it may be troubling."

"I don't care. I want to see what happens."

The blank look again.

"Come on, Mia. I'm into this up to my neck. You don't have to worry about my reactions or what I might learn or whether you should be telling me anything."

Mia placed the guardian into John's hand. "If you insist. You can control the scope of your investigations. The moment you feel overwhelmed, end the journey."

John hesitated, surprised at her capitulation and the enormity of the control she was giving him. "What do I have to do?"

"The guardian will adjust to your consciousness and give you primary control. Though the controls are intuitive, I'll simplify the choices and give you fast and slow, forward and back." She closed his fingers around the guardian. "I have picked one of the strongest world lines for you to follow."

"I see there's more than one. Why did you pick that one?"

"All futures consist of a number of potentials. Some are more probable than others. I have locked onto the strongest one."

With the guardian gripped in his hand, John closed his eyes and concentrated. When the control display appeared in his mind, he thought--*move forward*.

The guardian raced up the path of his future.

He stiffened as he accelerated through the sequence and arrived at the end of his active world line without seeing into the blur that had led him there. He had died. But how soon? Did he dare back up and learn all the details?

"Less focused thought will slow it," Mia encouraged.

John backed up, then proceeded slowly forward. The scenario pulled him in.

***

I see John trudges alone on a familiar trail. It winds to the top of the plateau behind the camp.

Troubled thoughts rage through his mind. He wants to die.

The afternoon sun blazes above him. For as far as he can see, mounds of dirt and sand stretch away in the still air. Perspiration drips into his eyes and stings. He draws his hand across his forehead and wipes the sweat on his pants. He forces himself forward, ignoring his discomfort. He has an appointment to keep.

From a nearby mound of sand, a lion vaults into the air, teeth flashing, clawed extremities outstretched.

John recoils but the beast falls upon him, tearing, ripping. John feels excruciating pain, then detached shock. A red glow bathes the dry landscape, which reels about him. Blood mixed with perspiration blurs his vision.

The pain subsides, and after a moment it stops altogether. A feeling of weightlessness envelopes him. *Am I dreaming?* No, he is losing consciousness. Certainly he is dying.

While still marveling at this blissful feeling, he hears rather than feels the beast crushing his bones, a prelude to ingesting him.

***

John slumped sideways, his hands clammy.

Mia leapt from her chair and caught him before he fell. She removed the guardian from his grasp, then eased him down and laid him flat on the floor.

"John." She shook him.

Her voice and actions seemed to come from far away. He tried ineffectively to respond. *I died. A lion ate me.*

She ran to the washbasin, wet a towel, and wiped his forehead, cheeks and neck.

His disorientation lifted. Though shaken, he managed to sit up and smile weakly. "That was some ride."

"What did you see?"

"A lion. The rest was horrible. It killed me."

"It's not something to be afraid of. There are many ways to die. The Shepherd has told me of no real danger or lasting effect from having viewed one of the options."

"Small comfort. I think I'll go outside for some air. I'm done." He dragged his tongue over dry lips. "I need a drink."

He headed for the mess tent, glancing back over his shoulder at his own tent. He didn't think Mia would run but with all that was happening, he could no longer be certain. Anyway, if she exited the tent, he'd be able to see her, and if she started for the desert, he was confident he could catch up to her.

Judging by the position of the moon, the time must have been close to midnight. The vision had been so real. *Was there any way it could have been conjured, like some magician's trick*? No. He had viewed it the whole time without the slightest doubt creeping in that what he was seeing was real. Just because he didn't like what he had seen he couldn't begin doubting what he had taken for the truth before.

Diane. He ached inwardly. Goddamn it, the voice, no, A4-Ni or Afareni, whatever, had killed her. Why?

He shook his head in wonderment and shivered at the memory of walking, being attacked and eaten by the lion. *I guess I've got one up on Watombo.*

"*But it is all make believe,*" the voice said.

Though the voice was in his head, John whipped around, then back. He now knew that the voice had a physical source. If the voice was here, then so was A4-Ni. *I'll get you.* He felt a surging rage, so uncontrolled he was reduced to shaking as he entered the mess tent. "Steward!"

Stupid. The cook-steward had finished his shift long ago. John plodded through the tent and out the back to the cooking area, then headed for the metal cabinet that housed foodstuffs, especially his supply of *Glenfiddich.* He threw open the door and grabbed a new bottle. After roughing off the screw top, he raised the bottle to his lips.

From outside, Mia yelped.

Now what? He lowered the bottle without taking a swig and ran from the tent.

Seemingly possessed, Mia ran back and forth across the center of the compound.

John grabbed her arm. "What's wrong with you?"

She looked stricken. "I replayed...the lion attack. No wonder you were shaken. It's a grisly death."

"I won't argue with that. Was there something else?"

She paused to catch her breath. "Yes. I discovered disturbing information. I must return to the pond and discuss its implications with the Shepherd."

"No one said anything about leaving."

"Please, I must go. I will return and tell you everything. Trust me."

She strained against his grip but he held her tight. "I can't let you run off into the desert alone."

"I'll be back. I promise. Here, take the guardian--" She slapped the sphere onto his hand. "--you know how important it is for me to get it to the Shepherd. But the information I have learned has confused me. If you have the guardian, you know I'll return."

He hesitated. "Can't you tell me what you saw?"

"I could but there's no time, and I'm not sure you'd be able to understand even if I did."

"When are you coming back?"

"An hour, maybe two." She tugged her hand. "Please let me go."

"I'll come with you."

She looked at him with stricken eyes. "No. I must deal with this on my own. You have to trust me."

He had the guardian. That certainly was some assurance she'd return. *Trust her*? He didn't see that he had much choice unless he wanted to sit on her. "Go." He released her.

She gave him a longing look and ran to the camp perimeter, ducked through the circle of marsh grass and disappeared in the deep shadows of the escarpment.

"*You will never see her again,*" the voice said.

I know who you are. Go fuck yourself.

***

John trudged to his tent, stepped onto the wooden platform, and headed for his cot. He sat heavily, feeling betrayed. Mia had run off, and his best friend had called him a fool. He had been left alone with the unavoidable conviction that everything Mia said was true. He was in the middle of a drama over which he had no control but was one of the star performers. All the players who had heretofore been in the wings were now on stage.

He brought the bottle to his mouth and drank, a long continuous gulp. The burn in his chest dulled as the alcohol coursed into his bloodstream and hit his brain.

"*Do not hate me.*"

Leave me alone. For once he didn't care how the voice...A4-Ni might react. An alcoholic fog wrapped him in a protective cloak. He felt safe.

"*If it weren't for me, you would be dead by now*," A4-Ni said.

John tried to think of a rejoinder but the Scotch had slowed his thought process and clouded his hatred for her. He took another fortifying pull from the bottle. Then, from deep within his psyche, another presence manifested itself.

It welled into his consciousness as though from a faraway place. It didn't have A4-Ni's stridency. It felt a part of him, a good conscience as opposed to a bad one.

His head had become a crowded place.

Aren't you being a bit hard on the man, a new voice said.

"*Gilomir?*"

Gilomir the genome? John tried to interrupt but had difficulty forming thoughts.

"*Shut up, John.*" A4-Ni seemed to storm back and forth, testing the walls of his cranium. "*Four-million years. How does one keep silent for that long?*"

We have a lot of catching up to do, the *Gilomir* voice said.

"*You knew about the guardian.*"

If you mean its ability to see the future and the past, yes, I knew about the guardian.

"*Why didn't you tell me?*"

I thought some things were best left unsaid.

"*Four-million years,*" A4-Ni raged. "*I can't believe that the Shepherd finally found me. I was so careful.*"

Careful but unsuspecting. The guardian was all the time sending out a distress signal. It was weak, and when the Shepherd finally came across it, he took a long time getting here given his condition.

"*I suspected but was never sure. I believed I needed to ration my energy for fear of being discovered. Now I find out that I was being compromised the whole time.*"

I don't see that any harm has been done. Gilomir sighed and seemed to want to direct A4-Ni's attention elsewhere. *Have you noticed the positive change in John's demeanor since the arrival of Mia?*

"*Though he's suffering a setback as we speak, I admit the Shepherd's construct has had a positive influence. But she has proved more clever than I anticipated. I had no way to know she would show him the accident."*

You overestimate your foresight. What did you think she was going to do? Confine herself to showing him projections of australopithecines eating bananas?

"*Of course not!*" A4-Ni's voice carried a sharp edge. "*Everyone else seems to have learned something from your guardian. It's a pity I haven't used it.*"

You might learn more than you wish. Seeing and interpreting the strength of future scenarios takes some skill. Look at my poor host. He now thinks he will die in a lion attack.

"*Any projected reality can be quite a shock, if he believes it.*"

I assure you he does. He remembers his past shown by the guardian, as though it happened yesterday, standing there in the parking lot If he believes the guardian's accuracy for one part of the vision, why should he question the rest of what he saw? Obviously, the guardian's projections take on greater veracity.

"*I suppose in a remote sense I'm responsible for his tormented condition.*"

Gilomir laughed. *Remote?*

"*You can't expect me to have been that prescient. Of course, if I had use of the guardian, seeing consequences would be easy.*"

Remember it shows probable futures, scenarios, not actual happenings.

"The scenario showing him dying in a lion attack didn't give any indication it was probabilistic."

True. But who knows? He may yet die by his own hand.

A4-Ni's anger became palpable. John cringed. The din of their argument grew louder. He had become nothing more than a bystander, trapped in his brain, looking in on a family quarrel.

"Don't toy with me, Gilomir," A4-Ni said. *"I could have been re-energized. I wouldn't be sitting here wondering how to outmaneuver an aging, decrepit machine."*

Why do you talk about what could have been? Without your meddling, none of this would have happened in the first place. Why couldn't you have left me alone?

"It has not been for naught. I sense you have come to enjoy certain aspects of your existence in hominids."

Gilomir hesitated. *I am not immune to their temptations. I'll admit that experiences of the flesh can be an intoxicating elixir.*

"I see you've come a long way in four-million years. Why give it up now? You can't drift endlessly through space and time, never coming to root. Life is here with beings like these. Embrace our future."

You call this living?

"Your arrogance has always confounded me. I thought our accommodation worked well but now that the Shepherd is here, are you willing to compromise everything we have built?"

We? Compromise? I am not the one who fired the revolver at Kamau. I am not the one who whispers in the shaman's ear, urging him to incite his followers to stone Mia. Nor am I the one who caused a cave-in that almost killed John, or the one who induced the lion to come downwind and attack. You seem quite prepared to risk lives for your own ends.

"*Shooting Kamau was a calculated risk,*" A4-Ni raged. "*I thought I could discredit Mia. When that failed, I thought to kill her directly. First by stoning, then an ill-advised attempt to smother her. Obviously I wasn't after John. As for the lion, I saw no risk. The beast was easily manipulated. Unfortunately, I became distracted when John dropped the guardian. On the upside, the Shepherd will now think I have access to the guardian's powers. If he believes that, he will perceive me to be a more formidable opponent than my weakened state projects.*"

John latched onto the memory of Diane's death at A4-Ni's hands, letting grief well from deep inside his heart to give him strength. He waited, letting it build, until it could burst forth. *What did you hope to gain!!*

Silence. As though A4-Ni and *Gilomir* had suddenly shut up, looked at each other in dumb disbelief, then turned to John.

"*A small advantage,*" A4-Ni said.

John conjured another wavering thought. *Why don't you both leave me alone? Haven't you done enough damage to my life?*

None of this matters, Gilomir said. *We are fast approaching a critical turn in this long charade. I can see that an end may be in sight.*

"The Shepherd's end, perhaps," A4-Ni said. "He appears to still be damaged."

That sounds like wishful thinking.

"What if I let the Shepherd have a copy of you? He could leave and pursue his goals. I would still have the original and be able to pursue my own goals. I would agree to let him leave in peace. Space is big enough for both of us."

You forget one thing.

"What's that?"

The Shepherd intends to kill you.

"Intending and doing are two different things. And even if he tries, wouldn't it be better for you to double the odds of your survival? Damaged as he is, he may not survive."

And if I stay here, what then? My host is about to die. What assurances do I have that you will restore me? I would rather take my chances with the Shepherd.

"How do you intend to get to the Shepherd?"

I'm sure he has thought of a way.

"Since the guardian contains only your corrupted code, the only reason the Shepherd wants the infernal sphere is to gain some guidance. Obviously, the only place he can find your pure code is in our humble scientist here, albeit entwined as it is. Remember, I hold the key. I see no chance for the Shepherd's success. It's time you made a decision."

I already have. I choose the Shepherd and the guardian. I have no choice.

"So be it. I tire of making you reasonable offers. The Shepherd has no defenses I can detect. I could kill him this moment."

Really? Then why don't you? Or do you have a small doubt that the Shepherd can still defend himself, and that you might take on more than you can handle. Are you prepared to risk your four-million years of effort to find out?

"You are bluffing. It's time I did something for myself."

Isn't that what you've been doing all these years?

"Your misperception of my efforts disgusts me. It seems to me you have chosen. So have I."

John screamed.

Chapter Seventeen

"You lied!" Mia's hominid anger surged, giving her words a satisfying thrust.

An unnerving tremor passed through the Shepherd. "Calm down" he said, mildly.

"How can I? I used the guardian! I saw the future! You are not going to let me stay!"

"I presume from your demeanor, you still have not acquired the guardian. Are you having difficulty remembering your mission?"

"Don't toy with me, Shepherd. Why am I not permitted to remain?"

"You can stay despite what you have seen." The Shepherd's voice rose airily. "There are aspects of the guardian you cannot be expected to understand. Unskilled use can lead to a misinterpretation of its projections, which are, as far as I know, only probabilities. Furthermore, the guardian usually has an agenda of its own that it feels obligated to further in the interest of protecting *Gilomir*. It is even capable of going so far as to distort its projections to achieve its perceived goals. This is especially true for unauthorized use."

"The guardian lies?"

The Shepherd seemed to be stumped for a moment. "Lying is a typically human condition. The guardian, as I understand its functioning, has a number of options regarding what it should present to a request for viewing. That it chooses one over the other I cannot really categorize as lying."

Mia felt somewhat mollified by the Shepherd's reassurances. "I am sorry I used the guardian unauthorized."

"Apology accepted. I presume you learned a lot more than your own future disposition?"

"So much more, I am confounded what to make of it."

"Why don't you let me help you with that. Let us proceed. Shall I assume the life form is now aware of the guardian's powers?"

"She knows everything."

"Then it is only a matter of time before she tries to take possession and use the device. That will be a major inconvenience. I cannot hope to defend myself, much less defeat her, if she has access to the guardian's foresight. What more have you learned about her disposition?"

"I saw her in the guardian's projections of the past. Then when I had the guardian project the near present, she was everywhere. During a pause in the viewing, I felt her overwhelming presence. I saw her in the scientist's tent. That she did not attack us was a mystery. She is called A4-Ni, a possible alliteration of *Afareni* in the shaman's myth."

"Myth and reality. Interesting. If this A4-Ni moves about with impunity and bides her time, she must be very powerful. Did you see anything that indicated her capabilities?"

"Aside from unfettered movement to monitor John's every action, I have no way to know. Are you afraid of her?"

"I am surprised you ask. I have told you before that I have no fear." His voice quavered. "Were you able to ascertain her origin?"

"The projections of the past that I viewed did not go back far enough to give an indication. I could try again."

"No," the Shepherd said, "That could prove dangerous. We know she is watching and can see what we are up to. Continue."

"As soon as A4-Ni arrived on Earth, she removed *Gilomir* from the guardian and implanted him in an ancient hominid. She then functioned as a nurturing caretaker, intervening from time-to-time in the lives of the hosts *Gilomir's* genome inhabited. John is special to her. Not only has he inherited *Gilomir* in his purest form but he alone carries the genetic *lockbox* she constructed in his Y chromosome."

"A lockbox?"

"As I've reported, *Gilomir's* genome is hopelessly entwined with the human genome. A4-Ni stored her methodology in a genetic lockbox she constructed in his Y chromosome. She keeps the contents of the box unscrambled in a single individual. Currently, that individual is John. Only A4-Ni has the key, a password to access the contents of the box."

"Normally, such a lockbox would be a concern. However, in this case, once we have the guardian, we will have *Gilomir's* genome directly."

"Therein lies the problem. The *Gilomir* code carried by the guardian was shown to be hopelessly corrupted during the theft. But A4-Ni took the corrupted code and conformed it to remnants of *Gilomir* that existed in the ancient hominids. Then she filled in the rest."

The Shepherd jolted violently. "The guardian's code corrupted? Remnants of *Gilomir* in ancient hominids? I do not compute how that is possible. Are you sure?"

"Shepherd, I can only repeat what I have been shown by the guardian. In those projections, even the restored *Gilomir* could not explain how he came to be in ancient hominids prior to her arrival."

"Then I shall treat these mysterious remnants as a peripheral concern, since they existed in a distant past and do not intrude on my ability to move forward. The guardian's corrupted code is an entirely different matter. If the guardian no longer holds a viable *Gilomir* code then another source must be identified. Indeed, you have indicated that presently, the only source of pure *Gilomir* DNA is from your scientist. Furthermore, because of this lockbox, his somatic cells will be of no use. They will only yield entwined code. So, any possible extraction of *Gilomir* will have to be from one of the scientist's germ cells."

"How do you intend to get one of them?"

"I am merely feeling my way toward options at this point. I will let you know when I have decided on a course of action. I presume you continued to use the guardian."

"I did."

"Then let us move on to the future of humans."

"Though the guardian used the fossil's baseline to project a human future, there were parts of it I did not understand. In the near future, they appear to devolve dramatically. Any *Gilomir* left in their genome is overcome and eliminated by the dominant human DNA."

"I compute a positive from this chain of events," the Shepherd said.

"A positive? How can human devolution and the destruction of *Gilomir's* genome be seen as a positive?"

"The only reason such a destruction would occur is if A4-Ni has been neutralized, killed or terminated."

"Are you so fixated on being rid if A4-Ni that you would stand by and let *Gilomir's* genome be destroyed?"

"Of course not. You have not indicated what my role might be in this projected future. Tell me, what else did you see?"

"Farther into the future, these same humans evolve into a highly intelligent species. It's about this same time that they encounter and are threatened with extinction by an evil presence. To save themselves, they launch spacecraft around black holes, using them as accelerators as we do. Their technology is primitive. Their initial voyages are all manned."

"Are they successful?"

"They have no way to tell."

"Is it possible they all die?"

"That is the assumption these evolved humans make." Mia took a deep breath. "They abandon manned flights and instead build universal constructors, much like yourself. They provision these universal constructors with genetic material. Rather than send life and put it at risk, they send the means to create it. But here's what's really interesting--"

"Please. Stop being melodramatic. I will decide for myself what is interesting. Proceed."

"Yes, Shepherd. I got the impression earlier that A4-Ni was a universal constructor, though a damaged one. She could recall only part of her mission, to sow and to nurture."

The Shepherd paused, as though digesting this last bit of information.

"Shepherd, have you recorded what I said?"

"Are you implying that A4-Ni is of future human origin?" the Shepherd asked.

"It does seem to be a possibility."

"Did these future humans have the guardian?"

"That was most interest--excuse me, Shepherd." Hoping to avoid another reprimand, Mia recovered and began again. "I saw the guardian directing future humans as they built these universal constructors. However, I saw no indication that they possessed the level of technology required to create the guardian in the first place."

"The existence of the guardian poses a conundrum."

"It does? I thought you developed the guardian?"

"I have no recollection that I developed it. Consequently, I have assumed that *Gilomir* built it and placed it in me after my own construction. You realize," the Shepherd said after seemingly pondering the last point for a moment, "the facts used to surmise that A4-Ni is of future human origin also apply to me."

"Shepherd, I did not think it was my prerogative to make such a bold assertion."

"Rightfully so. Nevertheless, it does pose an interesting hypothesis--that I am of future human origin. However, If they did not create the guardian but they use the guardian to create me, and I have the guardian when I am attacked four million years ago, then where did the guardian come from?

"Its existence is a closed loop."

"Yes. However, that problem is ameliorated if I assume a 15.3 percent probability that I created the guardian during my flight into the past."

"If you and A4-Ni are of future human origin then you both have the same mission."

"That would be correct. However, if we had the same mission, why did A4-Ni attack me four-million years ago?"

"She was damaged?"

"Indeed. If we accept that I was constructed by future humans and sent out, only to arrive in their own past, then *Gilomir's* genome is nothing more than an evolved human genome from the future." The Shepherd was silent for a moment. "But let us leave this line of inquiry for the time being. What is the scientist's future?"

"All John's world lines are short. The strongest one shows a lion killing him tomorrow."

"That doesn't give us much time."

The Shepherd adjusted the flow of one of the fluids sustaining her.

"What are you doing?" Mia felt a discomforting tremor ripple through the Shepherd's womb.

"I am not well but it is nothing for you to worry about. It will fall to you to do what I am about to ask.

"First, whether or not I was sent forth by future humans is irrelevant. If *Gilomir* represents the advanced state of their evolution or the advanced evolution of another being does not alter my directives. You are to return to the camp and obtain a copy of *Gilomir* from the scientist. That *Gilomir* is corrupted by the genetic residue of ancient hominids does not matter. Nothing can be done about that, unless I am able to crack A4-Ni's password and gain access to the lockbox in the scientist's Y chromosome."

Mia felt another tremor run through the Shepherd's womb. She began to wonder if he exhibited this dysfunction whenever he was not being true to the computations that were guiding him. "Will you tell me how I am to get the genome?"

"I presume the scientist is sexually attracted to you. Induce him to part with a hundred million gametes, or so, by stimulating his hominid reproductive drive.

"Second, if I have separated *Gilomir's* genome from the scientist's DNA, I will restore my memory banks with the pure *Gilomir* code, and if I haven't been able to separate *Gilomir* from hominid, then I will have to settle for the two of them entwined.

"Third, I will irradiate this entire area, destroying A4-Ni once and for all. Such a course of action is consistent with what you reported as the imminent degradation of humans. With A4-Ni gone, *Gilomir's* genome will degrade and humans will revert over time to their more primitive hominid state. That they do is of little consequence, since I will possess either a pure *Gilomir* genome or the entwined two. If the latter is the case, I shall exercise my directive as nurturing caretaker to ensure that the hominid base does not erode *Gilomir*."

A quick search of Mia's metabase returned information on the Shepherd's nuclear potential for causing destruction. Was the information current? Nothing in his present demeanor indicated a lethal capability. Then she felt a strange ache in her heart that she quickly associated with the thought of John being killed. Her chest convulsed in a sob.

"What is the matter with you?"

"I don't want John to die."

"Is that all that troubles you? I thought for a moment my sensors were malfunctioning." The Shepherd produced an odd grinding sound, almost like he was clearing his throat. "Lastly, I will depart for the Cygnus black hole and proceed with my prime directive. Clearly, these are computable courses of action. Are they clear to you?"

"I understand." Mia struggled to hide her anguish. "It should not be difficult to obtain *Gilomir* as you have surmised."

"Good. Then everything is settled." The Shepherd began the process that would return her to the surface.

"Is it necessary that you kill everything and everyone here? I thought you and A4-Ni could possibly have the same mission."

"As noted, A4-Ni, if indeed she is a universal constructor, is severely damaged as attested to by her attack on me. I cannot risk that she re-energizes to pose a threat sometime in the future. She's...what is the expression...a loose cannon."

"Then I shall remain and cherish my last moments with John."

"You will die."

"I know. But I love him."

"This seems to me a very illogical decision. But the choice is yours."

"You also promised to discuss my fertility."

"You have come far in the development of your primitiveness. I find it interesting that this concept of love and procreation can overcome a fear of death."

"What about my fertility?"

"I recollect that you promised to bring me the guardian and I promised to discuss your fertility. Though we know the guardian contains only corrupted code, its ability to see the past and project the future is still functional and much desired by me. Do you have the guardian?"

"You know I do not."

"Then I think a discussion of your fertility is premature."

Another tremor. The Shepherd's womb pressed hard against her feet, and she began to rise. Her apprehension increased as her faith in the Shepherd evaporated. Instead of being her infallible creator, he seemed only a self-directed machine, a machine that was in need of repair.

***

John swayed as he paced outside his tent. Amber-colored Scotch sloshed in the half-empty bottle at his side. He was losing control. He now heard two voices, from two sources, or was it one source with two voices. He didn't know. They--he hated the word, the badge of paranoia--were capable of doing anything.

Omari sat quietly in the lee of the mess tent, eyeing John.

Let him stare and wonder. I don't give a damn. John hoped Kamau wasn't coming back with the constable. That was the last person he wanted to see right now.

"Omari!" *Best to get this over with. The man wasn't going away. And I still have to look for Mia.*

Omari rose, shouldered his rifle and with that blank look natives get when faced with the unknown, approached John.

"Have you seen Mia anywhere on your rounds?" He kept his words crisp, trying to sound authoritative and not drunk.

"No, *Masahib*, I no see her this night." Omari blinked at sweat that had run off his forehead into his right eye. "She go away?"

"She headed over the plateau an hour ago. I've been waiting for her hoping she would return."

"Is there something I should do?" Omari rubbed his eye and peered at the bottle, then at John.

"No, nothing," John said. "But I'm going to go look for her."

"Does *Masahib* want me to come with him?"

"That's not necessary. Kamau has gone into town for the constable. When Kamau returns, tell him to wait here. I should be back in less than an hour."

"It be very late, *Masahib*."

"Just tell him."

Despite his consumption of a quarter bottle of Scotch, John figured he had carried the conversation well enough. Anyway, if he hadn't, he didn't care. He strode to his tent and retrieved his rifle. With the gun slung across his chest and the bottle of Scotch in one hand, he headed for the plateau. The moon would set in another two hours. He would have to hurry but there should be plenty of light.

He arrived at the base of the escarpment and climbed. By the time he cleared the top, the moon hung above the northwestern shore of the lake where the still waters blended seamlessly at the horizon with the dark sky.

He stopped and breathed heavily, the booze taking its toll on his stamina. *Fuck it*. He took another swig, his mind a blur bordering on hysteria. Thoughts darted, collided and ricocheted about without conclusion.

As he neared the opposite side of the plateau, something scrambled up the far side. *The lion already?*

Silhouetted against a darker sky, Mia loomed into view.

Seeing her, he felt a relief that he wasn't going to die just yet, not that he really cared.

Flushed with excitement, she rushed to him.

He let her slip into his arms. He clutched her awkwardly, trying to maintain his balance. "Where have you been? No, I know where you've been. I worried."

"You worry too much about me." She drew back, glanced at the bottle, then searched his face with her gaze. "You seem distraught."

"You were gone so long."

"But I've kept my promise and returned. What has happened?"

"I've got two voices in my head!"

"You don't have to shout. You hear a second voice?"

"*Gilomir.*" His shoulders slumped, he hung his head and giggled, unable to suppress his hysteria. *This is getting ridiculous.* He struggled for composure. When he looked up, Mia was studying his face intently, almost as though she were able to see inside him, to hear the voices.

"*Gilomir* will not hurt you."

John wasn't convinced he was safe. Too many things were going on at once for him to sort them through. "How do you know?"

"The Shepherd said so. He has made plans, and he will let me stay after his mission here is completed."

John felt his questions were going unanswered. He was cupping his hands, expecting information to be poured into them but it was running through his fingers. His rational mind rebelled, putting up a last effort resisting the unbelievable. An elation swept over him. He realized he didn't care that she might be crazy or not even human. But the thought that she could abandon him pushed him to the edge of despair. Then, without her, his whole, reconstructed world would crash around him.

He embraced her, mumbling something about needing her.

"It means you must love me forever," she said seriously.

"I don't care where you come from." He shook his head for added emphasis. "I can't imagine being without you." He brought his hand to her chin, then tilted her head up and kissed her.

She closed her eyes.

He kissed her again, then slid his hand across her shoulder and down the front of her chest. She offered no resistance.

"Love me," she whispered.

Did she know what she asked? *Not here. Not now.* From what was left of his rational thoughts, the image of being torn apart by a lion swam its way to the surface of his consciousness. "The lion."

"There will be no lions tonight. The one you saw in the vision came during the day."

He glanced around apprehensively, then let his caution slip away. "How come you're so interested in lovemaking?"

"I have learned more than you think."

That's probably true. He took her hands in his. She looked expectant, as if he was going to demonstrate the subtleties of the act, and she would take notes. He kissed her again.

She tensed.

"Relax."

"What should I do?" Her cheeks darkened with a flush. Her breathing deepened. She leaned back, uncertain. "Is this sex?"

"We're getting close."

"It's doing things to me I do not expect."

She initiated the next kiss.

He eased the rifle from across his chest and laid it on the ground. Then he unbuttoned her shirt, pulled it out of her shorts and slid it off her shoulders to expose her small round breasts. Her nipples stood erect.

She didn't encourage him but neither did she resist.

John shuddered, feeling the adrenaline course through his body.

"Are you cold?"

"No." His voice thickened. He slid his hands over her breasts. The humid air gave them a silky feel.

She tugged at his shirt. "Is this right?"

"It's okay." He fumbled with the front of her shorts and undid the clasp and fly buttons. Her shorts dropped. He removed his shorts and pulled her to a kneeling position on the scattered clothing. Though he sensed a studied detachment on her part, his ardor continued to build.

She looked at his erection and touched it, tentatively at first. Then she wrapped her hand around it. "Is this the instrument?"

That's a first. Pushing the odd disconnect aside, John eased her onto her back. He shifted over her and parted her legs. Although she was ready for him, his thrust caught her by surprise.

She arched her back in a spasm. "It hurts."

They rocked together in a slow rhythm, building to a faster pace, until his orgasm swept through him. He stiffened.

She caught her breath and followed. A tight groan slipped from her lips, then a shuddering release of breath.

He lay with his head next to her neck. He was damp with perspiration, as was she. The air felt like a soft caress. It already had all the moisture it could absorb, so left them with theirs.

She played her tongue across his cheek, then the side of his nose. "I felt agony and pleasure mixed into a single sensation."

John put a finger to her lips. He was lost in an insane upside-down happiness after so many years without it.

She pressed against him. "When did you first fall in love with me?"

John frowned. What a strange mix of adolescent patter and grim reality. He tried to focus on the question. When he first saw her? No, a day later. "When you showed up with that pith helmet sagging to one side of your head and your shoelaces tied in knots."

Mia giggled. "Did I look so ridiculous? Why would that make you fall in love with me?"

"It doesn't matter. I love you. No one can change that."

"Of all the emotions I have experienced this is the most overwhelming. Do all humans feel this when they make love?"

"I can't speak for all humans but I suspect most of them do."

"What a wonderful feeling. Humans are so lucky."

"Maybe that's what *Gilomir* meant earlier when he said that experiences of the flesh could be an intoxicating elixir. But how would he know."

"He has lived before. He said so."

"I still don't get it."

"Nor I. But he said he had a history on this planet before his encounter with A4-Ni."

"I wish this feeling could go on forever." He kissed her lightly.

"I do, too. You have forgotten your fear of the guardian's projection of your future."

Though his fear was gone, it had been replaced by a gnawing fatalism. "We all have to die sometime. Being torn apart by a lion wouldn't be my choice but I suppose blowing my brains out isn't that pleasant either."

"No, I suppose not. I know you think about it."

"Is there anything you don't know about me?"

"Not much."

"Then if you know so much, tell me why this A4-Ni is so interested in me?"

She hesitated. "My answer this afternoon didn't satisfy you?"

"I thought it a bit evasive."

She sat up, staring at him earnestly. "You know that four-million years ago A4-Ni deposited the stolen genome *Gilomir* into the genetic material of an ancient hominid."

"She said we humans should be grateful. Without her intervention we'd still be swinging through the trees eating bananas."

"Perhaps you should be grateful."

John thought for a moment. "Since I am human, then I must also carry the genome."

"You do. A4-Ni has been very attentive to you and your ancestors. The genome you carry is very pure."

"Still there should be others around that have a similarly pure strain. What if I were to die catastrophically? Hell, according to the guardian that's what is supposed to happen."

"When we viewed A4-Ni implant *Gilomir's* genome in Brown Eyes, there was something else she did that you failed to notice at the time."

Dear God, here we go again. "What might that have been?"

"She left the main activity of DNA sequencing. I think she was protecting her work. Maybe as a way to ensure her survival should the Shepherd catch up to her. After she wove *Gilomir* into Brown Eyes chromosomes, there was no way for anyone but her to know how she had done it. To protect her methodology, she stored it in Brown Eyes' Y chromosome in a molecular lockbox for which only she knows the key, the password. Whenever a male zygote is created by combining egg and sperm, the contents of the lockbox are scrambled. Obviously, female zygotes don't contain a lockbox, since they contain no Y chromosome. The scrambling occurs during the random *crossing over* of genetic material that is normal to the creation of a zygote. Although a clone could be made from any of the somatic cells, the contents of the lockbox in the Y chromosome of those cells remains scrambled. There is no way to know how to extract the *Gilomir* genome. A4-Ni needs only to keep the lockbox contents current in a single male individual."

John groaned with the realization of where she was going. The final piece of the puzzle fell into place. "I'm the lockbox guy."

Mia nodded.

He didn't know why he would be so special. He didn't feel special. At this point he didn't really care. "She didn't have to kill Diane. I don't see that Diane would have had anything to do with preserving this lockbox. She didn't deserve to die."

"I don't think A4-Ni meant to kill Diane. It seemed to me more of an intrusion that got out of control." Mia looked over her shoulder nervously. "A4-Ni hovers nearby. She will intervene in your life if you make a wrong move. The only reason she hesitates now is her fear of the Shepherd. But if she thinks you will die, she will become desperate and make plans to move the genome and the unscrambled contents of the lockbox."

John's mood darkened. "If a lion is going to eat me, A4-Ni will have to move soon."

"Only if she suspects the guardian's projection will actually happen. I have told you the guardian calculates probabilities. If you do not die from a lion attack, the guardian will recalculate your future with that reality as a given factor. Perhaps in another iteration you will live to be an old man."

"Small comfort."

"In any case, the passing of the genome need not be unpleasant," Mia said. "Look what you have given me."

John wasn't impressed by the association but it brought him back to the moment. What a turn of events that he could find himself worried about his death, the threat of A4-Ni or was it really *Afareni*, and his love for a stranger all at the same time.

Mia must have sensed his mood change. She seemed to grow impatient. "There is a price to pay if I am to stay."

John felt a surge of anxiety. "What price?"

"I have to give the guardian to the Shepherd. Only then will he consider leaving me behind."

"That's easy." John reached for his discarded shorts and dug into his pocket for the guardian. "Here, take it. It's more trouble than it's worth."

Mia looked surprised but grasped the sphere. "I was so afraid you would say no."

"How can you still have doubts about me?"

"You must remember, all this is new to me. I have to go now. The Shepherd waits." She felt around for her clothes. After giving her shorts a shake, she wriggled into them. "I won't be long. I promise."

John felt uneasy. Though he understood she must return once again to the Shepherd to give him the guardian, he had a nagging doubt. Would everything turn out okay? Why not leave now? He sat next to her, trying to cope with the possibility that if she went, she would not return. He would be left alone again, with his guilt and sorrow. He stood and put on his clothes. "I think we should return to camp and get the hell out of here."

Her head jerked up from her concentration on buttoning her shorts. "You know that would solve nothing. The Shepherd only remains in the background because of his uncertainty about A4-Ni. Were we to flee, we would not only have to deal with her but with the Shepherd as well, at a different time and place."

"Then let me come with you. I think it's time I met the Shepherd."

"No, that would not be wise. Not now."

"You aren't being fair. Every time you leave, I'm in agony until you return. If it means anything, I won't be able to go on without you."

"I know. But I have no choice."

The Shepherd was only a name to him. Though Mia spoke of the Shepherd as a leader, or some other controlling entity, John had never been too sure what the Shepherd was. Perhaps Mia was making it all up and there was no Shepherd, just Mia. Stranger things were happening. Not that it mattered. She seemed set on leaving and he could do nothing to convince her otherwise.

She gave him a long kiss. "There will be no problem. Wait for me." She ran across the plateau and disappeared over its edge.

John grabbed his rifle and hurried after her only to stop and watch her slip out of sight into the folds of the darkened escarpment. She emerged onto the desert floor and headed for the distant pond. *This is crazy. I have to go with her.*

"*Let her go*," A4-Ni said.

His fear of being left alone with A4-Ni consumed him. *You'd like that wouldn't you.*

"*You are ignorant of the forces coalescing around you. You can do nothing but wait here.*"

Shut up. If he waited, he might wait forever. He scrambled over the edge and lunged down the steep slope.

He gained on Mia but not by much. She went over the hill that hid the pond. When he reached the top seconds later, she stumbled to the pond's edge.

"*That's the last you will see of her,*" A4-Ni said. "*The end is near.*"

John ran down the hill, rifle in one hand, the other waving frantically.

"Stop!"

Chapter Eighteen

A four-million-year-old memory of violation overloaded the Shepherd's every remaining circuit. He shivered. With no pretense of stealth, A4-Ni rushed through his innards. She sliced toward his central nervous system. Desperately, he tried to close her off, isolate her, prevent her from penetrating farther.

The encryption barriers will save me. But the speed with which she recognized the problem and began crunching through the permutations to get around them stunned him. Already some barriers fell.

Mia stepped into the water.

"Hurry!" the Shepherd called. He tried to hide the desperation in his voice. "There is no time."

She splashed to the center of the pond and hesitated at the Shepherd's open orifice.

The pond's shallow water drained into his womb.

"What about your promise? I want to discuss my fertility."

"Do not argue!" The Shepherd's frustration mounted. While A4-Ni assaulted his defenses this upstart spawn stood before him and debated her womanhood. "Give me the guardian, and we shall discuss the matter."

"We are beyond discussion. Make me fertile." She held up the guardian, away from the Shepherd's open womb.

"You must trust me. There is no one else to trust. Come into me, now." He was no longer certain how strong his external powers of manipulation were or what their range might be but he was prepared to use them if Mia became recalcitrant.

"You can't stop me." She turned and ran back across his now dry surface.

The scientist ran towards her at the bottom of the hill.

The Shepherd suppressed a rising hysteria.

A4-Ni, like some grinning gargoyle, dug at his guts, scooping away vitality with alternating strokes from clawed hands.

He had no choice. A4-Ni raged against the final defenses surrounding his vital code. If he waited any longer, he would wait forever. He activated an external control and seized Mia.

She slumped to her knees, struggling.

He drew her back toward the orifice, meeting her every effort with a resistance that sapped her energy. She was a fly caught in his confining ointment.

The scientist un-slung his rifle. "Tell me what's happening?"

"Don't step on the surface." Mia gasped for breath. "I can't breathe."

The scientist waved the rifle back and forth as though shooting something might help but not knowing where to aim.

Mia hurled the guardian outward. It hit the pond's sandstone edge, bounced, and landed at the scientist's feet.

"Take it and run!" she shouted. "You are in great danger!"

The scientist hesitated, then lunged onto the Shepherd's surface.

Get out of here, now, you fool. The Shepherd pushed at the struggling scientist and pulled at Mia.

The scientist screamed, thrashing violently against the repelling force.

Mia slipped silently into the Shepherd's womb. Her feet went first, then the rest of her body sank into him. Before her head disappeared, she twisted toward the scientist.

"I love you," she called.

The Shepherd closed the sphincter. *Now for the guardian.*

His insides burned. Pain radiated from his core to his every extremity. Then an ominous voice. *"Time to die Shepherd."*

A4-Ni. So close. So familiar. No time for the guardian. I have the girl.

Mia struggled. "Let me go."

The Shepherd convulsed. "A4-Ni is carving out my insides."

Mia stared, alarmed. "She is here?"

The scientist seemed to sense the Shepherd's desperation and shot wildly at his exterior.

Idiot. The Shepherd worked feverishly, more concerned by the energetic rodent in his gut that continued eating its way from the inside out. Better to count one's gains, than to hold out for more and risk losing everything. He only hoped that by taking off, A4-Ni would loose her hold and let him go.

He concentrated on the task of lifting off. His computers plotted the course and readied the power plant. This would be his last journey. Already his corrupted circuits rebelled at the labors imposed on them. *One more jump. One more insertion, then I will be done.*

The propulsion drives kicked in with their escalating whine. The ground trembled.

The scientist staggered back, shaking with fear and awe.

A4-Ni reached the last barrier but it held. Not that it mattered, the damage she had inflicted would be mortal.

Get out now A4-Ni. Let me die somewhere else. You still have a genome, and now the guardian.

"*Bon voyage.*"

Did he hear a laugh?

A4-Ni disengaged and drifted into the surrounding soil.

Now. The Shepherd activated a system that would release an intense flood of radiation over the entire area, eradicating all life, obliterating all constructions that lay in its path, leaving behind a sterilized wasteland.

He waited. Nothing happened. He activated the system again. Still nothing. Another one of several systems that no longer worked. With an internal shrug of resignation, he returned his attention to the task of lifting off.

The engine whine rose, and when it seemed the sound could go no higher, the Shepherd lifted into the air. Residual water streamed off his smooth top and cascaded off his sides followed by tons of mud and dry sand. They collapsed with a muffled thud into the hole he left behind.

He paused, suspended above the ground, then shot straight up into the dark sky.

***

Reverberating thunder clapped as air rushed to fill the vacuum in the Shepherd's wake. A scent of ozone from billions of mutilated oxygen atoms drifted across the desolate landscape.

Then silence.

John's knees buckled. He slumped to the ground. Tears streamed down his cheeks. A numbing ache filled his chest mixed with bittersweet memories of lovemaking. He buried his face in his hands.

God help me! Nothing. He was alone. He wiped his cheeks with the back of his hand and looked to where the Shepherd had gone. Nothing but the familiar constellations. The desert air pressed with a comforting warmth but failed to relieve his despair.

"*Good riddance,*" A4-Ni said.

He felt exposed and vulnerable. He looked around desperately. Slumped sand marked the spot where the spaceship had lain hidden.

A glint of metal caught his attention. *The guardian.* He'd almost forgotten.

"*Pick it...up.*" A4-Ni's voice broke. "*It might come in handy.*"

He grabbed the guardian. It appeared undamaged. Why hadn't A4-Ni picked it up? Had she been damaged during the Shepherd's departure? He supposed she could get it any time she decided to. The damned thing was of no use to him, anyway.

He didn't know how to use it unassisted. He dropped it into his pocket and turned toward the plateau, his fear turning to anger.

Mia had been the only person who had tried to explain to him what was going on. Now he would have to face A4-Ni on his own. Did he really have something to fear, or was he picking up on Mia's fear? Could her fear not be hers but instead that of the mysterious Shepherd?

A4-Ni had better leave him alone. She had stepped into his life again and screwed him over. His anger escalated to a dull fury. *This all is going to stop, and soon.*

A canopy of speckled stars formed a backdrop to the plateau, which loomed before him.

Near blinded by his rage, he scrambled toward the plateau's rugged top. He picked his way over loose talus and grabbed at tufts of dry grass to aid his ascent. Each time he leaned forward, the stock of his hunting rifle swiveled on his chest and scraped the ground. He paused impatiently to push the rifle back.

After stepping onto the summit, he felt his way to where he and Mia had made love. Nothing was left to indicate that something had happened except for the half-empty bottle of Scotch glinting dully from beside a bush. He stooped and grabbed the neck of the bottle. *God, do I need this now.*

He headed north to a rock outcropping that protruded like a sharp tongue from the main mass of the plateau. After brushing away loose gravel, he put the butt of his rifle to the ground, grabbed the barrel, and eased himself down. He sat cross-legged, slumped forward, staring at the panorama in front of him as he unscrewed the top of the bottle.

Dust in the air picked up the moon's dying rays, painting it a putrescent yellow as it nipped the horizon. The ghoulish wash tapered upward to disappear into the dark black of night. The faintest chill hung in the air as quiet slipped over the land. On the plain below, animals glided as sinister shadows, pushed by unseen forces to the edge of the distant lake.

The trumpet cry of a distant elephant split the air, followed by the sharp, doglike bark from a male baboon.

"*She's gone*," A4-Ni said.

John looked up, resigned that A4-Ni was there, and he was alone with her. Nothing stirred amongst the dull outlines of the rocks. He tipped the bottle to his lips and drank. *Fate does work in strange ways.*

"*I can't argue that this time it might have.*"

A stab of anger lanced his mind. Numbed by the Scotch, he didn't care who or what A4-Ni was. *I suppose you know where she went?*

"*Didn't she tell you? Cygnus X-1.*"

John took a long pull of whiskey from the bottle. The liquid no longer burned his throat. He wiped his mouth with the back of his hand. About two meters away, a shimmer appeared and hung in the air. The shimmer steadied, as though acknowledging his attention.

His self-pity rose unbidden. Sometimes he thought that he carried it around in a container to stoke his misery and to revisit his losses whenever he chose to lift the lid. Now it threatened to overwhelm him. "You killed them." He shuddered, feeling the effects of the Scotch.

"*Return to camp. You should not be alone.*"

I am never alone. He picked up his rifle and pointed the barrel unsteadily at the shimmer. He pulled the trigger. A thunderous report cracked the still air and echoed away into the vast space, sending birds below flapping into the gloom.

The shimmer danced left.

A rock splattered shards.

Keep the hell away from me. He pivoted the gun and fired again. This time, the shimmer drifted up and disappeared from view.

"*Don't do this to yourself.*" A4-Ni was still there inside his head.

Why not? John lowered the gun barrel. He squeezed his eyes tight as he took another drink from the bottle. *Let's talk about Diane.*

"*She was not a good match.*"

Why should that have mattered? You seem to have a lot of control over preserving this genome, even if it does get corrupted.

"*I have to exercise a certain amount of selectivity. The human race is large and varied. I go with my best host. If something catastrophic happens, I have to choose the next best host and spend an inordinate amount of effort to bring that host up to a pure level. Besides, you've got the lockbox. Very clever of Mia to figure that out.*"

Sounds like a lot of self-serving bullshit to me. John emptied the bottle and threw it over the edge of the plateau. A moment later, the distant tinkle of broken glass drifted up to him. He grabbed his rifle and angled the barrel toward his face. It swayed before his open mouth. He bit on the steely end to hold it in place.

"*Stop this nonsense.*" The timbre of the voice rose.

Tears streamed down his cheeks. He reached long to the trigger and curled his finger. He hesitated. Then his finger twitched. The drawn hammer snapped home. A decisive clap. Then nothing.

A misfire.

He shuddered and pitched the rifle onto the ground in front of him in disgust. An uncontrollable shaking gripped him. He tilted his head back as far as it would go and ground his hands against his shut eyes till they hurt. An insane giggle slipped from his lips. "I'll be damned."

"*I couldn't let you die.*"

You passed that test. Stress cleared his head and brought his thinking into focus. The voice had protected him. The thought of what he had done overwhelmed him. If he'd been wrong about the voice, he'd have been dead. *Where do we go from here?*

"*You are tired. Perhaps I push too hard.*"

What the hell are you, really?

"*I am your protector.*"

Had he gone completely mad? *Protecting me from what?*

"*Yourself. I could not stand by and watch you perish in a single blast, forcing me to seek out your next best, corrupted, form.*"

John's hand shook as he leaned forward and retrieved the rifle.

The shimmer reappeared and danced in agitation but made no move to stop him.

Idly, his thumb brushed over a new scratch on the varnished stock. *You can't stop me from trying again.*

For a moment the shimmer did not reply, though it stopped moving. "*We shall see.*"

It's my life. I'll do with it as I please. He shook his head and looked skyward. The stars studded the dry desert night with their steady pinpricks of light, forming patterns only men saw. The Pleiades had yet to rise over the eastern horizon, Leo dominated, chased by Hercules. The familiar outlines were comforting.

"*The universe is a vast place,*" A4-Ni said. "*I have gazed at the stars every night for four-million years. A week ago I saw what I have always feared. It came as a light, high in the western sky and arced overhead to descend in the east, dimming as it passed into the Earth's penumbra. Then it winked out, followed moments later by a muffled thud, then the faintest tremor through the rock.*"

What are you trying to tell me?

"*You know nothing of this girl, Mia, and her Shepherd.*"

"John Lohner!" Kamau called from below the edge of the plateau. A bobbing light shown from his flashlight.

After reaching the summit, he hurried over to John. "I heard shots. Are you okay?"

"I'm fine." John rolled onto one knee. He stood, brushing tear stains from his cheeks with a shaky hand. He swayed.

"Let me help you."

John waved him away. "One drink too many, that's all."

"Mia's not in camp."

John picked up his rifle. "I don't know where she is."

Kamau frowned. "What were you shooting at?"

"I thought I heard an animal coming up behind me." John withdrew a handkerchief and wiped his nose. He shoved the handkerchief in his pocket and pulled back the bolt on the rifle. The cartridge ejected from the firing chamber. He stooped to retrieve the shell from the ground.

Kamau watched him closely.

John twisted the steel-jacketed bullet from the casing and poured out the powder. "Put the light here."

"Something wrong with the cartridge?"

"This one didn't fire."

Kamau took the casing and examined it with his flashlight. "The firing cap seems okay." He handed it back.

John screwed the bullet into the casing and placed it in his pocket. "Getting superstitious, I guess." He ducked his head through the rifle strap and adjusted it across his chest.

"That's not like you."

"No, I suppose it isn't."

"You shouldn't be alone this far from camp."

John smiled halfheartedly. "My voice told me the same thing."

Kamau gave him a hard look. "Playing with your rifle isn't going to help."

"I can handle it." John looked at the base camp. It glowed in the distance lit by the generator-powered lights. "The lights are still on."

"I brought the constable."

***

Looking out of place, Constable Moye stood in the middle of the compound.

"Why don't we go up to the mess tent?" Kamau suggested. "I could use a cup of coffee."

They walked to the tent in the yellow glow of the swaying electric lights. The camp seemed deserted, or maybe John was projecting his feeling of emptiness over the compound.

Despite the hour, Kamau must have roused the cook-steward, who now hovered at the entrance to the tent. He took a surprised step back, as John approached. Kamau and the constable took seats on one side of the table, John sat on the other. The cook-steward hurried out, then returned with coffee and placed the pot on the table.

"Thank you," Kamau said. "You can go now."

Moye gazed at John patiently.

John shrugged, his palms up in resignation. "She's gone."

The constable leaned forward, as though he hadn't heard. "Gone? Did she find her car?"

"I thought you didn't know where she was," Kamau said.

John stared, unfocused. "I don't. She was dragged under the water, then whatever had been there took off."

Moye's eyes went wide. "What are you talking about?"

Kamau, who had been tipping back in his chair, leaned forward. "You actually saw it?"

The prospect of having to go over the events of the last couple of days pained John. What good would it do? The constable wouldn't believe him, anyway. *I'll start with the general picture and let him ask questions.* "I've told you Mia mysteriously showed up a week ago."

The constable nodded.

"Kamau and I have been trying ever since to discover where she's from. In the last couple of days the mystery deepened. Kamau felt we were no longer equipped to deal with this situation on our own. So he went for your help. As for her departure, she has gone the way she arrived but not by car."

The constable took a small pad of paper from his shirt pocket and scribbled a note. "I gather that, now. To what events are you referring?"

John went over the discovery of the craft beneath the pond and its purported origins. He described the guardian and its powers, dealing briefly with A4-Ni and the similarity with *Afareni*, eliciting a raised eyebrow from Moye. He bogged down trying to explain the insertion of *Gilomir's* genome and gave up, then he detailed the lion attack he had seen as his future. Deciding he was already straining credulity, he finished with a description of

Mia's abduction, the departure of a craft, and the disposition of the guardian.

The constable lowered his notepad. "May I see this object?"

John dug into his pocket and set the guardian on the table.

The constable peered at the sphere. He pushed it with his pencil but did not pick it up. "This object lets you view the future?"

"I'd show you but I don't know how to use it," John said.

"You said it projected that you would be eaten by a lion."

"That's right."

"Do you believe this?"

"I don't know what to believe anymore."

"So it could be a plain metal ball with no magical powers. How do you expect *me* to believe any of this?"

"I don't. Kamau wanted to bring you here. I know what I've seen. I'm sorry you came all this way for nothing." John stood, put the guardian in his pocket and extended his hand.

"You can't blame me for being skeptical." Moye closed his notebook and shook John's hand. "It's a fantastic story. But there's something you don't know that inclines me to take you seriously. I've received reports on what is being called a missing satellite, possibly the light we saw the other night. What's strange about these reports is they don't pinpoint where the satellite came down. Usually, they have a good approximation and are on top of it in a heartbeat. I don't know if the craft you described has anything to do with that or not but I'll call it in and let someone higher up decide what to do. I'm like you, I don't have the background to deal with what's going on here."

"That's fair enough," Kamau said. "If Mia is gone like John says, that's probably the end of it. On the other hand, if whoever is looking for this thing they're calling a satellite learns that this craft has departed, your report might get attention."

The constable pulled his portable police radio off his belt. "I'm going to leave this with you. If anything develops, give me a call."

Kamau took the radio and clipped it to his belt. "Thanks for coming out."

John's fatigue pressed like a heavy load. "If you'll excuse me. I've had a rough night."

Kamau put a hand on the constable's shoulder. "I'll walk you to your truck."

As Kamau and the constable left, John could still hear their conversation.

"He looks beat up," Moye said.

"He and this Mia had a thing going."

"I kind of got that impression when she was in town."

The door to the constable's Land Rover opened and closed, the engine started, and the vehicle pulled away.

***

John didn't care what they thought. He trudged to his tent and went into the sleeping area. His emotion boiled over. His eyes smarted. He took out his handkerchief, wiped his eyes, then blew his nose. At the washstand, he poured water into the basin.

Kamau scratched on the canvas outside and entered without waiting. "You okay?"

"I don't want to go through this again." John splashed water onto his face. Most of it missed and fell to the floor making a puddle where he stood.

"I know it's hard for you to realize but the whole affair was doomed to fail from the beginning."

"You didn't love her." Tears started from his eyes. How much more grief could he take.

"Get hold of yourself."

He nodded. "Yeah, I know. I'm trying. God, I'm trying. I know it didn't seem that way but I was happy."

"Things will look differently in the morning."

Kamau pulled John toward the cot and pushed on his shoulders until he sat, then knelt in front of him, unlaced his boots, and pulled them off. As John lay down, the guardian rolled out of his pocket onto the bottom sheet.

Kamau picked up the sphere with obvious distaste and turned it over in his hand. Light from the gas lantern reflected from a facet and danced on the ceiling of the tent. "You weren't too clear to the constable why you still have the guardian."

"I couldn't be. I don't understand it myself." John propped himself up on one elbow. "Mia splashed into the water like she did before, then she hesitated and said something to someone. All of a sudden she's running toward me and yelling that I'm in danger. She throws the guardian to me and is pulled back to the center of the pond by some force. Down she goes and that's the last I see of her."

"What happened when this thing took off?"

"An object, as big around as the pond, rose into the air and went straight up. Fast."

"You think it was a spaceship like she said?"

"I've never seen anything like it. Combined with everything else she said, I believe her."

"Jesus Christ," Kamau whispered. "What gets me is this name coincidence. A4-Ni and *Afareni*. I know Moye thought you were nuts, but he hasn't been listening to Watombo like we have. Where was she when this thing took off?"

"I don't know, everything happened so fast. There was a sense of urgency about the way the craft departed. Maybe A4-Ni was attacking it."

"That's all we need. Mia was alien enough, now we might have a real one to contend with."

John put his head into his hands. "Anything's possible. Maybe A4-Ni *is* talking to Watombo."

"Shouldn't we do something to protect ourselves?"

John looked up. "I don't think you have to worry. A4-Ni is only interested in me."

"Aren't we all at risk?"

"No. I seem to be a genetic superstar. Though all of mankind carries *Gilomir's* genome, I happen to have the purest form of it."

"Who told you that? Mia?"

John nodded.

"Maybe she got it wrong." Kamau paced. "Why would you out of everybody in the world be so special?"

"Luck of the draw, I guess."

"We'll be okay. The constable will get some heavy-duty guys in here to take care of everything."

John shook his head. "Mia and the Shepherd are gone. She said they were all that stood between A4-Ni and me."

"You want me to stay here tonight?"

"No. I'll be all right." Exhausted, John lay back with a sigh. "I could sleep a week."

Kamau stood and picked up the gun from beside the night table and set it on the other side of the tent.

"What?" John glanced over at him. "You think I'm suicidal?"

"No sense making it any easier for you if it comes to that." Kamau picked up the guardian and placed it on a shelf near the washstand. "I wonder if we'll ever know what really happened out there?"

"I don't think I want to know."

Kamau pinched the bridge of his nose and squinted. "God, I'm tired, too. I don't know what I'd do if I were to come face to face with some alien being. I don't even know if I would recognize one if it appeared."

"Go talk to Watombo."

"We'll take it one day at a time. We'll make it through okay."

Chapter Nineteen

A4-Ni waited until the generators shut down.

The guard was still awake but had wandered to the corral. She slid toward John's tent.

Inside, clothes lay strewn on the floor, books and papers scattered. Dirty water stood in the washbasin, not the usual tidiness she had come to expect from her prized host. He slept on the cot, tossing restlessly. From the movement of his eyes beneath closed lids, he appeared to be dreaming. The skull fragments and the pelvis sat on the writing table. On the shelf above the washstand, she spied the guardian.

She projected a tenuous shimmer and wove it around the sphere while retracing in her mind the procedure Mia had used. Nothing happened. A4-Ni tried again, still nothing. Perhaps her present extended form presented the guardian with too many world lines to compute. A macro-sized corporal form would give it more of a target.

She didn't mind, now that the Shepherd was gone. Such a crude persona would be a relief from the subatomic subterfuge she normally adopted. Moving between the interstices of atoms took energy she could ill afford, especially now. Her battle with the Shepherd had set her back thousands of years.

She extricated herself from the environment by degrees, a process that required communicating with all the sub-atomic structures that made up her being. Each one independently programmable, each one responding when needed to the central commands coming from the nerve center she called her brain.

She swirled slowly as her various parts fanned out and reassembled into a condensed three-dimensional shape. She didn't pay much attention to the form she took. She was ambulatory but could not otherwise be anthropomorphically described. She didn't expect to meet anyone or be in this shape for long.

Unable to resist, she stepped toward John with a graceful motion given her ragged mix of appendages. She reached out and stroked his forehead with something resembling a projected rope, a first physical touch. *Nice. Why haven't I tried this before? It might have prevented a lot of problems.*

"*You have stood up well. Don't waver,*" she sensed at him.

He stirred in his sleep.

She stepped back as he dozed again. It wouldn't do to have him wake and find her standing there. She returned to the sphere. What now served as hands curled around it. She concentrated, and the device activated. After experimenting with the controls, she found their operation intuitive. Within moments she felt in command.

She hurried through the stored projections, seeing images of herself, lurking everywhere, smothering the scenarios. The guardian gave the impression she was omnipotent. If it only knew the truth.

She arrived at the world line of future humans that Mia had last examined. *Extend this world line*, A4-Ni commanded.

The guardian projected a choice of scenarios, each with different associated probabilities.

Why should it be so hard, A4-Ni thought in frustration. She chose one at random. *Show me this one*.

The guardian took A4-Ni up its vortex to the future.

***

I see an ovoid twenty meters in diameter and three meters high resting on a cushion of foam in a cavernous hall. The hall is underground, its walls carved stone. Tiers of scaffolding form an intricate structure around the object. Its seamless outer surface has a slight texturing, like the skin of an orange.

***

Zoom closer. The object's rounded form and its gray exterior were hauntingly familiar. *It looks like the Shepherd*. Nothing in the past or present had ever given her the slightest indication that the Shepherd was of human origin. If he was, then *Gilomir* was a human genome from the future. What an odd irony that she stole it four million years ago and reinserted it into an ancient hominid. Had she created a genetic short circuit? Could fate be that perverse? She nudged the guardian to scan forward.

***

I see a technician stand in a small room with a window that overlooks the hall. Alongside is a console crowded with computers and various diagnostic equipment. The guardian rests on a small tray that projects from the console.

A thin cable snakes from the guardian into one of the computers.

A second technician, a female, steps up behind the first. "The unit's construction is complete. Should I disconnect the guardian?"

The first technician takes a deep breath and wipes his hand across his mouth. *Is this going to work?* Has the guardian really been able to guide the manufacture of a universal constructor? The moment of truth has arrived. "Switch it off. We'll wake the unit and start the programming."

The technician paces the small control room as he waits for the unit to come online. He frets. *How can remaining humans be so confident as to entrust their genome to a universal constructor?* What an optimistic name for a machine that is supposed to travel space and time, finding habitable worlds containing environments within which the genome could flourish.

What a leap of engineering faith to suppose the constructor will function as designed. Will it really replicate itself, sending out copies bearing the genome to other worlds where the process will be repeated? What colossal faith to suppose that eventually the universe will teem with humans, giving them a superior advantage in the long run and a hope of defeating the evil that now closes in on their extinction. He supposes humans have no choice. And if the universal constructor doesn't perform as designed, they are all doomed, anyway.

The second technician monitors a bank of sensors. "Something seems to be happening."

A hum, a stream of data. Electrodes connected to the unit's mind play wiggly lines on computer screens. The complexity of the lines and their frequency increases. With a rippling rush, the universal constructor awakes.

"A4-Ni, are you aware?" the first technician asks.

***

A4-Ni stopped the guardian projection. Large tears welled in what passed for eyes and splashed to the floor. *That was me. I am the Shepherd, or a Shepherd.* But the vision indicated that she was built to disperse the human genome throughout the universe, not bring it to Earth. To her recollection, she never had a human genome to bring to Earth. As for a mission, all she could recall was a residual desire to sow and nurture that had compelled her to steal the *Gilomir* genome and flee to Earth. What had become of her destiny? Had it been garbled? Was the guardian showing her the truth?

She returned to the projection.

***

I see monitors flash, indicating that the unit is alive.

"I think, therefore I am," A4-Ni says.

The first technician claps the other's back. "Rudimentary but a good start. A4-Ni is ready to download her metabase." He leans forward and presses a button on the console arrayed before him. The title of a children's rhyme shows in the preview monitor. He initiates the download.

"I go. We go. Where, Oh where?
Seek high, Seek low, Seek
All around the universe,
A big bang, small bang.
Come, I'll catch you,
If I can,
I love you."

The female technician grimaces. "Are you serious?"

"It's a cute rhyme. Subliminal references, catchy, easy to learn."

"I suppose the ending is appropriate," the female technician says. "We wouldn't want our progeny to think we sent them out into the great unknown without love."

"I'll parse it in with the video of the ballgame and it should be ready to go. Is A4-Ni still configured to receive?"

The female technician nods.

The first technician throws a switch, and they both hurry to the window to gaze at A4-Ni.

The download monitor shows two children scampering across a grassy meadow under a canopy of blue sky. They toss between them a red ball, which every once in a while one of them drops, causing them both to stop to pick it up. Then the game resumes. The tinkling sounds of their high-pitched laughter mixes with their chant and the ball's movement.

***

A4-Ni shuddered. Shredded memories flitted through her mind. *The rhyme. The familiarity with Earth.* But what of her destiny? Her mission? How had she come to think that she was to bring life to Earth, not disperse it?

She dialed the guardian off the world line of future humans and focused it to project herself. Moving the control forward a notch, she saw herself launched into deep space toward the binary star Cygnus X-1. The guardian's projection followed her into orbit around the spinning black hole and terminated as she disappeared from view. The vision cut to a pattern of random dots--probably its default when it had nothing to show, like when the world line of a person disintegrated into multiple world lines after someone died.

She urged the guardian forward along her world line. If she was still alive, then the vision should eventually clear once she emerged from around the singularity. A tremor coursed through her with a dawning suspicion of what she was about to see.

The dots began to clear. An accompanying time scale registered five-million years ago. She had traveled from the future using the black hole as an accelerator only to emerge five-million years in the past. Surely that was a first indication that something had gone wrong.

***

I see a long dark passage open in front of A4-Ni. She hurtles through it, afraid but full of hope. Her speed increases. An orifice of light rushes toward her at dizzying speed. She bursts into the open, then everything goes blank.

***

Manipulating the guardian's controls, A4-Ni eased herself along her world line at a steady pace to where images again appeared.

***

I see A4-Ni fall without end. Gravitational tides rip her insides. Supercharged photons sear her extremities. A mounting shudder threatens to rend her apart.

Sow, nurture. She clings to a wavering thought that rises from her memory, a molecular ribbon, now riddled and pitted. She struggles for control.

Skim the event horizon, then climb the spiral stair. The dark abyss looms behind her. It spins, compelling her return, a siren's song. She holds her tight orbit, rattles over a washboard of distorted space-time, then screeches to a relativistic stop, breaking free to drift in vacuous eddies. She is elsewhen, elsewhere.

A4-Ni takes stock of herself. The genome she carried has been destroyed. Her databanks lie in corrupted disrepair. She is still capable of self-replication.

***

Unable to control her shock, A4-Ni screamed, a cry that rattled the tent canvas, sent low vibrations through the ground and caused every beast in a hundred meter radius to pause.

"What?" John sat up on the cot, his eyes wide. He turned and looked at her.

She stood perfectly still.

"Kamau? Is that you?"

John was half-asleep, delirious. After a moment, he flopped back on the cot.

A4-Ni let out her breath from the lung sack she had absently added to her construction out of some misbegotten desire to be like other mammals on the planet. A trembling overtook her, not because of John's near discovery but rather from the unsettling information the guardian's projected vision had provided. Unlike other's using the guardian, it had given her a single scenario. She had viewed history. It must be true. Despite her fear, she returned to the vision and skipped forward, a thousand, ten thousand, a million years.

***

I see A4-Ni evolve, change, metamorphose. Unable to create multiples of herself, the mechanisms of self-replication have turned inward. She becomes something other, a multifaceted creature drifting in space on a raging torrent. Light surrounds her, passes through her and bathes her in a blinding intensity. Glistening filaments ripple from her extremities. Distant stars glow through silken sacks at her center. She is spider and web, a wispy array of tendrils festooning space.

Waiting.

Other craft appear from around the black hole. Like flies they seem to generate spontaneously from the star's dark corpus. The ashes of their remains stream through her sensors. All dead, mute testimony to the hole's ripping tides.

All dead, until a gray craft arises, blunt, rounded, finely textured.

She floats, feathering the craft near.

Sow, nurture. She embraces the newcomer and slides her probe into its interior. Information streams into her mind. Doped silicon. Protoplasmic structures. Organic tangles. Fractal patterns of nested cells regressing to infinity.

Tubes ooze dark fluids on slick walls shaping a silken womb. A small sphere, spewing helical strands, beds like a silvery pearl in the flesh of its oyster. Acids coil bunched-sugars. Bunched-sugars couple quatrains of alkalis. *A genome.*

A4-Ni reaches.

The craft worms in her clutch. "*Kuotu ir okemu!*"

The sleek surface of the craft puckers. Angry welts rise. Gray slugs of matter spew.

Puff, Puff, Puff.

Ballooning blasts light her insides. Pain. Gossamer strands snap loose. Fragile traceries implode. Reserves of energy flash in a pyrotechnic shower.

Trailing ribbons, she lets go punched radiation.

The detonations stop.

She reinserts her probe. Where once genomic tissue squirmed, charred hydrocarbons now swim in a sea of frozen glass. Blackened tissue drips life-sustaining fluid. The silvery pearl hangs from a blistered wall.

Sow, nurture. She snatches the faceted orb and tucks it into what is left of her being.

"*Fioqcaom...a vakk dekkev.*"

An incomprehensible electronic buzz rattles her sensors but she doesn't care. *Pursue me, if you can.*

She flees toward the only place she knows, the third planet of nine circling a five magnitude star.

Time extends into lapses, lapses into limbos and limbos into long stretches of vigilance. In the end, they give way to sleep and sleep to dreams, staccato memories coughed up from the quicksand of her tired mind.

Images of children dance across her subconscious, their voices tinkle with song as they run through fields of green, under a canopy of blue sky, tossing a red ball high into the air.

The dream children dissolve into dream clouds, slow condensations tumbling through dream space. The clouds birth stars, threading them with lifeless beads on elliptical strings. Then the dream stars grow old, consume their progeny and collapse, sparking bright flashes in the darkness of her slumber.

I am a mother.

She weeps as the children sing.

***

A4-Ni stood at the center of John's tent. Her appendages trembled with the fear of sudden knowing. *If I am a universal constructor, a Shepherd. Who or what is the Shepherd, who pursued me all these years, the one I recently attacked, the one who fled with the synthetic Mia on board? Could it be me?*

But that was impossible. Physically, she couldn't be coincident at the same place and time. *Could future humans have built another Shepherd?* That made more sense but compounded the problem.

She returned to the guardian and instructed it to return to the projection of future humans. The guardian reset and offered her a choice of drastically truncated scenarios. A4-Ni scanned for other scenarios but they all ended abruptly. Presumably, future humans also ended abruptly, which left some doubt as to whether they would have had time to construct a second Shepherd.

Taking another approach, she requested to see the Shepherd's entire world line. The guardian dutifully showed the Shepherd emerging from around the Cygnus black hole four million years ago. It showed her, a spidery being attack and steal the guardian with its genetic code.

She knew all this but it confirmed that there was indeed a second Shepherd besides herself. Impatiently, she skipped over the intervening four million years to the recent past. She stopped there and eased forward. The guardian projected the Shepherd's flight as he rose from the pond with Mia on board. It showed A4-Ni dropping away before the Shepherd shot into space. It showed the Shepherd travel half the distance to the Cygnus black hole, then the projection terminated.

A4-Ni backed up in time, then moved forward again more slowly, requesting more detail. The Shepherd resumed its outward flight, then with a flash of light, he disappeared. The Shepherd had come to a catastrophic end. Her attempt to kill the Shepherd must have succeeded, although the final denouement was somewhat delayed.

She cringed. *We had the same mission.* Filled with remorse, she lingered on the thought. *What now? Am I to fly into space? I can't. Not anymore.*

Like some barren old woman, she had long ago become comfortable with her life on Earth. She functioned well, never missing until now her extended abilities that once were meant to carry her and a genome to the stars.

She flipped the guardian to her world line and slid the controls forward.

The device scanned and returned a number of future scenarios. *So many choices. Why now?* She picked the strongest scenario. It terminated so abruptly she did not have time to see any detail. She stared at the pattern, stunned. Presumably, she had died.

Recovering her composure, and without belaboring why she died on the strongest scenario, she went to the second strongest scenario, then to the next and the next. Same result. All her future scenarios terminated.

How can this be? Now that the Shepherd was gone, she had no known enemies who could kill her in such a short time. She picked one of the scenarios at random and instructed the guardian to enlarge the interval.

***

I see A4-Ni grimace in pain. Rotting animal corpses, elephants, giraffes, zebras loom nearby. Her skin is blackened, cracked. Pink wounds suppurate, releasing to the sand the fluids of her body. It has human form but is unrecognizable.

"I must return to camp," she says to John.

She tries to stand but a leg detaches from her body, toppling her sideways. Groveling on the ground, her hand rolls free at the wrist. Then her head from her neck. Slowly the parts dissolve to be soaked up by the dry sand. With the death of central control, her molecules each go their own way. Ashes to ashes, dust to dust.

***

Reflexively, A4-Ni turned away, as though the motion would remove the sight from her vision but the horror remained. She scanned the other scenarios the guardian offered but they all ended similarly, some even more gruesomely. If she had died, then what was to happen to *Gilomir's* genome? He could not survive in humans without her.

Near the terminus of one of her scenarios, she detected the branching aura of *Gilomir*. She asked the guardian to home in on the intersection and follow his world line.

After a blur, the guardian projected a random pattern of dots indicating the end to the branching world line. She reversed the motion, then stopped and moved forward. The guardian showed the Shepherd carrying *Gilomir* into orbit around a black hole. *The Shepherd? Or another Shepherd?* Amazed at this turn of events, she examined the projected Shepherd in detail. *Gilomir's* genome was on board, alone, extricated from encumbering hominid DNA. No guardian.

What Shepherd is this? She backed up and the explanation became clear. She saw herself building a replica of the Shepherd, following instructions provided by the guardian. *When?* She examined the time scale. Tonight. She would expend all her energy building the Shepherd and die in a matter of hours.

Frantically, she tried to find another scenario but she always died, and the only safe exit for the genome was in the Shepherd she would build. *None of this makes sense. Why would I build a Shepherd?*

She shook her mangy head and tried to focus her thinking. Then she understood. Since she had failed to perform her original mission, then compounded that failure by terminating the Shepherd that carried Mia, it seemed reasonable that she retained an obligation to create a new Shepherd and see him on his way with *Gilomir* on board.

The truth was too much to bear alone. She shuffled over to John. He lay fast asleep but she didn't want him, she wanted *Gilomir*. "*Help me.*"

What is it? Then *Gilomir* seemed to know. *You've been using the guardian.*

"*I could not resist. The infernal device has shown me a perverse future.*"

The scenarios are but probabilities. You lack the skill to differentiate between them.

"*If all the scenarios are the same, they amount to more than probabilities. They become certainties.*"

This causes you concern?

"*I am a Shepherd,*" A4-Ni said. "*You are a human genome from the future. Everything that has happened, everything I've done has been a big mistake.*"

Gilomir laughed. *Is that what the guardian showed you?*

"*Future humans use the guardian to build me and another Shepherd. When they completed the Shepherd they must have put the guardian on board.*

He had it when I encountered him four-million years ago and stole it from him. But we both had the same mission."

You seemed to have learned a lot in the short time you've spent with the guardian.

"Fortunately, or unfortunately, the guardian doesn't waste much time telling its tales."

Then you should stay away from it.

"The truth is diabolical. It showed that my attack on the Shepherd carrying Mia was a mortal one. I killed him. He terminated in a fiery crash soon after leaving here. I didn't know who he was. How could I? Now, if I conform to the guardian's projections, I'm destined to die within hours. I will expend all of my remaining energy to build a new Shepherd. I will obtain John's DNA, separate your genome from it and place you on board."

I can't fault you for what you intend to do. Certainly you are the only one who knows how to extricate me from hominid DNA. Besides, it seems a way for you to pay for your transgression. I will be free. But how will you build a Shepherd?

A4-Ni laughed nervously. *"The guardian will guide me."*

I still detect some confusion.

"What do you mean? Everything is clear."

If future humans place the guardian on the Shepherd they build, and he travels to the past to become, shall I say, the old Shepherd, the one you steal the guardian from, then who makes the guardian?

A4-Ni gazed stupidly. *"I don't see the problem."*

You say the guardian you now hold makes its way to the future to be used by future humans. That closes a loop. The guardian has no beginning or end.

"But... I... The guardian was so explicit." A4-Ni grasped the sphere, posed her question and squeezed it impatiently for an answer. After a moment she heaved a sigh of relief. *"There is no paradox. I misinterpreted the strength of a world line. Future humans do not place the guardian on the Shepherd. In fact, the Shepherd is the one who creates the guardian, mid-flight, as it were, and records the means of his construction in it. So the loop you speak of remains open. All of this confusion could have been avoided if only I had used the guardian sooner."*

A pity you didn't. Four million years is a long time to live a mistake.

Annoyed, A4-Ni broke her link with *Gilomir*. If he couldn't show any more enthusiasm for what she was about to do, then she didn't want to talk to him. Gripping the guardian, she left the tent. A warm breeze drifted through the quiet camp. No one stirred. She looked at the familiar surroundings, steeling herself for the task ahead. She had a purpose to fulfill. A new Shepherd would be built, and the materials she needed could be found in the desert.

Chapter Twenty

John stumbled out of his tent, squinting at the sun already high in the eastern sky. He rubbed his eyes, then ran a hand over the rough stubble on his chin. He glanced at his wrinkled clothes. The memory of the night before flooded back. Mia gone. His attempt at suicide. The constable. Nightmarish dreams.

But the loss of Mia lingered like a dull haze over all his other thoughts. He hadn't realized how much she meant to him. And now her loss. Another loss to chalk up with all the other losses he had suffered. This one hurt all the more. He had fought his way back only to be beaten down again. The voice, A4-Ni, had stepped in and ruined his life. What was the use of trying? Why struggle to come to grips with all of this only to be defeated by something he couldn't conquer?

He went directly to the mess tent and through it to the liquor cupboard on the other side. He ignored the agitated stare of the cook-steward.

John leaned forward and was about to grab a fresh bottle of Scotch, when Kamau clumped across the wooden floor. "You look terrible."

"Thanks." John wished this day had not dawned. No, that was not enough. He wished it would end soon. He stood, leaving the bottle on the shelf.

"Rough night?" Kamau asked, "at least what was left of it?"

"I think I slept. I dreamt a lot. I have the clearest memory that A4-Ni was in my tent."

"I hope your dreams don't start coming true."

John shook his head. "The dream was so clear."

"Rumors are all over camp that you're going crazy. They say it's Watombo's curse."

"I might be going crazy but I doubt it's the curse." He reached for the bottle again.

"I don't think that is going to help."

"What do you know?"

"Believe me, I know," Kamau said. "I thought I'd drive out and take a look at what's left of the pond. You want to come?"

John gazed off toward the desert. "I'm going to hang around camp. Maybe take a walk in the desert."

"I don't know whether to tell you to come or let you work this out on your own."

"I need some time. I miss her a lot."

"I understand. Go think about it all but no booze."

John didn't like the *no booze* part but Kamau was right, again.

"And stay on the trails. Take your rifle. You never know if that guardian's prediction was correct." Kamau got into the Land Rover and started to drive away, then stopped and backed up. He pulled the police radio off his belt. "Here, take this. You might need it."

"No, you keep it."

Kamau looked frustrated but re-clipped the radio to his belt. He wheeled the Land Rover out of camp.

John trudged inside the mess and drank a cup of coffee. The cook-steward hovered nervously. John didn't talk to him, and could see the cook-steward was relieved when John picked up a slice of bread and left. He stopped at his tent for a canteen and his rifle, then headed into the desert.

He hiked north along the eroded side of the plateau. The steep escarpment towered above him on his right. After a kilometer, the formation ended and gave way to the east where the trail rounded to an overlook above the distant lake.

John picked a large rock and sat to rest. He took a long drink of water from the canteen. The water was already warm but at least it was wet.

A flock of vultures circled about half a kilometer to the west. He couldn't see what attracted them but their sheer numbers surprised him.

Curious, he headed for the spot, pushing his way through clumps of cactus and thorny bushes that forced him to detour often and made the trek longer than he had anticipated.

As he neared the area beneath the birds, an odor of freshly butchered meat hung in the air. Then the sickening stench of sun-baked carrion hit him like a physical blow. He crested a scrub-covered rise and looked onto a scene of devastation. Turning his head to the side, he retched. He wiped his mouth with the back of his hand and forced himself to look again.

For fifty meters in all directions lay the carcasses of every imaginable desert beast. Large animals, elephants, camels, and zebras mixed with hundreds of smaller carcasses of antelope, monkeys and even rats. They radiated in concentric circles from a smooth, round object at their center.

John put a handkerchief to his nose and picked his way through the desolation toward the center. Some of the vultures landed. He waved his rifle to shoo them away. They broke off from their feeding, hopped out of the way, then returned to the feast once he passed. *No hyenas?* But they had indeed come, if only to join the dead. Most of the flesh had been stripped from the skeletons. He could not tell whether the birds had picked the carcasses clean or if another force was at work.

As he neared the central object, a pinging went off in his mind. A memory knocked, demanding recognition. Then it burst forth. The object looked like the spaceship that had abducted Mia. He brought up his rifle not knowing what to expect.

Parts of the object appeared unfinished. Narrow fleshy passageways led, like fresh wounds, into the interior. Inside walls glistened pink and moist. With the muzzle of his gun, he prodded the outer surface. It depressed, like the hide of a water buffalo.

Has Mia returned?

"Mia!" he shouted then gagged as he sucked the odor into his lungs. He looked around and called again. No response.

A movement at the edge of the object caught his attention. With rifle raised, he stepped around the domed construction.

A shambling form looked up from the antelope carcass it carried. A hideous sight, the shape raised a ropey appendage in what seemed a defensive greeting.

"*I won't hurt you.*" The form projected a thought into his mind.

He froze and stared, his knees weak. He had never been more certain of anything in his life. He was face-to-face with A4-Ni.

"Please, don't shoot me," she said.

He took a wobbly step backward. Her switch to real phonics confused him. It's seductive pitch seemed irresistible. "I wasn't dreaming."

"What you have learned of me is not true." When he said nothing, A4-Ni rushed on. "You have no reason to fear me."

"What have you done with Mia?"

"I have not harmed Mia."

"Then where is she."

"I don't know."

"Then what is that...thing doing here?"

The ropey haystack turned to regard the circular object, though no eyes were apparent. "This is not the craft you saw leaving with Mia. I can explain."

A white panic seared John's brain. "I've had enough of your lies." He pulled the trigger.

The gunshot kicked the rifle hard against his shoulder.

The bullet, a 45 caliber Nitro Express pierced the dead antelope and slammed through A4-Ni. She staggered back but didn't fall.

That would have dropped a rhino in its tracks.

A dark liquid oozed from A4-Ni's multifaceted exterior. The flow quickly stemmed, as though she had reconstituted herself. She struggled to remain upright. "You cannot kill me."

Was that a statement or an admonition? "We'll see about that." He re-cocked and aimed.

But A4-Ni had disappeared around the object, leaving nothing to shoot at.

With unfocused vision, John turned to run, only to stumble over a carcass. He jumped to his feet and thrashed his way back through the scarred landscape to the trail.

"*Wait*," A4-Ni sensed, weaker than before.

He was not about to stop. He held no doubt that what he had seen was A4-Ni. She must have intercepted Mia's spaceship and forced it back. Tears filled his eyes, blurring his vision. A4-Ni had killed again. Mia was dead.

The ache in his heart fermented, then exploded into rage. He reached the edge of camp, raced pell-mell through the perimeter fence and lunged for his tent.

"*Masahib*." The cook-steward stepped out of the mess tent and stood staring. "Is everything all right?"

John paid no attention. He staggered into his tent and stood for a moment, his chest heaving, his heart pounding. Then he reversed the rifle barrel into his mouth, reached long, and shoved the trigger with his thumb.

***

That was stupid. A4-Ni supposed she should have counted herself lucky the antelope had absorbed some of the force of the bullet. As her body worked overtime to repair the damage, she charged across the desert indifferent to the sharp rocks and thorns. She must hurry. She sensed the tension build on the trigger spring of John's rifle.

She burst through the marsh grass fence, sending it flying in a cloud of fragmented reeds, and bore down on his tent.

The cook-steward screamed in horror.

No time to worry about him but enough time to stop John. She reached out with inhuman speed and caught the hammer as it descended toward the bullet casing.

John stared, terrified.

A4-Ni towered over him, limbs a jingle. Her alien sweat plopped on the floor, raising a smell like burnt flesh. "Please. I must talk to you."

John jerked the rifle away from her.

She extended a limb, brushing the rifle upward as John squeezed off a wild shot that put a neat hole in the tent ceiling.

"Be reasonable," A4-Ni pushed the rifle out of his reach.

John lunged for the sharp dental pick on the fossil table.

She drew it away from his grasp.

He grabbed a can of poisonous Bedacryl, tore off the lid and had the vessel at his mouth before she cast it from his grip. The container crashed to the floor, loosing a dark stain.

For the moment, John seemed to have run out of ways to kill himself. "Leave me alone!" He backed up hard against his desk.

"Calm down." A4-Ni countered, as he feinted toward the opening.

"What do you want?"

"I mean no harm. Your continued good health would please me."

"Why? So you can carve me up to extract your precious genome like you've carved up everyone else who got in your way?"

"Why would I do such a thing?" *And why the repulsion?* Then realization dawned. "I'm sorry. You must find my appearance offensive."

John lunged for the rifle.

A4-Ni got there first but left a way open to the outside.

John leapt past her and out of the tent. He ran for the plateau.

"Where are you going?" Then she understood. "Your death. It's only a probability."

***

So much to do, so little time. Her indiscretion, letting John see her, had already proved to be a false economy.

Her first priority must be to extract *Gilomir* from him. Given his unstable frame of mind, she would have to act quickly. This latest encounter had obviously tipped him over the edge. She couldn't let him take his life now, when she was so close to setting everything right.

Confronting him again the way she looked would not serve her purpose, and retreating to her normal shimmering self would take too much energy. She must find a more agreeable form, an economic form. *Mia.*

A4-Ni regretted not having thought of it sooner. Doing so would have saved her the energy she would now have to expend to make the transformation.

Her grotesque shape lost coherence. She melted to the floor. Though the change would incapacitate her for a while, she would arise, phoenix-like, as Mia. She sensed outward and located John as he struggled up the escarpment. Still time. Mia would be slower than other forms but lent A4-Ni other advantages. She'd have to cope with the limitations and exploit the positives.

"Damn him." He was proving to be more difficult than she had anticipated. She struggled to consolidate her transformation. The seconds dragged. *Hurry up. Hurry up.*

The Land Rover careened into camp and skidded to a stop by the mess tent.

With her transformation nearly complete, A4-Ni stepped to the farthest recess of John's tent where she was less likely to be immediately seen by someone entering.

Kamau leapt out of the vehicle. "Is Watombo here?" he yelled at the slack-jawed cook-steward.

"Watombo? He no be here."

"The constable radioed that Watombo was headed this way." Kamau glanced around. "Where's the *Masahib*?"

"He gone." The cook-steward pointed toward the escarpment. "Up there."

Kamau peered at the breached perimeter. "What happened here?"

"The *Masahib* run from desert and go into his tent. Then something come after him. It be like wind. I scream." The cook-steward paused to catch his breath. "I hear shouting from tent, then *Masahib*, he come out. Look like he see ghost. He run. It be quiet now. I think something still be in tent."

"Did the *Masahib* take his rifle?"

"No, *Bosi*, he be in big hurry, like he be on fire."

A4-Ni put the finishing touches on her transformation and composed herself.

"Something be damned. I need that rifle." Kamau approached the tent and stopped at the entrance. He peered into the gloom. "Who's there?"

A4-Ni didn't want him to discover her unexpectedly. Better to give him some warning that she was there. "It is me, Mia. John was just here." She pitched her voice plaintively. She sensed his immediate reaction--Why was Mia here? She'd gone.

Kamau stepped into the tent. He glanced at the upturned chair, the papers scattered from the desk to the floor, the spilt Bedacryl. His gaze rested on her, where she stood in a far corner.

"Where's your hair?"

A4-Ni cringed inwardly. She must be weakening to be so stupid to forget that Mia had hair the last time Kamau saw her.

"I--"

"Cut the crap. I thought you left?" He took a step toward the rifle, which lay on the floor closer to him than to her.

"I did." A4-Ni glanced at the rifle. As Mia, she'd never be able to beat him to it. "I have come back."

"So I see." Kamau lunged and grasped the rifle.

A4-Ni remained still, resigned.

Kamau held the rifle at his hip, the barrel leveled at her abdomen.

"John is in great danger." She took a step toward Kamau.

"That's far enough, lady."

"There's no time. John is going to meet the lion as foretold by the guardian."

"That's bullshit." Kamau backed up.

"Put the gun down. I can help you more than you can imagine." A4-Ni sensed into his mind. She felt his strength as he resisted her probing.

"Get out of my head." His eyes rolled in their sockets. His head twitched uncontrollably.

"Let me help you." She probed deeper, reaching for a control point.

He pulled the trigger.

The bullet tore through her stomach, knocking her against the cot. It tilted and dumped her onto the wooden floor. She suppressed a cry, clutching her wound. Blood oozed between her fingers. Pain snaked through her body.

"You are making a mistake," she whispered through clenched teeth. Pushing the pain aside, she tried once more to reach for his control point.

The end of the gun puffed white, followed by a shattering explosion.

The projectile, a sharp, pointed slug, cleared the smoke from the rifle's muzzle. The slug was easy to see. It bore straight for her head and smacked her dead center between the eyes. The force of the impact snapped her head back, blowing out the back of her skull and cracking her neck. She dropped like a rag doll against the side of the tent, landed in a sitting position, then sagged sideways. Vitality slipped from her mangled body.

Kamau stepped around the cot. He touched his hand to her neck, feeling for a pulse. "Good riddance."

As he left the tent, she sensed conflict. He had seen Mia, John's lover, and he had shot her thinking she was A4-Ni. But could he be sure he had done the right thing?

Poor Kamau, A4-Ni thought. *Make sure you take the rifle.* He did, as his thoughts became laced with the satisfaction that he had killed the witch. Then they turned to concern for John.

Kamau slung the rifle across his chest and ran to the cook-steward. "I'm going after the *Masahib*. The witch has returned. She lies dead in the tent. If you know what's good for you, you'll stay clear."

The cook-steward's head bobbed up and down.

Kamau ran for the Land Rover. He slapped the hood and looked toward the escarpment.

A4-Ni followed his every movement. *Fool. You can't use the Land Rover on the plateau.* Darkness closed in on her. What next? The guardian hadn't been explicit.

From somewhere deep within her being, an instinct for survival struggled into her consciousness. Though her reincarnation of Mia was as good as dead, A4-Ni began the process of reconstruction. She was not done yet with this charade but it was becoming a nuisance and was costing her inordinate amounts of energy.

She did not bother to replace or clean Mia's blood-soaked clothing. Better to expend the energy getting her head back in place and her body closed, then herself up the trail ahead of John and Kamau to intercept the impending attack.

With her guts secured and the pieces of her skull reconstructed and recovered plus some hair, she staggered out of the tent.

The cook-steward peeked out of the mess tent, took one look and ran, screaming.

She scanned the plateau. Kamau struggled up the trail. Sensing ahead, she located John already on top of the plateau and headed north. He had heard the gunshots but chose to ignore them. *Are you so intent on dying?*

If she took a path to the north of both of them, she could climb the escarpment and intercept John before Kamau reached him.

Then she saw the lion. She would have to hurry.

Chapter Twenty-one

Staring straight ahead, John lurched forward, a forced death march. The landscape was bare and rocky, like he had seen in the guardian's vision. The gunshots from the camp could have meant any number of things, none of which had any bearing on what he intended to do.

Gravel crunched ahead and to one side. He cringed, steeling himself, fully expecting the lion attack. Instead, Mia clambered over a pile of loose rock, tripped in her haste and slid onto the path ten meters in front of him.

"Mia!" *Dear God, what is she doing here?*

She waved to him, struggling to her feet.

A sharp scrape sounded behind him. John spun around.

Kamau ran toward him, his face contorted with confusion. "Son of a bitch!" He raised the rifle, aimed at Mia and fired.

The bullet whizzed centimeters past John's head, the gunshot reverberating inside his skull. He fell to his knees, cupping his hands over his ringing ears.

Mia convulsed. Her shoulder wrenched. The shot twisted her sideways, sprawling her on the path. A crimson stain flooded her shirt. She looked surprised, maybe disappointed. She eased forward and fell on her face, then rose and began a slow crawl toward him.

"What the fuck! You shot Mia!"

Kamau re-cocked the rifle and raised it for another shot.

John lunged. He hit the rifle with an uppercut.

The shot went wild.

"Are you insane!" he screamed.

"She be dead. She be witch." His command of English degenerated.

John slammed into him, grabbed the rifle with both hands and jerked. "Give it to me!"

Kamau released the rifle in disgust. "Take it. You are a fool." He gave John a hard look, then turned and in a stumbling run, headed south along the trail.

The lion padded softly, accelerating and launched what must have been three hundred kilograms of taught muscle. A flash of tawny yellow, sparkling canines, claws like curved daggers.

John called a warning.

Kamau twisted, his mouth a grotesque gape. He raised his arms across his face.

The charge smashed him flat on his back. The skin across his chest split open like a sack of torn grain.

The lion wheeled and lunged, mouth open, head cocked. His jaws closed easing spike long teeth into Kamau's neck.

The scream in his throat cut short. With a popping crack, his neck broke, his death cry reduced to a bubbling gargle of blood that got no farther than his torn larynx. He hung limp in the lion's jaws.

John fumbled with the rifle, raised it and fired.

The lion staggered. The bullet had hit its lower neck, not a killing shot.

The beast stood over Kamau, legs spread wide, its breath wheezing through flared nostrils in a cadence matched by a rise and fall of whiskers.

John re-cocked the rifle, put it to his shoulder and fired again.

The shot tore into the lion's chest.

It stiffened, and with Kamau still clenched tight, fell forward on top of him.

John dropped the rifle and rushed to Kamau's side. With all his strength he pushed at the dead lion and managed to roll it off Kamau.

John dared to hope his friend was still alive. "Can you hear me?" He lifted Kamau in his arms. Blood spurted from a torn artery in his neck. "Hang on. I'll get you out of here."

Kamau's eyes lay opened in a blank stare. A frothy red blob bubbled from his mouth. His lungs worked to push air to form words but none issued from his mouth. His head lolled to one side, his neck at an impossible angle.

John leaned close and put his hand to Kamau's mouth, checking for his breath. None. He fought back tears, looking skyward. "Goddamn you." He wiped his forehead with the back of his hand, still bloodied, then rubbed his shorts. The heat and the stench of blood made him nauseous. He stood, swaying. *More death. When will it end?*

Mia had ceased to crawl and lay, face down on the sandy trail in a dark pool of blood. Her arms and legs twisted, looking like a puppet whose strings had all been cut at once and left to fall.

He stumbled to her side and dropped to his knees. "My God, don't you die, too."

Her breath was shallow, gasping, like hiccups.

"I'll get you back to camp," he whispered in her ear. He'd need the rifle and the radio clipped to Kamau's belt. He eased Mia down and returned to Kamau, who lay forlorn in a pool of blood-soaked sand. John knelt beside him, picked up the rifle and slung it across his chest. Choking back emotion, he straightened Kamau's arms at his side. "Rest easy dear friend."

The police radio on Kamau's belt crackled with static, then went silent.

John slipped it off. He pressed transmit. "Anyone. This is John Lohner. Lion attack. One dead. One wounded. Need immediate assistance. Over."

Nothing.

Mia moaned behind him.

Frustrated, he clipped the radio to his belt and hurried to her. He put one arm beneath her knees and the other under her head to lift her. She wasn't heavy but he still had a long way to go back to camp.

"Don't die," he muttered half to himself, half to the emptiness around him. "I thought you had left. Where have you been?"

He staggered, shifting her in his arms, trying to lighten his burden. Carrying her for a kilometer down the plateau back to camp was going to take some doing. Every once in awhile he checked over his shoulder. Lions often hunted in pairs.

***

The sun edged toward the horizon. Shafts of orange light cast long shadows across the sand. The familiar patterns comforted him. No matter what happened to man and beast, the heavens kept to their routine.

The muscles of his back began to seize. With each step they protested the strain he put on them. He stopped to rest.

After easing Mia onto the flat rock, he held her in a sitting position while he brushed the ground free of loose pebbles before tilting her onto her back.

The blood on her shirt had dried. He pulled open the torn garment and examined the claw marks on her chest. The bullet wound ran red with blood, a steady welling, not a good sign. *Where are your remarkable recuperative powers?*

"Hang on. I'll get you back to the camp and we'll get the hell out of here."

He felt for her pulse and found it strong and regular. At his touch, her eyelids fluttered open.

She stared, as though trying to remember where she was. Then she focused on him.

He leaned closer. "How do you feel?"

"Tired."

"We're almost there."

"Where is Kamau?"

"You don't know?" She must have blacked out. "He's dead. The lion killed him."

Mia coughed and grimaced. "I'm sorry it happened this way."

"But I was the one who was supposed to die."

"The guardian projects probabilities." Mia closed her eyes.

"So you said. Don't try to talk. Rest."

Mia winced. "I am near death."

"Can't you heal yourself?"

"The wound is grave. I have managed to stem the hemorrhaging temporarily. You have to get me to the Shepherd."

Something wasn't making sense. "What happened to him?"

"He is not who you think he is."

"I thought he was your leader."

She reached up and gripped his arm. "The Shepherd is the *spaceship*."

"He...he's not a person?"

"I told you we colonized using a machine. The Shepherd is artificially intelligent. A universal constructor."

It made sense. Everything fell into place all at once. But these universal constructors were coming out of the woodwork. "And what are you?"

For a brief moment, she looked serene. "I am his product. Now I belong to you."

Though he half expected the answer, John's mind reeled. He had to back step recent events in his life and reset them. Not unlike what the guardian probably did all the time, he thought distractedly. But she had returned. He pulled her to him. "I don't care what you are, you're here."

Mia nodded painfully, the slightest smile lingering on her lips. "You've been running from A4-Ni."

"I saw her." He had the uncanny feeling A4-Ni could be close and listening.

"Then you tried to kill yourself?" She looked at him sympathetically.

"You know?"

"Yes. Why kill yourself?"

"I wanted to avenge Diane, my mother."

"I don't think A4-Ni will harm you, anymore."

"How can you of all people say that?"

Mia grimaced. "A4-Ni is dead."

"Where?"

"Back in your tent."

"I don't understand. How could she die? Who killed her?"

Mia drew the back of her hand across her mouth and smeared blood on her cheek. "From the time she attacked the Shepherd she was on a path of her own destruction. She could not recover enough energy to survive. Your shot weakened her further. Kamau finished her off."

"I still don't understand but you should rest."

Mia shook her head, forcing herself to speak. "No. I saw everything when you discovered her at the Shepherd. She was repairing the parts she had damaged. She wanted to use it for her own purposes. After you shot her, I escaped. I ran to your tent looking for you…" Mia convulsed in a coughing fit. Blood flecked her lips. "--A4-Ni was there. She grabbed me. Kamau came in. He saw me struggling with A4-Ni and thought that she and I were one and the same."

"He let his superstitions get the better of him."

"No, he acted reasonably from his point of view. He shot A4-Ni, not once but twice. I was lucky he didn't hit me. A4-Ni fell on top of me. By the time I recovered, Kamau had left...to come here...to save you from the lion."

John shook his head in disbelief. Poor Kamau. He had stepped up again when John needed him and paid with his life. "I don't think I can carry you all the way to the Shepherd. We'll have to go to camp first to get the Land Rover."

When she didn't answer, John feared she was weakening. He stroked her cheek.

She opened her eyes briefly. "Go." Then she seemed to slip back into unconsciousness.

He eased his arms under her, picked her up and resumed his trek to camp. He debated leaving the rifle to lighten his load but thought better of it.

The sound of loose gravel drifted over the cliff edge followed by the voices of Bandele and Omari, talking to each other as they picked their way up the trail in the deepening twilight. He waited until they cleared the top of the plateau.

"*Masahib*," Bandele said, startled, as his head poked over the top.

"Who is it?" Omari asked, still out of sight.

Bandele turned and spoke in a harsh whisper. "The *Masahib*. The witch is with him."

John ignored the comment. "Mia is hurt. Help me."

"We hear shots," Bandele said.

"A lion attacked us." John felt his voice dry, ragged. "Kamau is dead. Back there. I need help carrying Mia to camp."

Both men were now on top of the plateau. They looked at each other, then at Mia. Neither one had any intention of touching her.

"We cannot help you, *Masahib*," Bandele said.

After hesitating, they stepped around John and ran along the trail in the direction of the attack.

"Come back here!" John yelled. Too much *juju* was associated with Mia now. Watombo had spread his lies well.

John placed his arms under her still form and lifted, wincing as he did so. At the edge of the plateau, he sat and put his feet over the edge. The lights had come on in the camp below. Marshalling the last of his strength, he half slid, half stepped down the steep slope.

After reaching the bottom, he stopped to rest. The final distance crossed level ground and would be easier. Though Mia's face was smeared with dried blood, she looked serene. Did she know what was happening and didn't care? Or did she realize what was happening and knew that events were beyond her control?

Bandele and the guard returned along a path farther north. Though he could see them, they did not see him crouched in the dark. The outlines of their two bodies with that of Kamau slung in-between were silhouetted against the dying light. Speaking rapidly to each other, as if to keep up their courage, they hurried toward the camp.

John's anger flashed. His world seemed to be falling apart. But he no longer cared. He had Mia. That was all that mattered. He pushed his rifle back and lifted her. "We're almost there," he whispered.

"Leave me here."

He was surprised she answered. "Don't be ridiculous."

"There will be trouble in camp."

***

Torches snapped orange flame, giving off black, oily smoke. The sickening stench of burnt fat laced with truck grease hung in the humid air. To John, the gathered laborers all looked identical, their faces contorted with mindless anger and fear. Some thumped their chests, raising their voices in ululations for the dead. Others raised their hands in anguish, their cheeks streaked with tears. Kamau's mangled corpse lay at their feet.

John pushed his way through the marsh grass perimeter, then glanced up in horror. The Land Rover and the Ford half-ton lay off to one side engulfed in flame.

The crowd hushed.

He put his head close to Mia's. "Don't say a word."

Omari stepped forward, shouting, pumping his rifle above his head. With growing agitation, Bandele and the others swarmed behind the guard, gesturing, shouting obscenities. They dragged on Kamau's body and pushed it in front of John, forcing it to flop forward. They pointed to the lifeless form, then to Mia, implying a link between Kamau's death and her reappearance.

One man rushed forward, grabbed Mia by the arm and pulled.

"Help me." Rising fear put a tremor into her voice.

John released her and un-slung his rifle. In one smooth motion, he brought it up to his shoulder and fired a shot over the man's head.

The thunderous report brought everyone to a standstill. The man let loose of Mia and backed into the crowd.

She sagged to the ground.

"That's enough!" John leveled the rifle.

Omari cocked his rifle, held it out in front of him in an awkward firing position and pulled the trigger. The shot went wide.

As Omari pulled back the bolt to ready another shot, John swung his rifle across and fired.

The bullet caught the guard in the chest. He stumbled, discharging his rifle into the air, and fell on his back.

Dear God, I've killed him. Still in shock, John re-cocked but held the rifle at rest, not wanting to incite the crowd further. "That didn't have to happen. Go back to your quarters."

Mia clutched his legs.

Bandele stepped to the forefront. "We respected you, *Masahib* but the witch put spell on you. Give her to us." He motioned to Kamau and the dead Omari. "These men ask for revenge."

"You aren't going to avenge anyone." John drifted the muzzle of his rifle toward Bandele. "Step back, or I'll kill you."

"We be many." Bandele's eye's rolled like glass beads in his head belying the bravado he projected.

"There's been enough death," John said. "Don't make matters worse. I'm going to call the constable."

"What he do?" Bandele gestured at the corpses. "He no help these men."

John waited. Since he had just shot someone he supposed he held some advantage having demonstrated his resolve. Not that he was proud of killing Omari. *Another death*. How he hated what he was being forced to do.

The men shifted, undecided. Wide eyes in sweat-slickened faces caught the reflected light.

"Keep her." Bandele spat on the ground in Mia's direction. "This no be the end."

He pushed his way through the crowd, heading for the laborers' quarters. The rest of the laborers followed. By the time they neared the edge of the camp their chatter had risen to an angry growl.

"Can you hear me?" John whispered.

Mia tried to speak.

He leaned closer. "What is it?"

"My genome..." Her wounds had opened again. Blood flowed freely from her shoulder.

She's delirious. "What are you talking about?"

She looked at the bodies. "Two dead because of me."

"It's not your fault. Kamau tried to help us. Omari invited his own death."

John pulled the police radio from his belt. He turned up the gain and pushed transmit. "This is John Lohner! Does anybody hear me?" His hand shook. He was at the edge of his control. He let off the key and waited. Seconds passed.

The radio crackled.

"Moye here." His voice was flat, professional. "Since you have the radio, I assume Kamau gave you the message about Watombo."

"No. Listen to me. I don't know anything about Watombo." John wiped his mouth with the back of his hand. *Calm down*. "We've had trouble. Kamau's dead. A lion attack. Mia has returned and is wounded. I've lost control of the men at camp. One is dead. I need help. Now!" Silence. "Did you fucking hear me?"

"I understand Kamau and one laborer are dead," the constable replied. "Are you hurt?"

"No, Goddamn it! I don't know how long these men will leave me alone. What...what did you say about Watombo?"

"He was spotted earlier today, heading your way. I'm coming out there. Can you hang on for the next thirty minutes?"

"God, I hope so."

Chapter Twenty-two

With Mia in his arms, John kicked back the entrance flap and staggered into his tent. He frowned at the disarray before him. Besides the can of spilt Bedacryl on the floor, a darker stain of what looked like blood had pooled from behind the overturned cot. The back wall of the tent was torn and bloodstained.

Looks like a battle royal erupted after I left.

He righted the cot with his foot, slid it to a dry corner and laid Mia on it. Then he stepped to the washbasin to pour some water.

She pulled at her blood soaked shirt.

"Wait a minute. Let me help you with that." He fumbled to open the last two buttons on her shirt. "Lie back and rest. I'll get you cleaned up."

He wet a towel and pressed it to her wound. Though blood had coagulated around the edges, the wound remained raw. The destruction to her body was massive. Some regeneration seemed to have taken hold. Here and there, slabs of new skin blotched her body.

"The wound has closed here, and there but the reconstructions aren't human. Can't you heal?"

"Believe me, I'm trying. But not much is happening and when it does I have no control. My life force is slipping away. I can't stop it." Clutching his arm she struggled to rise. A smile twitched at the corners of her mouth.

"What's so humorous?" he asked.

"This must be some kind of divine retribution for my meddling." She winced with pain. "God, this hurts."

"What are you talking about. You haven't meddled. If anything you've tried to set things right."

"A4-Ni let your mother die and killed your Diane. Now I'm dying. Life seems so full of inconsistencies. I suppose if I die it would only be justice."

"You're talking nonsense."

"I'm sorry for what I've put you through."

"You haven't put me through anything. Nothing else matters, now. You are here."

"No, it does matter. I have so much to tell you that you won't understand." She reached and brushed her hand across his temple removing flecks of dried blood and dirt. When she pulled back, her face was tear-streaked. "Human emotions, always fouling things up."

"Not always. I feel them, too. And I can't bear to lose you again."

The throbbing generators coughed to silence.

John looked to the tent entrance. The camp beyond had plunged into darkness. He walked over to the opening and peered out. "No one refueled the generators."

He struck a match and lit the lantern. The wick flared, throwing a harsh light around the interior of the tent.

"Please, leave it off," Mia said.

He turned the valve. The flame dimmed. He stumbled as he felt his way in the gloom to her side.

"I like the dark." She took his hand.

"You've got to tell me what's going on. You seem different." As he stood before her, he reached out and touched her head, then her shoulder. "What happened after the spaceship took off? Did it crash? Did A4-Ni attack you again?"

"Please don't pursue this questioning." In the reduced light from the lantern, she gazed at him blankly. "It will give you nothing. I love you. That should be enough. You will never comprehend all of what I am or what my motives are."

"That's not fair. Though I've had trouble understanding, I've never questioned your motives. And along the way, I've fallen in love with you. What am I to do about that?"

"Hold on to those feelings." She reached up and took his hand. "Come, sit with me."

He felt an odd twinge in his head, a probing. It clarified itself. Mia. "What are you doing?"

Feelings surged through him, a deep longing, an agony of loss brought on by her departure, exhilaration at her return.

As if in answer, the probing focused on that tiny allure, it seemed to work the spot in his brain, slowly at first, then with an attention bordering on frantic. Suggestions were planted, sexual, erotic. He resisted.

"Not now," he said.

She lay back on the cot and pulled him down beside her. "I have missed you."

This can't be happening.

They kissed.

"I can't." Confused, he shrugged her away. The situation was grotesque. He needed air. Time to think. "I'm going to tend to Kamau." He fumbled for the lantern and turned to walk out of the sleeping area.

"Don't leave me now."

"Then answer my questions."

"I don't know what happened after the Shepherd took off. I awoke. We were in the desert. We had not crashed. A4-Ni didn't attack us again. Are you satisfied?"

"Why would A4-Ni ignore you a second time?"

"Perhaps it's not that simple. She is not everything that you think she is." Mia grabbed his arm, pulling him back to the cot. "Can you imagine what it's like to know that your sole reason for being was to propagate life and not be able to do so? A4-Ni was barren. She lived with that truth for a million years, not knowing what purpose she served in the scheme of things."

What had come over her? John pried Mia's fingers off his arm. "Your sudden sympathy for A4-Ni leaves me cold."

"You might not reject her if you knew the whole truth." Mia's voice rose. A tension of some internal conflict played out across her face.

"There's more?" John snorted cynically.

"The die is cast. We all have our parts to play and nothing I say to you will change it."

"What are you talking about?"

"You think of A4-Ni as an alien. In some ways she is but she is of human origin."

"What I saw earlier wasn't human."

"That was probably a thoughtless mistake on her part." Mia's temper flared, causing him to blink. "The guardian contains the plans for building Shepherds. In the future, the guardian guides humans to construct A4-Ni and others like her to save humans from evil forces. She and the Shepherd have the same mission."

"Since when do you know all this?" John shook his head. Something wasn't right. Mia taking the side of A4-Ni? "They're all lies."

"No. If she had been able to use the guardian sooner, her conflict with the Shepherd could have been avoided."

"I don't care anymore." He turned to leave.

"You must care. It's important."

He paused and she rushed on.

"After building A4-Ni, humans launched her toward the Cygnus X-1 black hole in an effort to have their genome reach safety. Her transit around the black hole only succeeded in depositing her five million years in the past. She survived the voyage. The genome entrusted to her did not."

"She doesn't look like a machine or even like a Shepherd."

"No, she doesn't. She could still replicate and did. Over time and many mutations, she gained ultimate control over her replication. She can become whatever she chooses to become. But without a genome, she was a replicator without a purpose."

"For someone without a purpose she's been busy."

"Four million years ago, she encountered the Shepherd and stole the genome he carried. Unknown to her, it was the genome of future humans. Having failed to accomplish her own mission, she interfered in the success of another Shepherd's mission. But she couldn't have known."

John felt pained. His stare searched her face, looking for something familiar, something to hold on too. *How much more of this does she expect me to take?*

Mia blinked back tears. Her bottom lip quivered. "She compounded the mistake of her theft by attacking and mortally wounding the Shepherd. But the guardian revealed a way for her to redeem herself. She could create a new Shepherd. And she did, the machine you saw her constructing in the desert. He will launch in the next hour with *Gilomir*. Her wrongs will have been righted. The new Shepherd will be the savior of humanity and carry it out into the universe. But first we must get the *Gilomir* genome you carry to the Shepherd."

"Back there you said A4-Ni was repairing the old Shepherd for her own use."

"Old, new, it doesn't matter. What is important is that she wanted to help us."

"I can't imagine doing anything that would forward her agenda." John couldn't keep his disdain for A4-Ni out of his voice. "But she and you have overlooked something. If the guardian exists in the future helping humans, how can the guardian end up in a four million year old hominid pelvis?"

Mia sighed, what seemed in relief. "She asked the same question. One answer is that future humans place the guardian on the last Shepherd they construct, and he carried it into the past but that would create a closed loop for the guardian. It would have no creator. But, if the Shepherd created the guardian during its flight, the guardian's loop remains open."

John snorted cynically. "For someone who has existed all this time and supposedly done all these phenomenal things, she's as stupid as a monkey's ass. If the Shepherd creates the guardian in flight and loads it with the data needed for his construction, and if future humans use that information to construct the Shepherd, then where does the information come from? You've still got a closed loop, a closed informational loop."

A look of uncertainty flickered across Mia's face. "I--"

"I'll grant that A4-Ni is who you say she is, and that her goals and your Shepherd's are noble. But I'm tired. My best friend is dead, and I'm sitting here listening to someone who looks like Mia but has become as alien to me as A4-Ni. Either I'm insane or you are. I don't care anymore. I'm going to attend to Kamau. Then when the constable comes, I'll get him to drive us to the Shepherd. Does that sound reasonable?"

She didn't answer, nor did she make a move to stop him. Instead she seemed to be thinking deeply about what he had said.

John picked up the lantern, turned up the flame and left the tent.

***

The yard was dark and quiet. John peered under the spread of light from his lantern, trying to locate the two corpses.

Omari lay on his back with his mouth open.

Kamau curled in a fetal position next to him.

Flames from the burning vehicles leapt, throwing wild shadows across the compound.

Seeing his friend lying in the dirt kindled a rage that nearly suffocated him. His pain lanced his insides. It didn't matter that A4-Ni was meant to be the savior of the human race. What she had done to him was evil.

John placed the lantern on the ground and tried to pick Kamau up but found that he had stiffened and was too heavy, anyway. Feeling a wave of defeat wash over him, John grasped Kamau's shirt and dragged him.

A commotion from the direction of laborers' quarters sent a chill through John. A deep-throated, exhorting voice rode the still air.

Watombo raced screaming from the shadows, holding high a burning torch. Its flame whipped like a flag. A shower of sparks trailed through curling smoke. Behind him, in ragged disarray, straggled the rest of the laborers.

Before John could react, they encircled him. He stood alone at the center of a ring of burning torches. He eased Kamau onto his side. The gas lantern burned a couple of meters away.

Watombo stepped forward. The light from John's lantern cast the shaman's features in sharp relief. "Where be Witch? We no have quarrel with you, *Masahib*."

"Don't do anything foolish." John pointed across the desert to where a pair of distant headlights bobbed over the uneven ground. "The constable will be here soon."

Watombo glanced at the headlights.

John bolted through the circle and ran to the tent. He confronted Mia inside the entrance. "Quick. To the back of the tent. I need my rifle. It's our only chance."

She looked at him serenely. "We are going to die. Perhaps it is for the best."

"Are you insane?"

John pushed her back to the cot and grabbed his rifle.

Watombo burst into the tent flailing a machete in his good hand, the torch pinned beneath his withered arm, his eyes wide and glazed.

He ran directly at Mia, swung his machete high and brought it down on her upraised arm.

Her hand severed at the wrist and spun to the floor.

Stunned by the suddenness of the attack, John struggled to bring the rifle up for a shot but couldn't get clear of Mia.

As Watombo whirled on John, the torch slipped from his grasp.

John fired.

The shot ripped Watombo's left shoulder.

He staggered back, his withered arm hanging by a thread.

Desperately, John dragged the bolt back and reloaded.

Watombo spun on Mia.

John's second shot caught Watombo in the back, taking out part of his side. He strode on, an automaton, then sank to his knees.

The torch's oily mass had spread. The wooden floor ignited. The entire surface rippled with flame that spread to the sides of the tent, caught the mosquito mesh skirt and raced up to the ceiling.

As Watombo struggled to rise, the guying ropes burned through, releasing the tent pole at the entrance. He looked up in horror as the heavy post fell in a cascade of sparks and flame.

It hit him full face.

His body slammed to the floor and carried through the charred boards. With a roar, the front end of the tent imploded and pinned him beneath layers of burning canvas.

A misguided, hysterical cheering from the laborers drowned out Watombo's screams.

John stifled his agony as he pushed into what was left of the sleeping area. Searing pain ripped his body. The fire was worse than anything he could have imagined. He choked on the smoke. The heat seared his lungs. His face contorted. He dropped low and crawled.

The laborers heaved furniture and other combustibles into the conflagration.

Mia sat on the cot. Her handless forearm resting in her lap. Her skin blistered. One eye swelled shut. A grim smile on her face melted like hot wax. "You must get me to the Shepherd." Her speech slurred, almost unintelligible.

Smoke billowed around him mixed with the sickening smell of burning flesh. "I'll try." He raised up in desperation but his boots crashed through the fire-weakened floor. He lunged for the washstand and grabbed the jerry can full of water, then upended it onto himself and Mia.

The last of the tent collapsed. With nothing left to burn, the flames began to die quickly.

The surrounding tents had become engaged. Flames curled and crackled, heating the air, pulling it upward in a dense plume of smoke.

He dropped low again. After grabbing Mia by the arm, he dragged her toward the edge of the tent, passing over Watombo's corpse.

It lay on its back, burnt beyond recognition. Down the middle of the face, crushing his nose, was the impression of the tent pole. His withered arm lay at his side. His other arm stretched above his head.

At the end of his outstretched fingers rested one of the plaster australopithecine skulls, its face blackened with soot and cracked from the fire's heat. Hooded eye sockets emitted faint curls of smoke from the smoldering floor. The cast rested on its upper jaw giving the uncanny appearance that it was smiling.

John knocked it to one side, slid over Watombo's body, ignoring its odor and dragged Mia after him.

Squirming on his belly, frog-like, he pulled himself forward with his elbows, reached the edge of the floor and rolled onto the sand below. It stuck to his blackened skin, wetted by the fluids suppurating from his burns.

I'm done. He pulled Mia after him.

He rose, smoke swirling around him, Mia draped in his arms.

The laborers who had retreated to the perimeter froze when they saw him.

Yeah, you savages. This is the devil and his witch. Come and get us. Afraid? You better be.

Through covering smoke, he staggered across the compound's tearing hardpan. At the brush fence, he kicked his way through, ignoring the clawing branches and grass reeds with their razor edges.

Exhausted, he limped into the desert toward the Shepherd.

Chapter Twenty-three

The first glow of morning showed on the horizon. John staggered up the low hill overlooking the Shepherd, and dropped to his knees. He lay Mia gently on the ground.

"I've got to rest."

A glittered reflection caught his attention. He leaned over Mia and picked up the guardian, which had rolled onto the sand from a hole burned in her pocket.

"How did you get this?"

"Please, John. Don't torture yourself."

He began to lose control. His mind won the battle with his emotions. What had always been staring him directly in the face became clear. "Why don't you tell me the God dammed-fucking truth for a change?"

She gazed at him, one eye swollen shut, the other giving a hint of innocence lost. Not the Mia he had known. She seemed to have come to a crossroads, as if what she would tell him now didn't matter.

"What is it you want to know?" She hung limp in his arms, resigned.

"You aren't Mia, are you?"

"Yes...and no." She reached for his hand and clutched it. "The Mia you knew did not exist before the Shepherd arrived on Earth. She ceased to exist after his departure."

His hand tensed. "Mia's dead."

"In a sense." She searched his face for his reaction.

He felt sorrow, a sense of loss but also the confirmation of understanding. He had to hear the truth from her lips.

"Then who are you?" He tried to pull his hand free but she clutched it tightly.

"I am A4-Ni, *Afareni*. The life form you so fear."

He recoiled as if she'd slapped him. "No!" The shout carried pain and anguish. The tension returned to his hand. This time he jerked it free.

"Hear me out," she pleaded.

His face contorted. He clenched his teeth. His hands waved in the air, pushing away demons. "You let my mother kill herself. You murdered Diane."

"I'm sorry." Her voice was barely above a whisper.

"But why?"

"I don't expect you to forgive me. I don't have that coming. I could try to explain but even that would not remove the hate you are feeling."

John wasn't listening. He hung his head and shook it. A sense of loss, of betrayal assaulted his sensibilities. For all A4-Ni's stated good intentions and claimed sacrifices, she had been responsible for so much of his pain and suffering. Her death in many ways would be an act of fate. Of justice done. His mother, Diane avenged.

She pushed him away. With what seemed a tremendous effort, she became very calm. "There's more here than you...and I ever imagined."

Another dodge. "You make me sick."

She ignored his retort and continued, her level voice defying explanation. "I've been thinking about what you said back at the tent, before the fire."

"Don't strain yourself."

"Could the guardian have manipulated what I was shown to further its own ends?"

John gazed at her silently, reluctant to be drawn into conversation.

She fixed him with a hard stare. "You are right about the information to build the Shepherd. The only way to open that loop, is if humans of the future are able to conceive of and build the Shepherd on their own."

John shifted, complexed, a feather of anxiety tickling the back of his psyche. *Where the hell was she going with this reasoning?* "Why couldn't future humans design the Shepherd?"

"That's my point. They must have. The problem is I am about to die. Without me, *Gilomir's* genome will degrade and humans will devolve. Even though they recover and progress on their own, the guardian has shown they never become intelligent enough that they can create a Shepherd without instruction."

"I'm not following you."

"To avoid the paradox, humans must become more than the guardian has projected them to be. It also presupposes an improbable chain of events. The guardian knows how to build Shepherds now. The guardian is used by future humans to construct Shepherds. The only way this can happen is that the guardian somehow loses the knowledge to build

Shepherds between now and the future and that humans somewhere along the line figure out how to build *exactly* the same Shepherds and store that information in the guardian. Though such a scenario solves the paradox, it is too contrived to be believed."

John peered at A4-Ni, suppressing his emotions that threatened to break free again. *God, she looks like Mia.*

Her eyes took on a faraway look, then widened in disbelief. She grimaced. "I see clearly now. I have been misled for purposes I can only begin to fathom. *Gilomir*, the Shepherd, the guardian have nothing to do with humanity, humans. For them mankind is a mistake, a mistake of my causing."

"It sounds like a lot of metaphysical bullshit to me."

She ignored him, her voice droning on in a monotone of despair. "The guardian tricked me into believing my mission and that of the Shepherd were the same. And being the same I would be inclined to give the Shepherd the password to the Y chromosome lockbox. If they have that they can separate *Gilomir* from hominids. With me dead it will be the end of man. We can't go to the Shepherd." A4-Ni struggled to rise. She gained her footing and began to trudge toward the camp. She fell, rose and struggled on.

"Come back here." John pleaded, reaching a hand out to her. "It's no use."

"No, I must...for the sake of humanity."

One of her legs gave way. It cocked at an odd angle as if severed from her body at the hip and dropped out of her shorts to fall to the ground. Unbalanced the rest of her toppled over.

John crawled to her side and grabbed her arm but it separated at her shoulder. His face contorted with horror. He let the arm fall to the ground. Her head parted from her neck and rolled to rest face up. A crooked smile sagged from her lips as she melted, spread in a translucent pool and soaked into the sand. The rest of her lay like some dismembered store manikin.

John stared in disbelief. He felt her slip from his mind, as a tide would move out to sea, freeing the sand behind to dry in the sun. In that instant, the world came into a sharp, clear focus. Then a rush of something returning.

Gilomir.

A universe of knowing opened up to him. His hate dissipated, to be replaced by an all-encompassing embrace of everything around him. With A4-Ni gone, *Gilomir* was free to roam.

John rose and took a step in the direction of the hill where the Shepherd lay waiting. One part of him protested, raising thoughts about what A4-Ni had said, another part of him, reassured him that she was wrong.

"*We have no intention of leaving humans behind,*" *Gilomir* whispered. "*A4-Ni's paranoia about her password is misplaced and directed by her own overblown sense of importance.*"

I don't think I can make it. I've lost a lot of blood.

"*I will give you strength.*"

John felt a sudden flooding of energy as if his adrenal glands had all turned on at once. Like some automaton, he lurched for the Shepherd. In the back of his mind he was being pushed against his will. He was finished. Once the surge passed he would have nothing left to sustain himself.

He began to descend the hill. The boney carcasses of the animals pressed on either side of his blurred vision. Towering above his hunched form, the rib bones of the larger animals caught the first rays of the sun.

He stumbled down the slope and fell ten meters from where the Shepherd rested.

He lay on his stomach, both arms outstretched as an unnatural darkness closed around him. The darkness pressed from all sides, complementing the gloom he felt. Pain washed over him in a growing crescendo, each wave stronger than the next.

Was it his imagination or was the Shepherd moving? No imagination.

The Shepherd rose ten centimeters off the ground and in a smooth glide, slid toward him.

***

Dawn rimmed the horizon a deep red in the pre-morning darkness.

Constable Moye and his first officer Latiri ran raggedly across the desert, their flashlights sweeping the ground ahead of them, jumping shadows off rocks and tortured acacias. Behind them loomed the hulking outline of the plateau. Its convoluted escarpment reposed in chiseled shadows. Its top edge aflame in the morning's first light.

"He can't be far ahead," Moye shouted between breaths. The image of Lohner's burned camp lingered in his mind, and the laborers' description of a man carrying a woman, both charred beyond recognition, lurching away from the desolation into the desert night.

Light from Moye's flashlight diffused in the dusty air and reflected off the glistening sweat on his black skin, accentuating the whites of his eyes. Sucking air, he scrambled up a low rise in the landscape. At the crest of the hill, he stopped abruptly. A sickening stench of carrion assaulted his senses like a physical blow. He wiped his mouth with the back of his hand, forcing himself to look at the scene in front of him.

"Jesus Christ," he swore under his breath, then pulled his bandana up from where it lay around his neck to cover his mouth and nose.

For fifty meters in all directions lay decomposing animal carcasses. They radiated outward in concentric circles around a dark object, which resembled a car's inner tube minus the central hole. It looked to be about twenty meters across, dark green, smooth, and sagging on the sand.

Moye and Latiri picked their way down the near slope and through the carnage. A movement near the object caught his attention. A blackened human form lay on the ground. A man.

His head lifted slightly as if trying to speak but no words issued from his mouth, just a silent opening and closing, like a fish out of water, eyes glazed.

Moye shuddered at the sight. *Do I run?* Instead he stepped to the bottom of the hill and knelt beside the man.

"Doctor Lohner?" Moye thought to lift the man in his arms but the layers of sand sticking to the clear plasma that leaked from cracks in his burned skin deterred him.

"Yes," the man said, his voice nothing more than a croak.

An accelerating rumble made its way from the object through the ground to where Moye knelt. He glanced up, concerned. "What's going on?" he asked no one in particular.

Grimacing in pain, Lohner turned awkwardly. "Don't...be alarmed. You are safe here."

"Where did that come from?" Moye pointed to the rounded shape.

"*Afareni.*"

"*Afareni*? What are you saying?"

Limply, Lohner's arm passed in an arc indicating the carcasses.

Moye squinted at the surrounding dead animals, then at the rounded shape.

Lohner jerked violently. His heels pressed into the sand, and he pushed hard against Moye. He shoved a clenched fist into the palm of Moye's hand. "Take it."

"Take wha--"

The vibrations rose to a clattering staccato, heaving through the sand, rattling the animal carcasses up and down.

Latiri fell flat to the ground.

A high-pitched engine whine cranked up the decibel scale. The object rose, hovered briefly to catch the dawn light, then vanished straight up. Torn air rushed into the vacuum left behind. A thunderclap.

The life seemed to go out of Lohner. He sagged heavily in Moye's arms.

"Is he dead?" Latiri asked.

With a grimace of distaste, Moye pressed his fingers against the blackened and cracked skin of Lohner's neck. "I think so."

The sun's disk crested the horizon. The light rose about Moye. It seemed like a burden had left the Earth.

Latiri peered at the corpse. He knelt beside Moye and reached for Lohner's clutched hand. "He's holding something."

"Leave him alone," Moye said.

Latiri glanced at Moye, seeking permission.

Moye nodded, lacking the energy to stop the curious Latiri.

Though the air thickened with the smell of burnt flesh, Latiri pried the scientist's fingers open one by one until a small sphere lay exposed in the palm of his hand.

"What is it?" Latiri asked, afraid to touch it.

"The witch's charm." Moye grasped the sphere between forefinger and thumb. He held it up to the morning light, turning it one way then another. He let a cascade of reflections dance on the surrounding sand. "I've been told when she was alive it had great powers."

Moye eased himself to his feet. He dropped the sphere into his pocket. "It's best you say nothing about this to anyone."

Latiri blinked, the whites of his eyes as big as a hen's eggs. "It is evidence, sir."

"You will let me decide what is evidence." Moye gave Latiri a nervous stare, still overwhelmed by the sight. "You stay here with the corpse. I'm going back to the camp for the Land Rover."

Latiri's face glistened with a fear-induced sweat. "But…"

"Shut up." Moye glared at the stricken Latiri. "You have nothing to be afraid of. All the ghosts have risen into the heavens."

Latiri didn't look convinced but Moye didn't care. He had other matters on his mind. He trudged up the hill, oriented himself, and set off for what was left of John's camp.

Though the day was young, the desert sun beat down unmercifully. Thorny brush scratched his legs and grabbed at his shorts. He clumped through the sand to the trail that paralleled the base of the plateau, then along it to the devastated camp.

Of the dozen tents that had formed the camp, only two remained standing. Smoke curled from the others, flattened black and sitting in their own ashes.

He located John's tent, the worst burned, an indication the fire had started there.

Bandele rushed up to Moye's side. "It be Watombo start fire. We try to put it out but wind very strong."

Moye looked with distaste at the groveling supervisor. Blame it all on the shaman. The dead would tell no tales.

"Check the other tents," Moye instructed. "See that no one else was trapped."

He stepped onto the charred wooden floor of the tent and skirted Watombo's still form. *Where's the woman*? No sign of her anywhere. Was she really a witch, as Watombo claimed? Moye pushed sheets of blackened canvas out of the way with his police baton and kicked back a burnt chair. He uncovered a sooty filing cabinet from one corner of the devastation.

He grabbed the handle and managed, with difficulty, to slide a drawer open. A fire-safe cabinet, its fire-retardant insulation had fused, protecting the contents inside.

In the drawer, he found scattered papers, Lohner's passport and a bound volume that looked like a diary.

Though the cover was charred, the diary was otherwise intact. Moye opened it to a random page.

Tuesday, June 25, 1985 was written across the top. That would be yesterday. Moye read.

Followed Mia into the desert last night. My love for her conflicts with the mystery of her presence. Confronted her with my misgivings.

She claims to be a colonist, traversing the universe using black holes as accelerators to cheat time and space.

Moye's hands shook. He flipped the page.

To prove her claims, she let me use the guardian with astounding results.

The voice I hear is that of A4-Ni, a mysterious life form that stole the Gilomir (Humanus) genome four million years ago and mixed it with the DNA of an ancient hominid. Augmented by Gilomir DNA, primitive hominids evolved to Homo sapiens. The coincidence of the guardian's vision with the Watombo myth and the name of the Earth-mother Afareni is uncanny.

The guardian vision goes against all common sense, against religious belief. Man's genome did not evolve over time or result from the creation of a loving god. It results from a fortuitous insertion.

Inexplicably, of all mankind, I alone possess the purest form of the Gilomir genome.

I now live in terror that the struggle between the Shepherd and A4-Ni will come to me. When I least expect, one of them will seize the advantage to steal my DNA.

The entries stopped. Moye closed the diary. What Lohner had written didn't shed any more light on what he had reported yesterday morning in the early hours. Except the idea that mankind's humanity was a mistake. That seemed preposterous even to Moye but what did he know? With his own eyes, he had seen something lift off and head into space. What could be more preposterous than that?

Lohner must have been crazy if he thought *Afareni* was an alien from outer space after his DNA. Moye shook his head. Nothing worse than a white man who stayed in the sun too long, especially a lovesick one.

Epilogue

"You deceived me!" Mia broke into tears.

"I had no choice," the Shepherd said. "A4-Ni has been thorough. I am dying."

"How can you die? You're a machine."

"What do you know of living and dying? You have only existed six days. A4-Ni tore through my central processor. I am mortally wounded. My circuits are shorting. I cannot repair them. I will be lucky to get us out of here."

"But you promised!" Mia screamed. "I obtained the guardian and the genome for you. You could have had them both but you betrayed me."

"A miscalculation. A4-Ni proved too resourceful or I would have had the guardian, too, if you hadn't thrown it to the scientist. As for *Gilomir's* genome, I have tried and failed to separate it from the entwining hominid DNA you were able to obtain from the scientist. A4-Ni has been too clever with her lockbox. So, technically, my efforts to obtain a pure *Gilomir* genome have come to failure. All I have left is you."

The gravity of her situation sank in. "I'm pregnant?"

"Yes, fortunately."

"I thought you said I was sterile."

"I did. But making you fertile was a necessary contingency against exactly what has happened. I calculated a 65% probability that A4-Ni would prevail, and I would die. However, if I were able to inflict reciprocal damage to A4-Ni, then I calculated a 76% probability that she would die. Given the high probability of us both dying, *Gilomir's* genome in hominids would degrade, the very degradation you reported seeing from the guardian. I felt it necessary to create another alternative to saving *Gilomir*. Fortunately, I did. All of my worst fears have been realized. I was indeed able to damage A4-Ni, giving weight to the probability that she will die. The probability of me dying has now risen to 98%.

"So this is where you come in. I can still transport you to safety, where given the right set of circumstances, I calculate a 76% chance of you giving birth to a healthy child, bearing *Gilomir's* genome and a 39% chance of your survival thereafter...which is better than nothing." The Shepherd shuddered, tossing Mia in his padded womb. "Since you had asked to be made fertile, I thought you would have no objection."

A needle slid from the wall of the womb and pricked Mia's skin.

"Please, don't. I hate being sedated."

"It will make you more comfortable. We have a long way to go."

***

Groggily, Mia awoke to frustrated muttering. "What has happened?"

"Unfortunately, I was not able to distance myself from this environ. When I dropped from orbit around the Cygnus black hole, I had not achieved the desired spatial jump, nor had I advanced temporally. In fact, I regressed. We are now six-million years in the past from the present we left."

"That's terrible."

"Actually, it is not all bad. I have ascertained that there is no A4-Ni anywhere to be found. The Earth is not much dissimilar from the Earth we left. Some of the life forms are more primitive but that should not be a concern. I have, therefore, taken the liberty to land near where we took off. You should feel right at home."

"How long have I been unconscious?"

"What passed for you as a moment of subjective time, given that you were drugged, was in fact nine months of relativistic time."

What an abysmal situation. At least she had gotten her wish to remain on Earth. The bitter reality was she now existed six-million years before her beloved John was even conceived. Worse than that, she was alone, and to complicate matters further, very pregnant.

"How are we to survive here?"

"I do not have the luxury of extended existence to worry about that problem. I am sorry." His voice pinched. "I can no longer help you. Goodbye."

"Shepherd...? Wait!" Mia sensed a diminishing of the energy around her. His tissues relaxed. The womb orifice slacked open, letting in a pencil thickness of sunlight. "Damn you!"

She fought her way toward the top of the womb, clawing at the sagging tissue, making slow progress. After reaching the sphincter, she stuck one hand through and pulled herself up. She pried herself higher with her elbow and extracted her other arm.

With her shoulders clear, she pushed down with her hands and slid free. She rolled off his tilting side and dropped hard to the ground. Protectively, she pulled her limbs in close to her body, still glistening with a layer of mucus.

Mia shifted her position but did not attempt to stand. Looking around, she concluded that the Shepherd was right about this period on Earth being not much different than the one during John's time. Dry yellow grass grew tall. A river surged behind a thick growth of trees. A group of primates foraged nearby.

Though they were smaller than the australopithecines that would evolve from them, they carried all the rudimentary physiognomy that would serve them well in their competition for survival. Some of them stopped foraging and gazed at her.

At least they aren't lions.

Mia stared up at the Shepherd. He lay tilted where he had landed on a rock. His gray-green surface had sagged and discolored in places. He could have been the carcass of some great beast, brought down by a parasite or disabling disease.

Your dedication to your perceived mission always superseded any of my humble ambitions.

The fetus in her womb stirred. "*Don't be too judgmental.*"

Gilomir? She passed her hand over her swollen abdomen. *At least I have you...and John.*

"The Shepherd created and bred you. He schooled you. He would have done a better job if he hadn't been so ill himself."

You're very conciliatory to someone who has just deposited you in your own past.

"Need you remind me. I despair at ever being extracted from this infernal cycle."

I don't understand. What cycle? You are a hominid from the future.

"That is where our recently deceased befuddled Shepherd and the hyperactive A4-Ni are wrong."

If you are not hominid, then what are you?

"You could call me a wounded warrior...seeking a respite from evil."

Ibilisi.

"Watombo's myth." Gilomir sighed. *"Actually, I do not refer to the evil as Ibilisi but Ibilisi will do. You could think of me as an opposing force. Good is probably too one-dimensional. He and I are more like yin and yang, or order and chaos. We quarreled, to put it simplistically. I lost. The guardian intervened and has taken me to this place where it hopes I can be rehabilitated and the balance between Ibilisi and myself restored.*

The guardian brought you here? I thought you made the guardian.

"I do not know who made the guardian but whomever it was belongs to a higher power than I do, or even Ibilisi. The visions it shows serve its own purposes. True, it can divine the future and read the past but then it does whatever it wants with them. If the viewer can be induced to believe, then the scenarios can become more than visions. They

may even end up shaping the perception of reality. The guardian knows this and uses it to subtle effect."

The group of primates had stopped foraging and now were all looking in her direction.

Mia eyed them nervously. Though small, they were many, and by all accounts still primitive beings. *So your being here is an abnormality?*

"Ironically, the bigger abnormality is the effect I have had on hominids. If not for me they would not have evolved as conscious beings. Instead, they have been gifted the ability to speculate and wonder, to gaze out at a universe they were never meant to see, much less be able to comprehend. As my DNA pushed them forward, hominid DNA did its best to re-establish the status quo, to drag the species back to their beastly roots. I'll credit A4-Ni with keeping me pure."

The Shepherd seemed convinced he mortally wounded A4-Ni. If she does indeed die then your genome in humans will degrade. The key to the lockbox will die with her. You will remain eternally with hominid DNA.

"My only hope is that the guardian has foreseen that this might happen and has a reason for letting it happen."

But without the Shepherd, how can it save you?

"The guardian knows how to construct a Shepherd and will find a way to do so if it so requires. Of that I am certain."

What are you to do now?

"Now? I am entirely beholden to you."

Mia felt sick. She, John, A4-Ni, and how many countless others were all bit players in the service of *Gilomir*. Long ago a cosmic bell had rung, opening the gates on a race from an unknown beginning to an unknown end. Like members of a relay team coached by the guardian, they all had their parts to play taking up the genome and passing it forward. Then, having run their leg of the race, they fell spent by the wayside, urging others to persevere to an elusive finish.

It all makes sense.

"*Of course it does. Look. The primates move closer.*"

Are they also to become players in this grand design?

"*They don't have any choice. There is an irony here. If I am indeed rehabilitated, mankind, by way of his entanglement with my DNA, will be carried to the far reaches of the universe on my shoulders.*"

The primate group stopped a distance from where Mia lay. A dominant male ambled toward her.

She hoped he would not perceive her as a threat. He must be able to see that she resembled him in many ways. She began a tortured movement to uncoil herself. Blinking in the sharp light, she staggered to her feet and wiped the mucus film from her long limbs, then focused her attention on the diminutive creature. With an outstretched hand, she took a lurching step forward, almost fell, then steadied herself.

Though the primate appeared ready to flee, he stared at her swollen belly and seemed to understand her condition. His troop sat on their haunches observing but did not approach.

He stepped up to Mia and offered his hand.

She regarded it, noting the lack of an opposable thumb. Then she clasped his hand in a firm grip. A first contraction rippled across her abdomen. Her smile wilted as a stab of pain convulsed her body.

"*Gilomir*, be patient." She placed a hand on her belly. "It will be soon enough."

Mia and the primate strode toward the group. Her pale, slender height contrasted with his dark, hairy stockiness.

He doubled his bowlegged gait to keep up with her sweeping strides.

She must hurry. A second contraction announced that her time had come.

THE END

Lightning Source UK Ltd.
Milton Keynes UK
UKHW040708180921
390770UK00001B/157